Nola's Worlds #2

ferrets and ferreting out

THANK YOU TO KIM AND POP FOR CONTINUING THIS ADVENTURE, WHICH IS STILL JUST AS ENCHANTING. AND A HUGE THANK YOU TO ALICIA AND GAËL, MY LITTLE FERRETS.

TO MARCUS B., JOANNA S., AND HUGO V.,
TO ERIC T. AND STUDIO 5265,
TO FRANCIS H. AND LA COMIX JAM,
THANK YOU TO EVERYONE ♡ FOR THE WELCOME TO MONTREAL.
KARELLE, THANK YOU FOR YOUR HELP WITH THE COLORING. :)

A BIG THANK YOU TO KARELLE AND LÉA FOR THEIR ASSISTANCE AND AN ITTY-BITTY THANK YOU TO KURI FOR HER ITTY-BITTY ASSISTANCE.
THANK YOU TO KIM, TO MATHIEU, AND ESPECIALLY TO GATE AND JAMES FOR THEIR PRICELESS SUPPORT.
AND THANK YOU TO ALL THOSE WHO LOVED BOOK 1.
I HOPE THAT BOOK 2 WILL PLEASE YOU AS MUCH.
HAPPY READING! ^.^

STORY BY MATHIEU MARIOLLE
ART BY MINIKIM
COLORS BY POP
TRANSLATION BY ERICA OLSON JEFFREY AND CAROL KLIO BURRELL

First American edition published in 2010 by Graphic Universe™.
Published by arrangement with MEDIATOON LICENSING — France.

Alta Donna 2 — Furets et fureteuse
© DARGAUD BENELUX (DARGAUD-LOMBARD S.A.) 2009, by Mariolle, MiniKim, Pop.
www.dargaud.com
All rights reserved

Graphic Universe™
A division of Lerner Publishing Group, Inc.
241 First Avenue North
Minneapolis, MN 55401 U.S.A.

Website address: www.lernerbooks.com

Library of Congress Cataloging-in-Publication Data

Mariolle, Mathieu.
    Ferrets and ferreting out / by Mathieu Mariolle ; illustrated by MiniKim ; colored by Pop. — 1st American ed.
        p.   cm. — (Nola's worlds ; #2)
        Summary: As her once perfect and boring hometown Alta Donna becomes increasingly turbulent and dangerous, Nola determines to find the reason and its possible connection to her mysterious new friends Inés and Damiano.
        ISBN 978–0–7613–6504–4 (lib. bdg. : alk. paper)
        1. Graphic novels. [1. Graphic novels. 2. Supernatural—Fiction. 3. Characters in literature—Fiction. 4. Ferrets—Fiction.] I. MiniKim, ill. II. Pop, 1978– ill. III. Title.
    PZ7.7.M34Fer 2010
    741.5'944—dc22

2010012412

Manufactured in the United States of America
1 – DP – 7/15/10

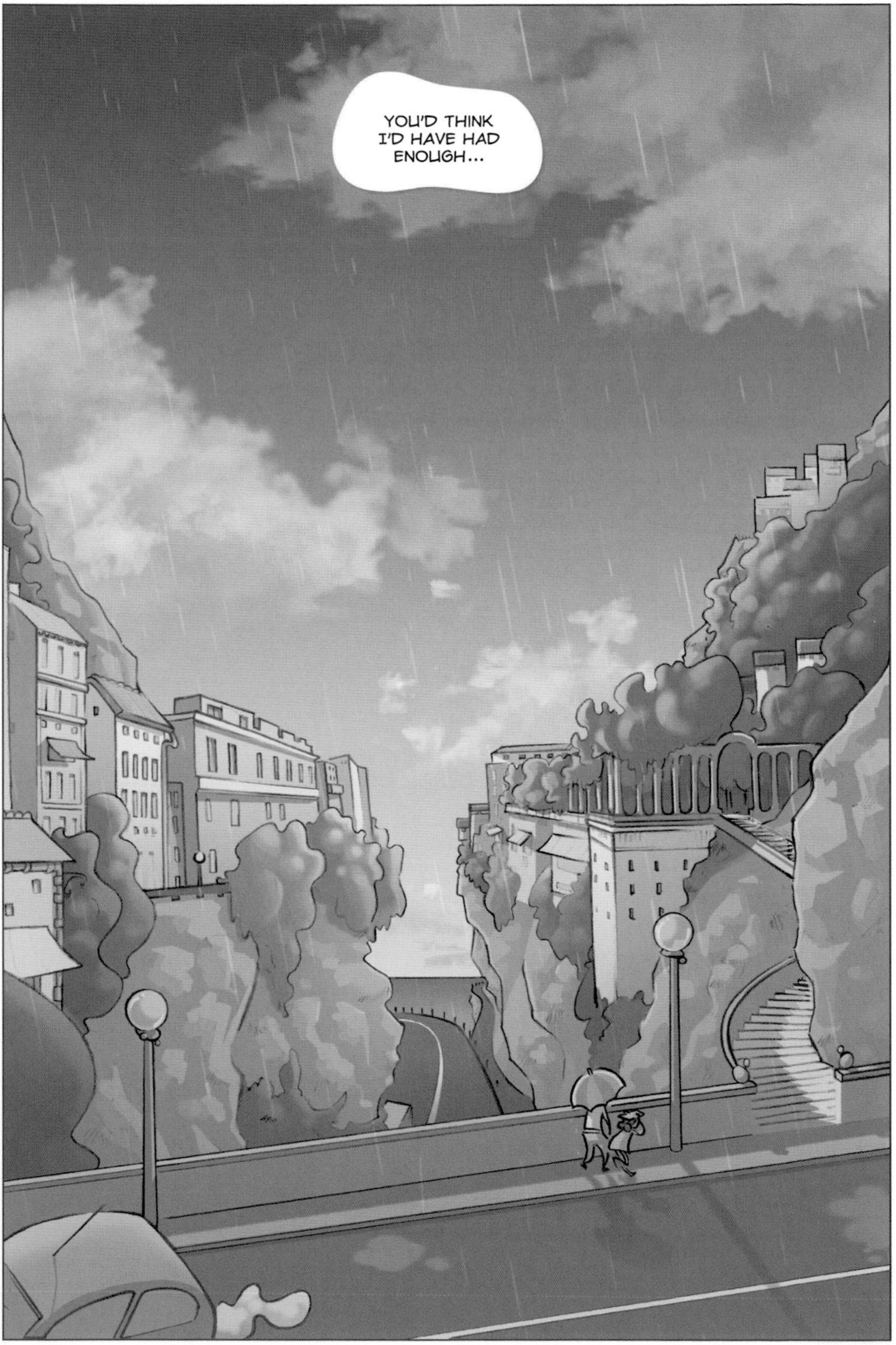
YOU'D THINK
I'D HAVE HAD
ENOUGH...

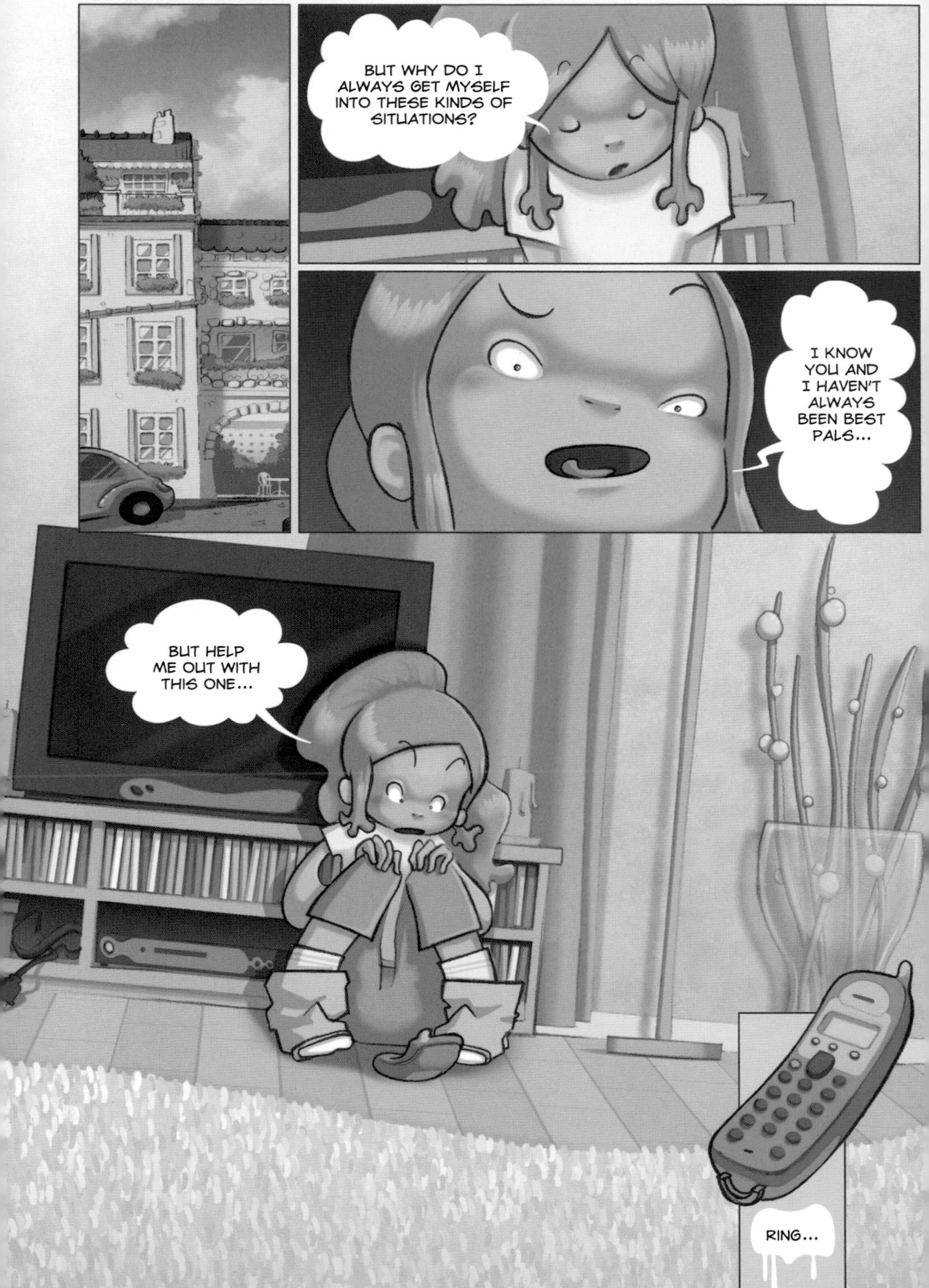
BUT WHY DO I ALWAYS GET MYSELF INTO THESE KINDS OF SITUATIONS?
I KNOW YOU AND I HAVEN'T ALWAYS BEEN BEST PALS...
BUT HELP ME OUT WITH THIS ONE...
RING...

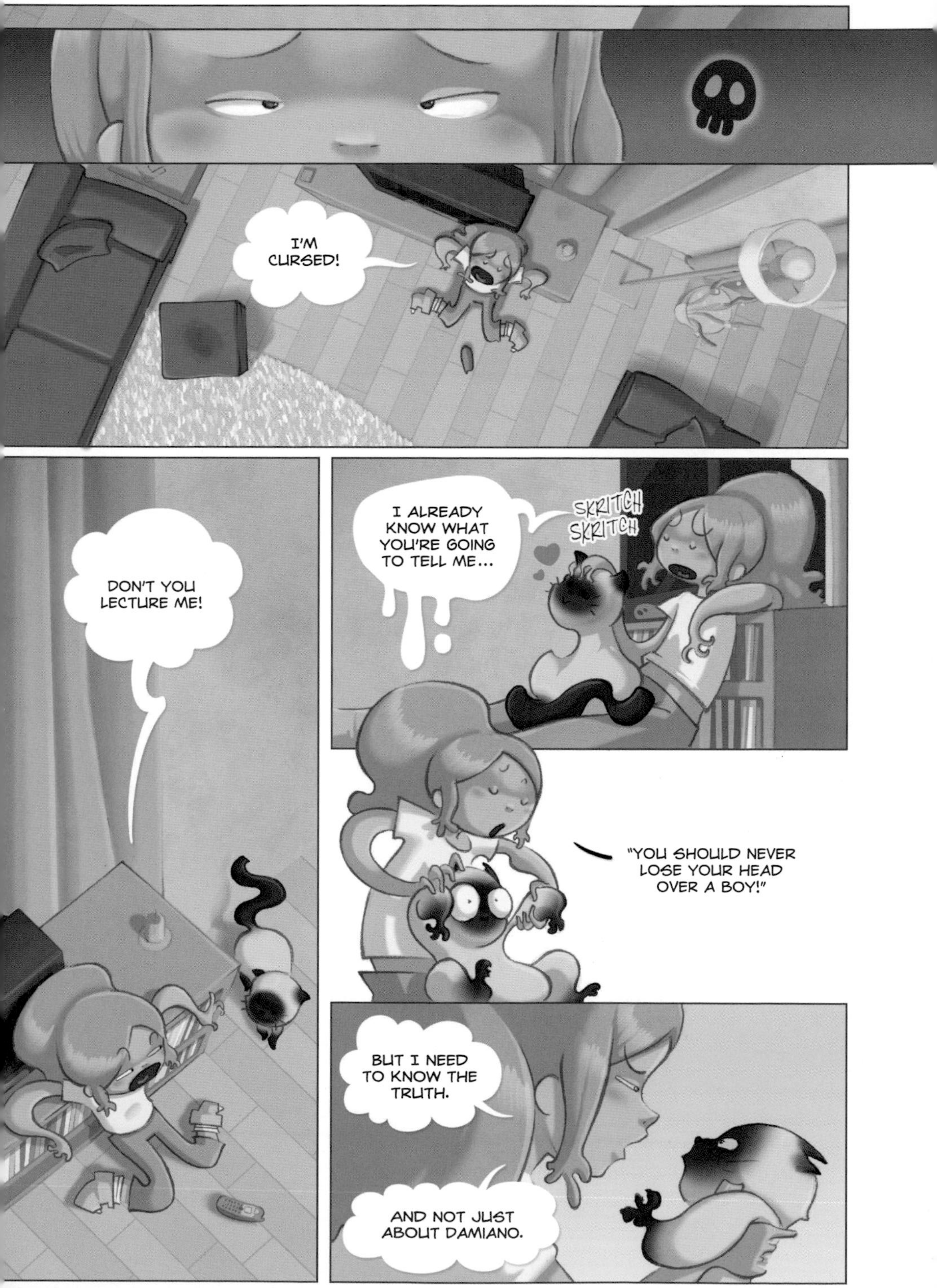
I'M CURSED!
DON'T YOU LECTURE ME!
I ALREADY KNOW WHAT YOU'RE GOING TO TELL ME...
SKRITCH SKRITCH
"YOU SHOULD NEVER LOSE YOUR HEAD OVER A BOY!"
BUT I NEED TO KNOW THE TRUTH.
AND NOT JUST ABOUT DAMIANO.

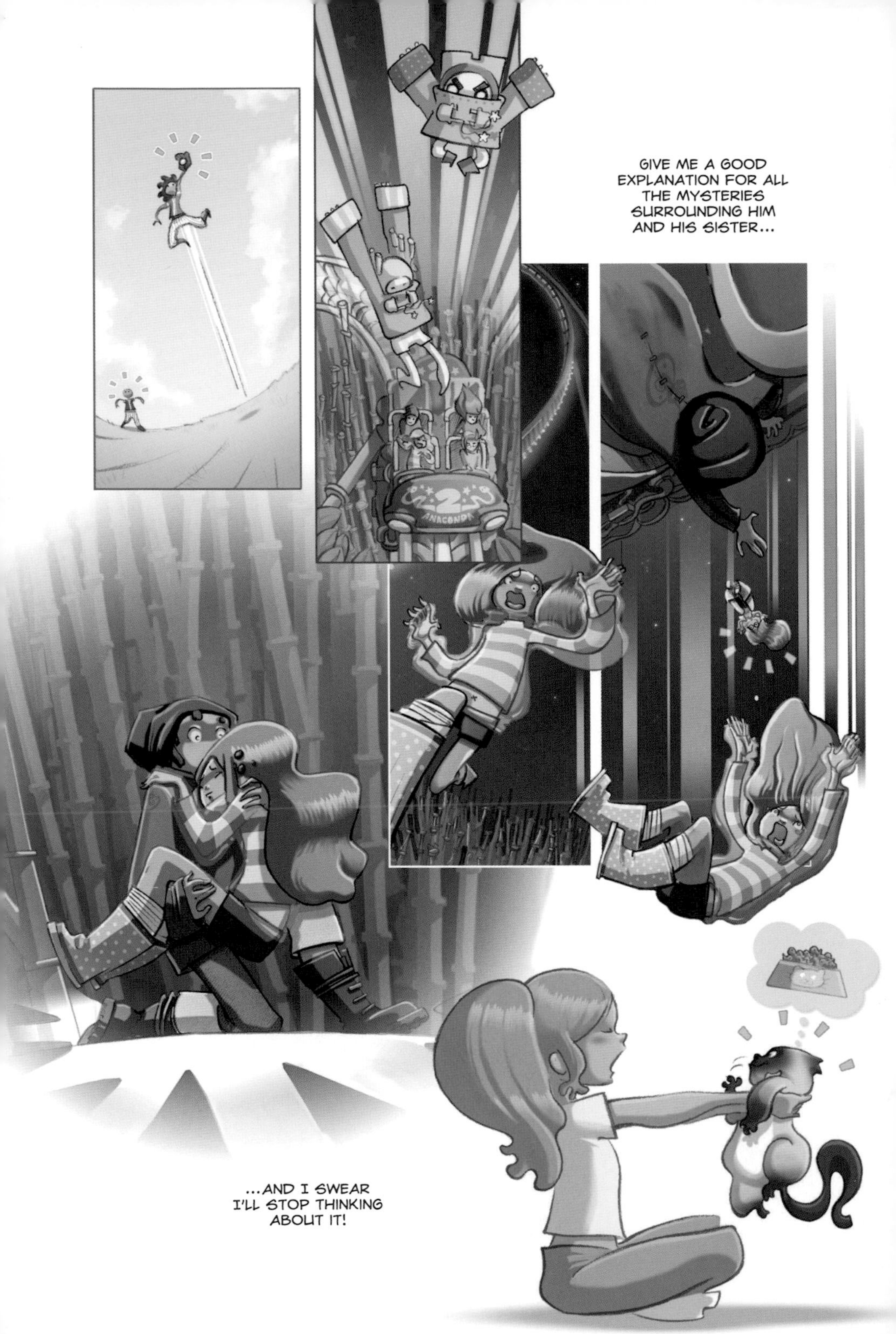
GIVE ME A GOOD EXPLANATION FOR ALL THE MYSTERIES SURROUNDING HIM AND HIS SISTER...
...AND I SWEAR I'LL STOP THINKING ABOUT IT!

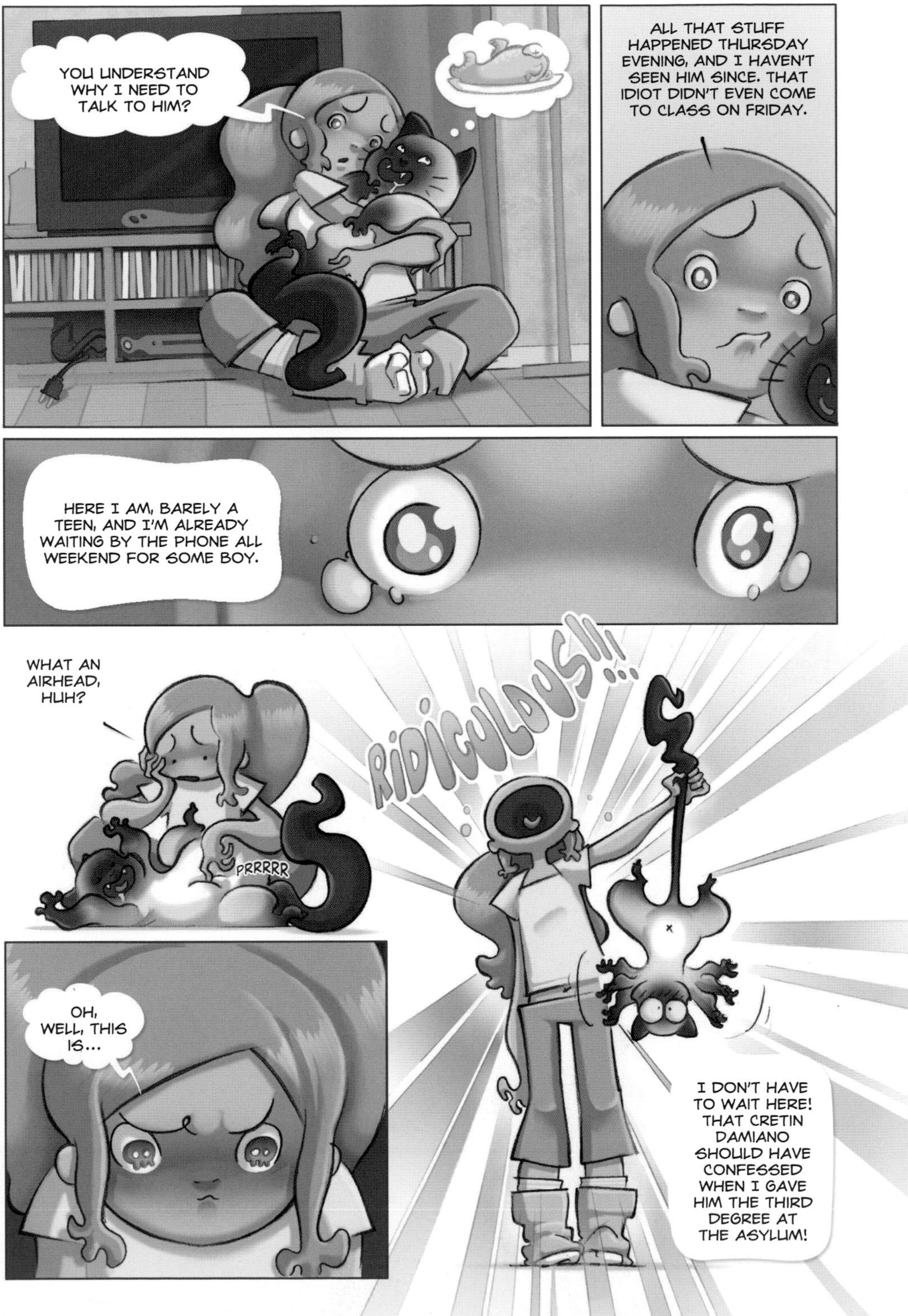
YOU UNDERSTAND WHY I NEED TO TALK TO HIM?
ALL THAT STUFF HAPPENED THURSDAY EVENING, AND I HAVEN'T SEEN HIM SINCE. THAT IDIOT DIDN'T EVEN COME TO CLASS ON FRIDAY.
HERE I AM, BARELY A TEEN, AND I'M ALREADY WAITING BY THE PHONE ALL WEEKEND FOR SOME BOY.
WHAT AN AIRHEAD, HUH?
PRRRRR
RIDICULOUS!!!
OH, WELL, THIS IS...
I DON'T HAVE TO WAIT HERE! THAT CRETIN DAMIANO SHOULD HAVE CONFESSED WHEN I GAVE HIM THE THIRD DEGREE AT THE ASYLUM!

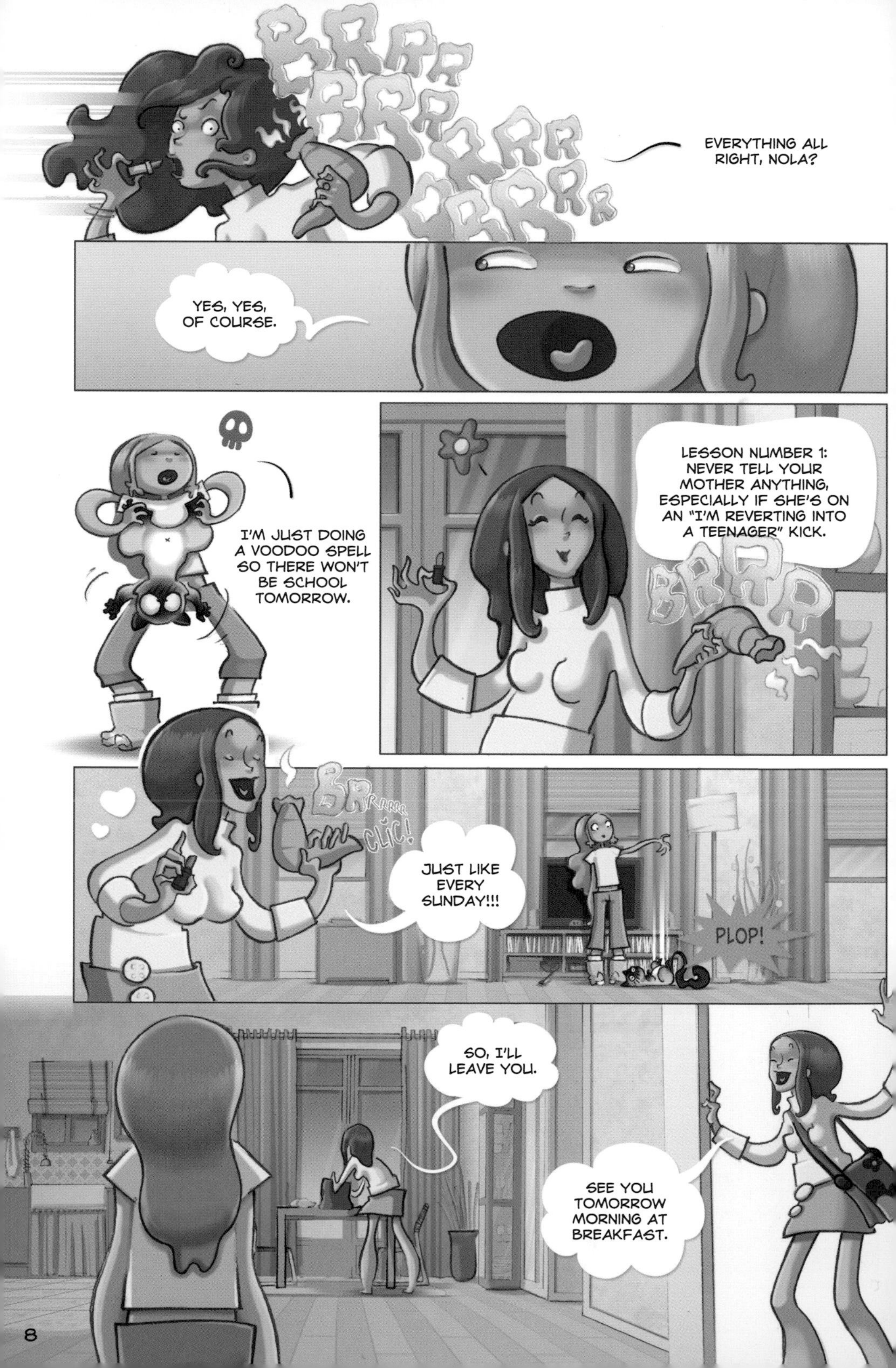
BRRRR
BRRRR
BRRRR
EVERYTHING ALL RIGHT, NOLA?
YES, YES, OF COURSE.
I'M JUST DOING A VOODOO SPELL SO THERE WON'T BE SCHOOL TOMORROW.
LESSON NUMBER 1: NEVER TELL YOUR MOTHER ANYTHING, ESPECIALLY IF SHE'S ON AN "I'M REVERTING INTO A TEENAGER" KICK.
BRRR
BRrrrrr
CLIC!
JUST LIKE EVERY SUNDAY!!!
PLOP!
SO, I'LL LEAVE YOU.
SEE YOU TOMORROW MORNING AT BREAKFAST.

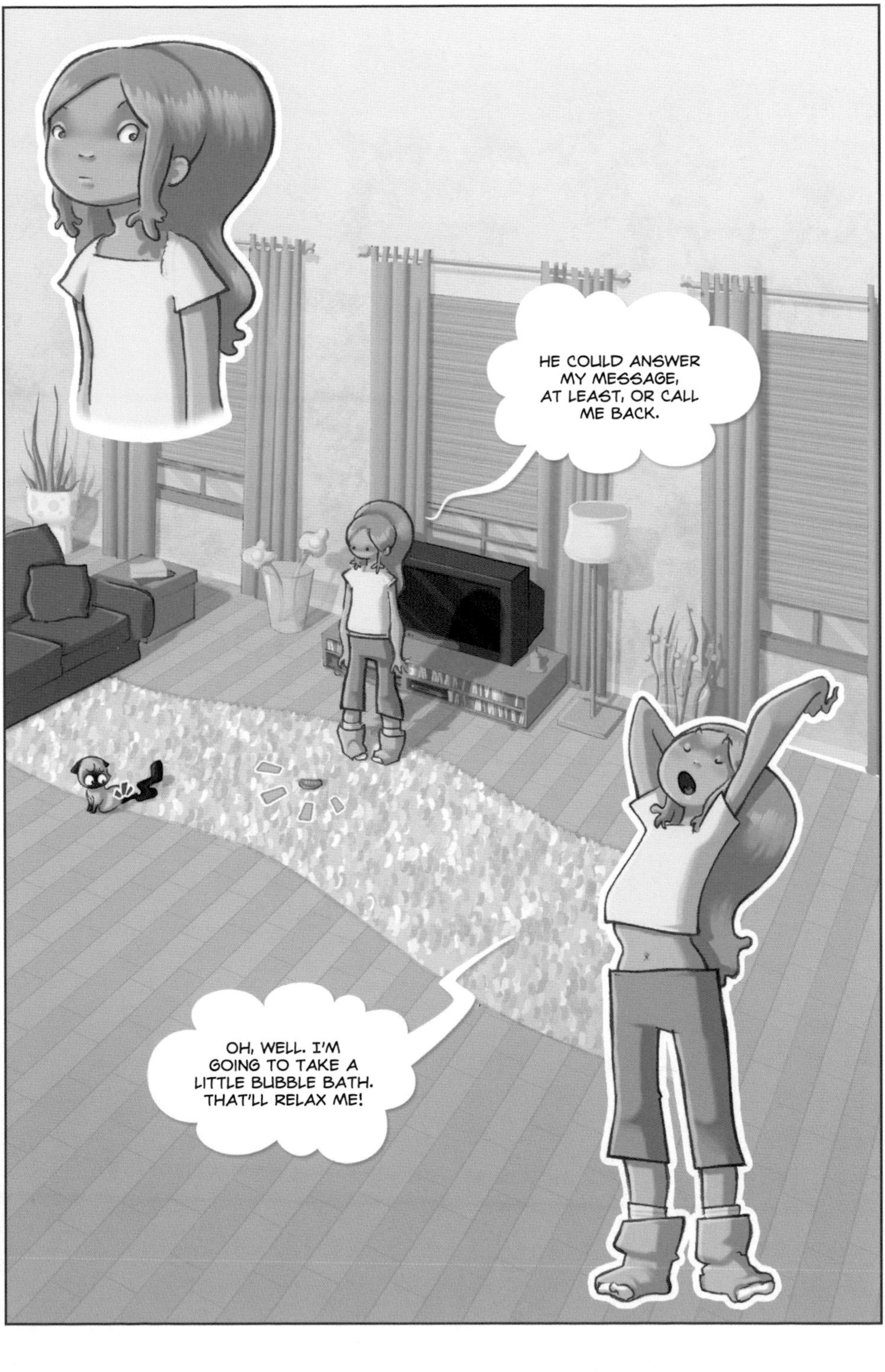
HE COULD ANSWER MY MESSAGE, AT LEAST, OR CALL ME BACK.
OH, WELL. I'M GOING TO TAKE A LITTLE BUBBLE BATH. THAT'LL RELAX ME!

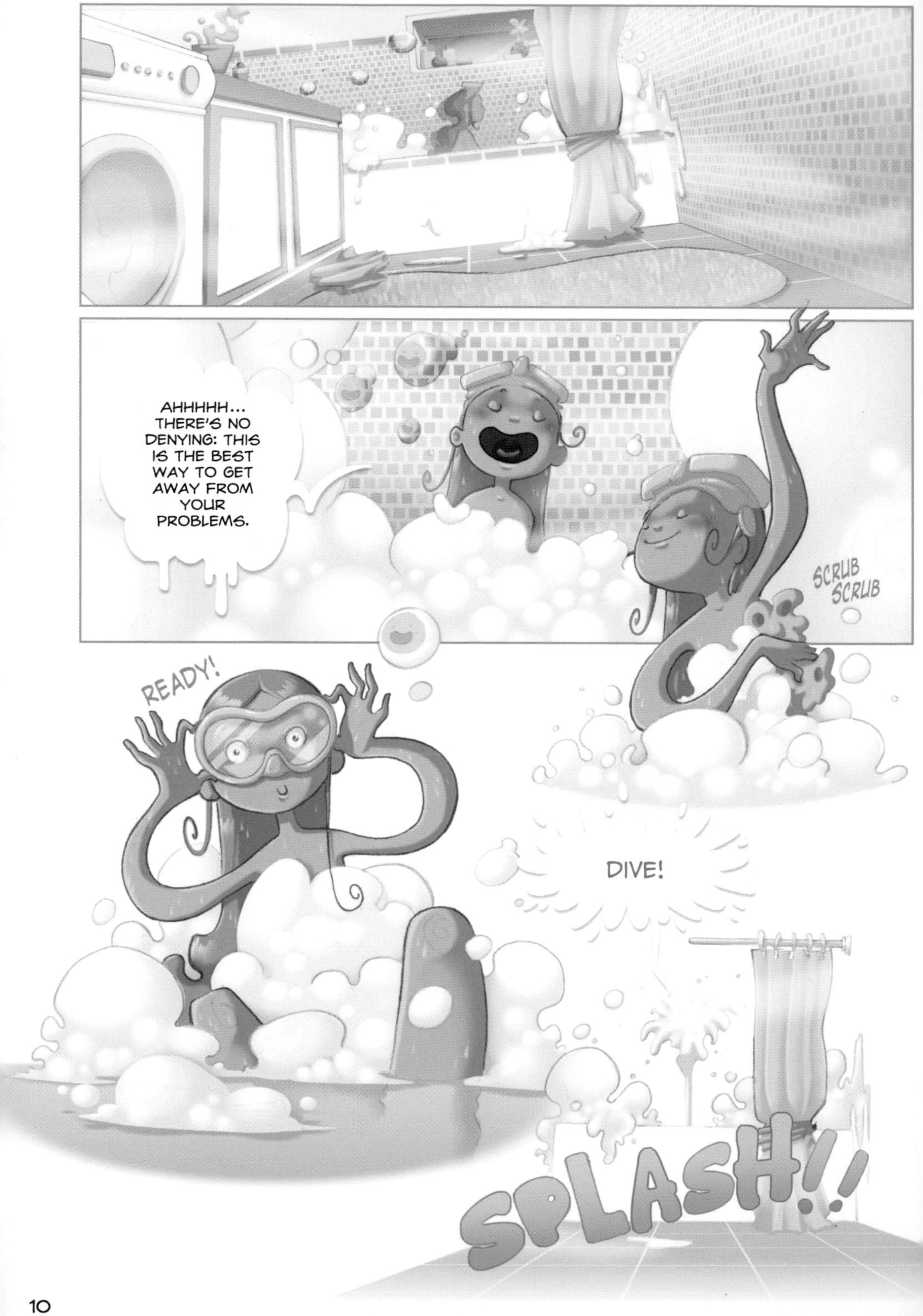
AHHHHH... THERE'S NO DENYING: THIS IS THE BEST WAY TO GET AWAY FROM YOUR PROBLEMS.
SCRUB SCRUB
READY!
DIVE!
SPLASH!!

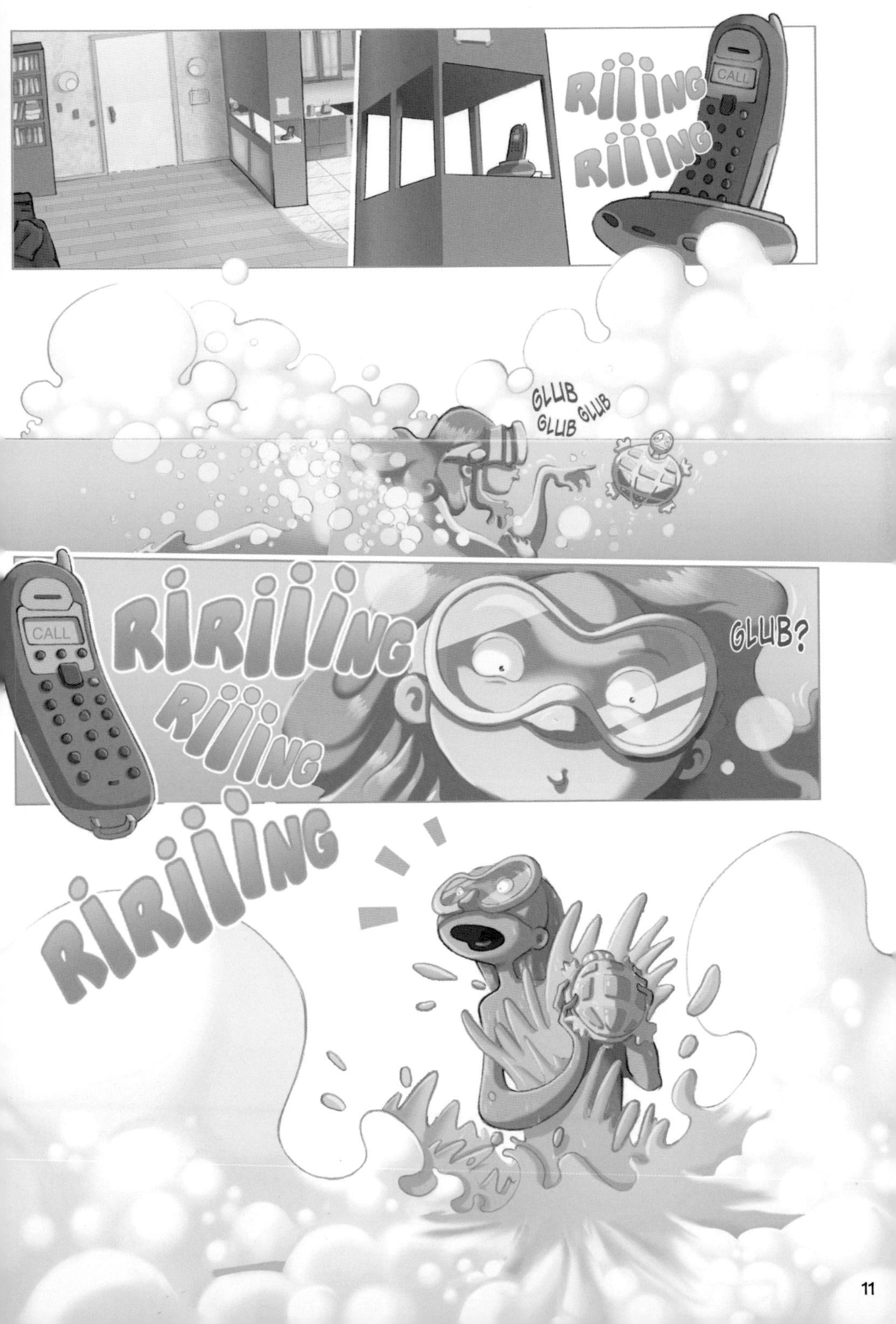
CALL
RIIING
RIIING
GLUB
GLUB
GLUB
CALL
RIRIIING
RIIING
GLUB?
RIRIIING

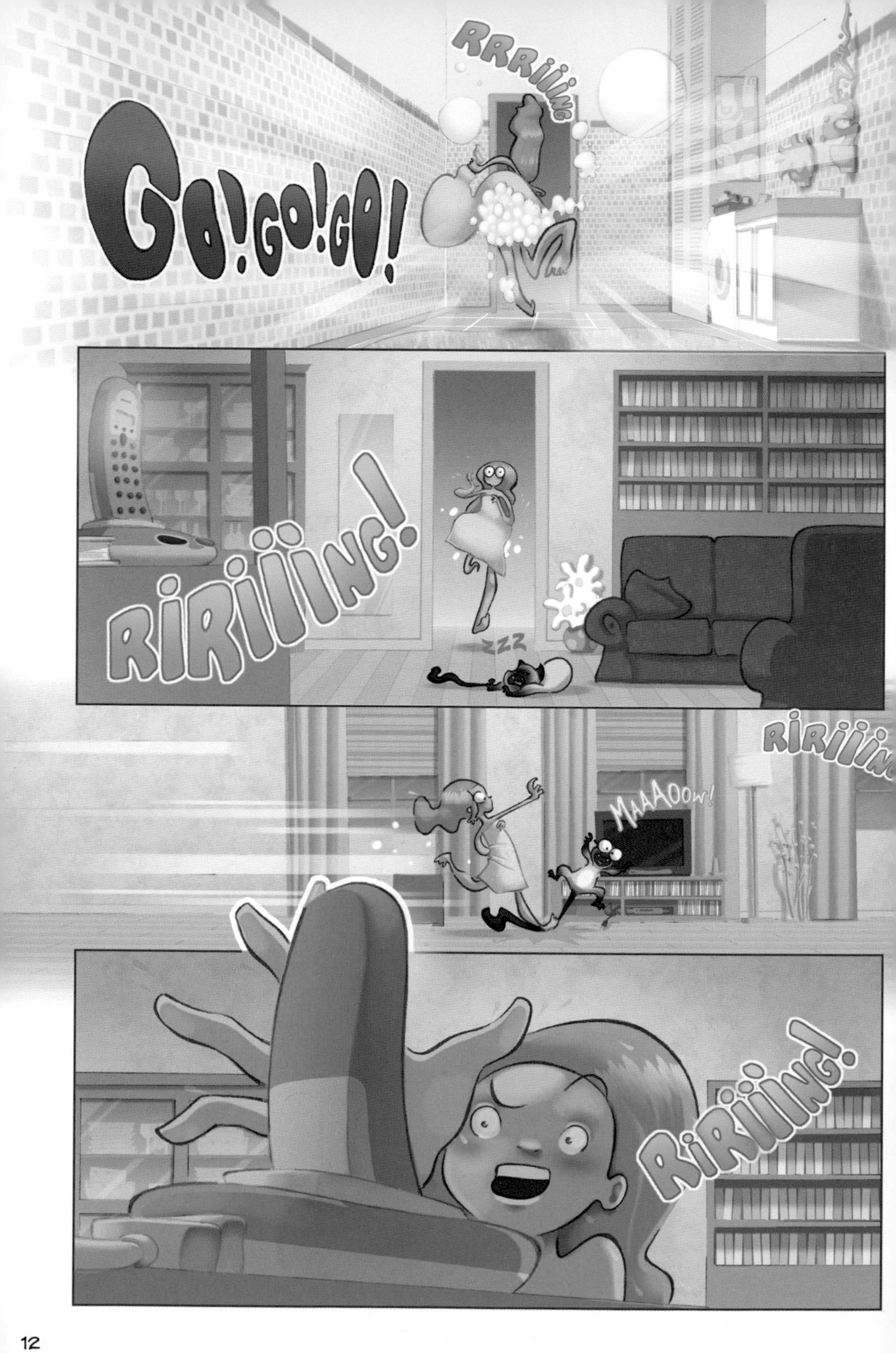
GO!GO!GO!
RRRIIING
RIRIIING!
ZZZ
RIRIIIN
MAAAOOW!
RIRIIING!

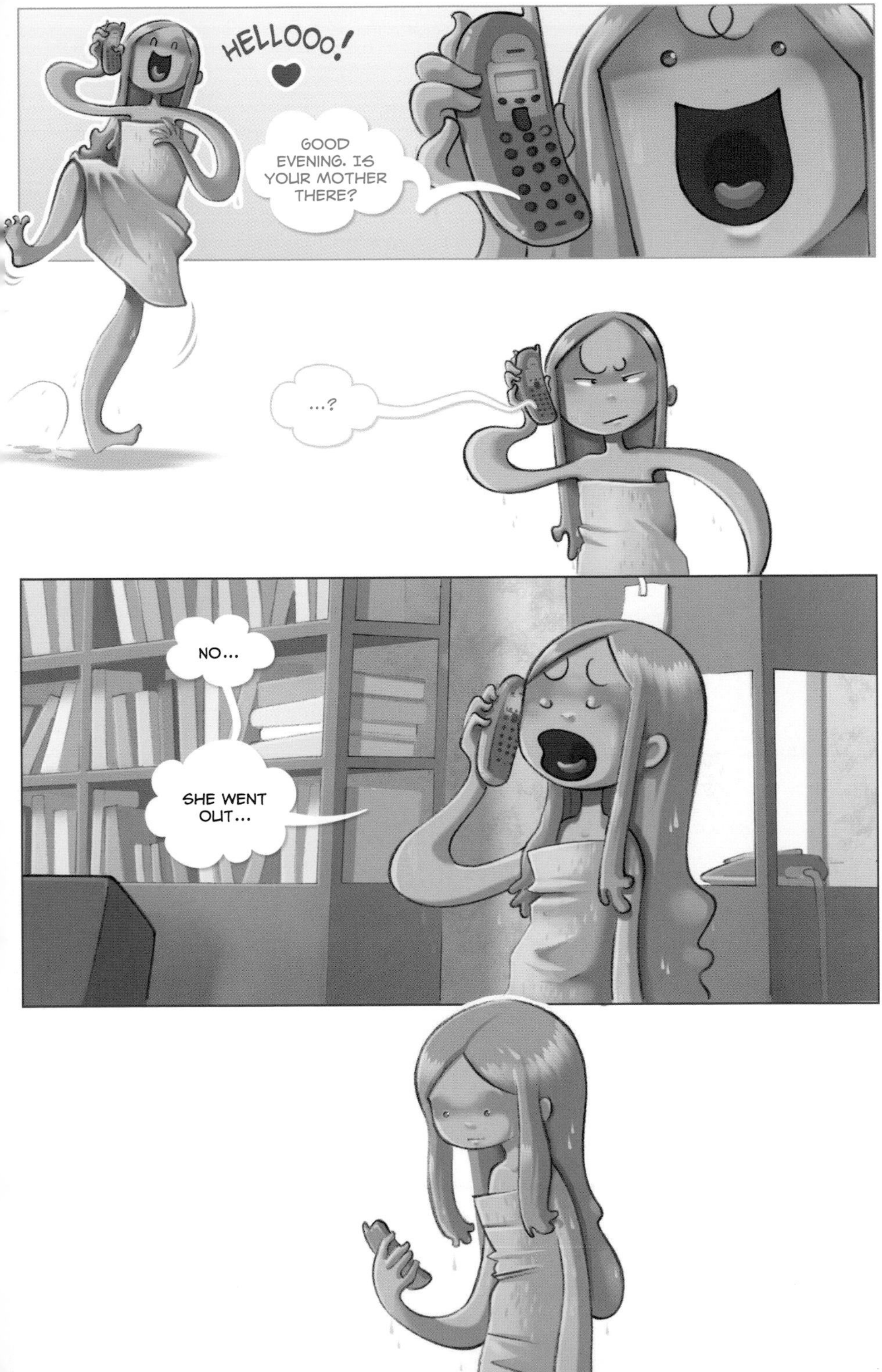
HELLOOO!
GOOD EVENING. IS YOUR MOTHER THERE?
...?
NO...
SHE WENT OUT...

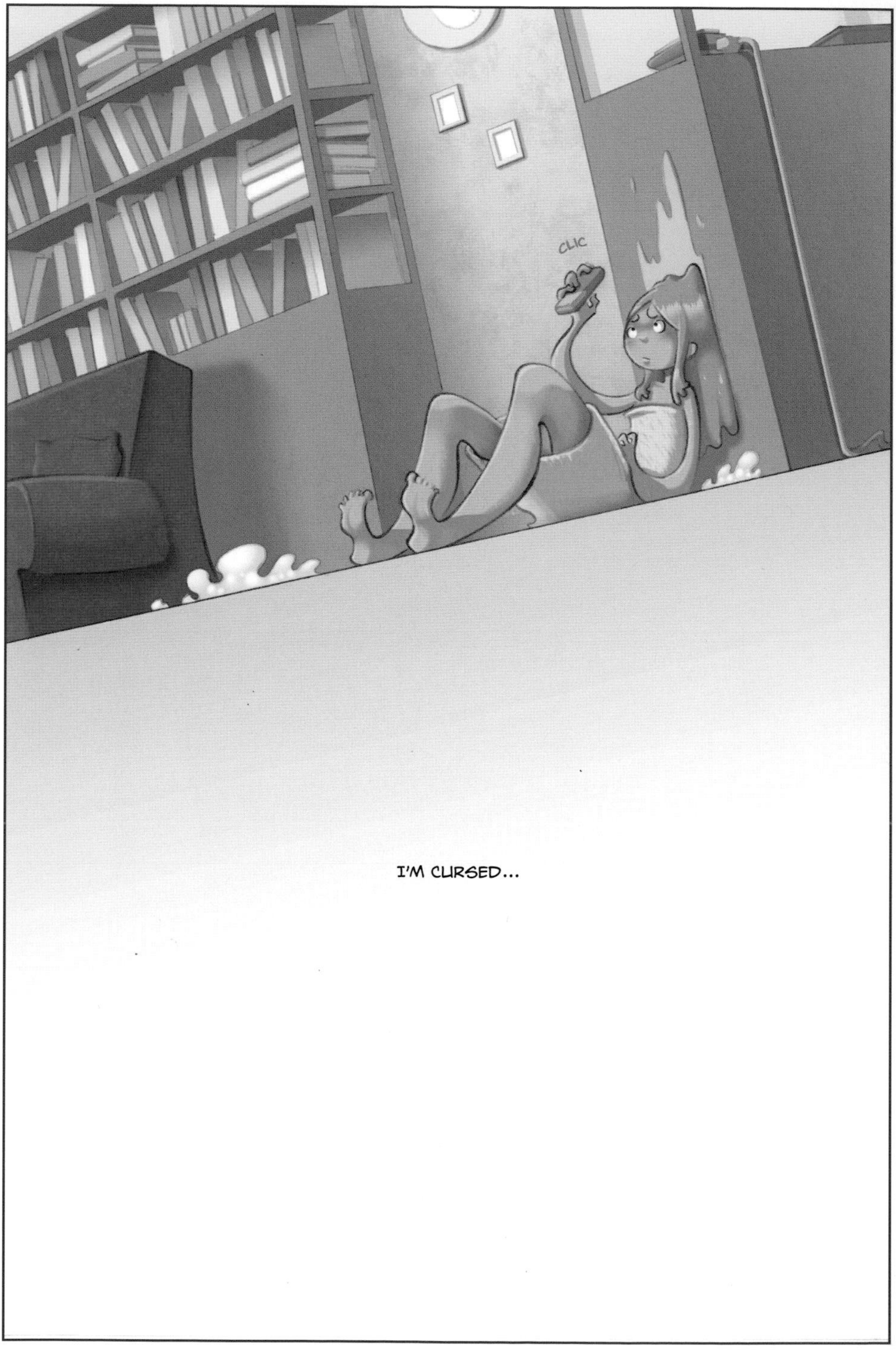
CLIC
I'M CURSED...

Nola's Worlds #2

ferrets and ferreting out

minikim ★ mariolle ★ pop

GRAPHIC UNIVERSE™ · MINNEAPOLIS · NEW YORK · LONDON

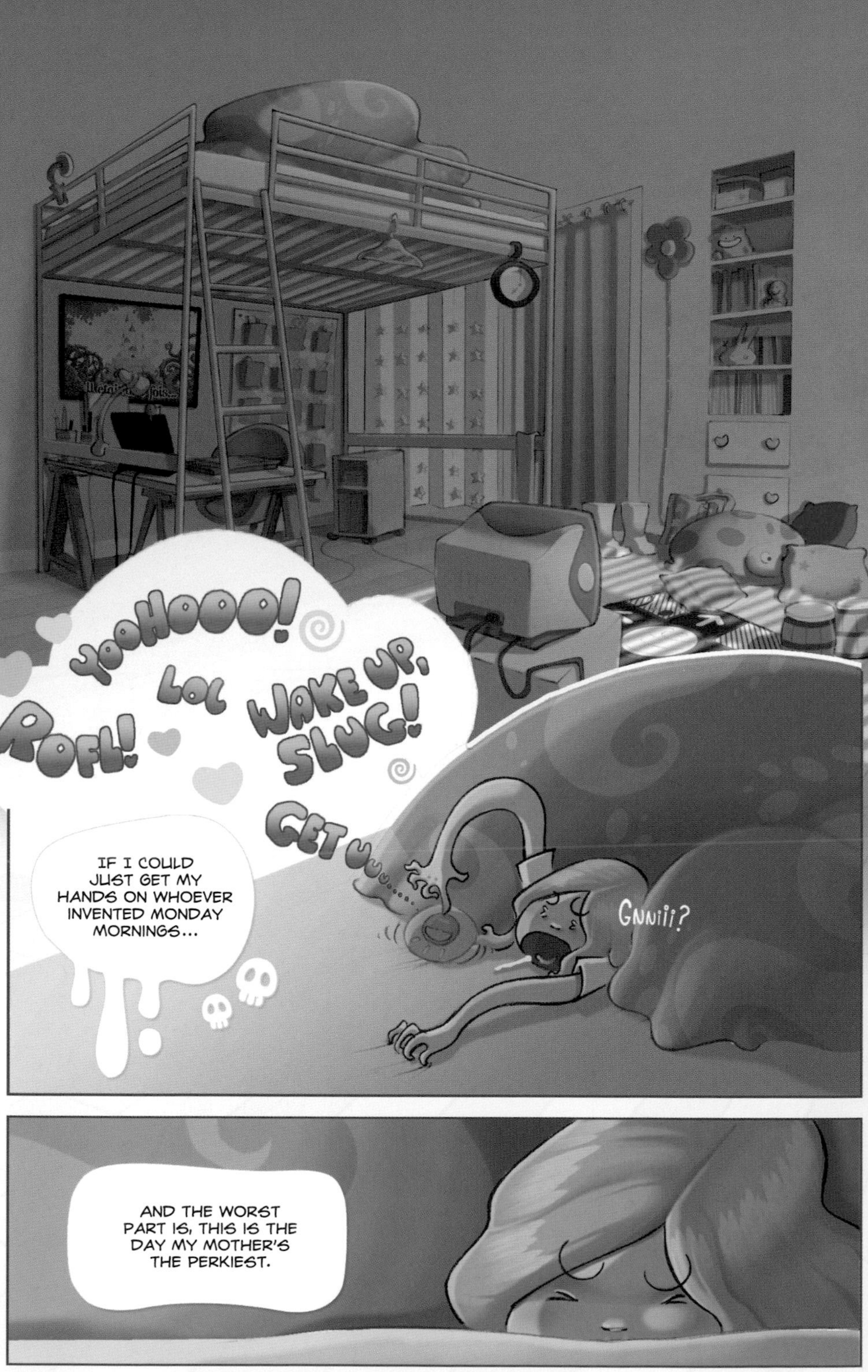
YOOHOOO!
ROFL!
LOL
WAKE UP, SLUG!
GET UUU.....
IF I COULD JUST GET MY HANDS ON WHOEVER INVENTED MONDAY MORNINGS...
GNNIII?
AND THE WORST PART IS, THIS IS THE DAY MY MOTHER'S THE PERKIEST.

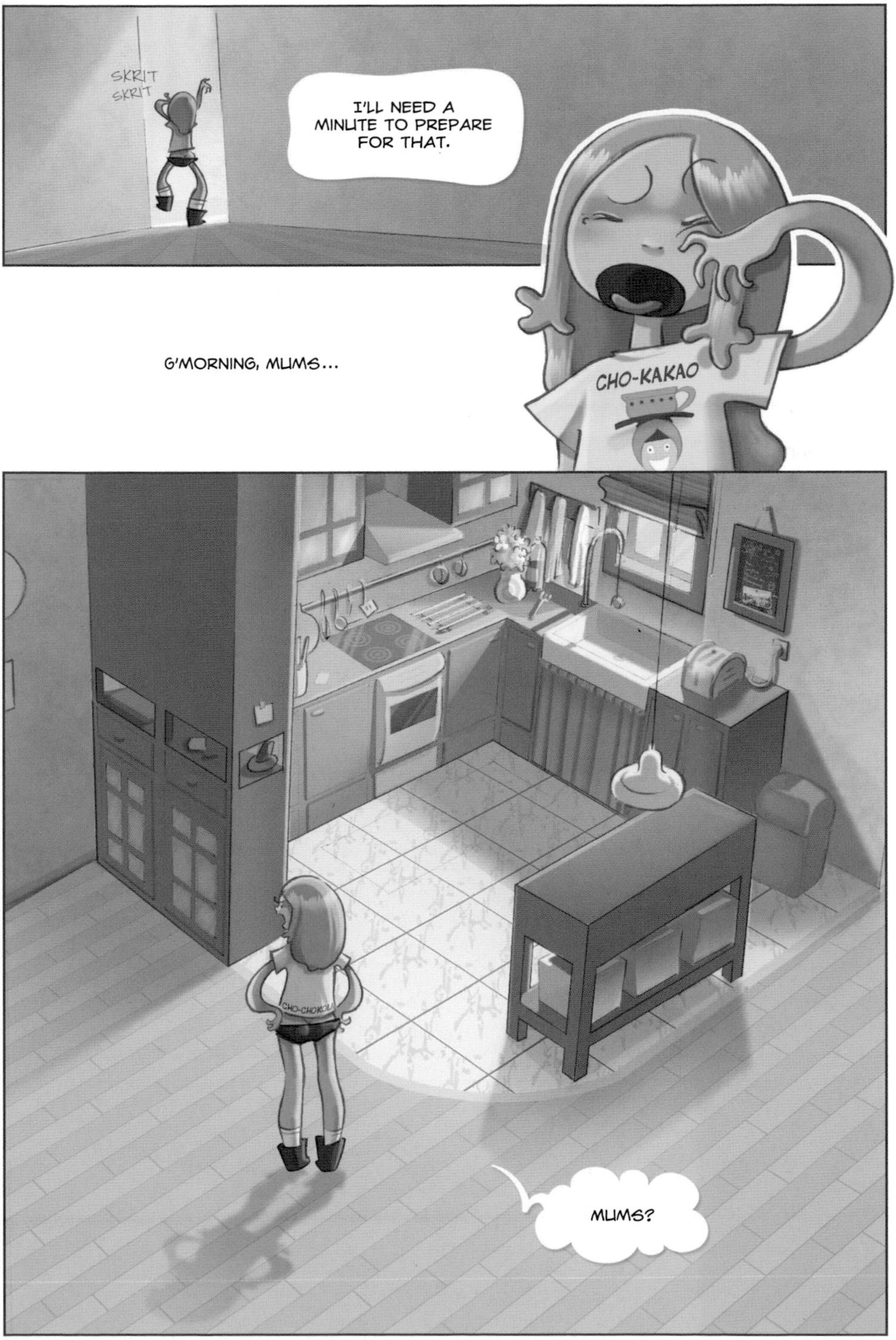
SKRIT
SKRIT
I'LL NEED A MINUTE TO PREPARE FOR THAT.
CHO-KAKAO
G'MORNING, MUMS...
MUMS?

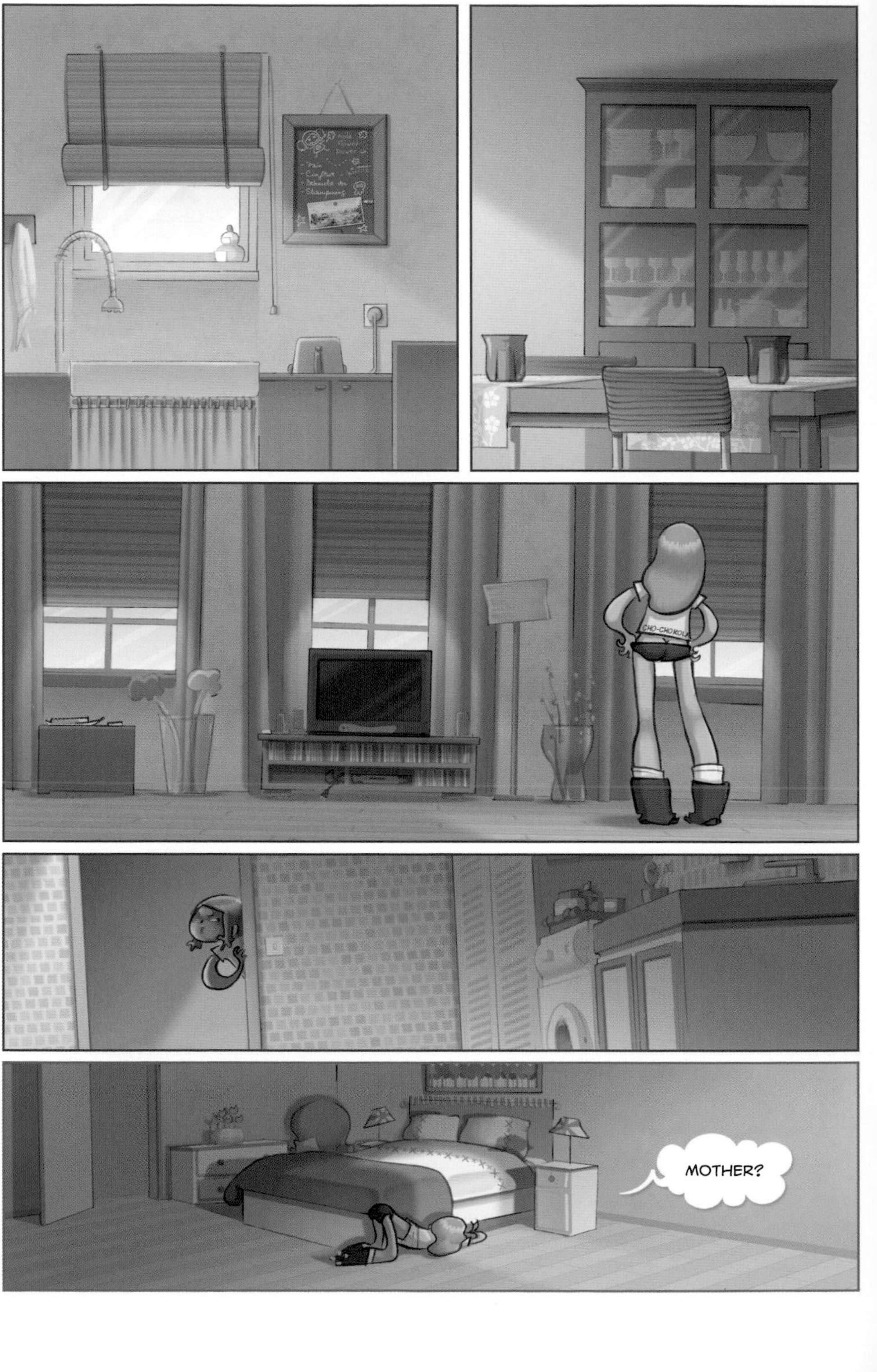
CHO-CHOKOLA
MOTHER?

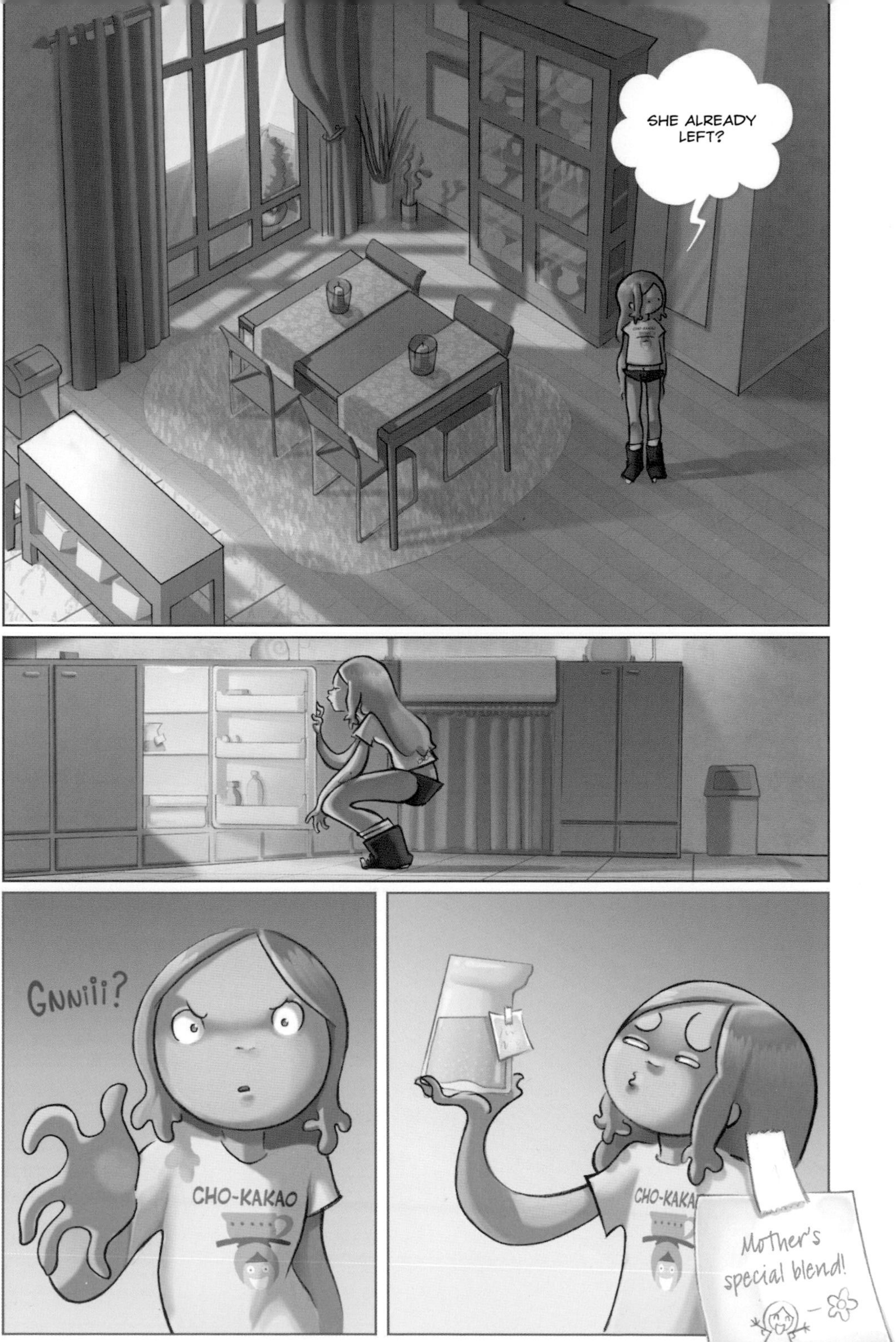
SHE ALREADY LEFT?
GNNIII?
CHO-KAKAO
CHO-KAKA
Mother's special blend!

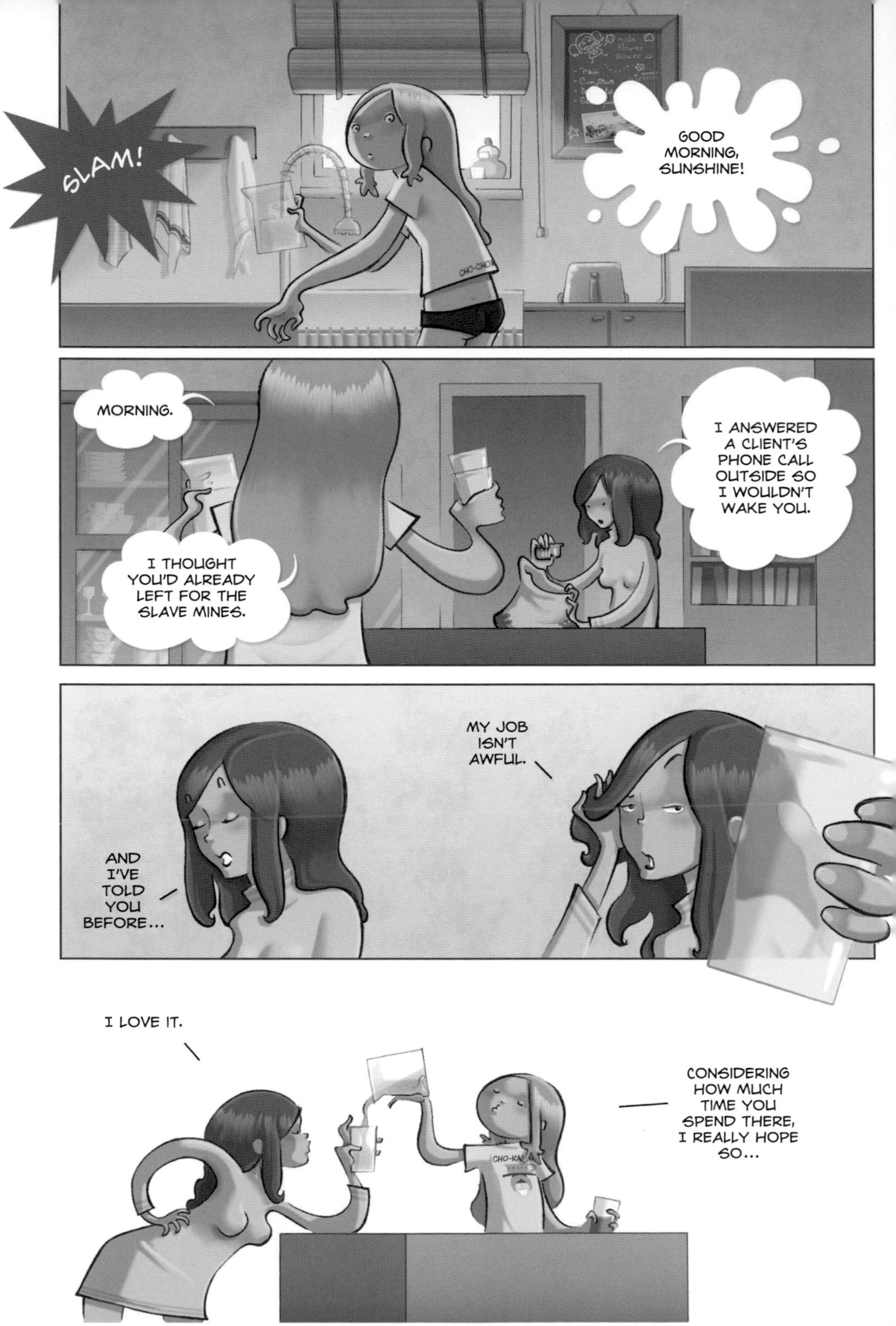
SLAM!
GOOD MORNING, SUNSHINE!
MORNING.
I THOUGHT YOU'D ALREADY LEFT FOR THE SLAVE MINES.
I ANSWERED A CLIENT'S PHONE CALL OUTSIDE SO I WOULDN'T WAKE YOU.
MY JOB ISN'T AWFUL.
AND I'VE TOLD YOU BEFORE...
I LOVE IT.
CONSIDERING HOW MUCH TIME YOU SPEND THERE, I REALLY HOPE SO...

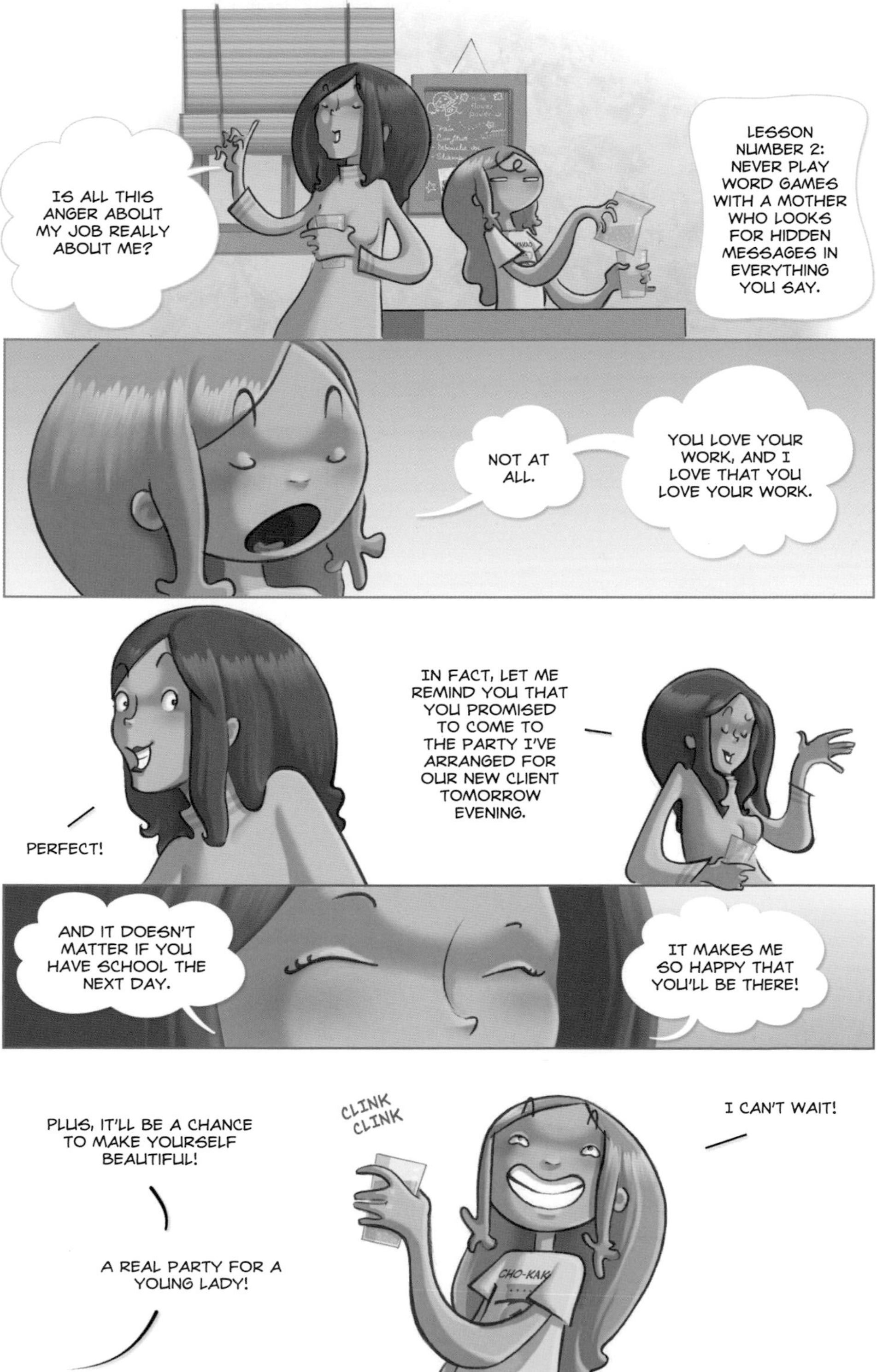
IS ALL THIS ANGER ABOUT MY JOB REALLY ABOUT ME?
LESSON NUMBER 2: NEVER PLAY WORD GAMES WITH A MOTHER WHO LOOKS FOR HIDDEN MESSAGES IN EVERYTHING YOU SAY.
NOT AT ALL.
YOU LOVE YOUR WORK, AND I LOVE THAT YOU LOVE YOUR WORK.
IN FACT, LET ME REMIND YOU THAT YOU PROMISED TO COME TO THE PARTY I'VE ARRANGED FOR OUR NEW CLIENT TOMORROW EVENING.
PERFECT!
AND IT DOESN'T MATTER IF YOU HAVE SCHOOL THE NEXT DAY.
IT MAKES ME SO HAPPY THAT YOU'LL BE THERE!
PLUS, IT'LL BE A CHANCE TO MAKE YOURSELF BEAUTIFUL!
A REAL PARTY FOR A YOUNG LADY!
CLINK CLINK
I CAN'T WAIT!
CHO-KAK

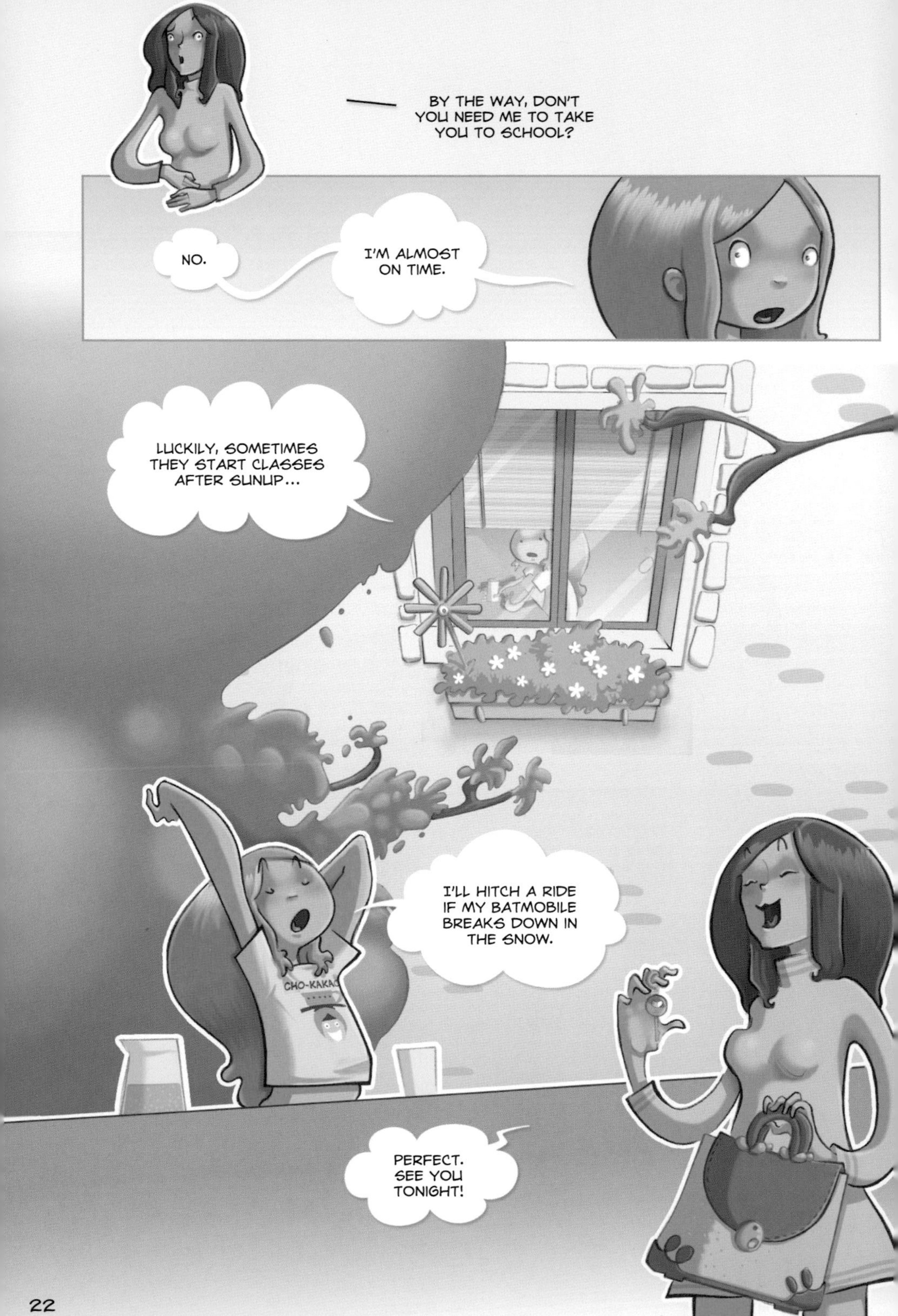
BY THE WAY, DON'T YOU NEED ME TO TAKE YOU TO SCHOOL?
NO.
I'M ALMOST ON TIME.
LUCKILY, SOMETIMES THEY START CLASSES AFTER SUNUP...
I'LL HITCH A RIDE IF MY BATMOBILE BREAKS DOWN IN THE SNOW.
CHO-KAKAO
PERFECT. SEE YOU TONIGHT!

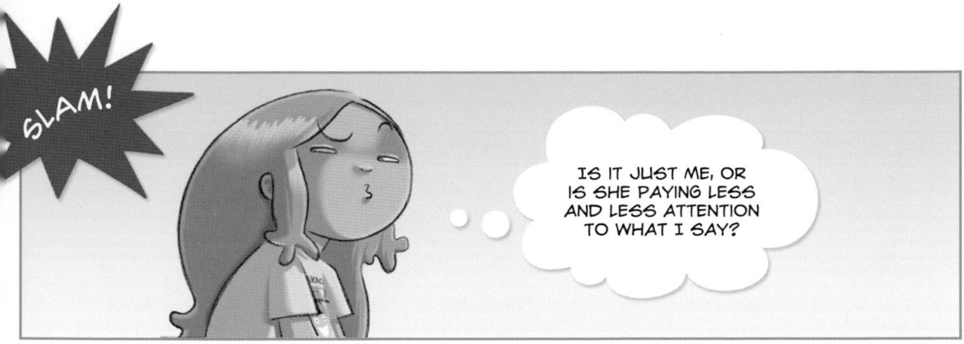
SLAM!
IS IT JUST ME, OR IS SHE PAYING LESS AND LESS ATTENTION TO WHAT I SAY?

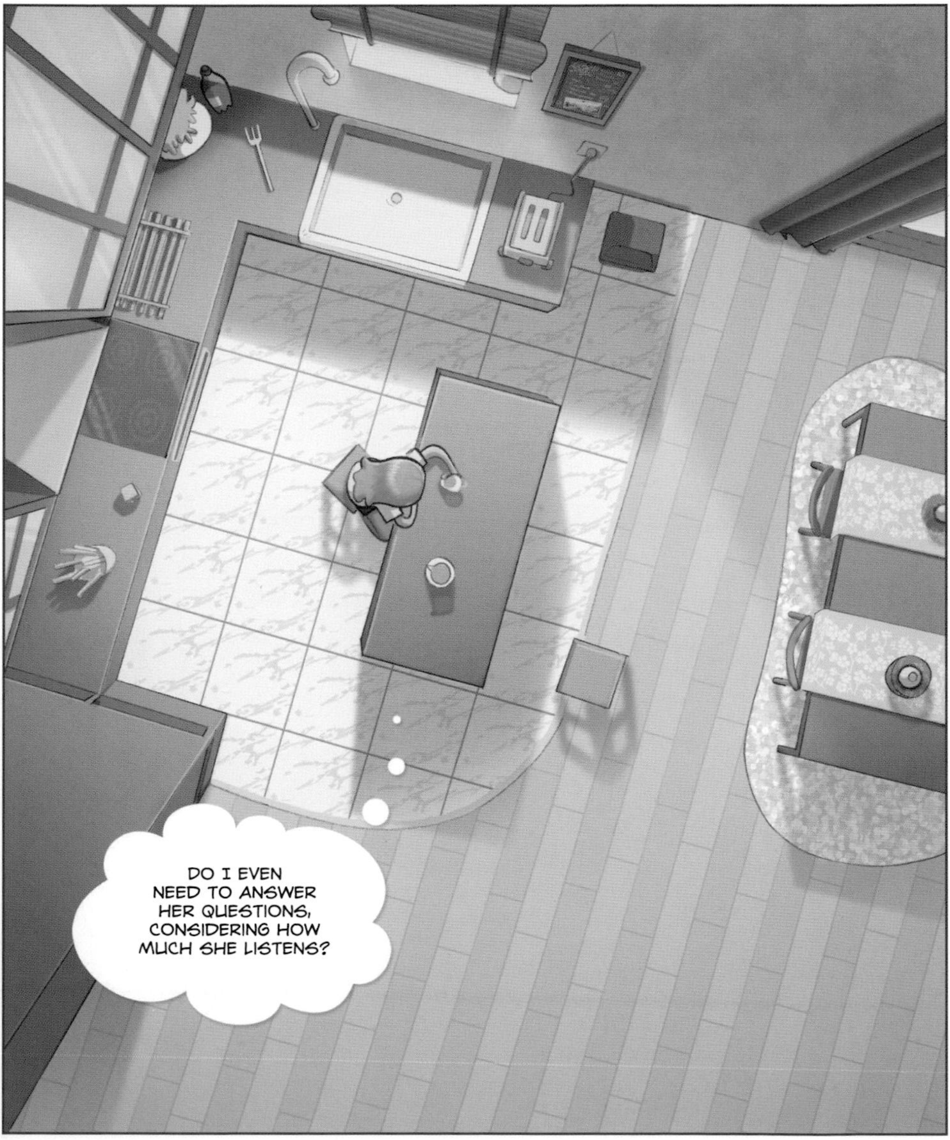
DO I EVEN NEED TO ANSWER HER QUESTIONS, CONSIDERING HOW MUCH SHE LISTENS?

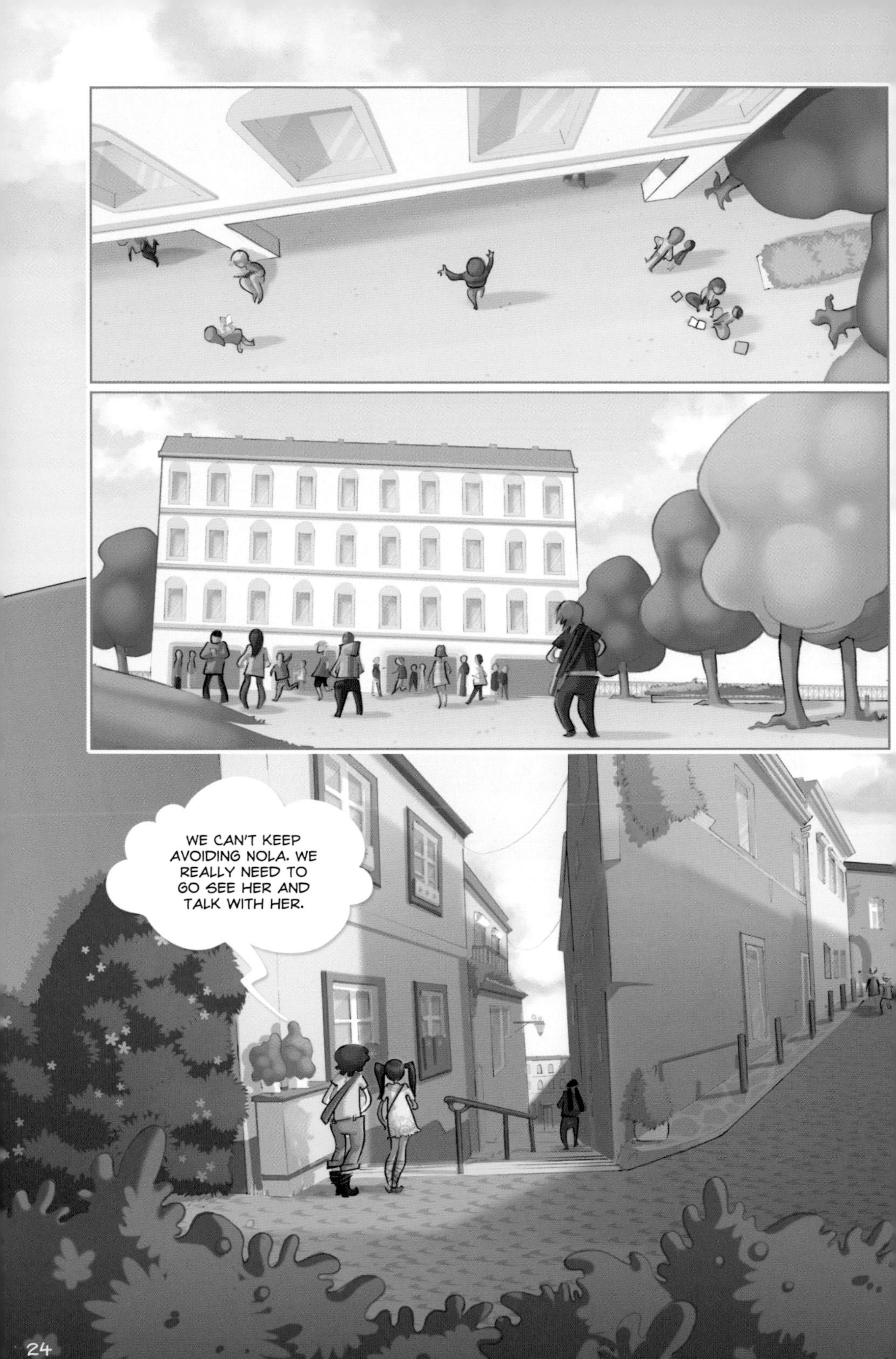
WE CAN'T KEEP AVOIDING NOLA. WE REALLY NEED TO GO SEE HER AND TALK WITH HER.

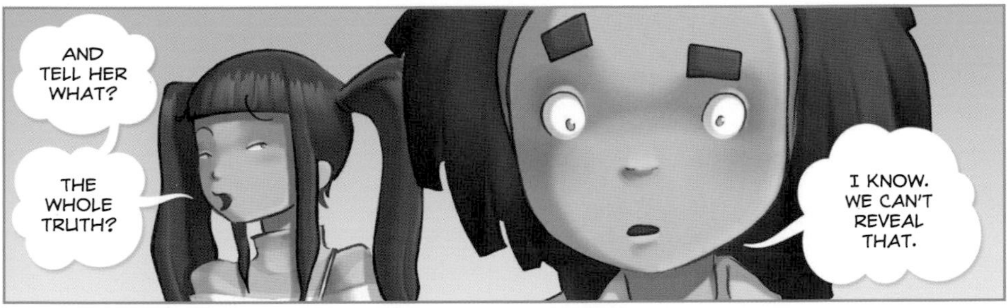
AND TELL HER WHAT?
THE WHOLE TRUTH?
I KNOW. WE CAN'T REVEAL THAT.

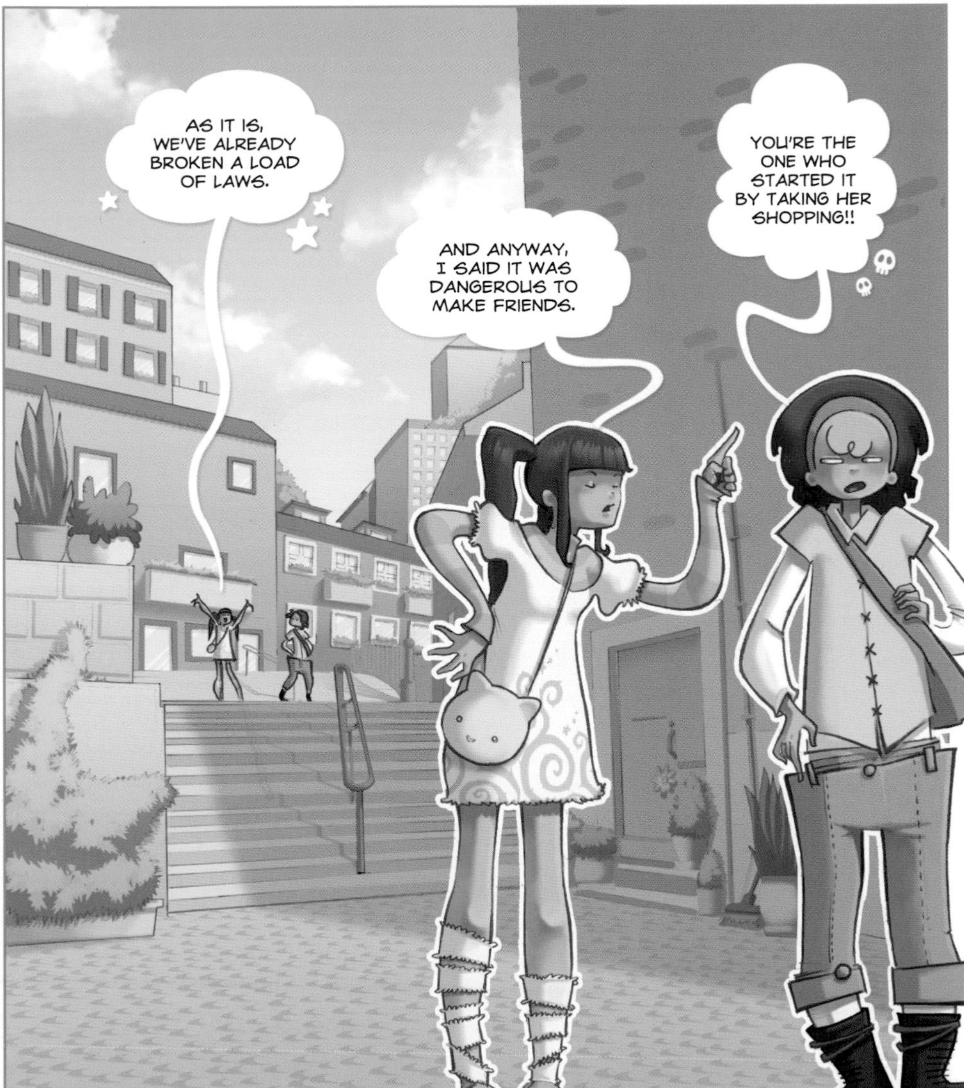
AS IT IS, WE'VE ALREADY BROKEN A LOAD OF LAWS.
AND ANYWAY, I SAID IT WAS DANGEROUS TO MAKE FRIENDS.
YOU'RE THE ONE WHO STARTED IT BY TAKING HER SHOPPING!!

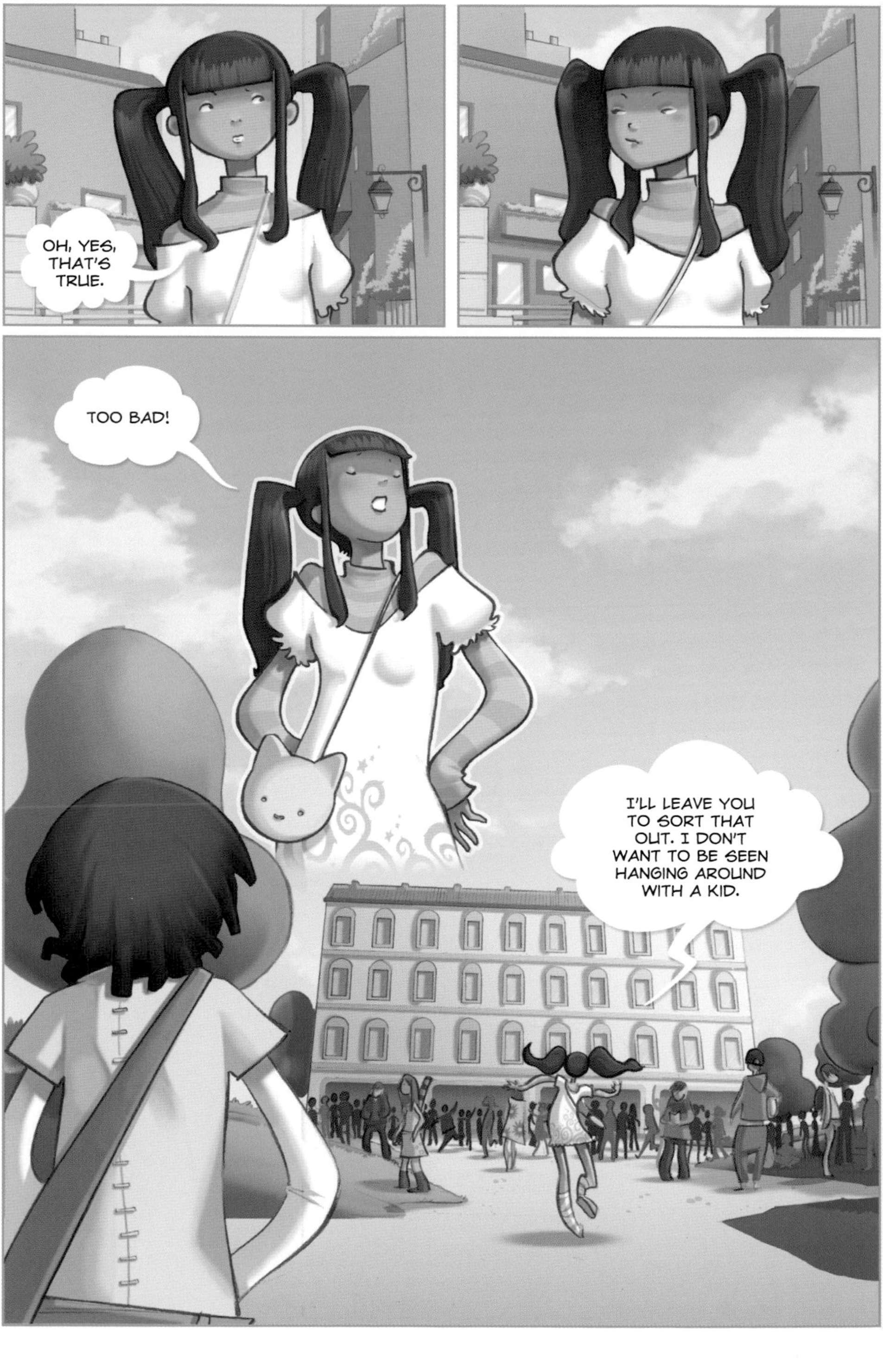
OH, YES, THAT'S TRUE.
TOO BAD!
I'LL LEAVE YOU TO SORT THAT OUT. I DON'T WANT TO BE SEEN HANGING AROUND WITH A KID.

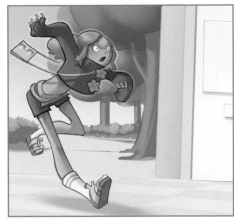

COME ON, IT WON'T BE SO BAD. JUST ATTACK THIS HEAD-ON.

ABOVE ALL, DON'T THROW MYSELF AT HIM. DON'T LOOK DESPERATE. I NEED TO LET HIM COME TALK TO ME FIRST.

AFTER ALL, I HAVEN'T DONE ANYTHING WRONG. I EVEN SAVED HER LIFE.

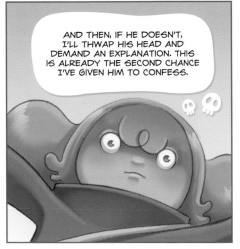

AND THEN, IF HE DOESN'T, I'LL THWAP HIS HEAD AND DEMAND AN EXPLANATION. THIS IS ALREADY THE SECOND CHANCE I'VE GIVEN HIM TO CONFESS.

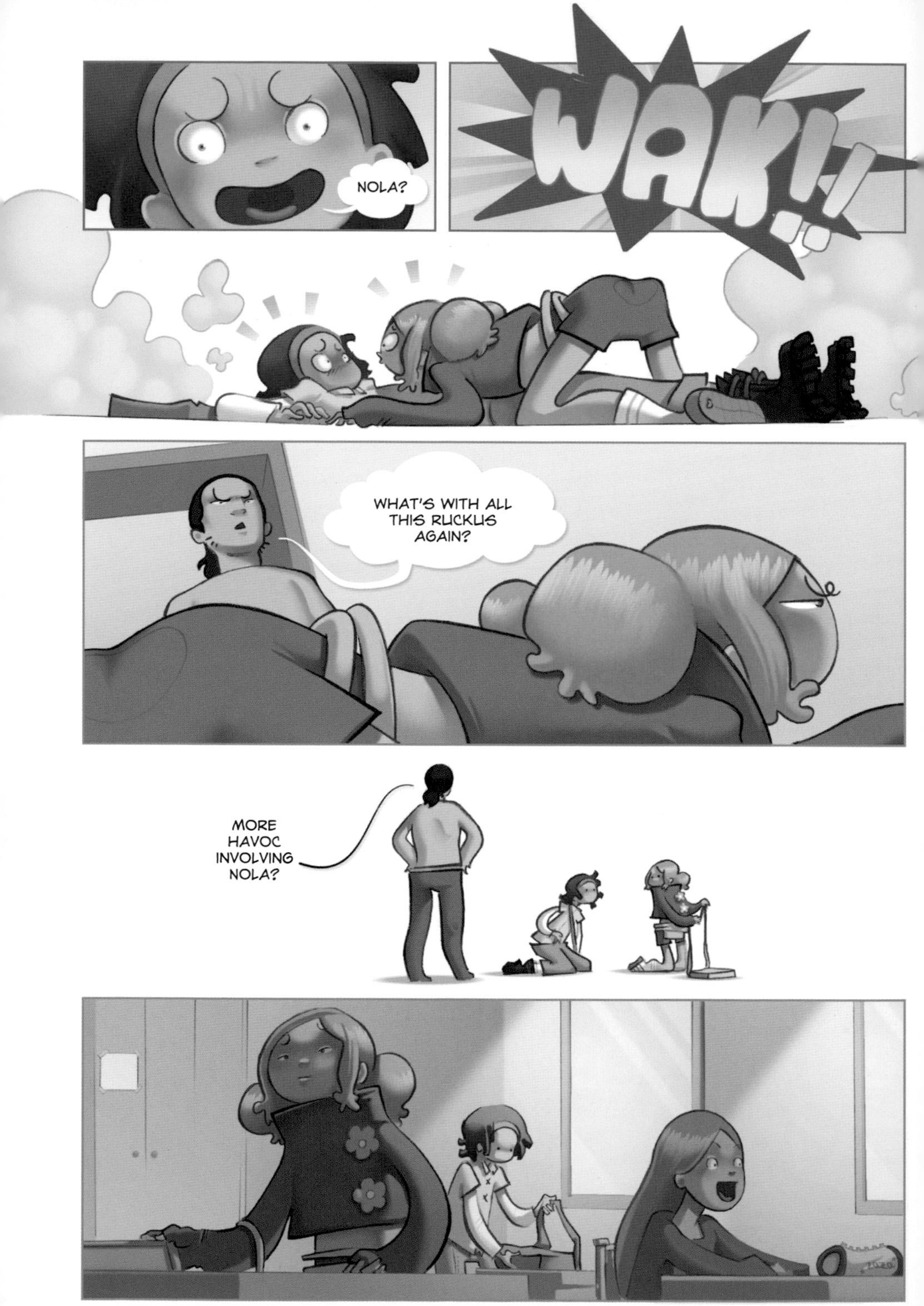
NOLA?
WAK!!!
WHAT'S WITH ALL THIS RUCKUS AGAIN?
MORE HAVOC INVOLVING NOLA?

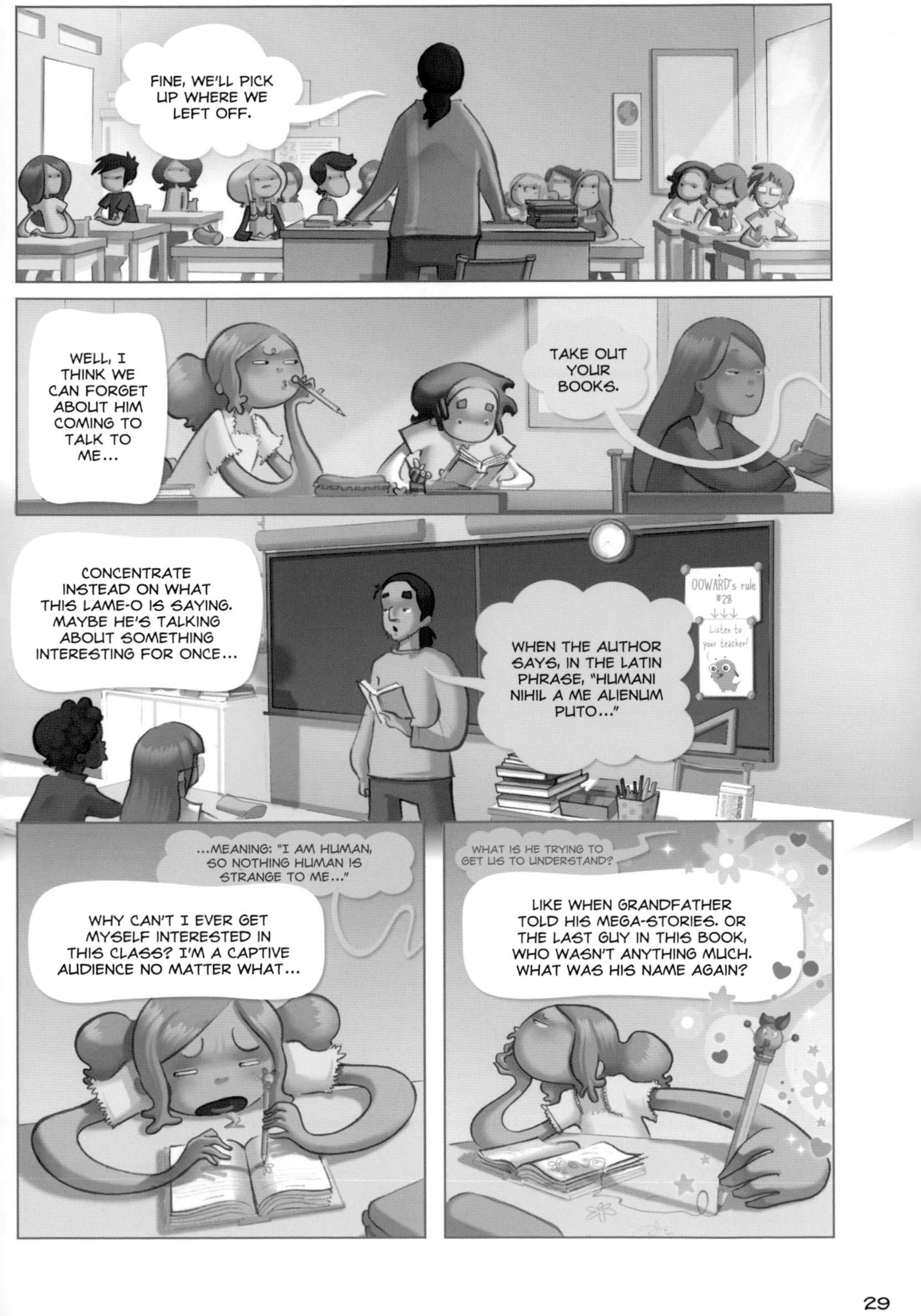

FINE, WE'LL PICK UP WHERE WE LEFT OFF.
WELL, I THINK WE CAN FORGET ABOUT HIM COMING TO TALK TO ME...
TAKE OUT YOUR BOOKS.
CONCENTRATE INSTEAD ON WHAT THIS LAME-O IS SAYING. MAYBE HE'S TALKING ABOUT SOMETHING INTERESTING FOR ONCE...
OOWARD's rule #28
Listen to your teacher!
WHEN THE AUTHOR SAYS, IN THE LATIN PHRASE, "HUMANI NIHIL A ME ALIENUM PUTO..."
...MEANING: "I AM HUMAN, SO NOTHING HUMAN IS STRANGE TO ME..."
WHY CAN'T I EVER GET MYSELF INTERESTED IN THIS CLASS? I'M A CAPTIVE AUDIENCE NO MATTER WHAT...
WHAT IS HE TRYING TO GET US TO UNDERSTAND?
LIKE WHEN GRANDFATHER TOLD HIS MEGA-STORIES. OR THE LAST GUY IN THIS BOOK, WHO WASN'T ANYTHING MUCH. WHAT WAS HIS NAME AGAIN?

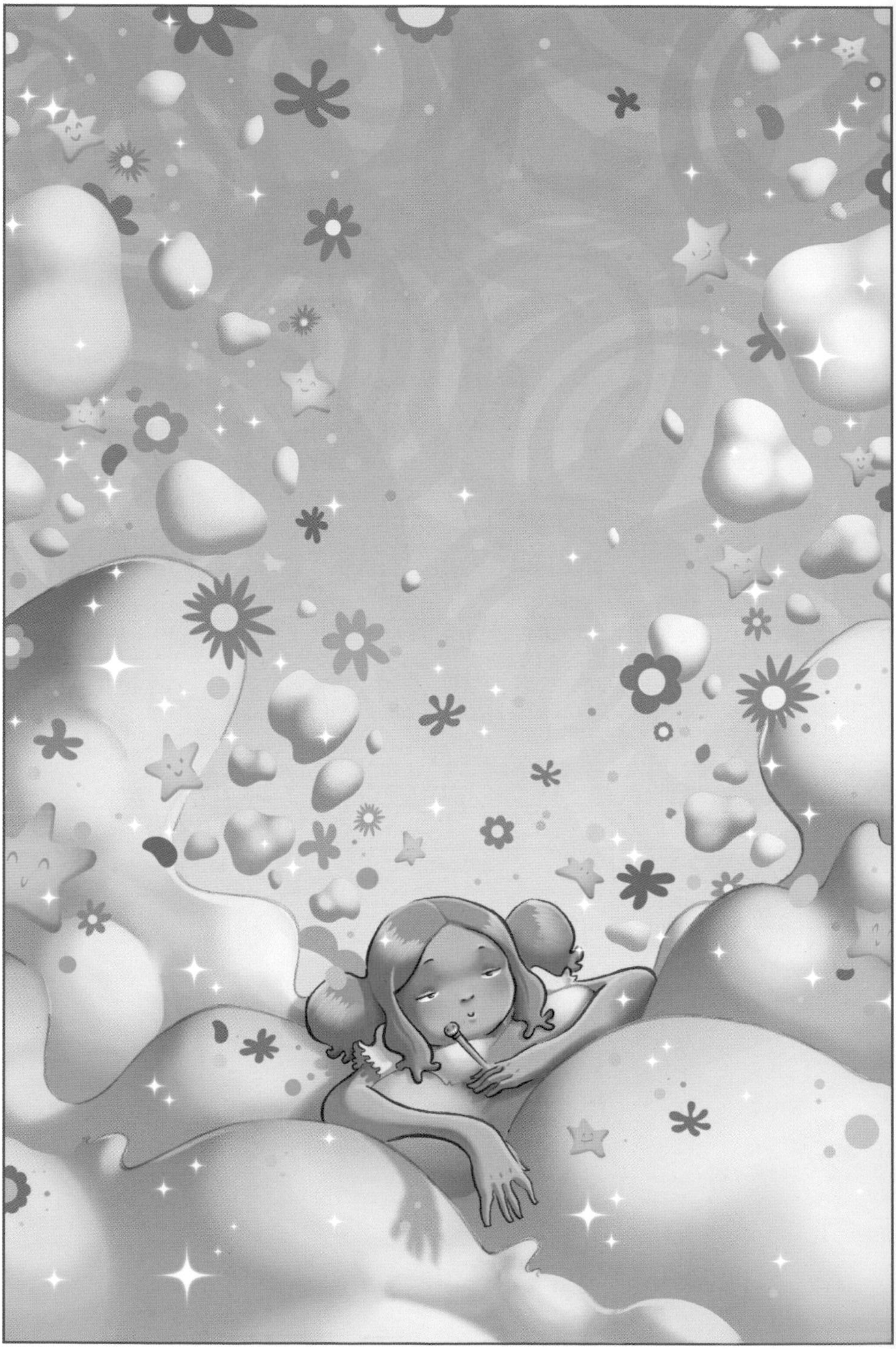

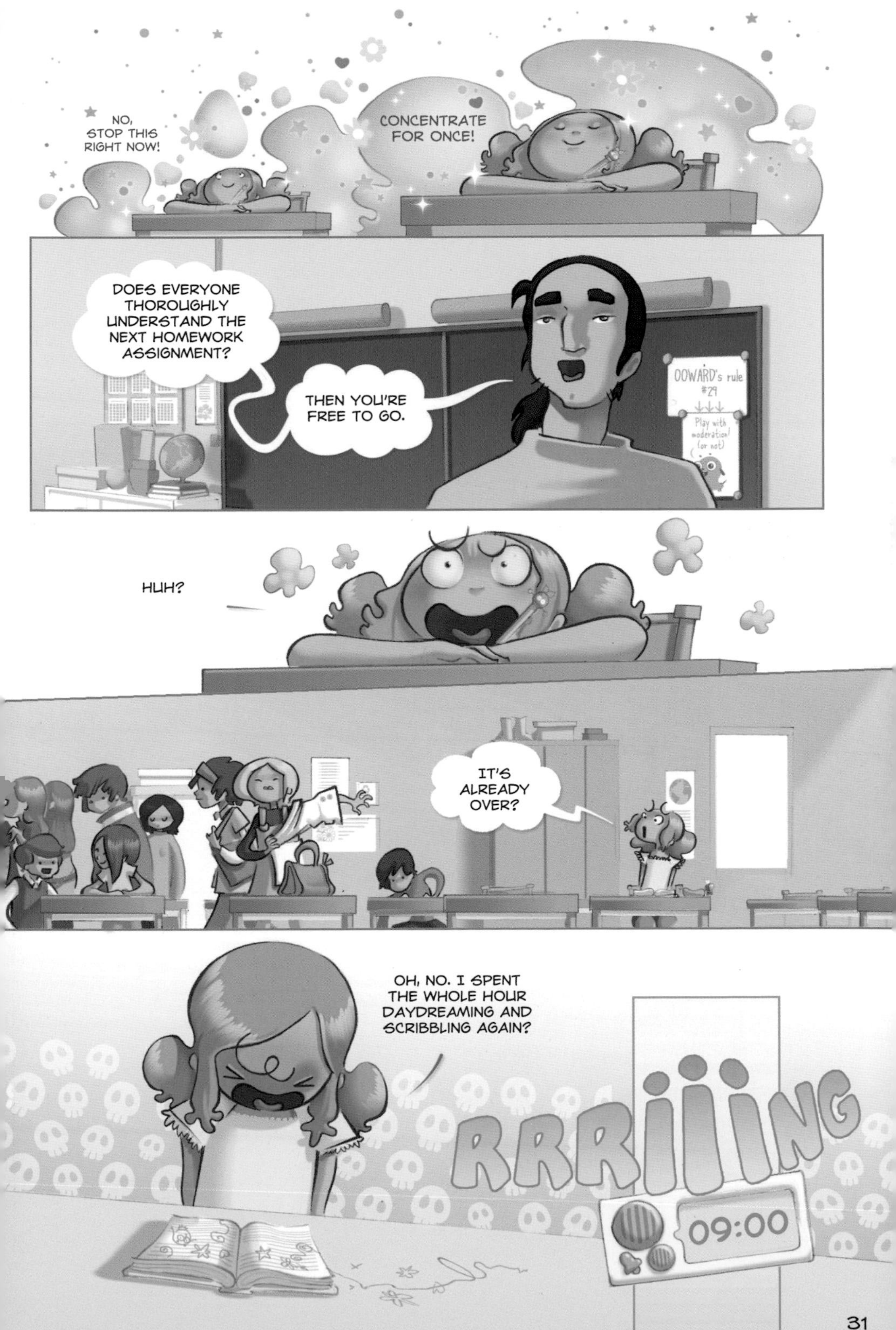
NO, STOP THIS RIGHT NOW!
CONCENTRATE FOR ONCE!
DOES EVERYONE THOROUGHLY UNDERSTAND THE NEXT HOMEWORK ASSIGNMENT?
THEN YOU'RE FREE TO GO.
OOWARD's rule #29
Play with moderation! (or not)
HUH?
IT'S ALREADY OVER?
OH, NO. I SPENT THE WHOLE HOUR DAYDREAMING AND SCRIBBLING AGAIN?
RRRIIING
09:00

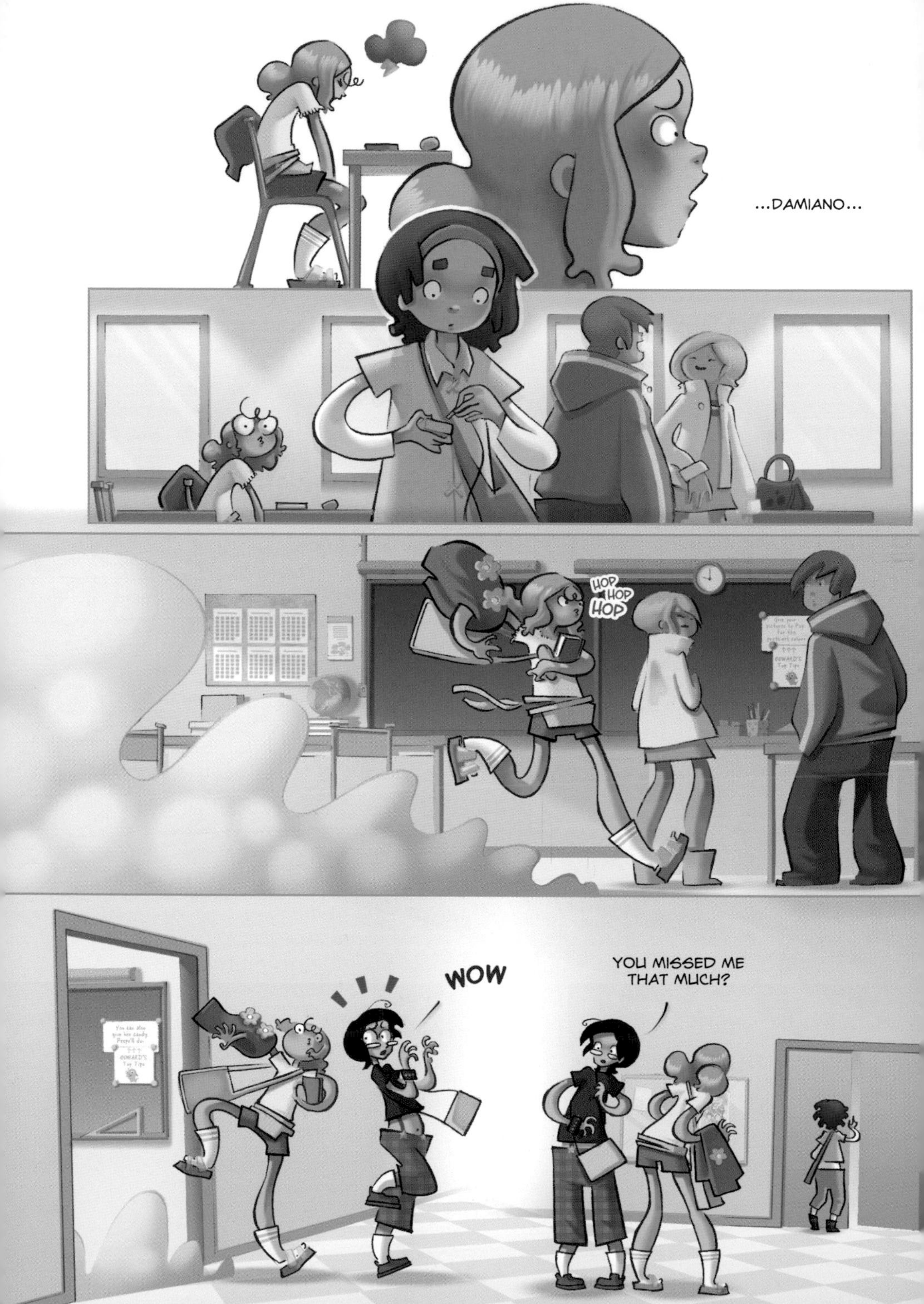
...DAMIANO...
HOP HOP HOP
WOW
YOU MISSED ME THAT MUCH?

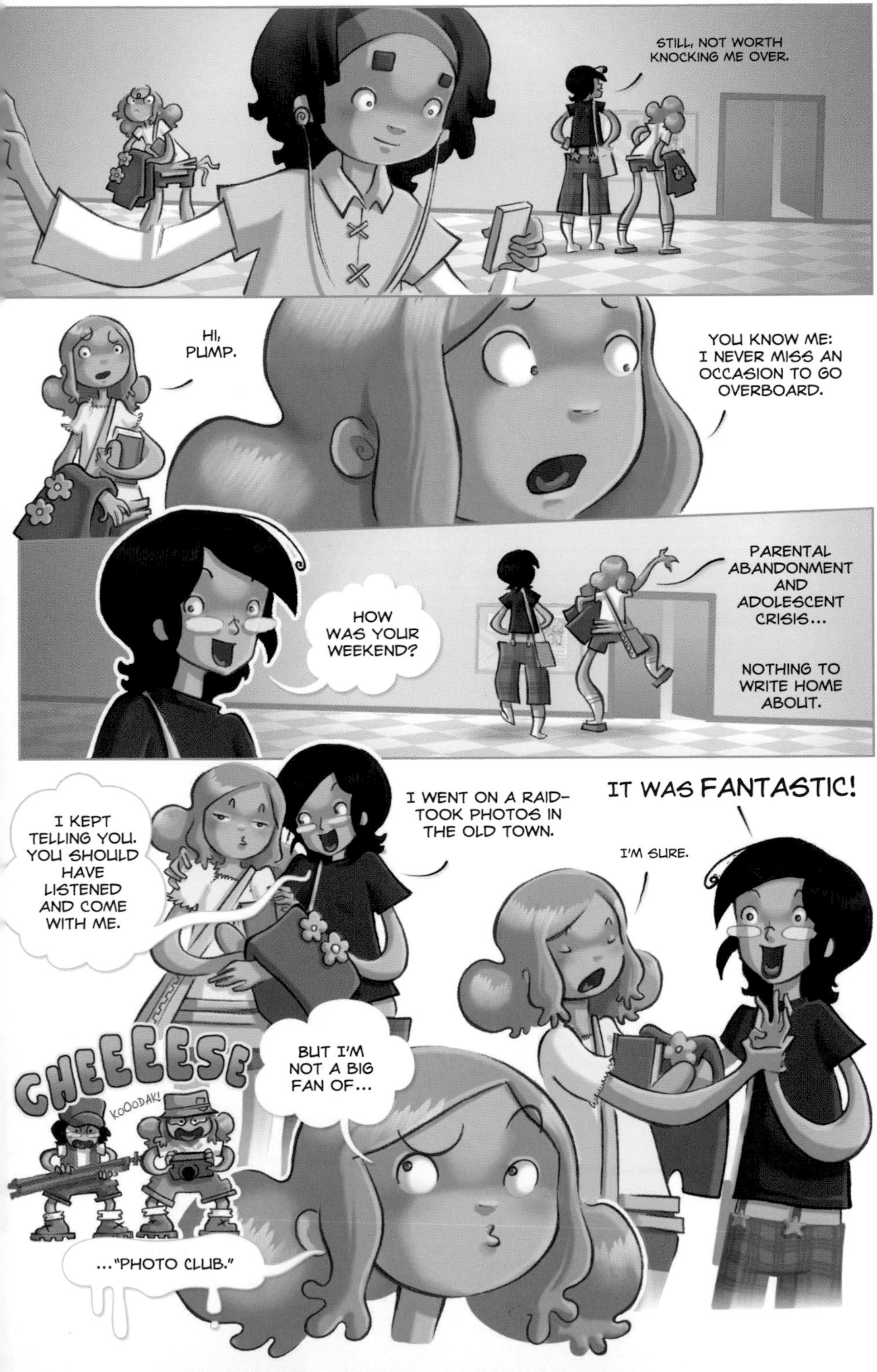
STILL, NOT WORTH KNOCKING ME OVER.
HI, PUMP.
YOU KNOW ME: I NEVER MISS AN OCCASION TO GO OVERBOARD.
HOW WAS YOUR WEEKEND?
PARENTAL ABANDONMENT AND ADOLESCENT CRISIS...
NOTHING TO WRITE HOME ABOUT.
I WENT ON A RAID-TOOK PHOTOS IN THE OLD TOWN.
IT WAS FANTASTIC!
I'M SURE.
I KEPT TELLING YOU. YOU SHOULD HAVE LISTENED AND COME WITH ME.
BUT I'M NOT A BIG FAN OF...
CHEEEESE
KOOODAK!
..."PHOTO CLUB."

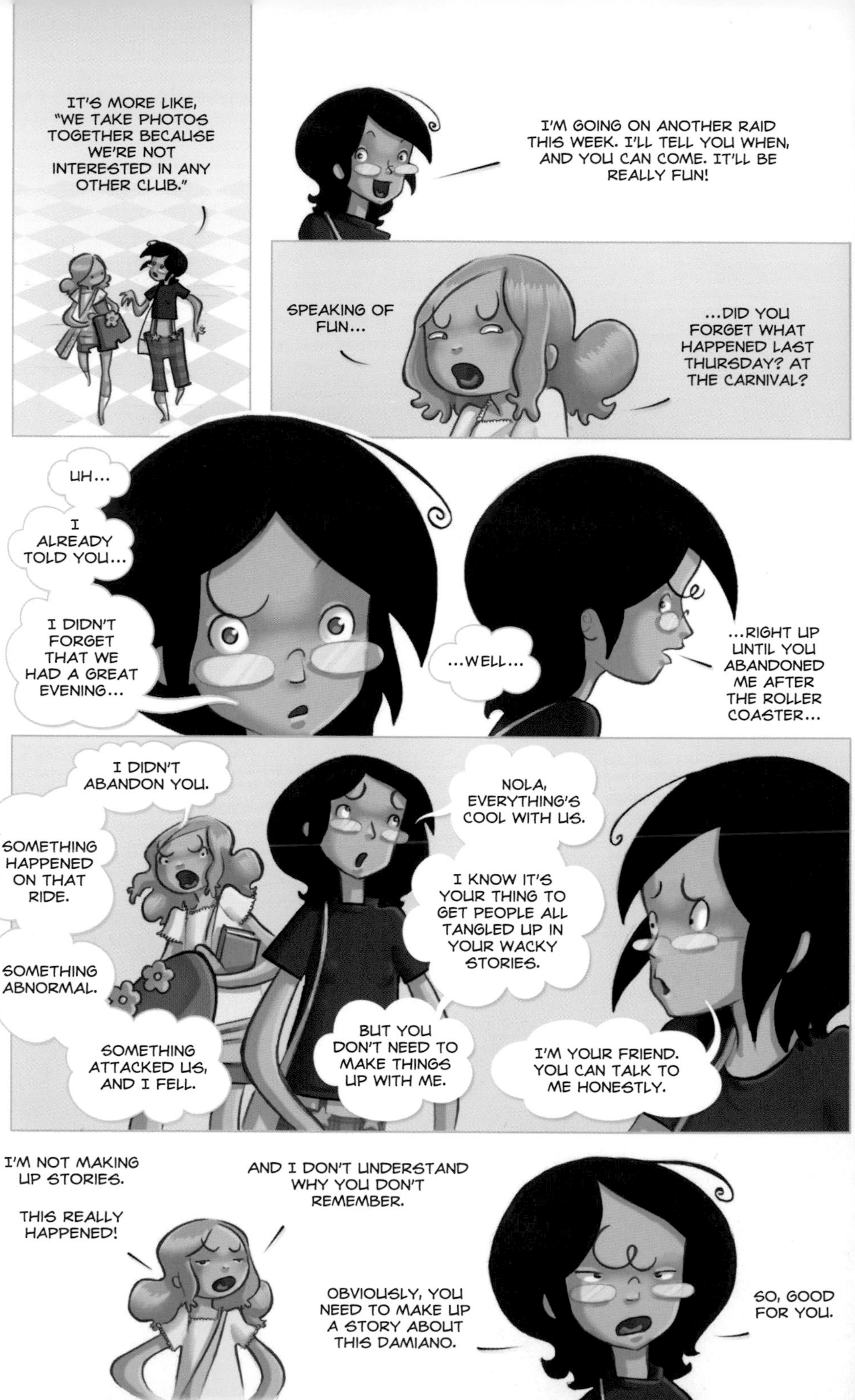
IT'S MORE LIKE, "WE TAKE PHOTOS TOGETHER BECAUSE WE'RE NOT INTERESTED IN ANY OTHER CLUB."
I'M GOING ON ANOTHER RAID THIS WEEK. I'LL TELL YOU WHEN, AND YOU CAN COME. IT'LL BE REALLY FUN!
SPEAKING OF FUN...
...DID YOU FORGET WHAT HAPPENED LAST THURSDAY? AT THE CARNIVAL?
UH...
I ALREADY TOLD YOU...
I DIDN'T FORGET THAT WE HAD A GREAT EVENING...
...WELL...
...RIGHT UP UNTIL YOU ABANDONED ME AFTER THE ROLLER COASTER...
I DIDN'T ABANDON YOU.
SOMETHING HAPPENED ON THAT RIDE.
SOMETHING ABNORMAL.
SOMETHING ATTACKED US, AND I FELL.
NOLA, EVERYTHING'S COOL WITH US.
I KNOW IT'S YOUR THING TO GET PEOPLE ALL TANGLED UP IN YOUR WACKY STORIES.
BUT YOU DON'T NEED TO MAKE THINGS UP WITH ME.
I'M YOUR FRIEND. YOU CAN TALK TO ME HONESTLY.
I'M NOT MAKING UP STORIES.
THIS REALLY HAPPENED!
AND I DON'T UNDERSTAND WHY YOU DON'T REMEMBER.
OBVIOUSLY, YOU NEED TO MAKE UP A STORY ABOUT THIS DAMIANO.
SO, GOOD FOR YOU.

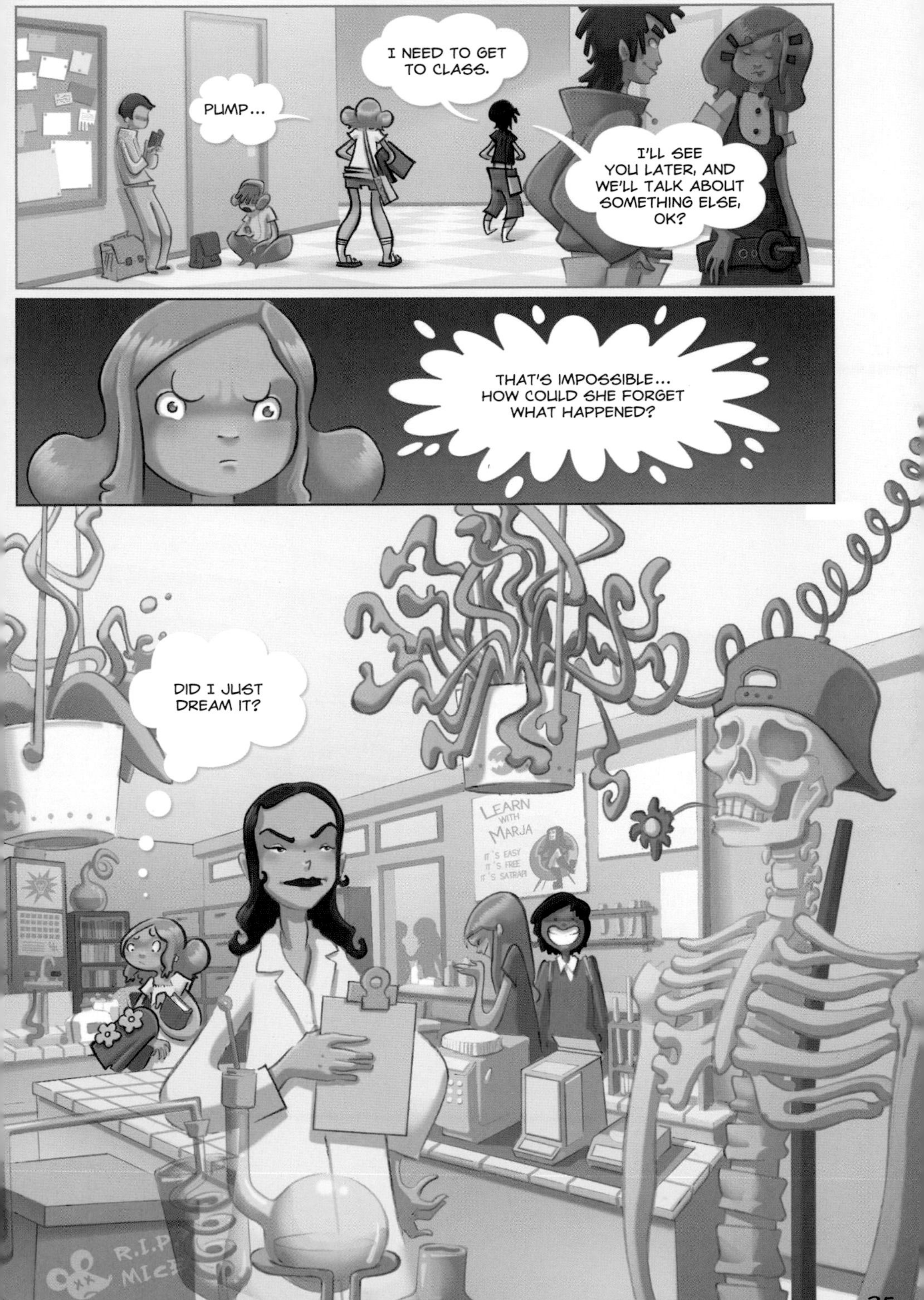
PUMP...
I NEED TO GET TO CLASS.
I'LL SEE YOU LATER, AND WE'LL TALK ABOUT SOMETHING ELSE, OK?
THAT'S IMPOSSIBLE... HOW COULD SHE FORGET WHAT HAPPENED?
DID I JUST DREAM IT?
LEARN WITH MARJA
IT'S EASY
IT'S FREE

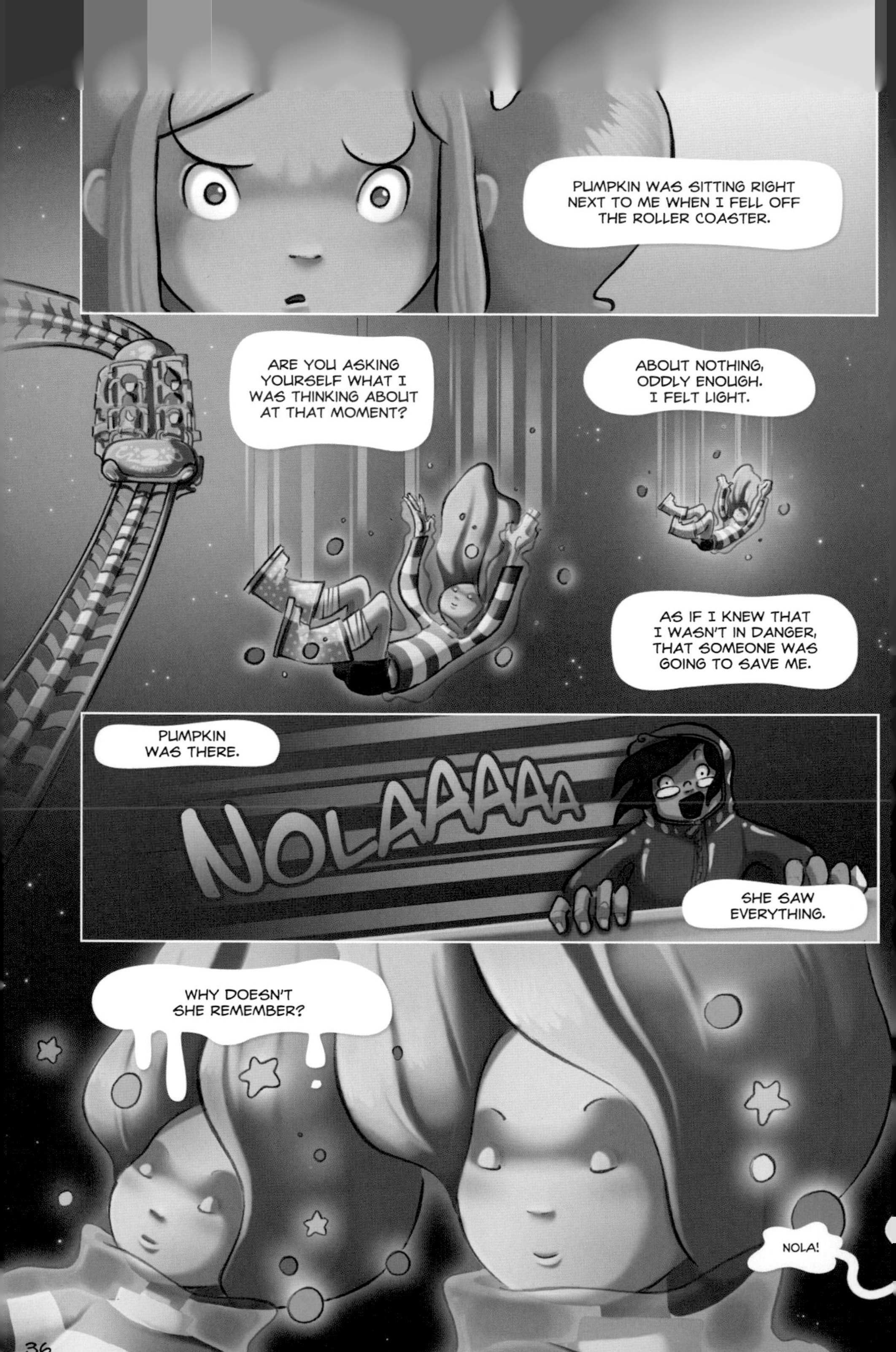
PUMPKIN WAS SITTING RIGHT NEXT TO ME WHEN I FELL OFF THE ROLLER COASTER.
ARE YOU ASKING YOURSELF WHAT I WAS THINKING ABOUT AT THAT MOMENT?
ABOUT NOTHING, ODDLY ENOUGH. I FELT LIGHT.
AS IF I KNEW THAT I WASN'T IN DANGER, THAT SOMEONE WAS GOING TO SAVE ME.
PUMPKIN WAS THERE.
NOLAAAAA
SHE SAW EVERYTHING.
WHY DOESN'T SHE REMEMBER?
NOLA!

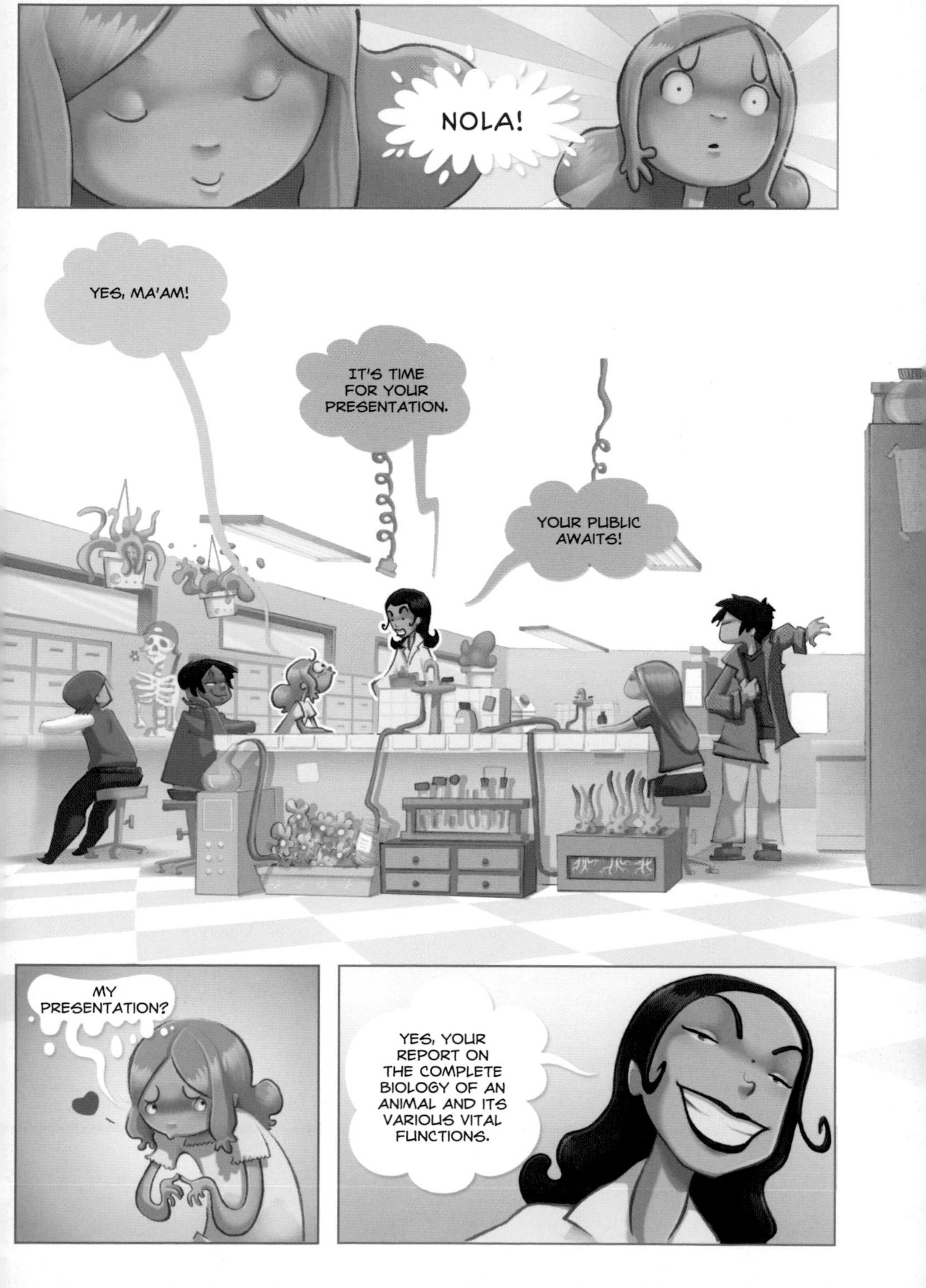
NOLA!
YES, MA'AM!
IT'S TIME FOR YOUR PRESENTATION.
YOUR PUBLIC AWAITS!
MY PRESENTATION?
YES, YOUR REPORT ON THE COMPLETE BIOLOGY OF AN ANIMAL AND ITS VARIOUS VITAL FUNCTIONS.

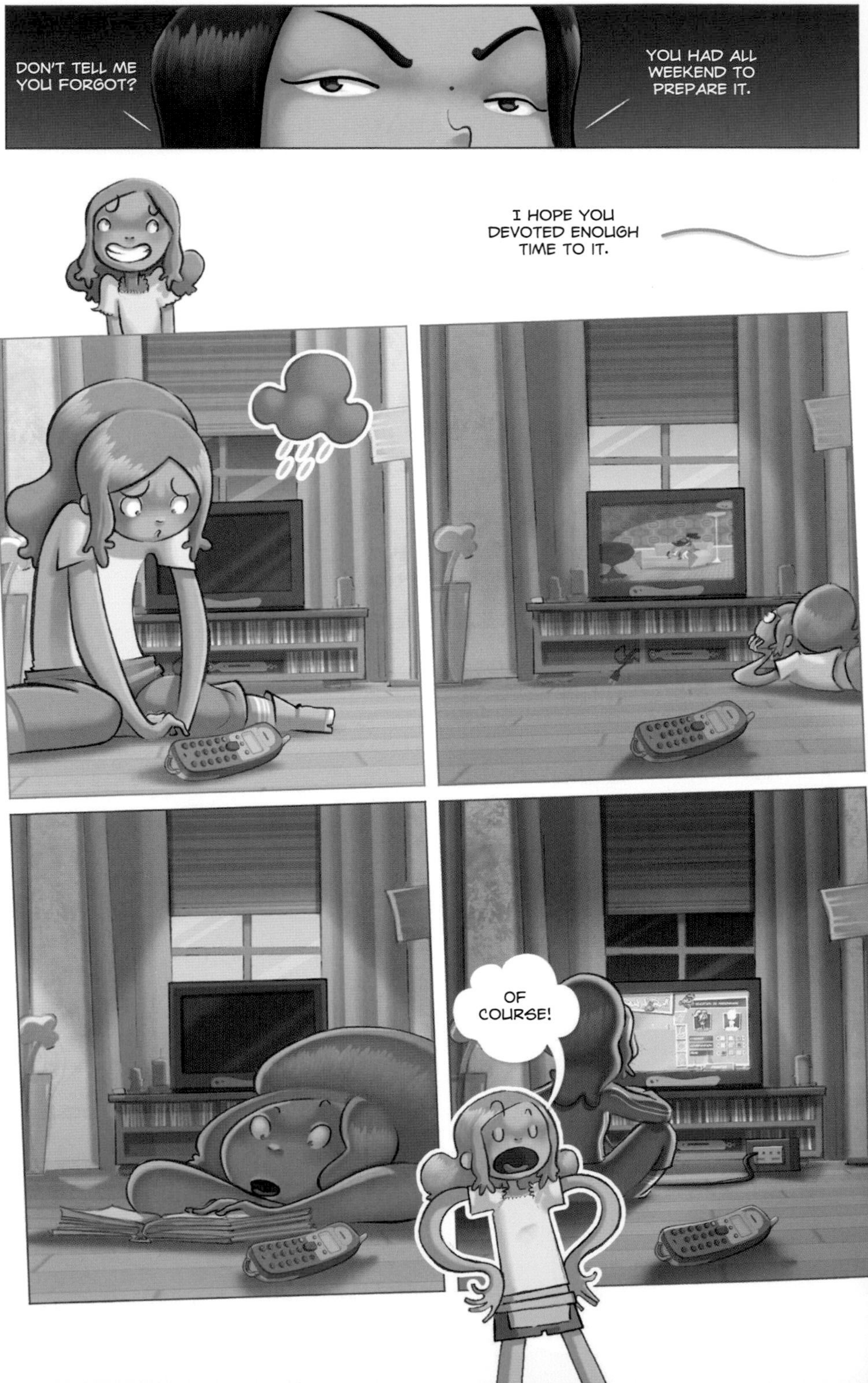
DON'T TELL ME YOU FORGOT?
YOU HAD ALL WEEKEND TO PREPARE IT.
I HOPE YOU DEVOTED ENOUGH TIME TO IT.
OF COURSE!

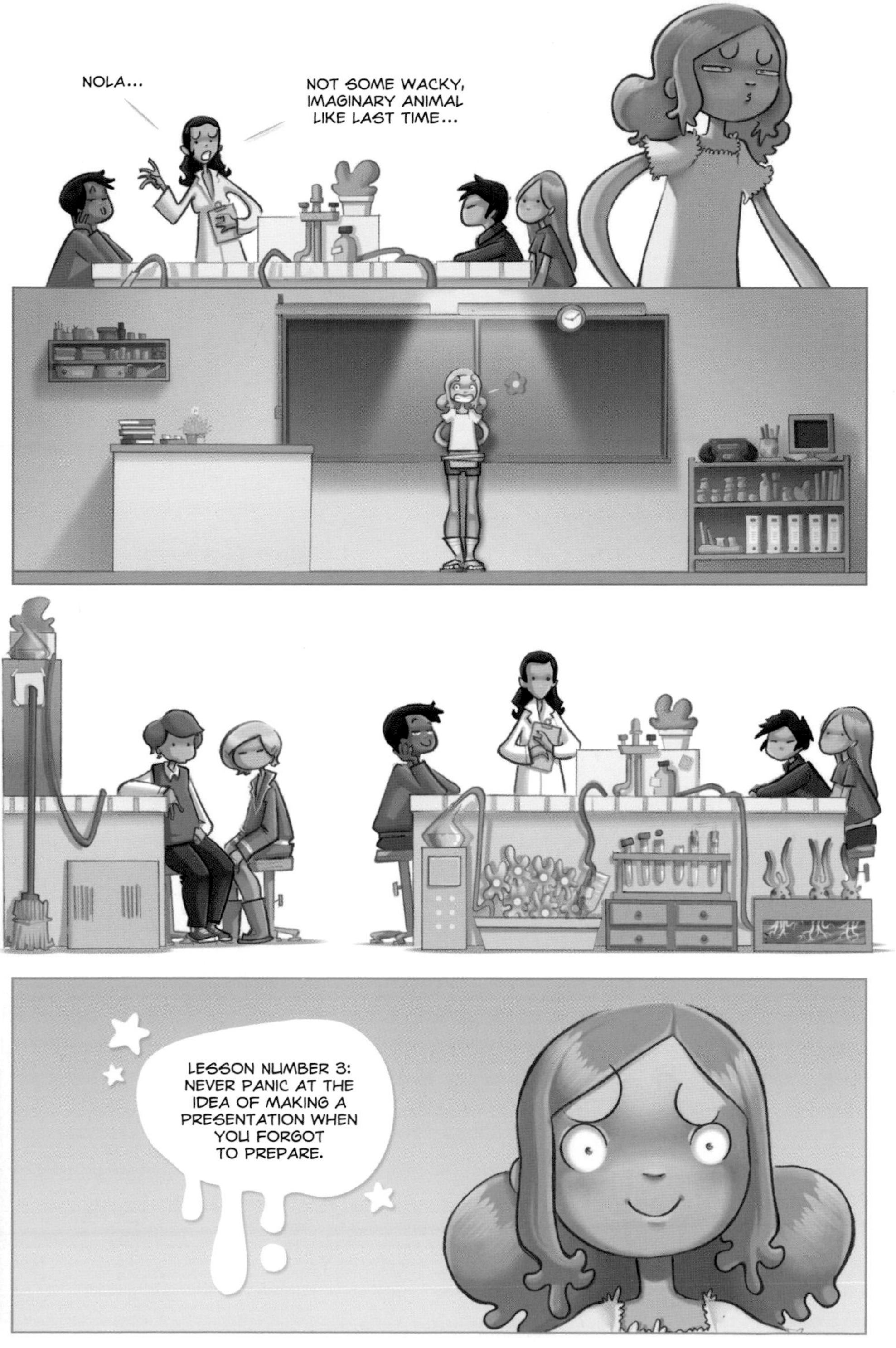
NOLA...
NOT SOME WACKY, IMAGINARY ANIMAL LIKE LAST TIME...
LESSON NUMBER 3: NEVER PANIC AT THE IDEA OF MAKING A PRESENTATION WHEN YOU FORGOT TO PREPARE.

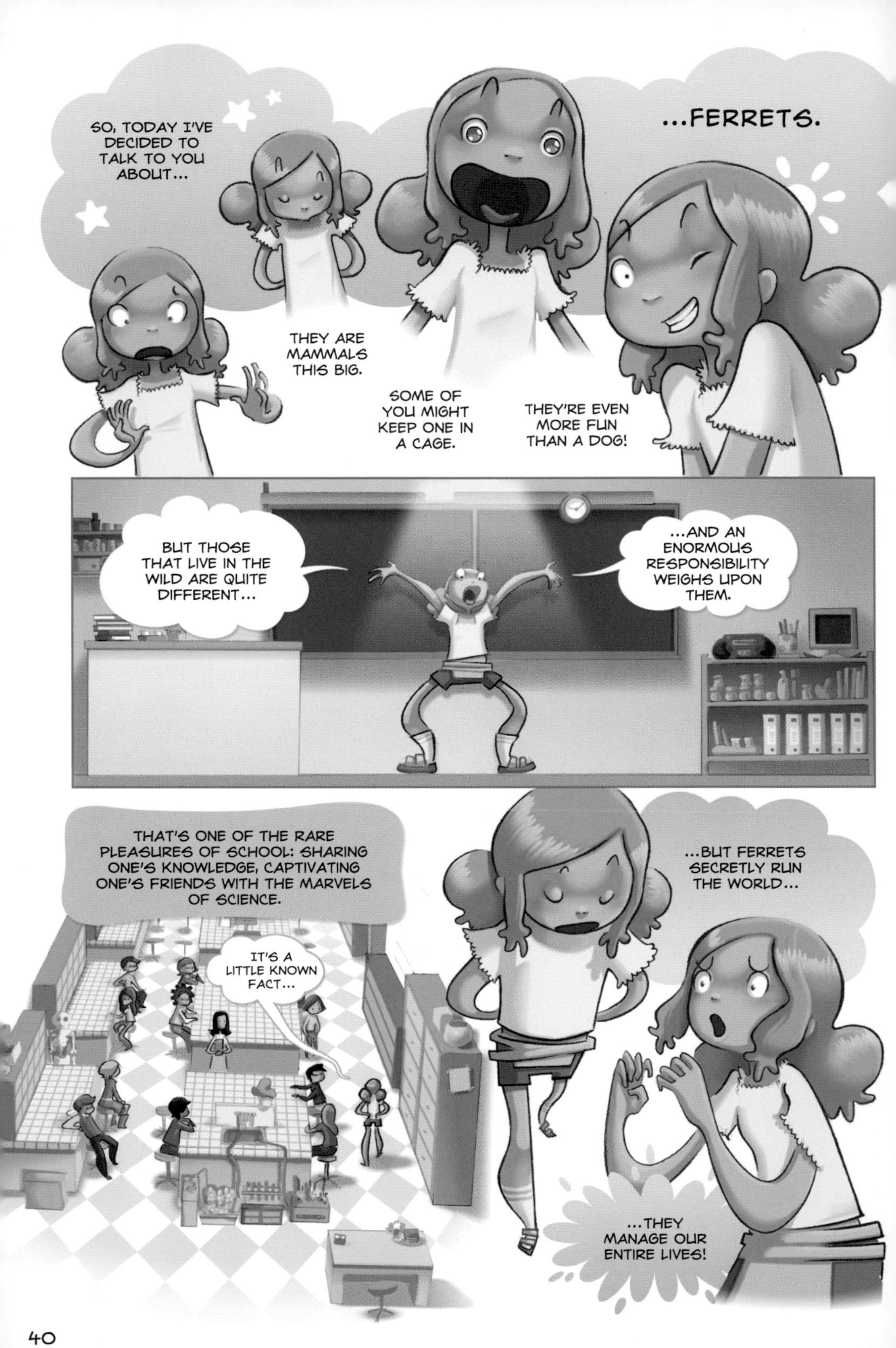
SO, TODAY I'VE DECIDED TO TALK TO YOU ABOUT...
...FERRETS.
THEY ARE MAMMALS THIS BIG.
SOME OF YOU MIGHT KEEP ONE IN A CAGE.
THEY'RE EVEN MORE FUN THAN A DOG!
BUT THOSE THAT LIVE IN THE WILD ARE QUITE DIFFERENT...
...AND AN ENORMOUS RESPONSIBILITY WEIGHS UPON THEM.
THAT'S ONE OF THE RARE PLEASURES OF SCHOOL: SHARING ONE'S KNOWLEDGE, CAPTIVATING ONE'S FRIENDS WITH THE MARVELS OF SCIENCE.
IT'S A LITTLE KNOWN FACT...
...BUT FERRETS SECRETLY RUN THE WORLD...
...THEY MANAGE OUR ENTIRE LIVES!

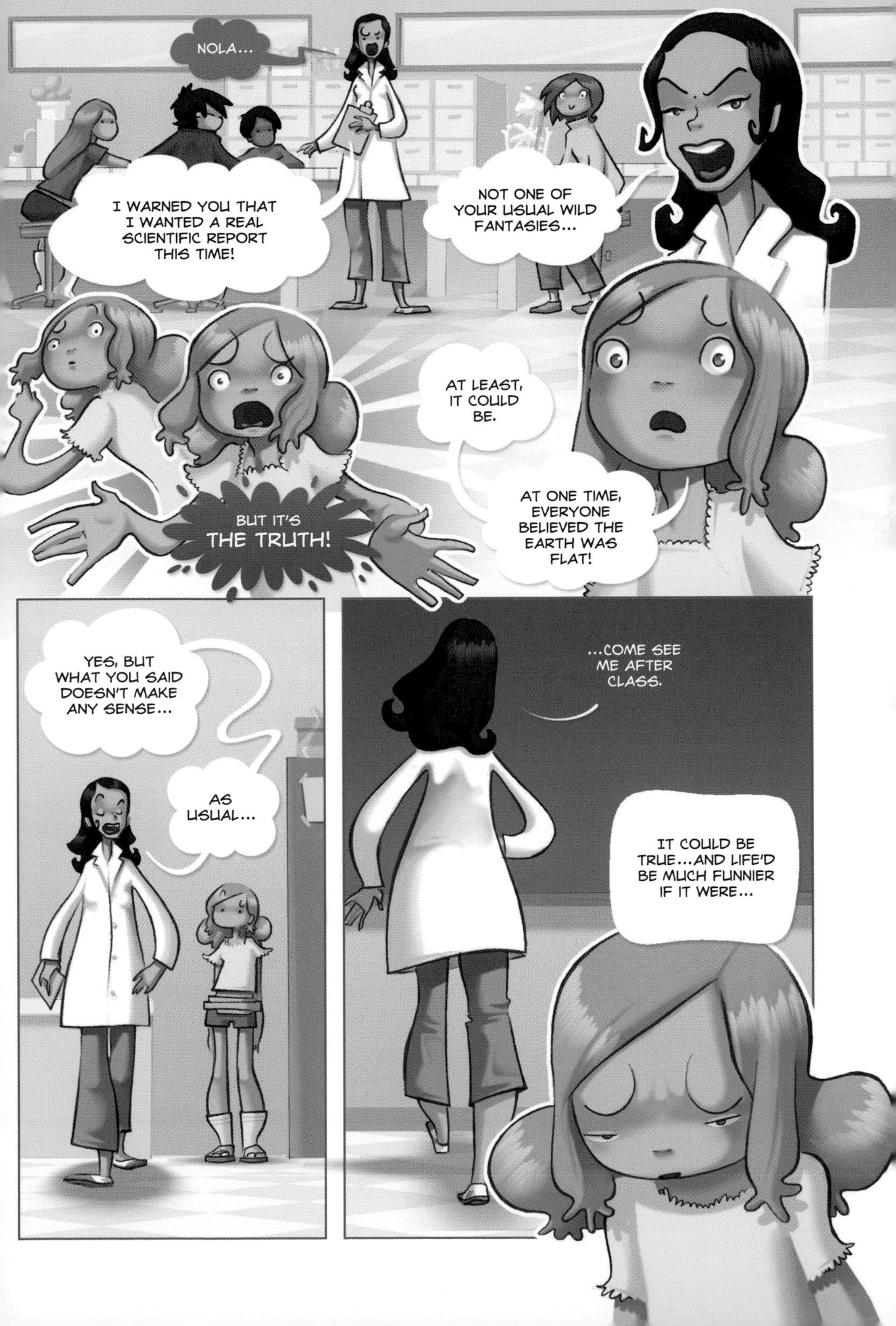
NOLA...
I WARNED YOU THAT I WANTED A REAL SCIENTIFIC REPORT THIS TIME!
NOT ONE OF YOUR USUAL WILD FANTASIES...
BUT IT'S THE TRUTH!
AT LEAST, IT COULD BE.
AT ONE TIME, EVERYONE BELIEVED THE EARTH WAS FLAT!
YES, BUT WHAT YOU SAID DOESN'T MAKE ANY SENSE...
AS USUAL...
...COME SEE ME AFTER CLASS.
IT COULD BE TRUE...AND LIFE'D BE MUCH FUNNIER IF IT WERE...

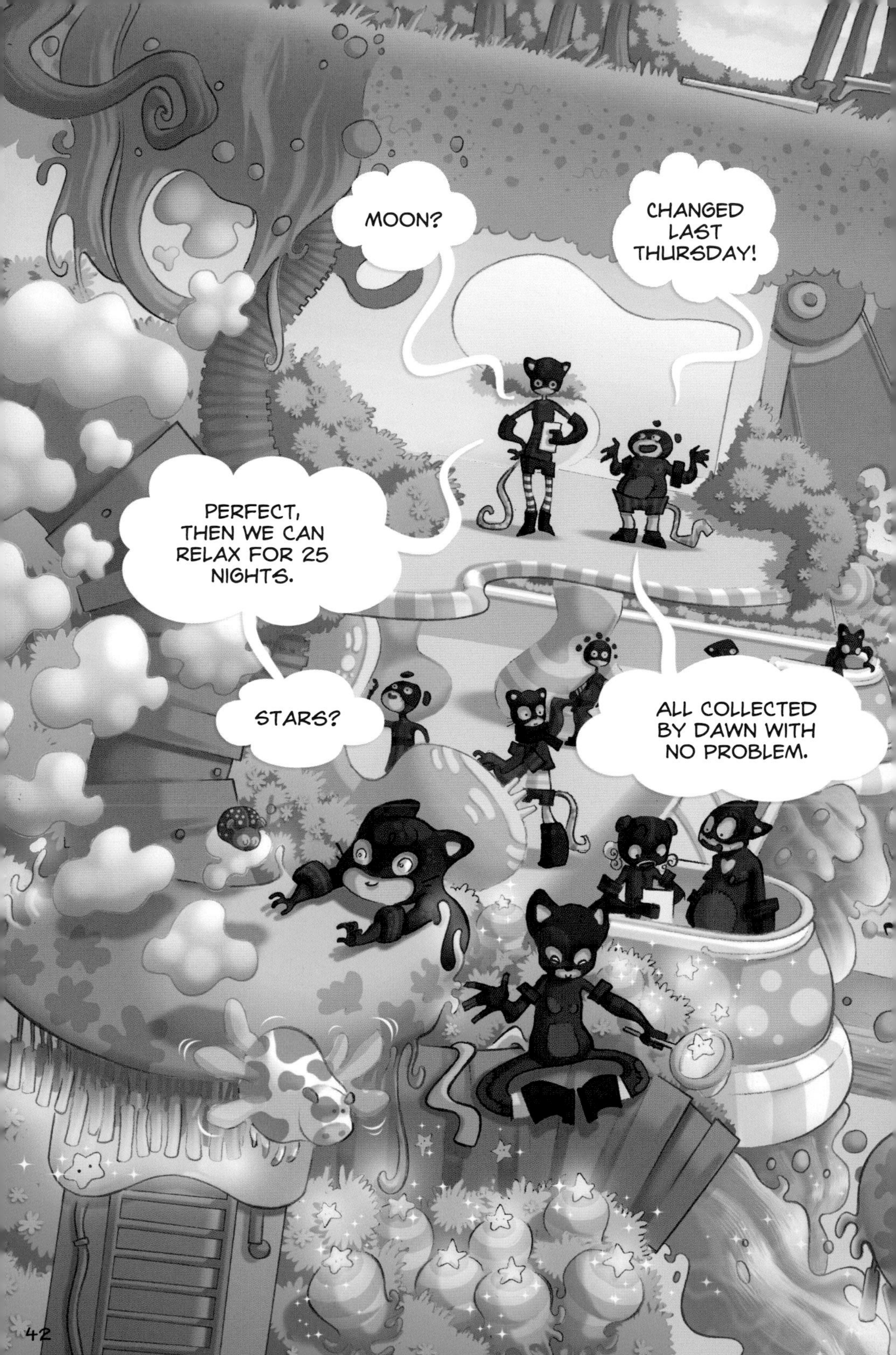
MOON?
CHANGED LAST THURSDAY!
PERFECT, THEN WE CAN RELAX FOR 25 NIGHTS.
STARS?
ALL COLLECTED BY DAWN WITH NO PROBLEM.

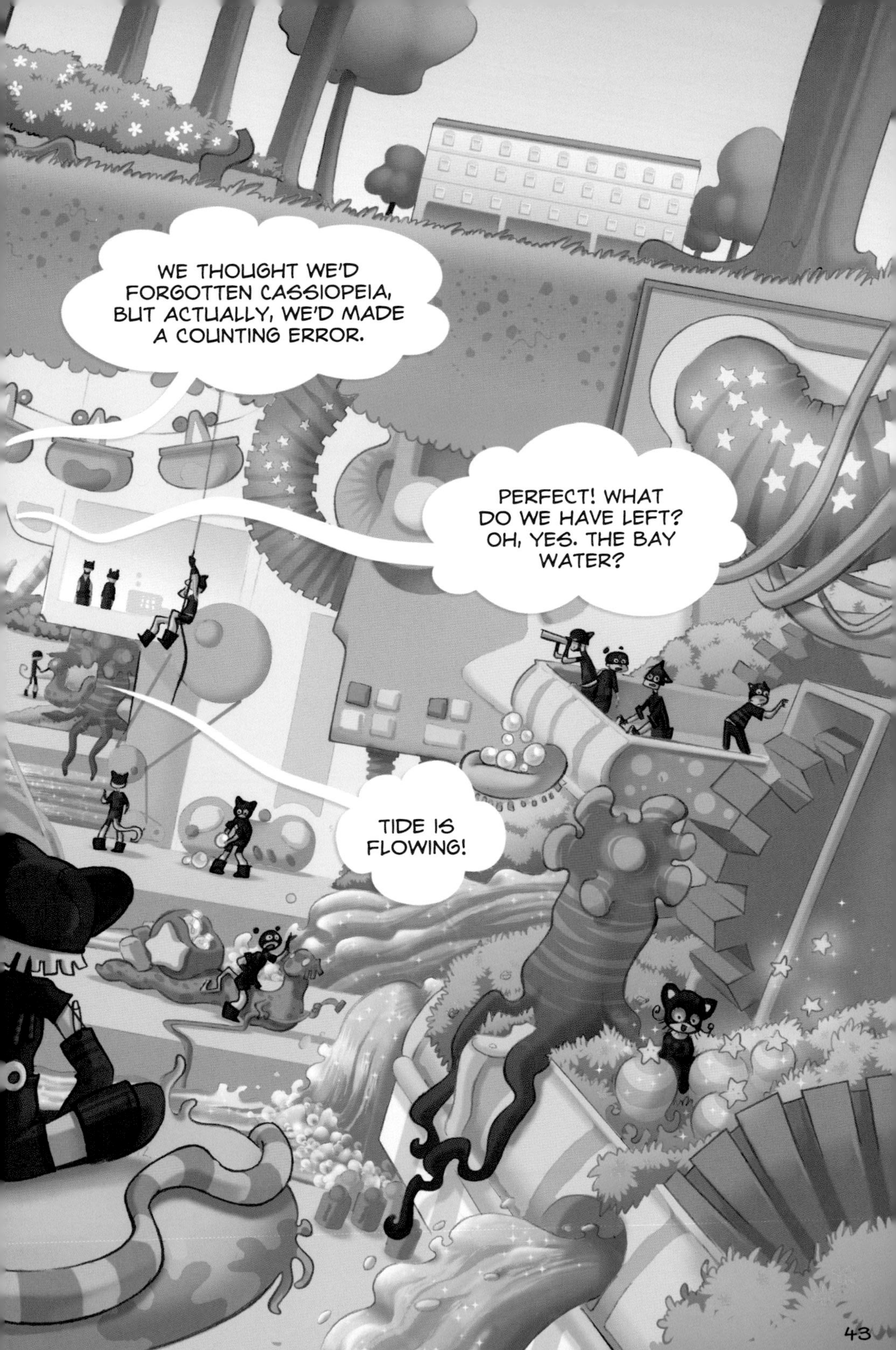
WE THOUGHT WE'D FORGOTTEN CASSIOPEIA, BUT ACTUALLY, WE'D MADE A COUNTING ERROR.
PERFECT! WHAT DO WE HAVE LEFT? OH, YES. THE BAY WATER?
TIDE IS FLOWING!

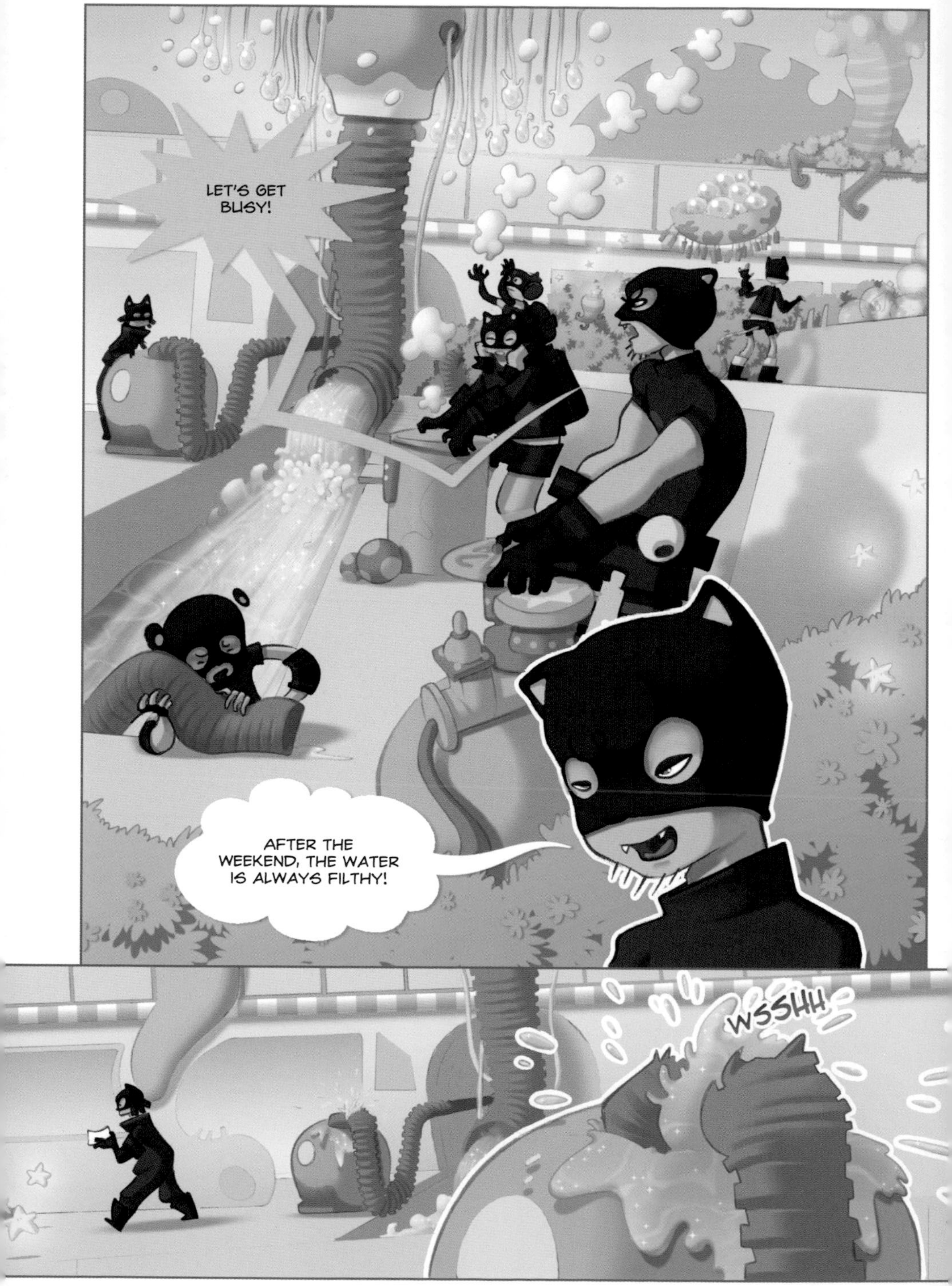
LET'S GET BUSY!
AFTER THE WEEKEND, THE WATER IS ALWAYS FILTHY!
WSSHH

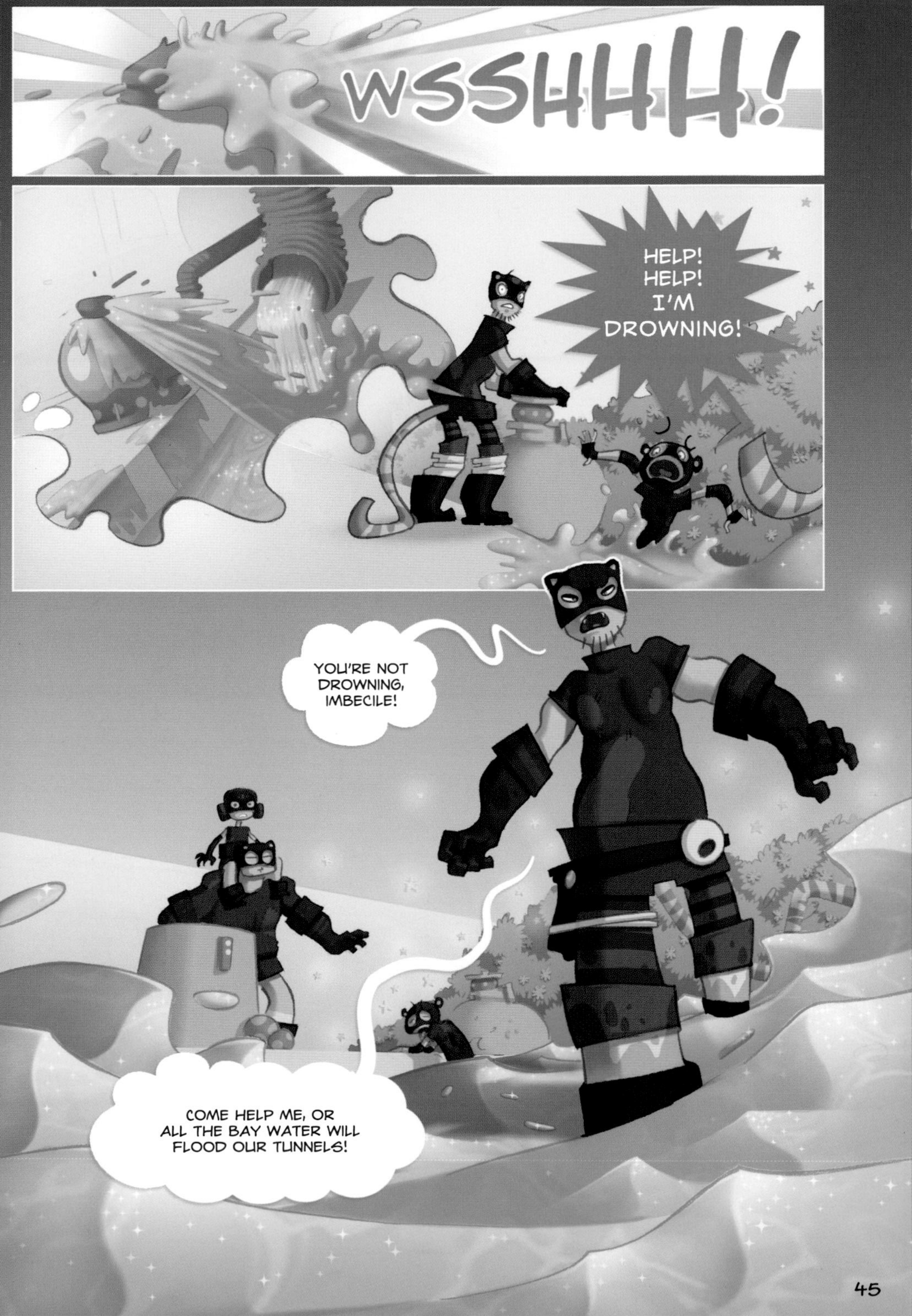
WSSHHH!
HELP! HELP! I'M DROWNING!
YOU'RE NOT DROWNING, IMBECILE!
COME HELP ME, OR ALL THE BAY WATER WILL FLOOD OUR TUNNELS!

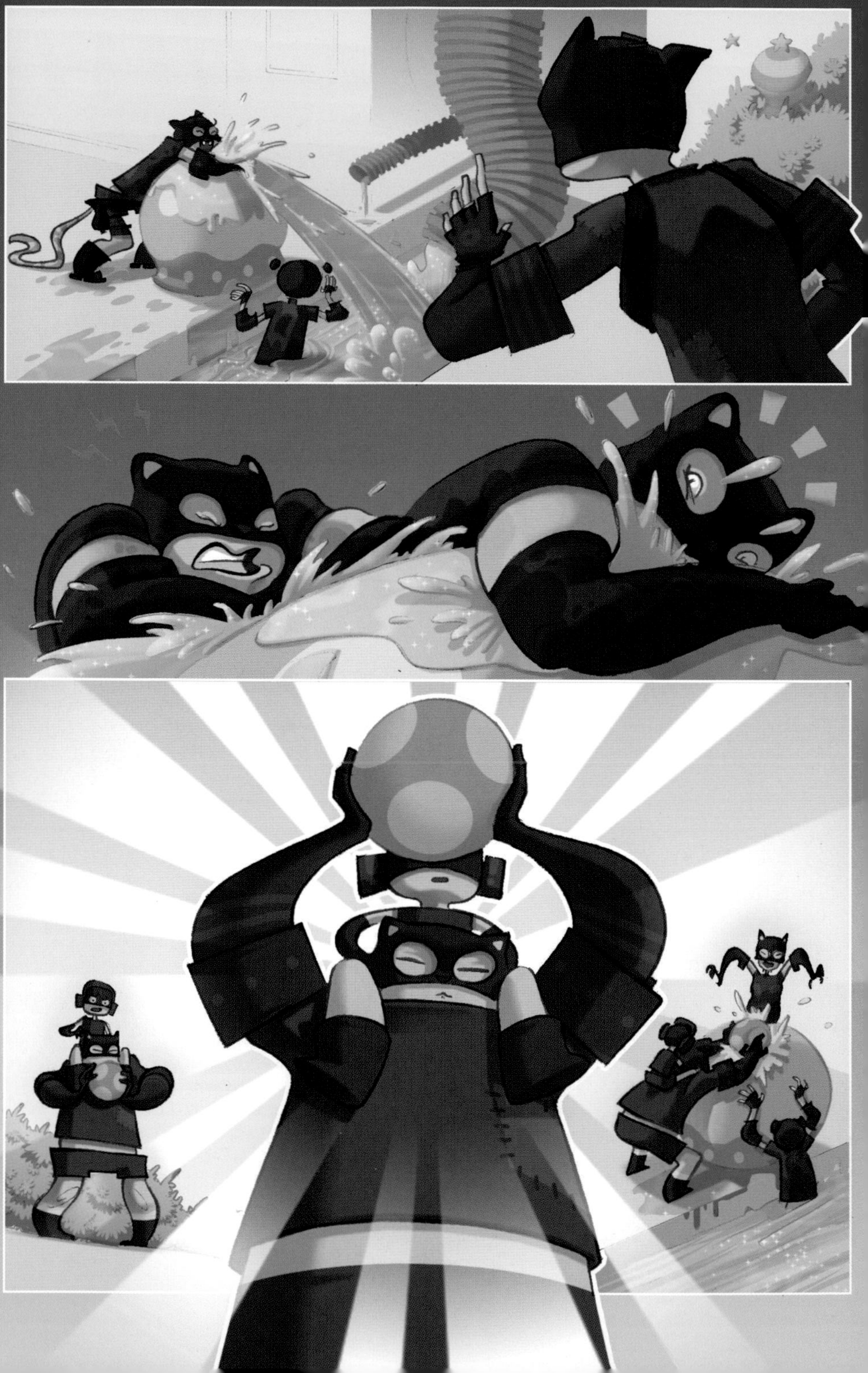

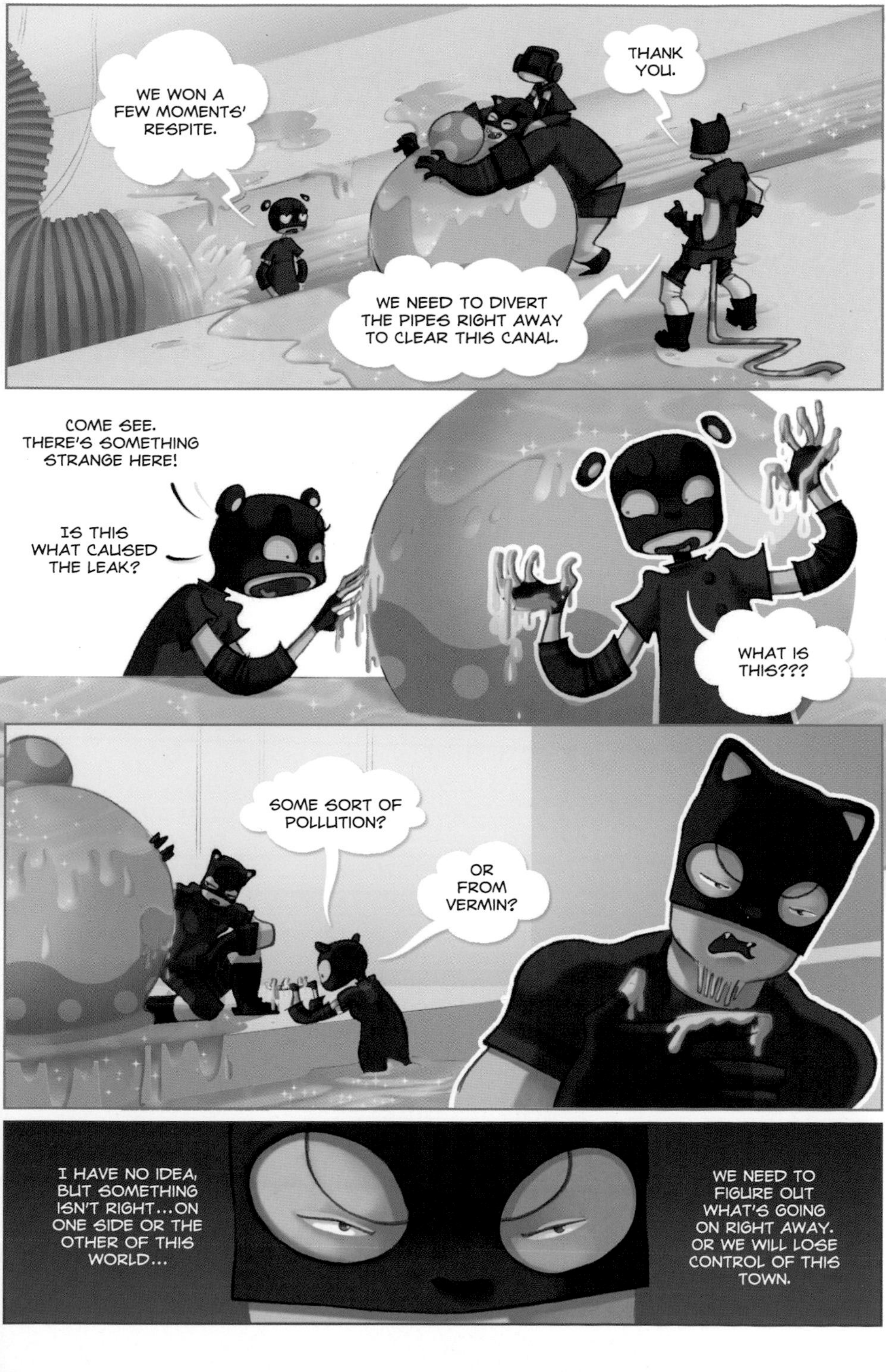
WE WON A FEW MOMENTS' RESPITE.
THANK YOU.
WE NEED TO DIVERT THE PIPES RIGHT AWAY TO CLEAR THIS CANAL.
COME SEE. THERE'S SOMETHING STRANGE HERE!
IS THIS WHAT CAUSED THE LEAK?
WHAT IS THIS???
SOME SORT OF POLLUTION?
OR FROM VERMIN?
I HAVE NO IDEA, BUT SOMETHING ISN'T RIGHT...ON ONE SIDE OR THE OTHER OF THIS WORLD...
WE NEED TO FIGURE OUT WHAT'S GOING ON RIGHT AWAY. OR WE WILL LOSE CONTROL OF THIS TOWN.

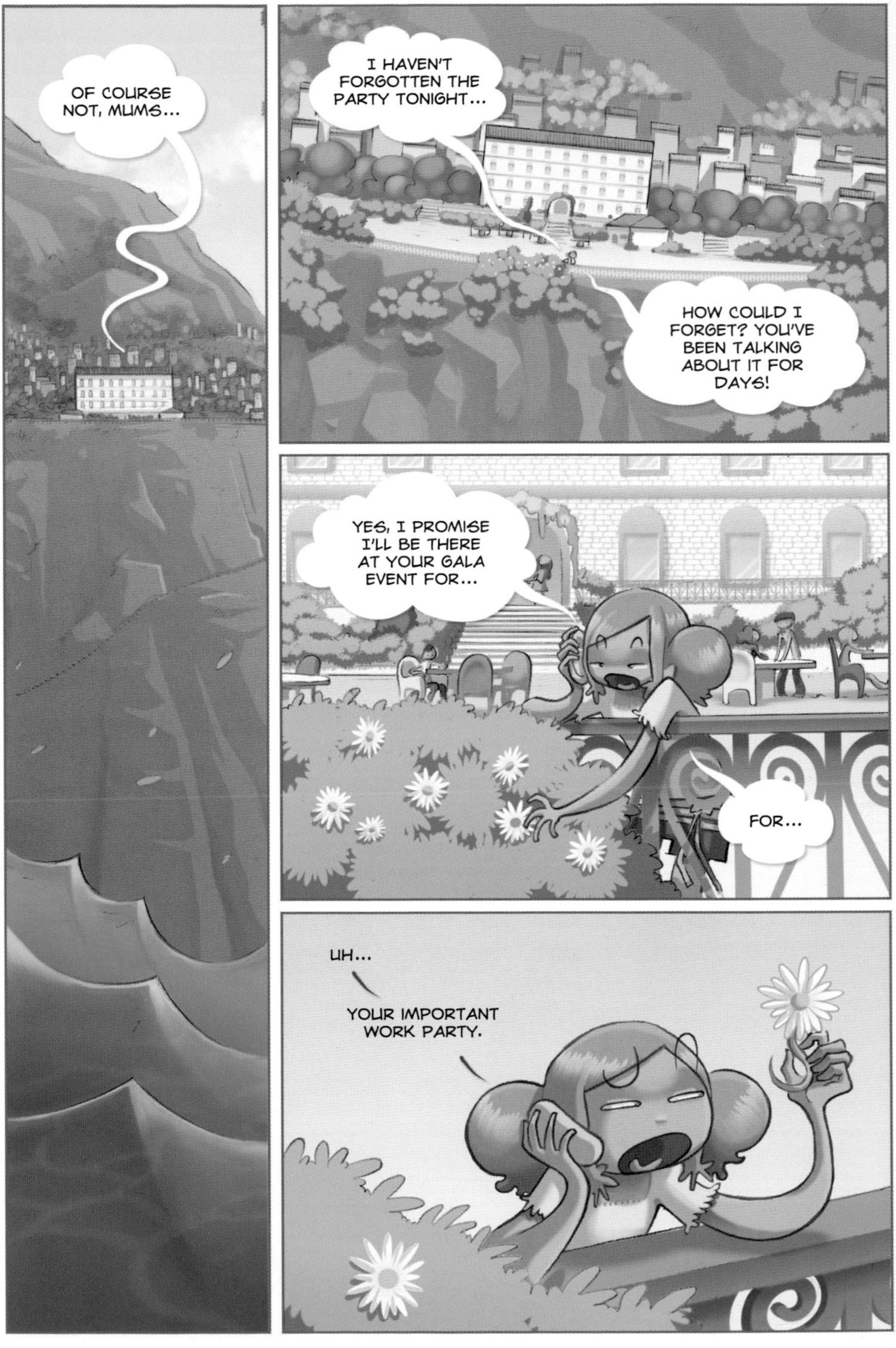

OF COURSE NOT, MUMS...
I HAVEN'T FORGOTTEN THE PARTY TONIGHT...
HOW COULD I FORGET? YOU'VE BEEN TALKING ABOUT IT FOR DAYS!
YES, I PROMISE I'LL BE THERE AT YOUR GALA EVENT FOR...
FOR...
UH...
YOUR IMPORTANT WORK PARTY.

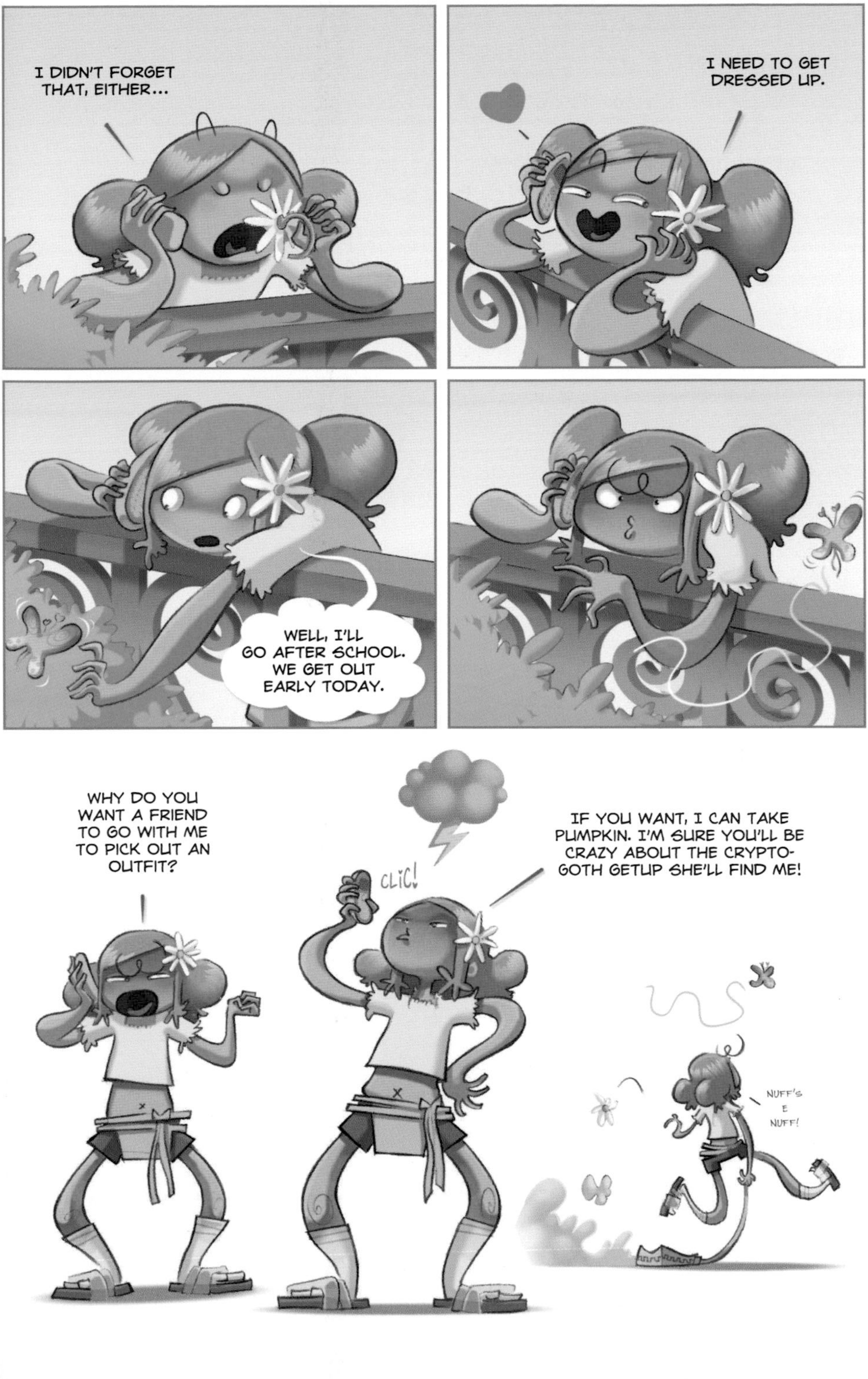
I DIDN'T FORGET THAT, EITHER...
I NEED TO GET DRESSED UP.
WELL, I'LL GO AFTER SCHOOL. WE GET OUT EARLY TODAY.
WHY DO YOU WANT A FRIEND TO GO WITH ME TO PICK OUT AN OUTFIT?
CLIC!
IF YOU WANT, I CAN TAKE PUMPKIN. I'M SURE YOU'LL BE CRAZY ABOUT THE CRYPTO-GOTH GETUP SHE'LL FIND ME!
NUFF'S E NUFF!

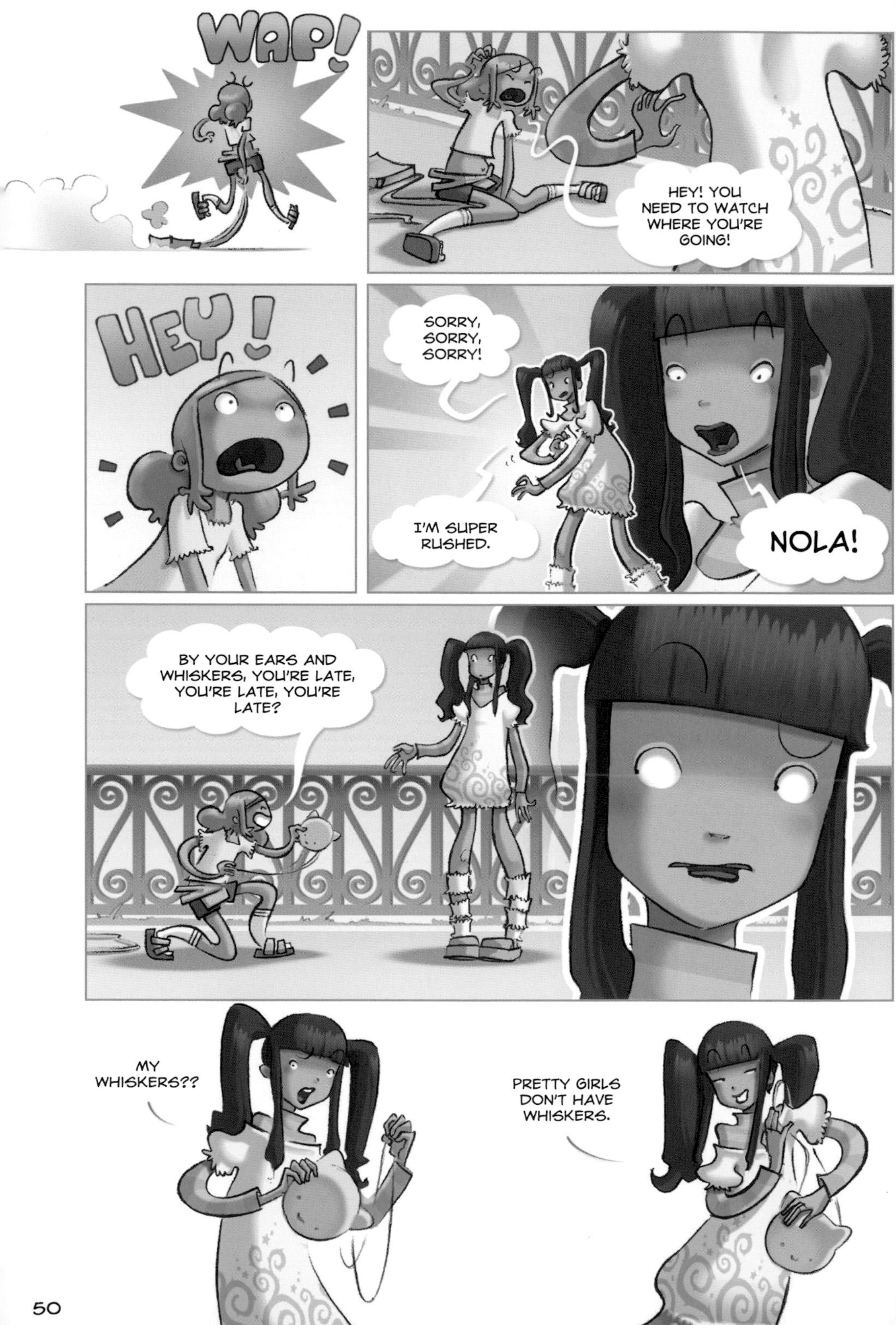
WAP!
HEY! YOU NEED TO WATCH WHERE YOU'RE GOING!
HEY!
SORRY, SORRY, SORRY!
I'M SUPER RUSHED.
NOLA!
BY YOUR EARS AND WHISKERS, YOU'RE LATE, YOU'RE LATE, YOU'RE LATE?
MY WHISKERS??
PRETTY GIRLS DON'T HAVE WHISKERS.

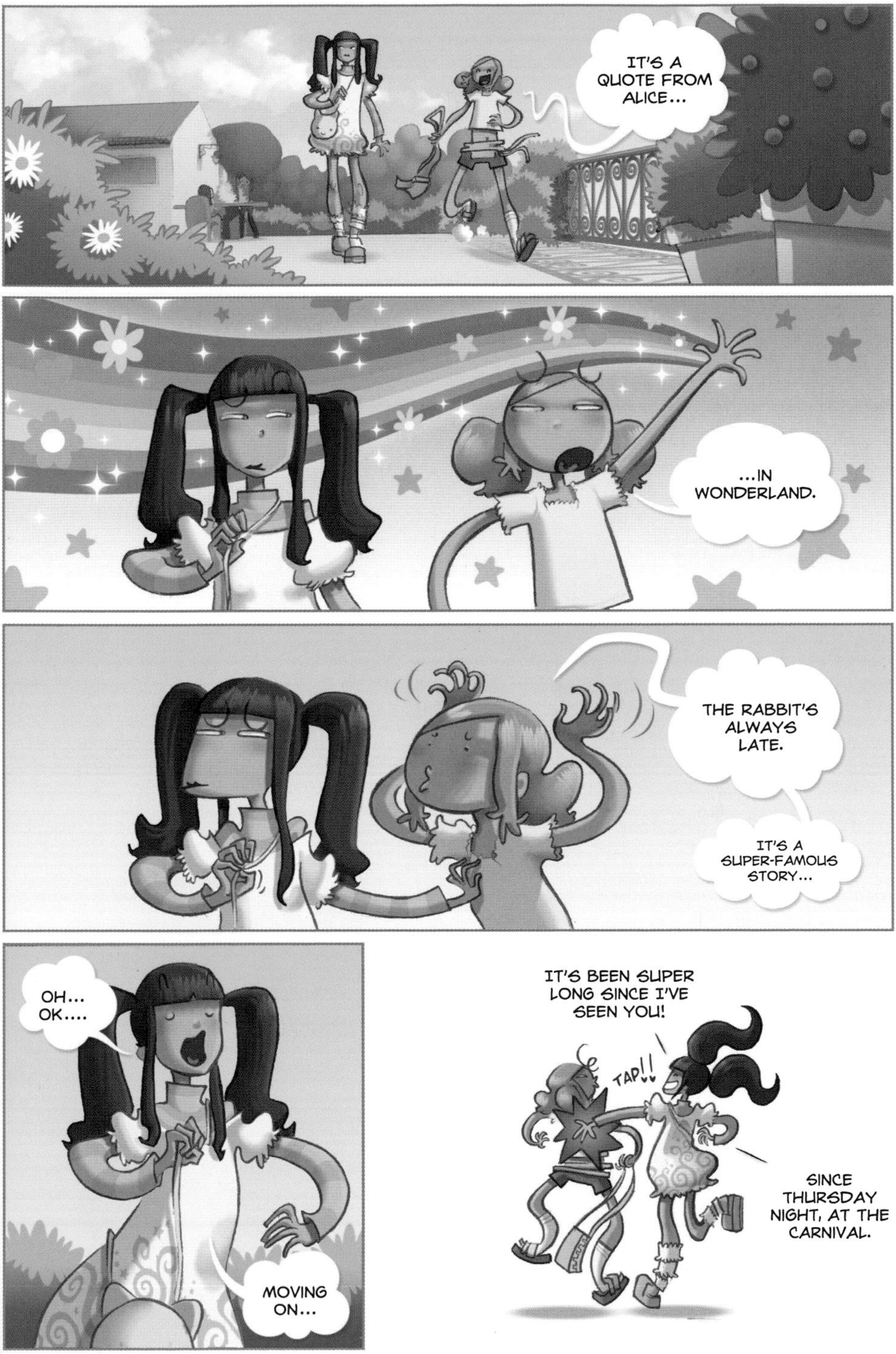
IT'S A QUOTE FROM ALICE...
...IN WONDERLAND.
THE RABBIT'S ALWAYS LATE.
IT'S A SUPER-FAMOUS STORY...
OH... OK....
MOVING ON...
IT'S BEEN SUPER LONG SINCE I'VE SEEN YOU!
TAP!!
SINCE THURSDAY NIGHT, AT THE CARNIVAL.

OF COURSE, AS USUAL, DAMIANO AND I HAD A FANTASTIC THREE-DAY WEEKEND.

WE HUNG OUT ON A SAILBOAT.

IT WAS AMAZING. I'VE NEVER SAILED BEFORE.

AND THAT IDIOT DAMIANO ALMOST GOT SICK BECAUSE HE PIGGED OUT ON FISH.

I WAS DYING FOR A NICE, BIG LOBSTER.

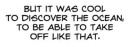

BUT IT WAS COOL TO DISCOVER THE OCEAN, TO BE ABLE TO TAKE OFF LIKE THAT.

SO...SHE'S NEVER BEEN TO THE OCEAN. A CLUE?

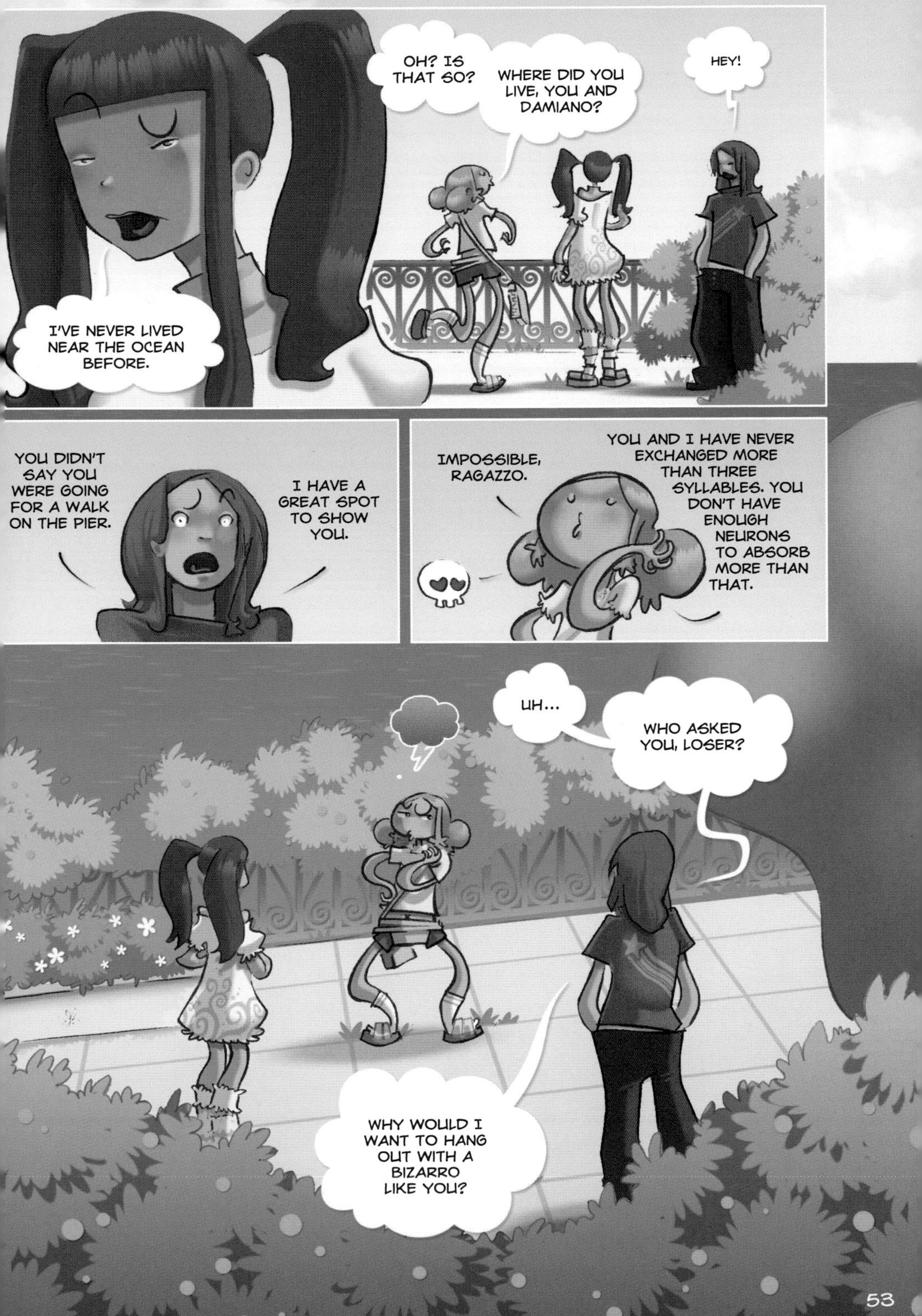
I'VE NEVER LIVED NEAR THE OCEAN BEFORE.
OH? IS THAT SO?
WHERE DID YOU LIVE, YOU AND DAMIANO?
HEY!
YOU DIDN'T SAY YOU WERE GOING FOR A WALK ON THE PIER.
I HAVE A GREAT SPOT TO SHOW YOU.
IMPOSSIBLE, RAGAZZO.
YOU AND I HAVE NEVER EXCHANGED MORE THAN THREE SYLLABLES. YOU DON'T HAVE ENOUGH NEURONS TO ABSORB MORE THAN THAT.
UH...
WHO ASKED YOU, LOSER?
WHY WOULD I WANT TO HANG OUT WITH A BIZARRO LIKE YOU?

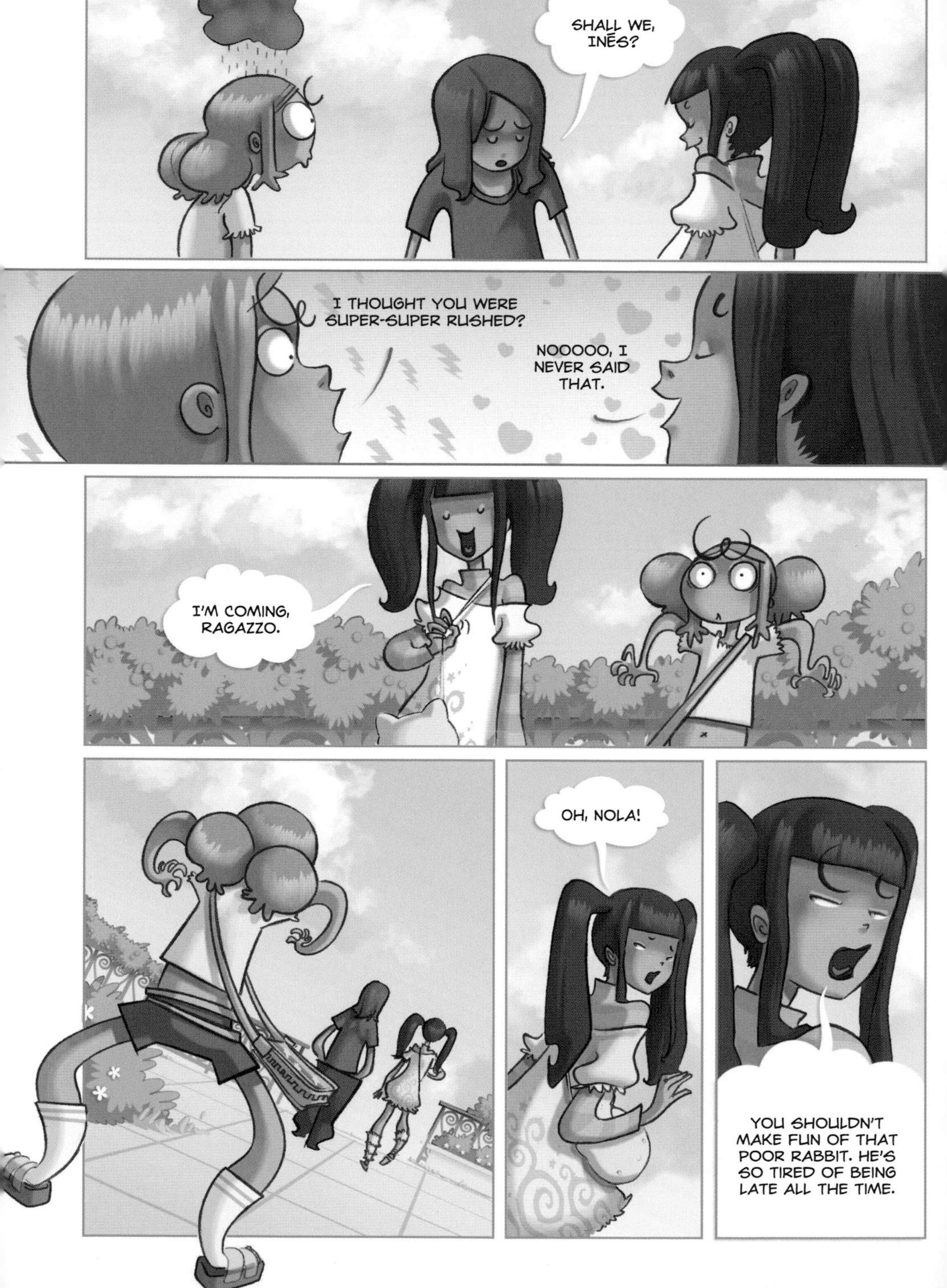
SHALL WE, INÉS?
I THOUGHT YOU WERE SUPER-SUPER RUSHED?
NOOOOO, I NEVER SAID THAT.
I'M COMING, RAGAZZO.
OH, NOLA!
YOU SHOULDN'T MAKE FUN OF THAT POOR RABBIT. HE'S SO TIRED OF BEING LATE ALL THE TIME.

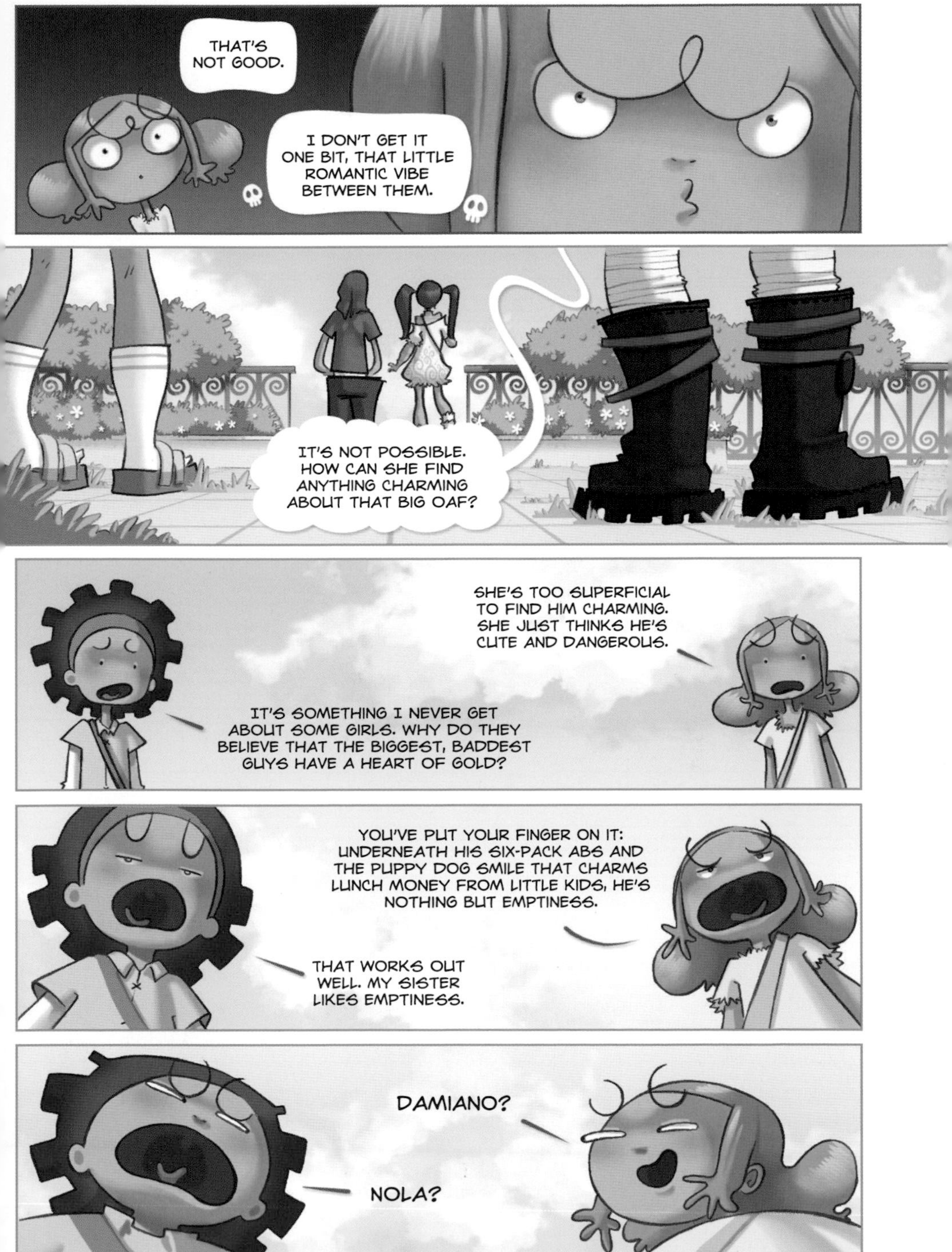
THAT'S NOT GOOD.
I DON'T GET IT ONE BIT, THAT LITTLE ROMANTIC VIBE BETWEEN THEM.
IT'S NOT POSSIBLE. HOW CAN SHE FIND ANYTHING CHARMING ABOUT THAT BIG OAF?
SHE'S TOO SUPERFICIAL TO FIND HIM CHARMING. SHE JUST THINKS HE'S CUTE AND DANGEROUS.
IT'S SOMETHING I NEVER GET ABOUT SOME GIRLS. WHY DO THEY BELIEVE THAT THE BIGGEST, BADDEST GUYS HAVE A HEART OF GOLD?
YOU'VE PUT YOUR FINGER ON IT: UNDERNEATH HIS SIX-PACK ABS AND THE PUPPY DOG SMILE THAT CHARMS LUNCH MONEY FROM LITTLE KIDS, HE'S NOTHING BUT EMPTINESS.
THAT WORKS OUT WELL. MY SISTER LIKES EMPTINESS.
DAMIANO?
NOLA?

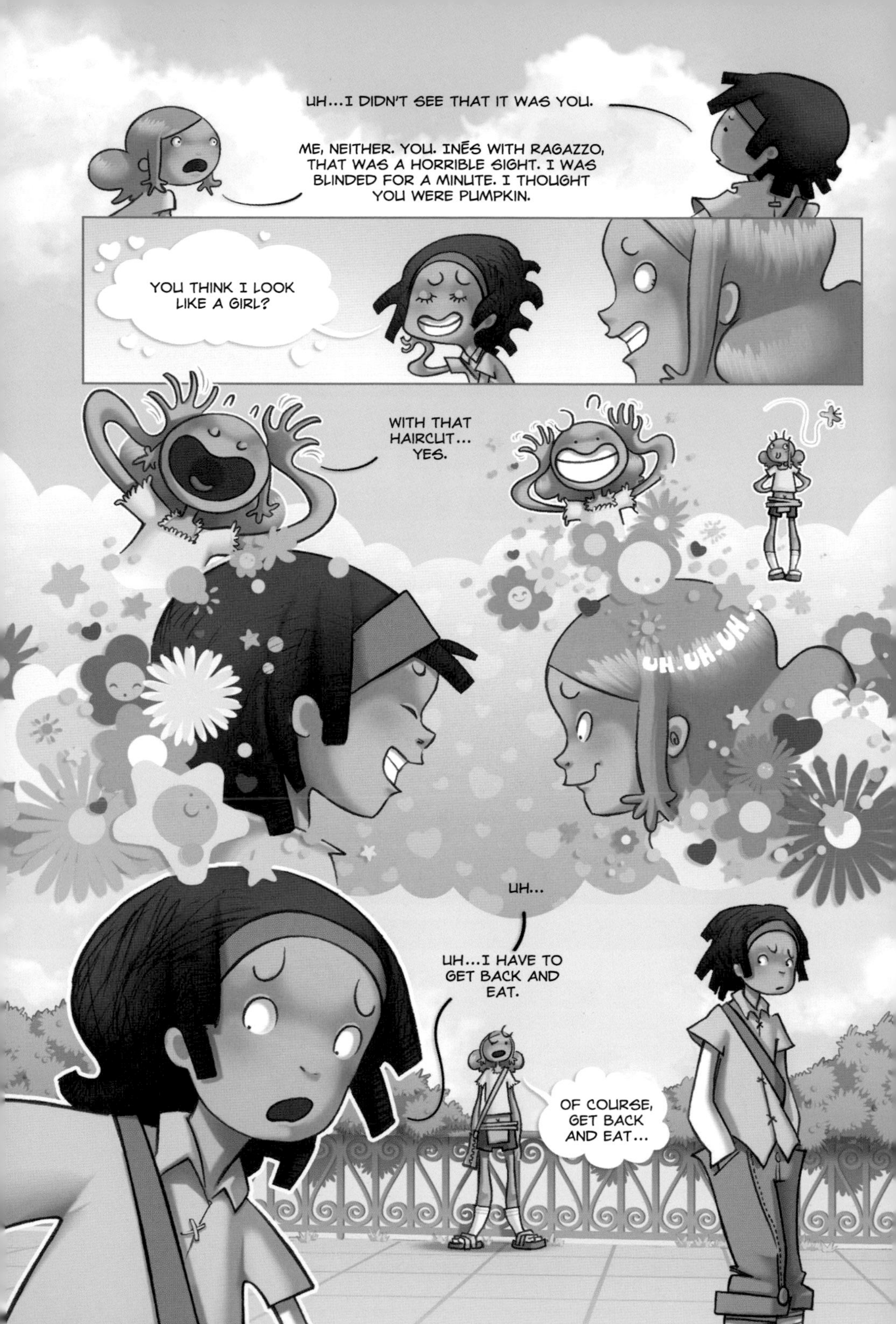
UH...I DIDN'T SEE THAT IT WAS YOU.
ME, NEITHER. YOU. INÉS WITH RAGAZZO, THAT WAS A HORRIBLE SIGHT. I WAS BLINDED FOR A MINUTE. I THOUGHT YOU WERE PUMPKIN.
YOU THINK I LOOK LIKE A GIRL?
WITH THAT HAIRCUT... YES.
UH.UH.UH..
UH...
UH...I HAVE TO GET BACK AND EAT.
OF COURSE, GET BACK AND EAT...

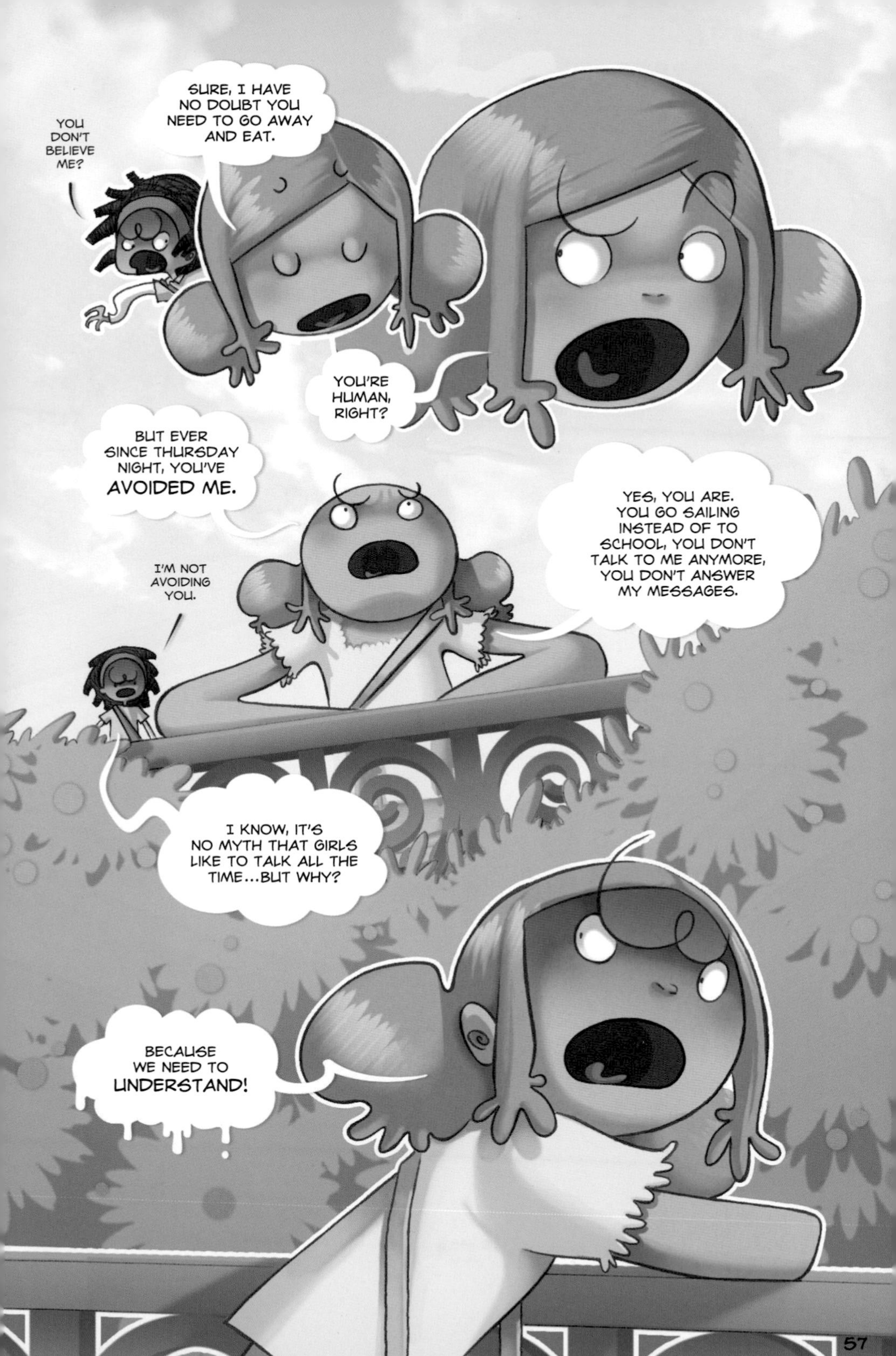
YOU DON'T BELIEVE ME?
SURE, I HAVE NO DOUBT YOU NEED TO GO AWAY AND EAT.
YOU'RE HUMAN, RIGHT?
BUT EVER SINCE THURSDAY NIGHT, YOU'VE AVOIDED ME.
I'M NOT AVOIDING YOU.
YES, YOU ARE. YOU GO SAILING INSTEAD OF TO SCHOOL, YOU DON'T TALK TO ME ANYMORE, YOU DON'T ANSWER MY MESSAGES.
I KNOW, IT'S NO MYTH THAT GIRLS LIKE TO TALK ALL THE TIME...BUT WHY?
BECAUSE WE NEED TO UNDERSTAND!

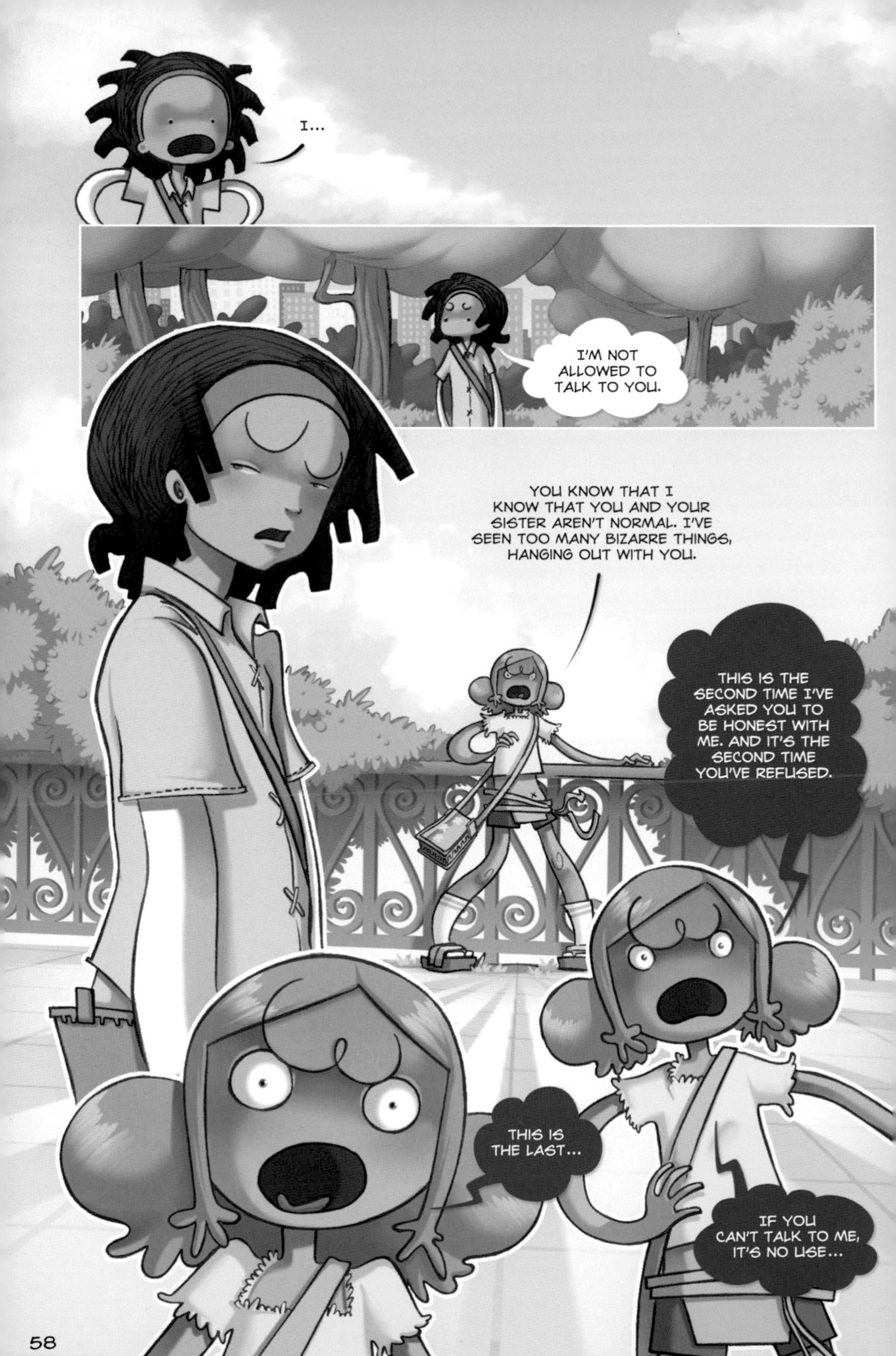
I...
I'M NOT ALLOWED TO TALK TO YOU.
YOU KNOW THAT I KNOW THAT YOU AND YOUR SISTER AREN'T NORMAL. I'VE SEEN TOO MANY BIZARRE THINGS, HANGING OUT WITH YOU.
THIS IS THE SECOND TIME I'VE ASKED YOU TO BE HONEST WITH ME. AND IT'S THE SECOND TIME YOU'VE REFUSED.
THIS IS THE LAST...
IF YOU CAN'T TALK TO ME, IT'S NO USE...

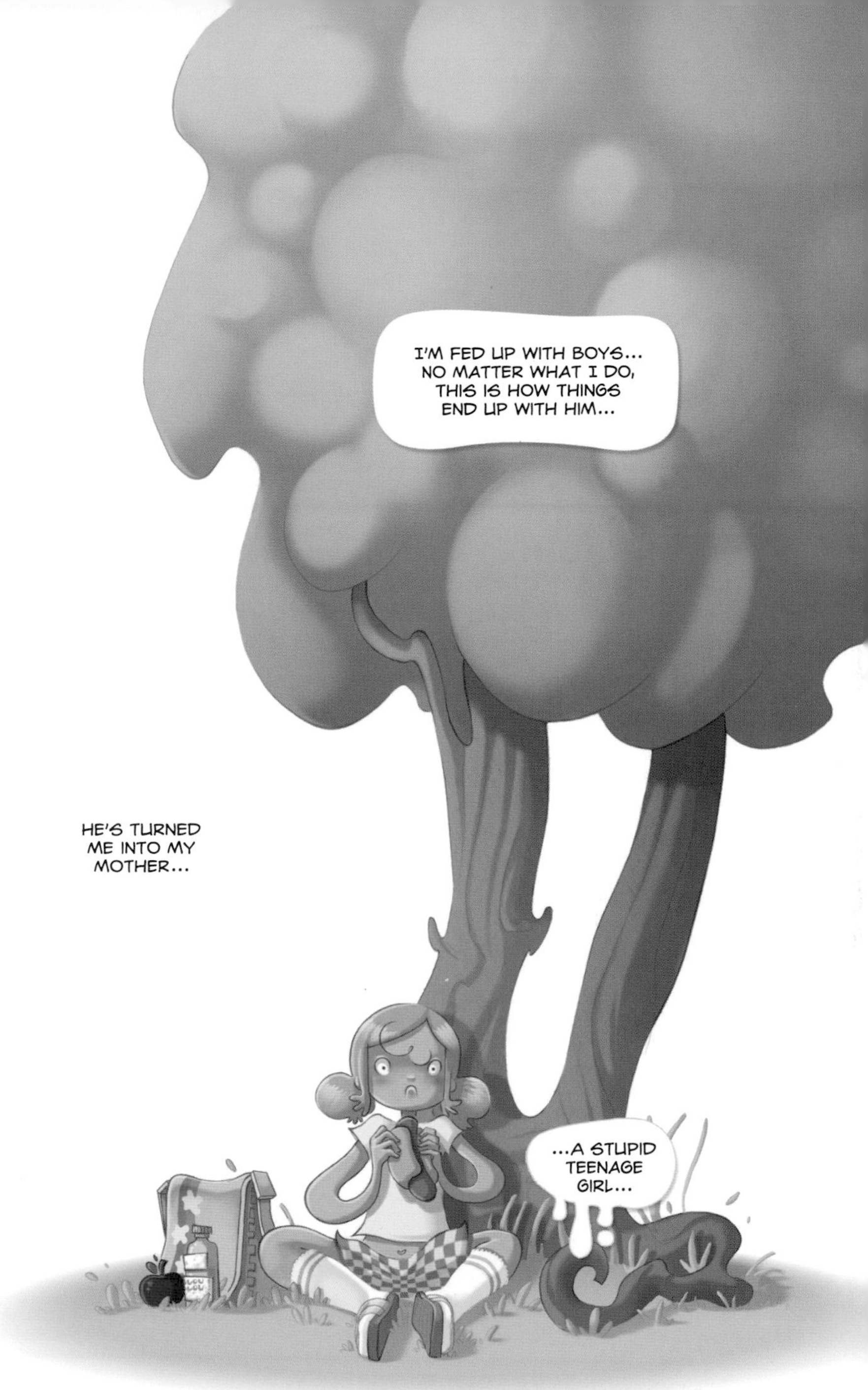
I'M FED UP WITH BOYS... NO MATTER WHAT I DO, THIS IS HOW THINGS END UP WITH HIM...
HE'S TURNED ME INTO MY MOTHER...
...A STUPID TEENAGE GIRL...

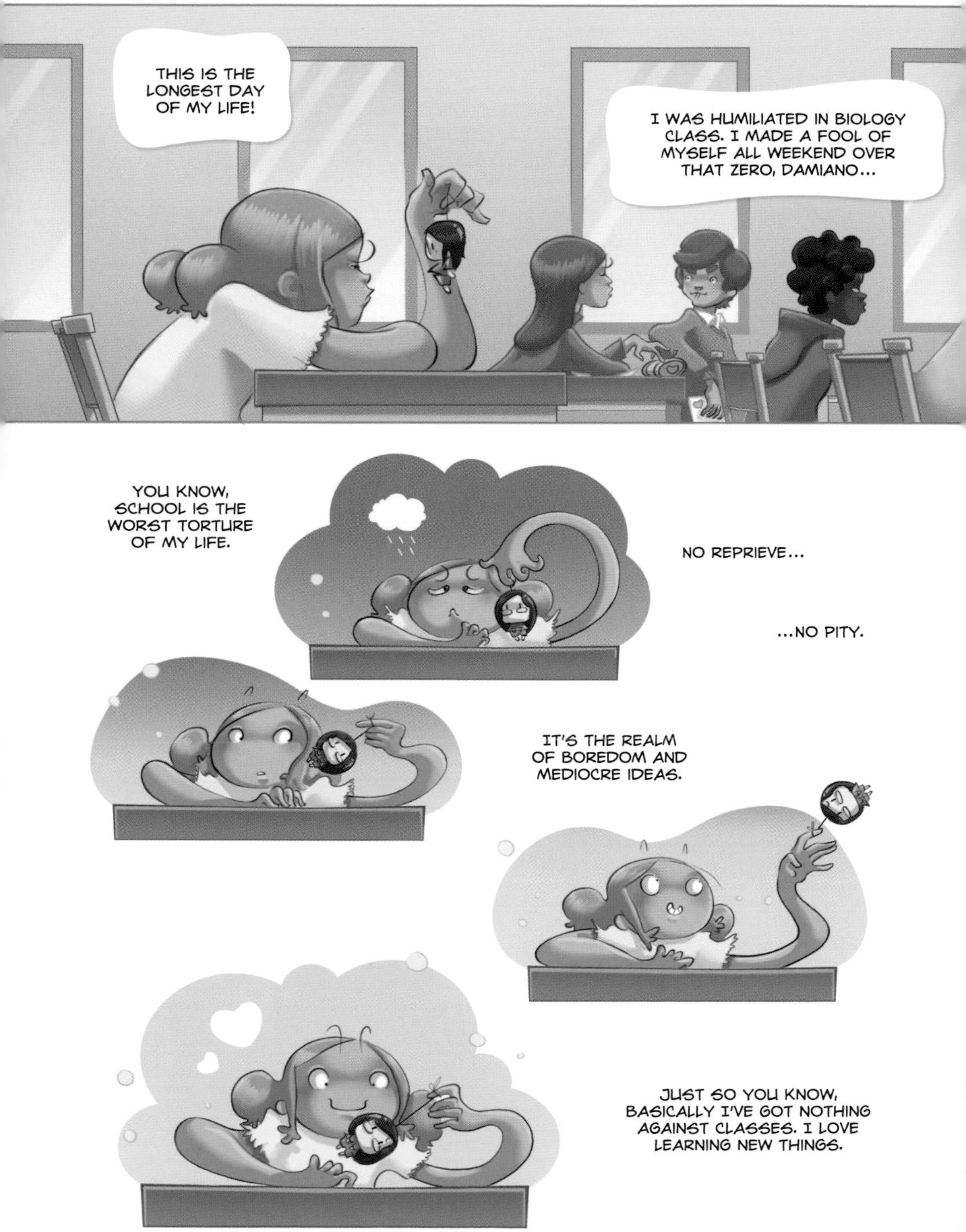
THIS IS THE LONGEST DAY OF MY LIFE!
I WAS HUMILIATED IN BIOLOGY CLASS. I MADE A FOOL OF MYSELF ALL WEEKEND OVER THAT ZERO, DAMIANO...
YOU KNOW, SCHOOL IS THE WORST TORTURE OF MY LIFE.
NO REPRIEVE...
...NO PITY.
IT'S THE REALM OF BOREDOM AND MEDIOCRE IDEAS.
JUST SO YOU KNOW, BASICALLY I'VE GOT NOTHING AGAINST CLASSES. I LOVE LEARNING NEW THINGS.

IT'S JUST THE WAY THEY TEACH US ALL OF THIS.

IT'S CRUELLY LACKING IN...

...FANTASY.

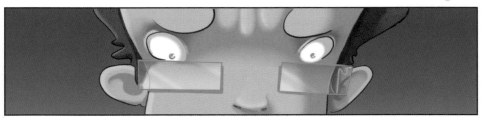

WHEN I HAVE MORE TIME, I'LL TELL YOU HOW MY HISTORY TEACHER TEACHES US ABOUT WARS.

AND I'LL EXPLAIN HOW I'D DO IT BETTER THAN HE DOES.

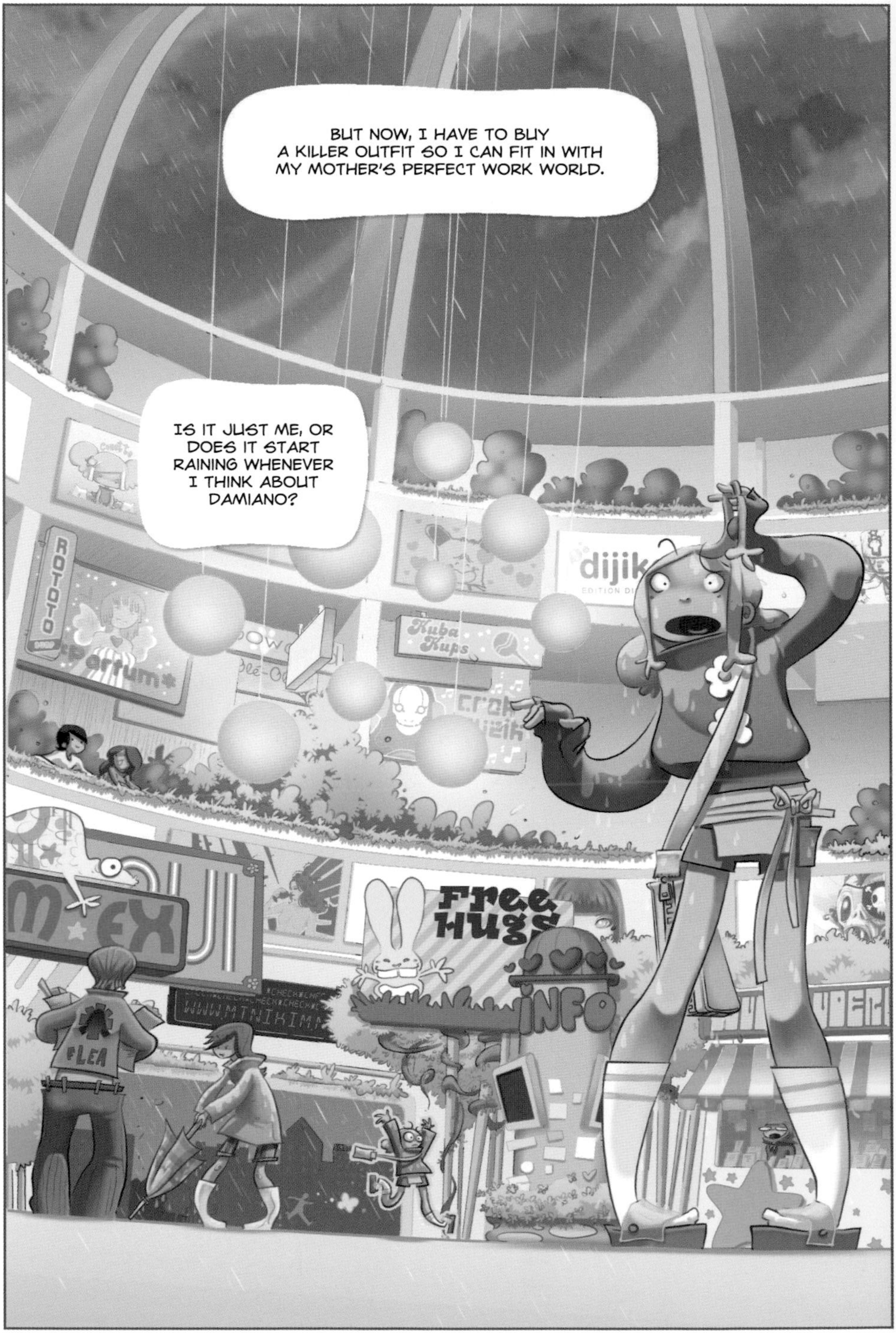
BUT NOW, I HAVE TO BUY A KILLER OUTFIT SO I CAN FIT IN WITH MY MOTHER'S PERFECT WORK WORLD.
IS IT JUST ME, OR DOES IT START RAINING WHENEVER I THINK ABOUT DAMIANO?
Free HUGS
INFO
FLEA
ROTOTO
dijik

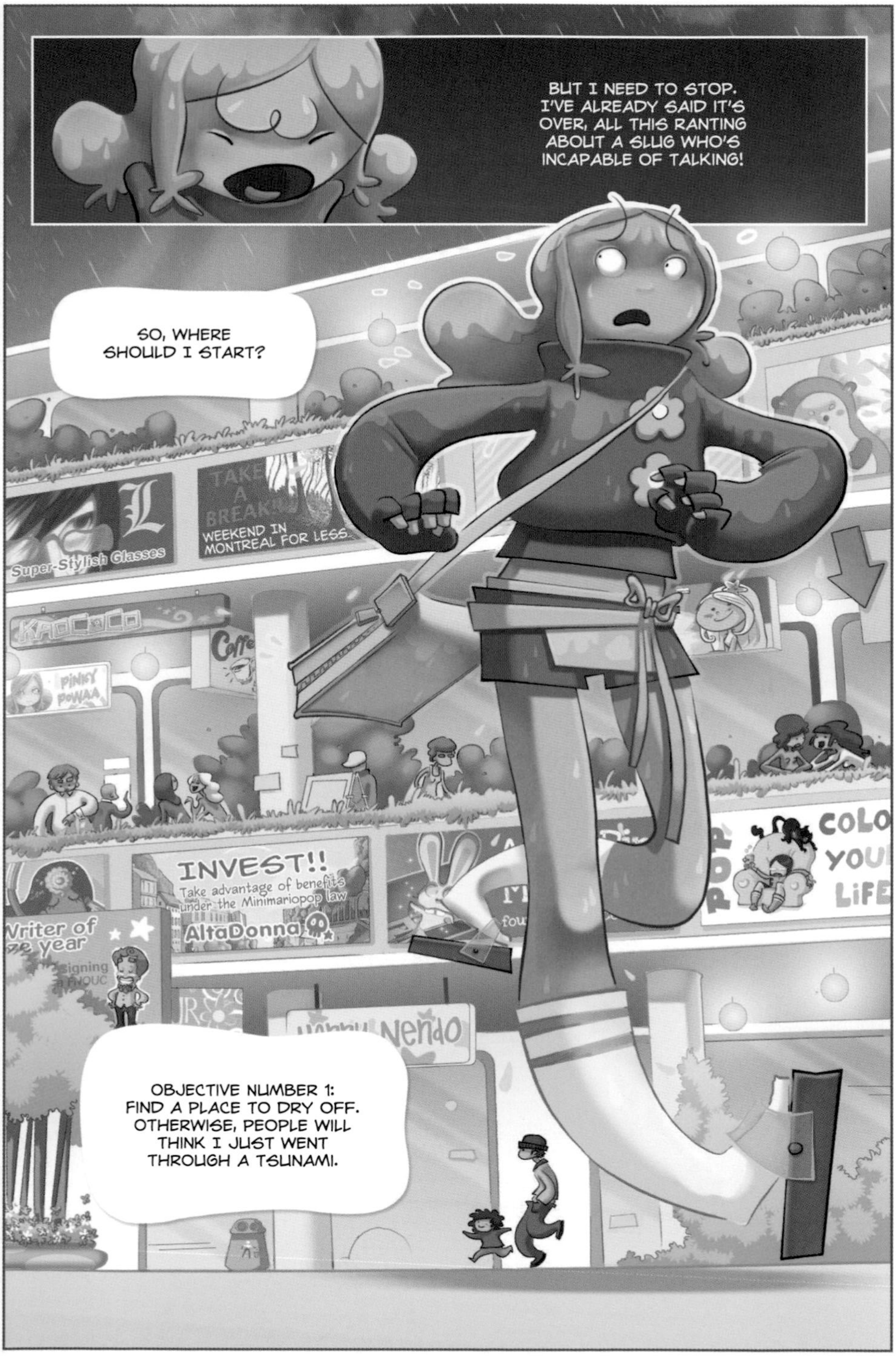
BUT I NEED TO STOP. I'VE ALREADY SAID IT'S OVER, ALL THIS RANTING ABOUT A SLUG WHO'S INCAPABLE OF TALKING!
SO, WHERE SHOULD I START?
OBJECTIVE NUMBER 1: FIND A PLACE TO DRY OFF. OTHERWISE, PEOPLE WILL THINK I JUST WENT THROUGH A TSUNAMI.
Super-Stylish Glasses
WEEKEND IN MONTREAL FOR LESS
INVEST!!
Take advantage of benefits under the Minimariopop law
AltaDonna
PINKY POWAA

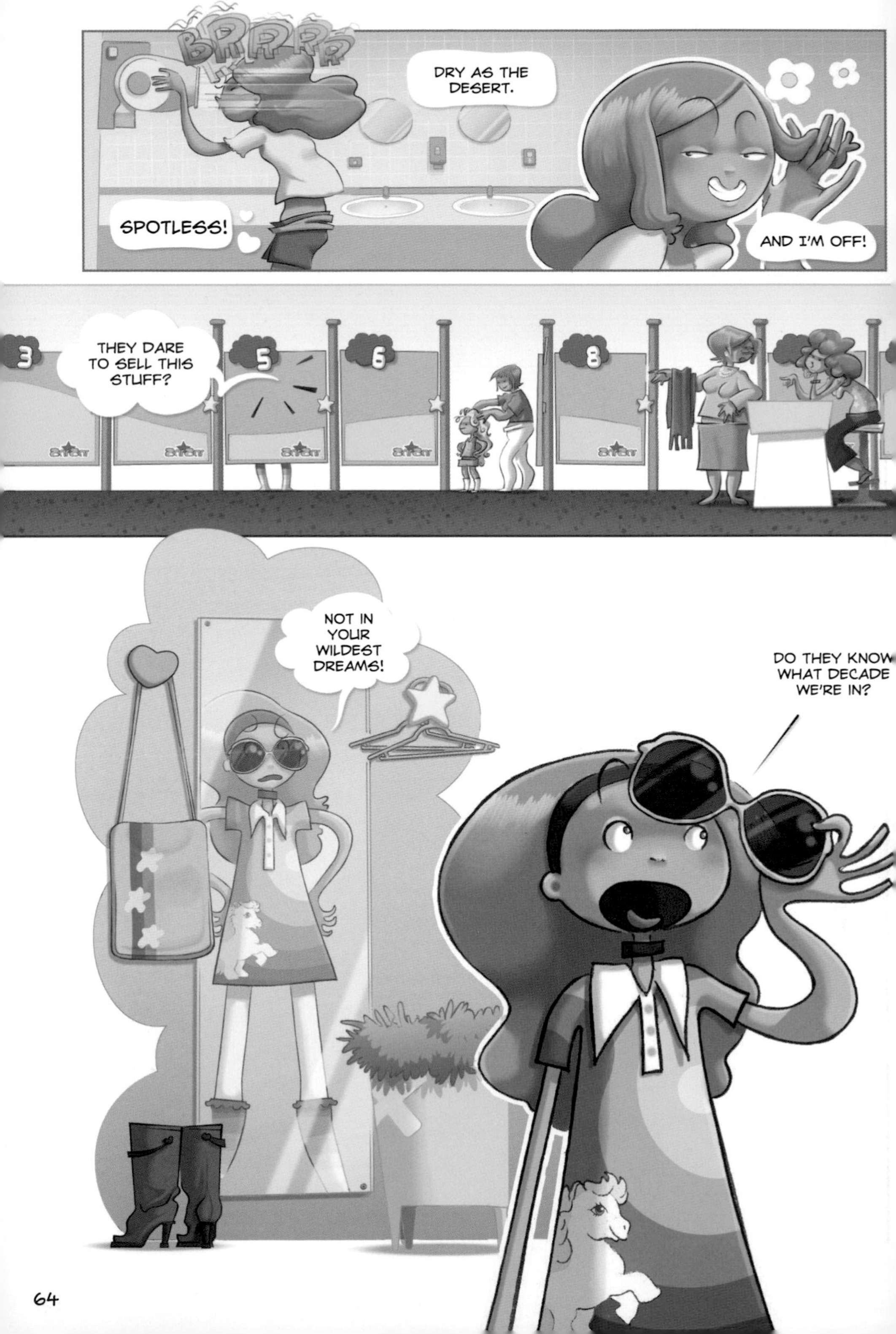
BRRRR
DRY AS THE DESERT.
SPOTLESS!
AND I'M OFF!
3
THEY DARE TO SELL THIS STUFF?
5
6
8
NOT IN YOUR WILDEST DREAMS!
DO THEY KNOW WHAT DECADE WE'RE IN?

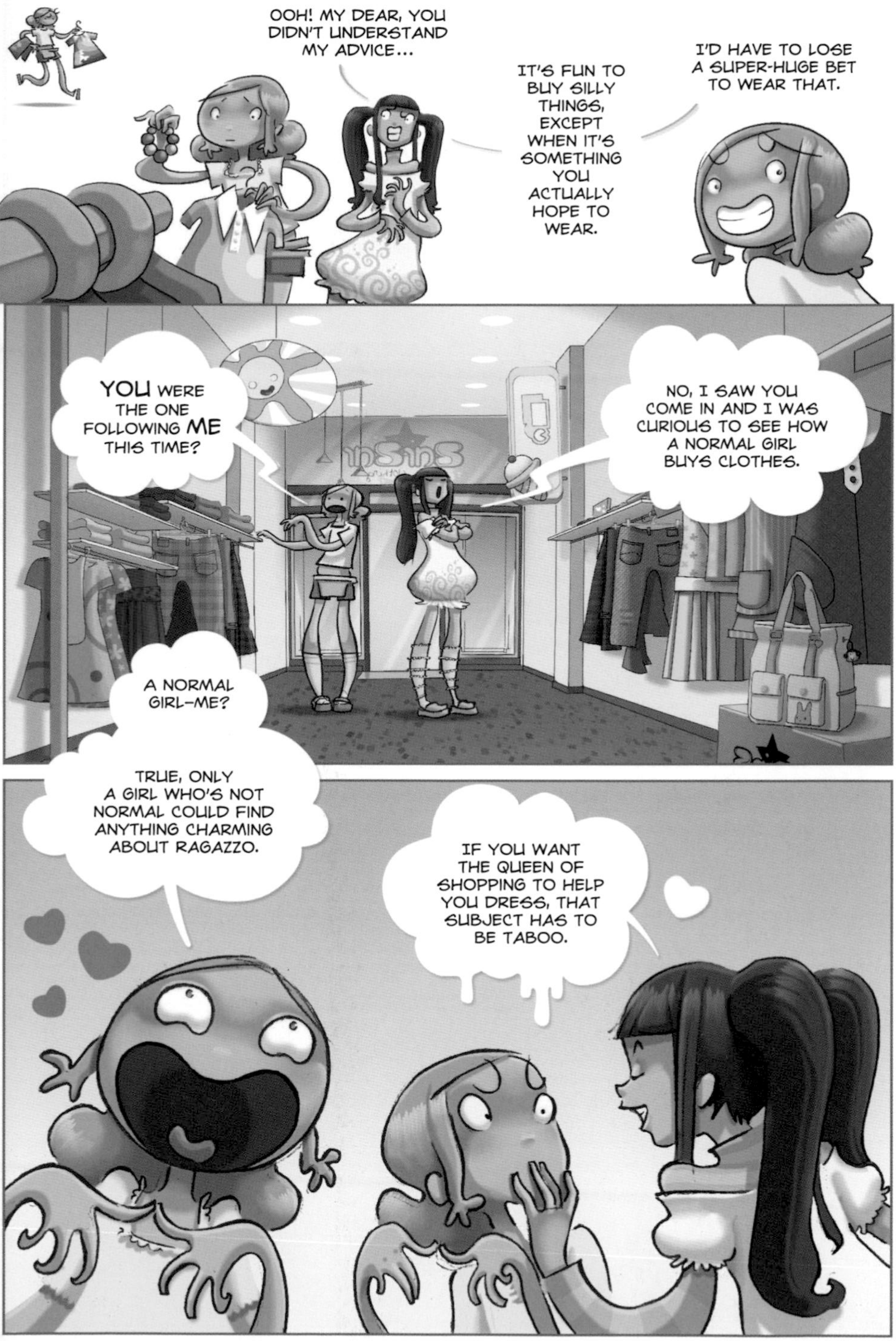
OOH! MY DEAR, YOU DIDN'T UNDERSTAND MY ADVICE...
IT'S FUN TO BUY SILLY THINGS, EXCEPT WHEN IT'S SOMETHING YOU ACTUALLY HOPE TO WEAR.
I'D HAVE TO LOSE A SUPER-HUGE BET TO WEAR THAT.
YOU WERE THE ONE FOLLOWING ME THIS TIME?
NO, I SAW YOU COME IN AND I WAS CURIOUS TO SEE HOW A NORMAL GIRL BUYS CLOTHES.
A NORMAL GIRL—ME?
TRUE, ONLY A GIRL WHO'S NOT NORMAL COULD FIND ANYTHING CHARMING ABOUT RAGAZZO.
IF YOU WANT THE QUEEN OF SHOPPING TO HELP YOU DRESS, THAT SUBJECT HAS TO BE TABOO.

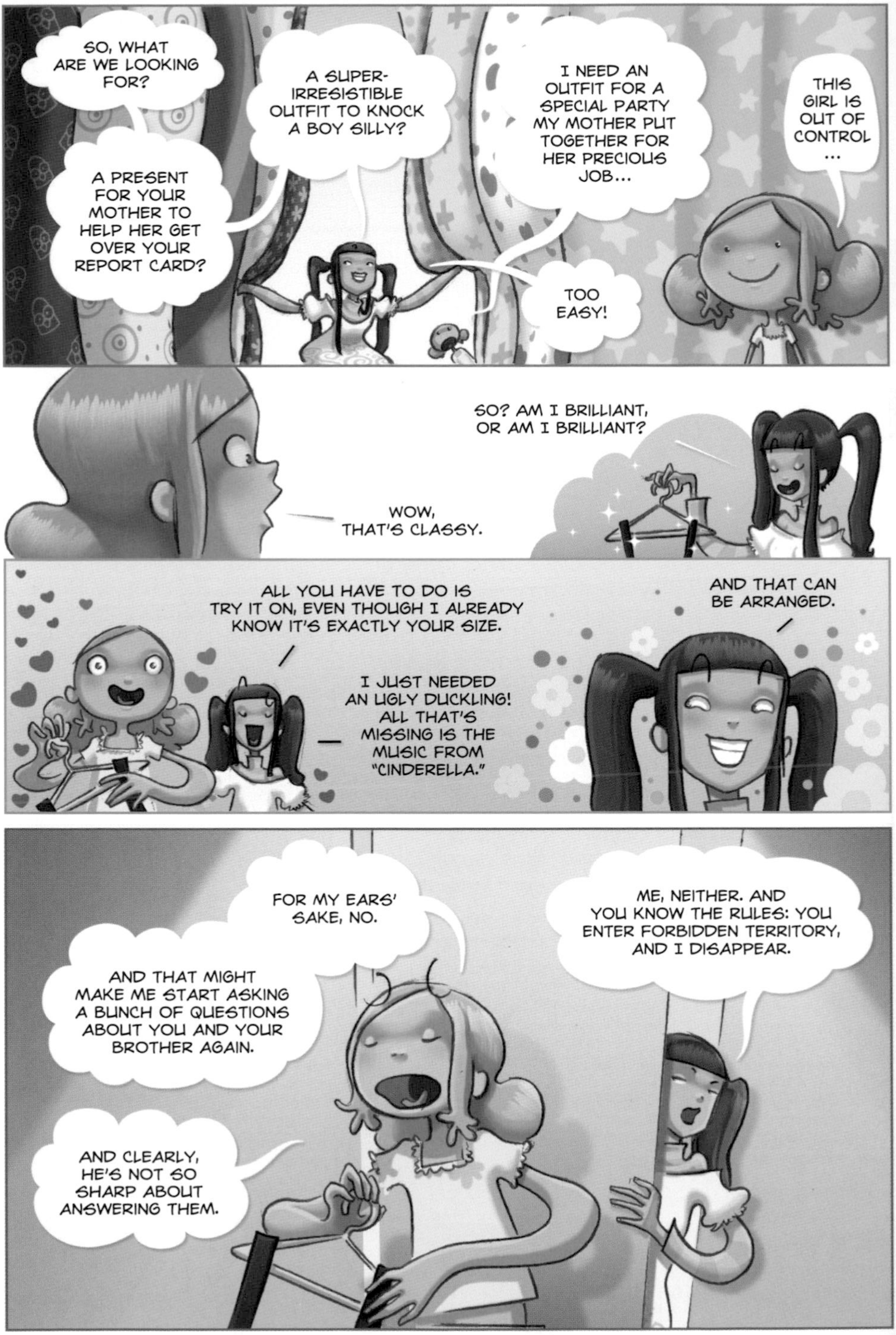
SO, WHAT ARE WE LOOKING FOR?
A SUPER-IRRESISTIBLE OUTFIT TO KNOCK A BOY SILLY?
A PRESENT FOR YOUR MOTHER TO HELP HER GET OVER YOUR REPORT CARD?
I NEED AN OUTFIT FOR A SPECIAL PARTY MY MOTHER PUT TOGETHER FOR HER PRECIOUS JOB...
TOO EASY!
THIS GIRL IS OUT OF CONTROL ...
SO? AM I BRILLIANT, OR AM I BRILLIANT?
WOW, THAT'S CLASSY.
ALL YOU HAVE TO DO IS TRY IT ON, EVEN THOUGH I ALREADY KNOW IT'S EXACTLY YOUR SIZE.
I JUST NEEDED AN UGLY DUCKLING! ALL THAT'S MISSING IS THE MUSIC FROM "CINDERELLA."
AND THAT CAN BE ARRANGED.
FOR MY EARS' SAKE, NO.
AND THAT MIGHT MAKE ME START ASKING A BUNCH OF QUESTIONS ABOUT YOU AND YOUR BROTHER AGAIN.
AND CLEARLY, HE'S NOT SO SHARP ABOUT ANSWERING THEM.
ME, NEITHER. AND YOU KNOW THE RULES: YOU ENTER FORBIDDEN TERRITORY, AND I DISAPPEAR.

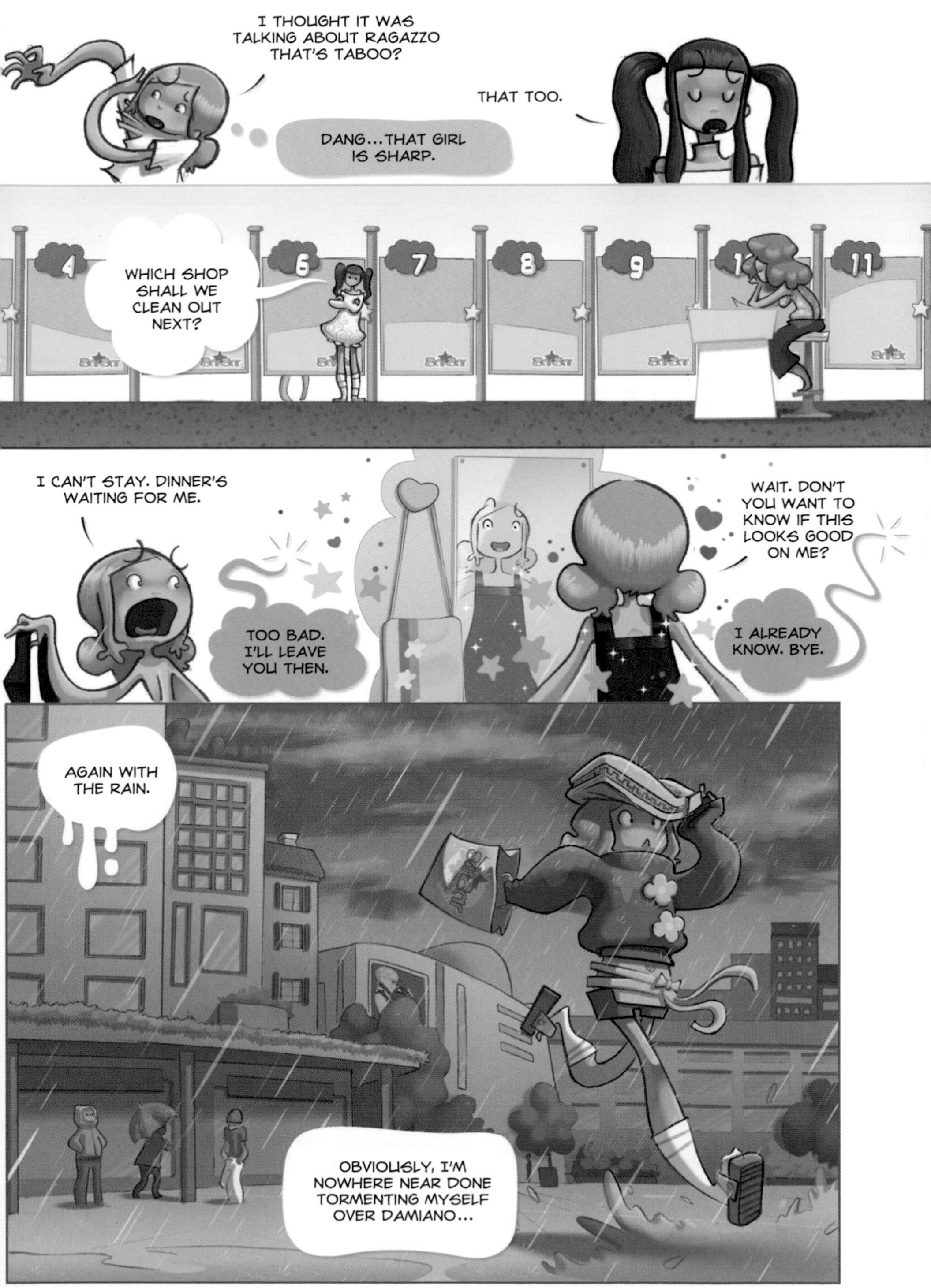
I THOUGHT IT WAS TALKING ABOUT RAGAZZO THAT'S TABOO?
THAT TOO.
DANG...THAT GIRL IS SHARP.
WHICH SHOP SHALL WE CLEAN OUT NEXT?
I CAN'T STAY. DINNER'S WAITING FOR ME.
TOO BAD. I'LL LEAVE YOU THEN.
WAIT. DON'T YOU WANT TO KNOW IF THIS LOOKS GOOD ON ME?
I ALREADY KNOW. BYE.
AGAIN WITH THE RAIN.
OBVIOUSLY, I'M NOWHERE NEAR DONE TORMENTING MYSELF OVER DAMIANO...

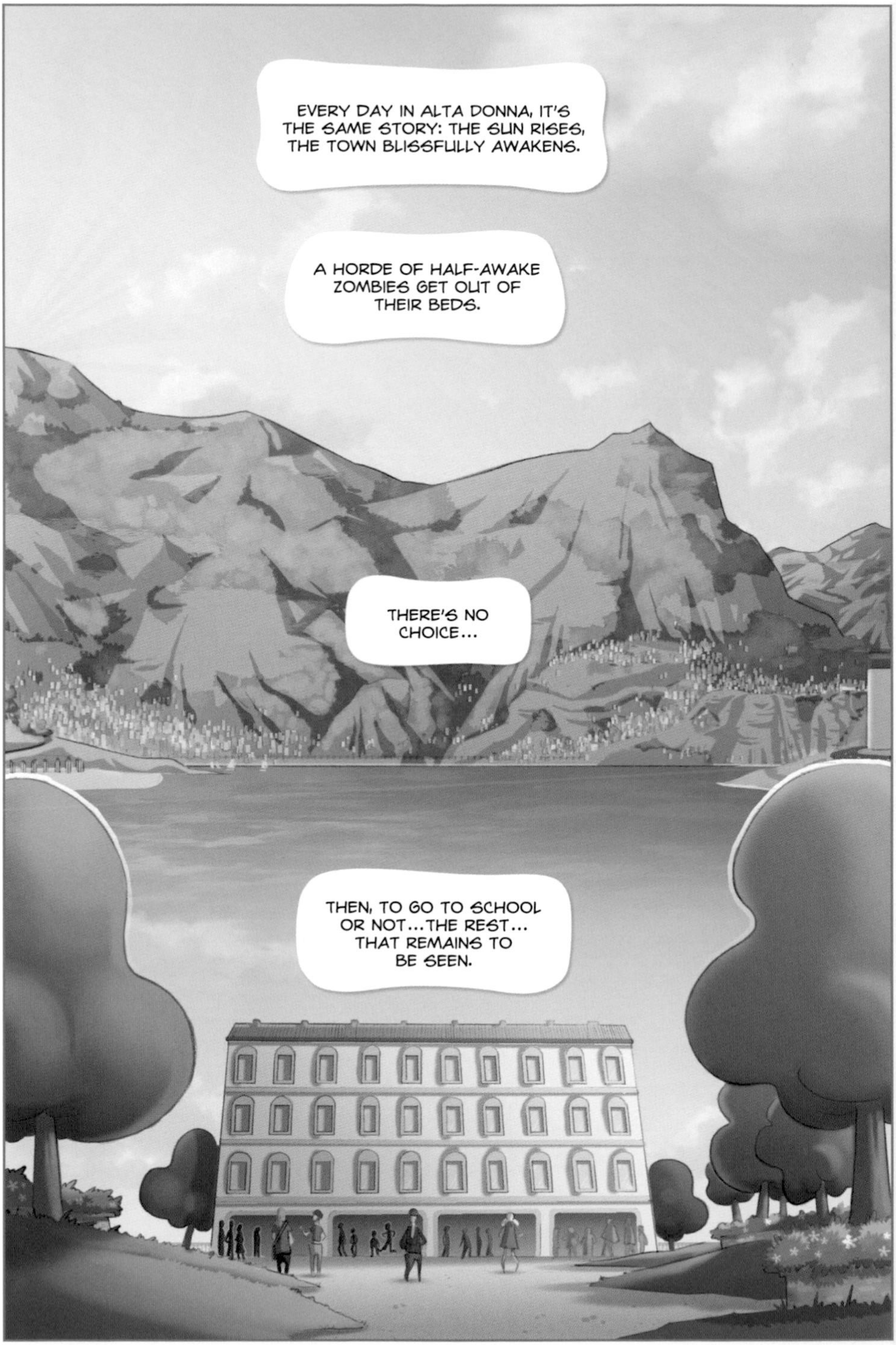
EVERY DAY IN ALTA DONNA, IT'S THE SAME STORY: THE SUN RISES, THE TOWN BLISSFULLY AWAKENS.
A HORDE OF HALF-AWAKE ZOMBIES GET OUT OF THEIR BEDS.
THERE'S NO CHOICE...
THEN, TO GO TO SCHOOL OR NOT...THE REST... THAT REMAINS TO BE SEEN.

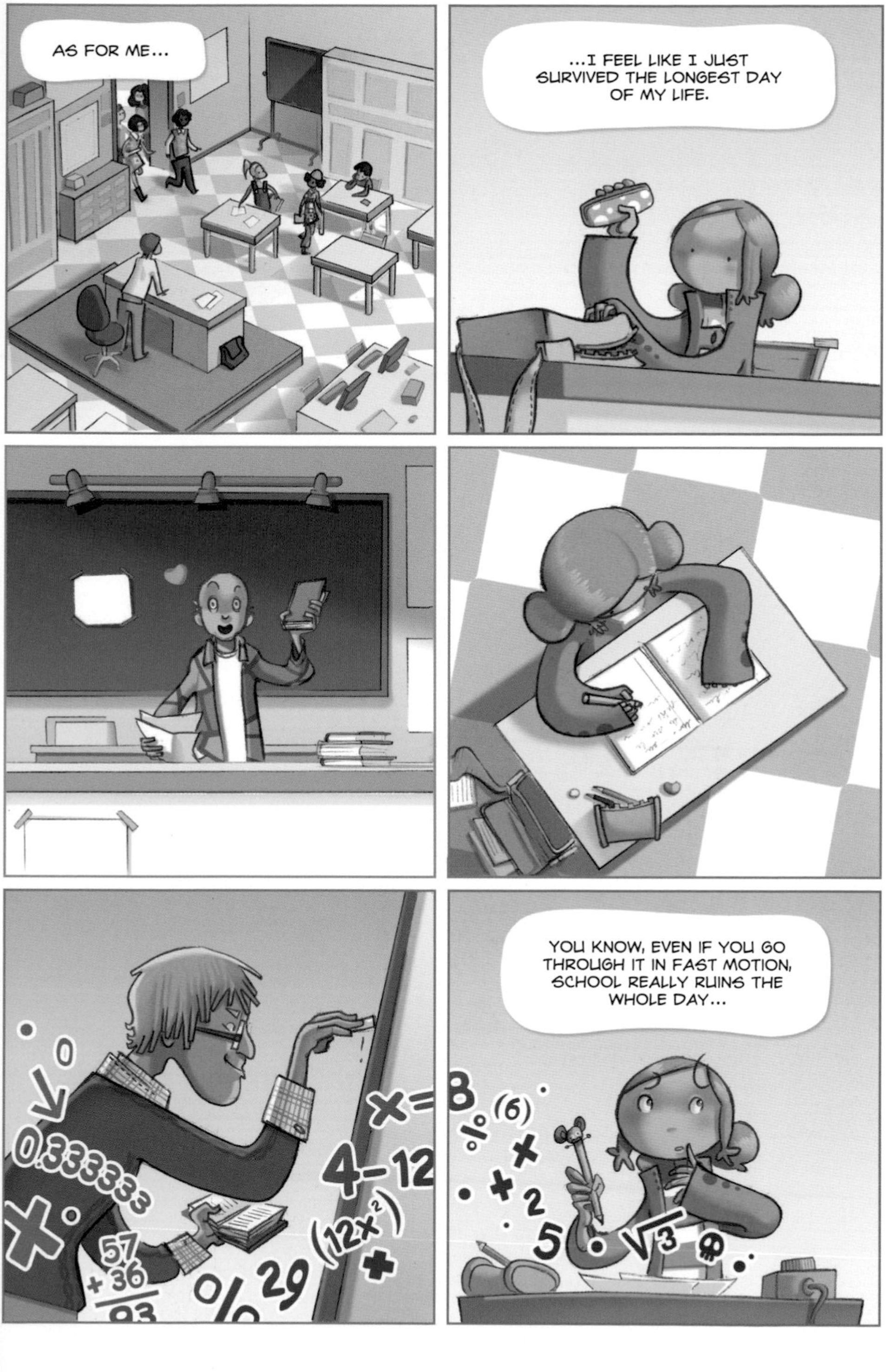
AS FOR ME...
...I FEEL LIKE I JUST SURVIVED THE LONGEST DAY OF MY LIFE.
YOU KNOW, EVEN IF YOU GO THROUGH IT IN FAST MOTION, SCHOOL REALLY RUINS THE WHOLE DAY...

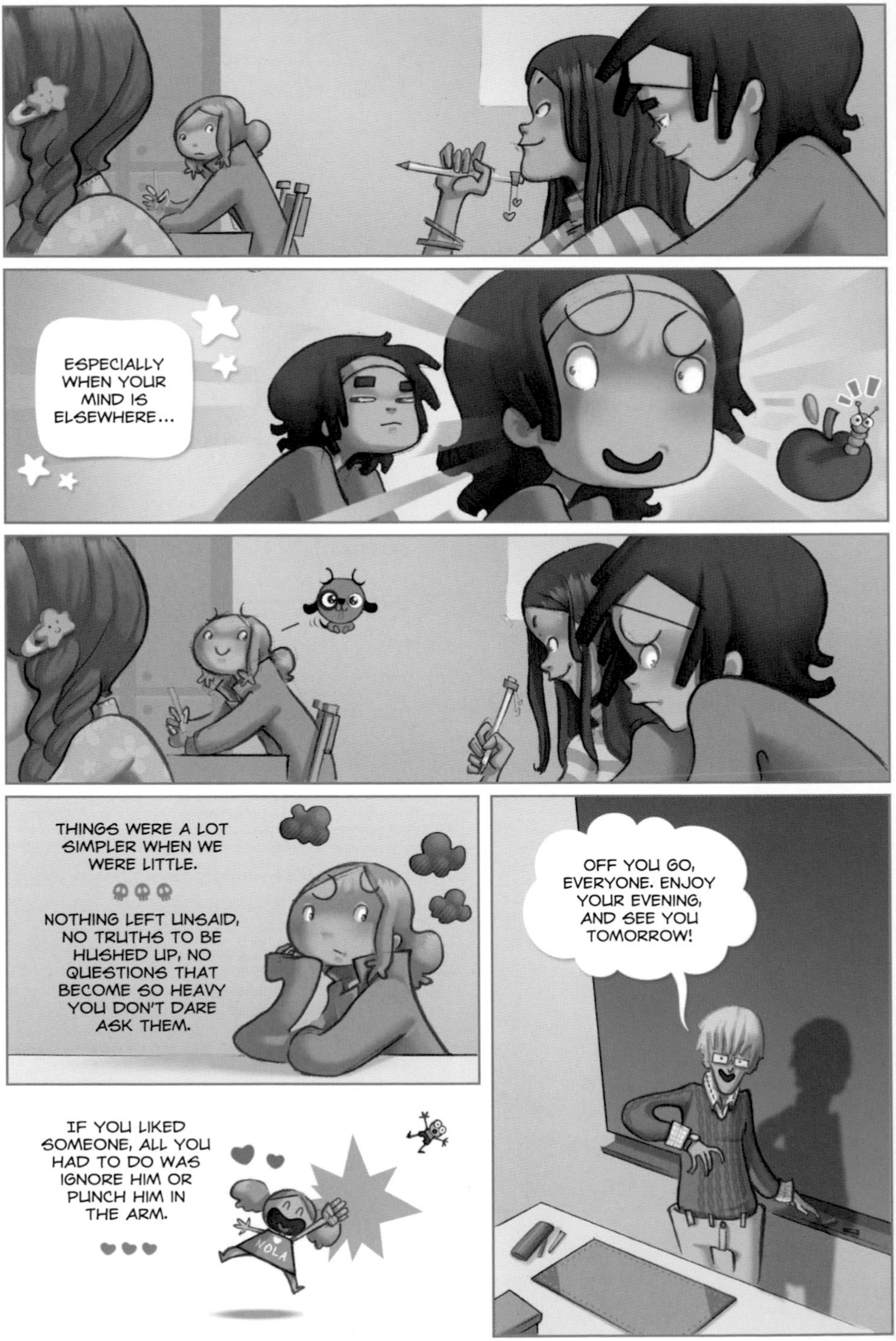

ESPECIALLY WHEN YOUR MIND IS ELSEWHERE...
THINGS WERE A LOT SIMPLER WHEN WE WERE LITTLE.
NOTHING LEFT UNSAID, NO TRUTHS TO BE HUSHED UP, NO QUESTIONS THAT BECOME SO HEAVY YOU DON'T DARE ASK THEM.
OFF YOU GO, EVERYONE. ENJOY YOUR EVENING, AND SEE YOU TOMORROW!
IF YOU LIKED SOMEONE, ALL YOU HAD TO DO WAS IGNORE HIM OR PUNCH HIM IN THE ARM.
NOLA

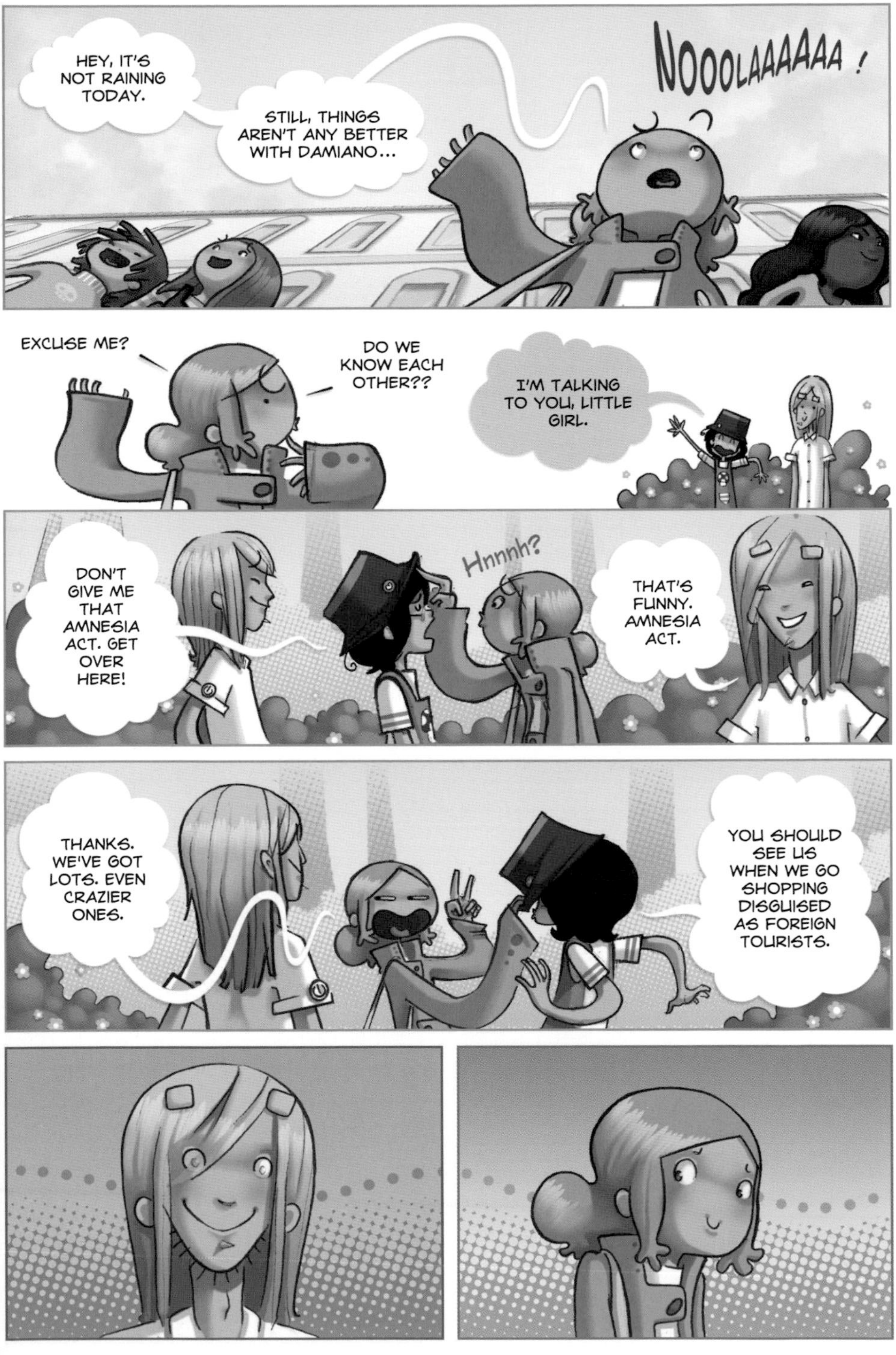
HEY, IT'S NOT RAINING TODAY.
STILL, THINGS AREN'T ANY BETTER WITH DAMIANO...
NOOOLAAAAAA !
EXCUSE ME?
DO WE KNOW EACH OTHER??
I'M TALKING TO YOU, LITTLE GIRL.
DON'T GIVE ME THAT AMNESIA ACT. GET OVER HERE!
Hnnnh?
THAT'S FUNNY. AMNESIA ACT.
THANKS. WE'VE GOT LOTS. EVEN CRAZIER ONES.
YOU SHOULD SEE US WHEN WE GO SHOPPING DISGUISED AS FOREIGN TOURISTS.

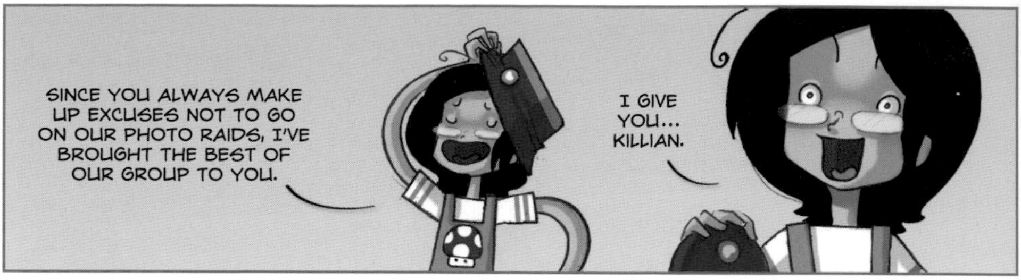
SINCE YOU ALWAYS MAKE UP EXCUSES NOT TO GO ON OUR PHOTO RAIDS, I'VE BROUGHT THE BEST OF OUR GROUP TO YOU.
I GIVE YOU... KILLIAN.

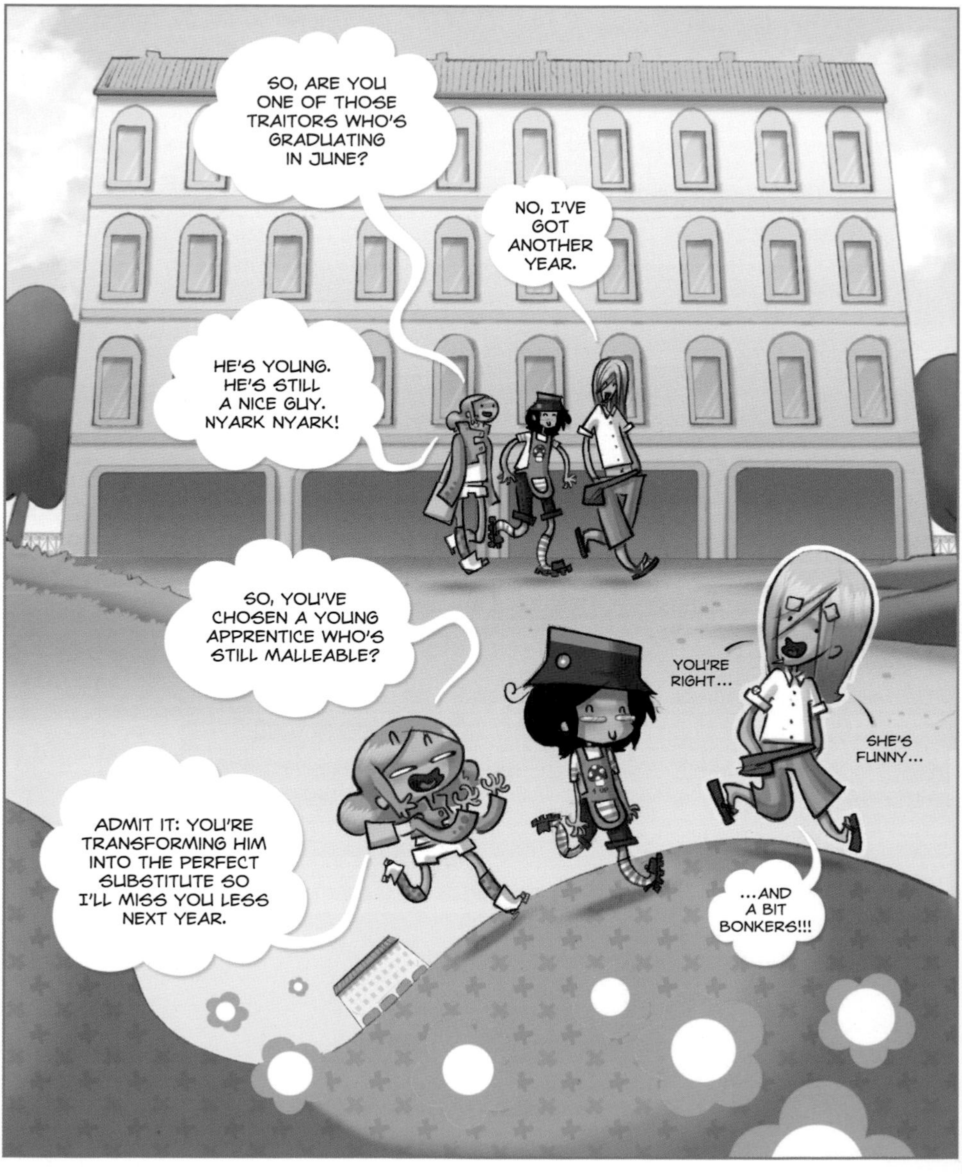
SO, ARE YOU ONE OF THOSE TRAITORS WHO'S GRADUATING IN JUNE?
NO, I'VE GOT ANOTHER YEAR.
HE'S YOUNG. HE'S STILL A NICE GUY. NYARK NYARK!
SO, YOU'VE CHOSEN A YOUNG APPRENTICE WHO'S STILL MALLEABLE?
ADMIT IT: YOU'RE TRANSFORMING HIM INTO THE PERFECT SUBSTITUTE SO I'LL MISS YOU LESS NEXT YEAR.
YOU'RE RIGHT...
SHE'S FUNNY...
...AND A BIT BONKERS!!!

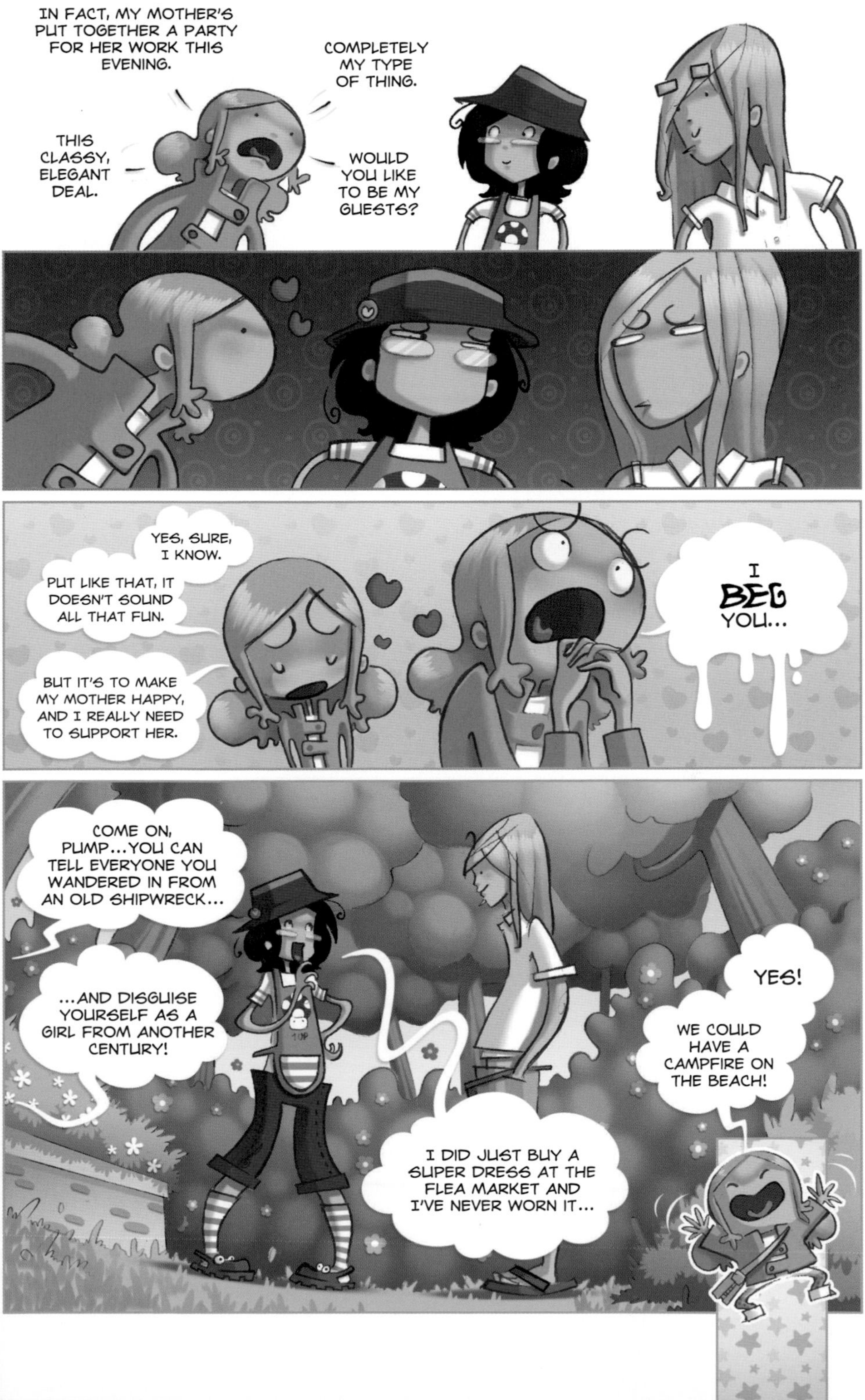
IN FACT, MY MOTHER'S PUT TOGETHER A PARTY FOR HER WORK THIS EVENING.
THIS CLASSY, ELEGANT DEAL.
COMPLETELY MY TYPE OF THING.
WOULD YOU LIKE TO BE MY GUESTS?
YES, SURE, I KNOW.
PUT LIKE THAT, IT DOESN'T SOUND ALL THAT FUN.
BUT IT'S TO MAKE MY MOTHER HAPPY, AND I REALLY NEED TO SUPPORT HER.
I BEG YOU...
COME ON, PUMP...YOU CAN TELL EVERYONE YOU WANDERED IN FROM AN OLD SHIPWRECK...
...AND DISGUISE YOURSELF AS A GIRL FROM ANOTHER CENTURY!
I DID JUST BUY A SUPER DRESS AT THE FLEA MARKET AND I'VE NEVER WORN IT...
YES!
WE COULD HAVE A CAMPFIRE ON THE BEACH!

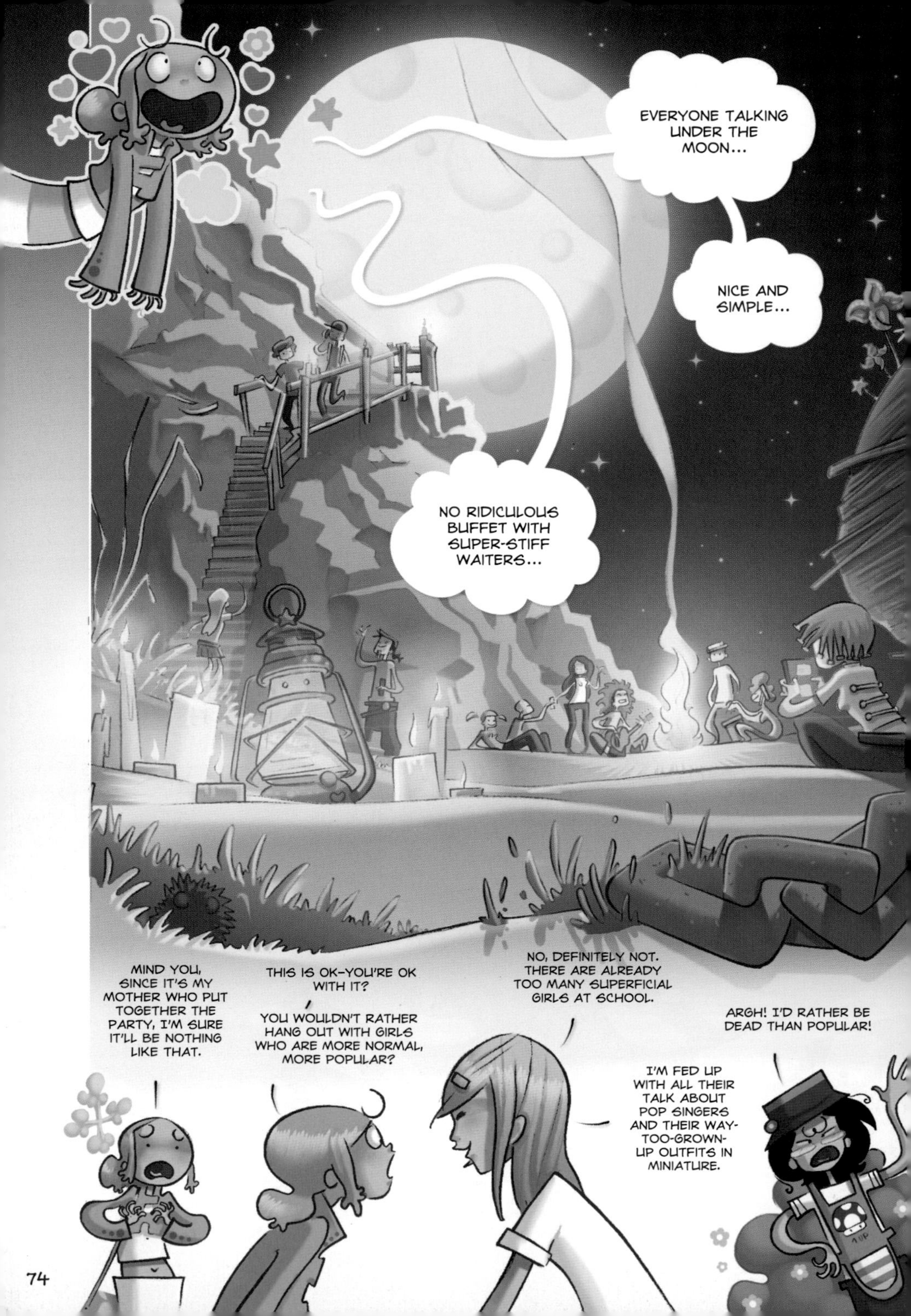
EVERYONE TALKING UNDER THE MOON...
NICE AND SIMPLE...
NO RIDICULOUS BUFFET WITH SUPER-STIFF WAITERS...
MIND YOU, SINCE IT'S MY MOTHER WHO PUT TOGETHER THE PARTY, I'M SURE IT'LL BE NOTHING LIKE THAT.
THIS IS OK–YOU'RE OK WITH IT?
YOU WOULDN'T RATHER HANG OUT WITH GIRLS WHO ARE MORE NORMAL, MORE POPULAR?
NO, DEFINITELY NOT. THERE ARE ALREADY TOO MANY SUPERFICIAL GIRLS AT SCHOOL.
I'M FED UP WITH ALL THEIR TALK ABOUT POP SINGERS AND THEIR WAY-TOO-GROWN-UP OUTFITS IN MINIATURE.
ARGH! I'D RATHER BE DEAD THAN POPULAR!

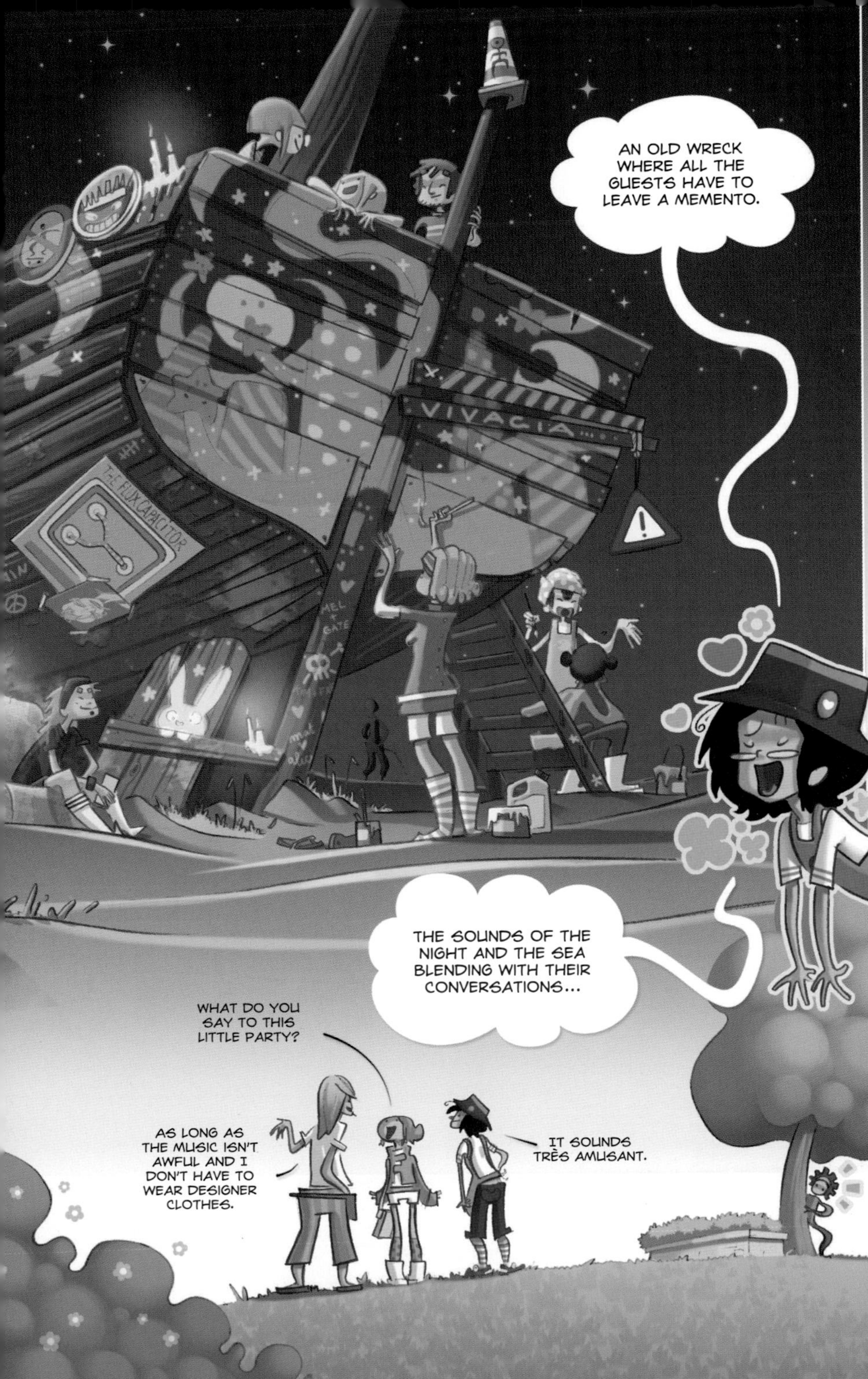
AN OLD WRECK WHERE ALL THE GUESTS HAVE TO LEAVE A MEMENTO.
VIVACIA...
THE FLUX CAPACITOR
THE SOUNDS OF THE NIGHT AND THE SEA BLENDING WITH THEIR CONVERSATIONS...
WHAT DO YOU SAY TO THIS LITTLE PARTY?
AS LONG AS THE MUSIC ISN'T AWFUL AND I DON'T HAVE TO WEAR DESIGNER CLOTHES.
IT SOUNDS TRÈS AMUSANT.

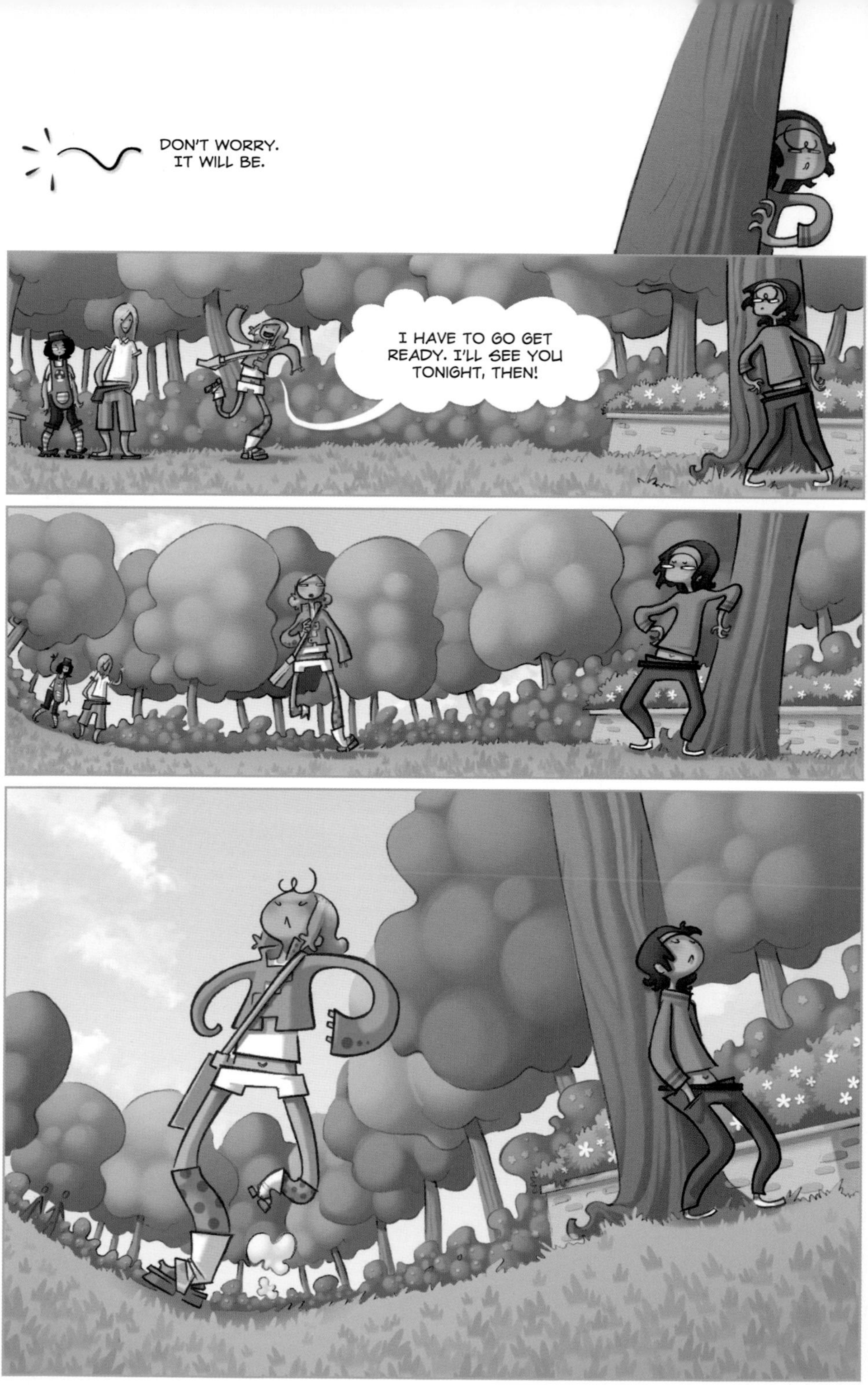
DON'T WORRY.
IT WILL BE.
I HAVE TO GO GET READY. I'LL SEE YOU TONIGHT, THEN!

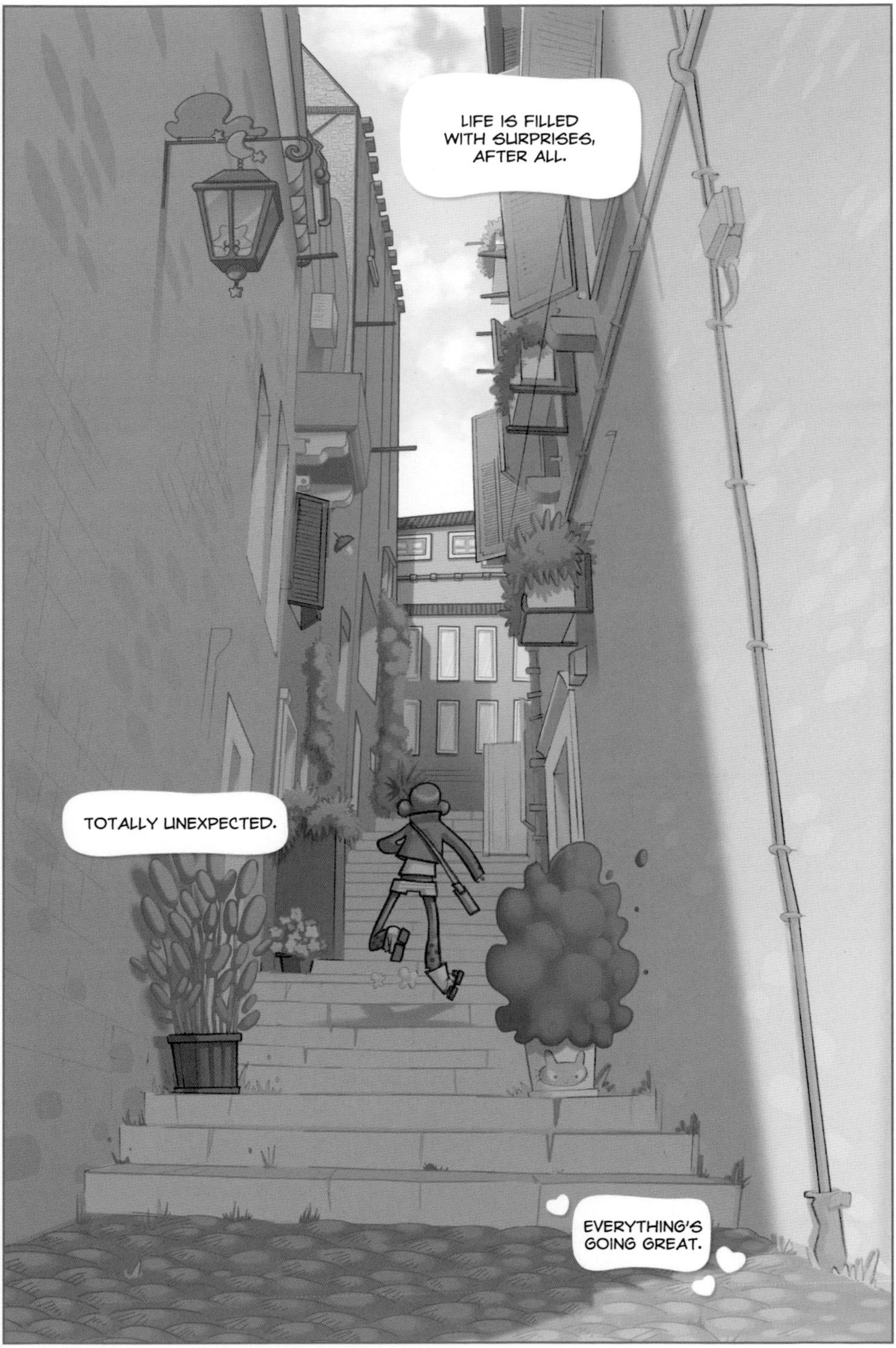
LIFE IS FILLED WITH SURPRISES, AFTER ALL.
TOTALLY UNEXPECTED.
EVERYTHING'S GOING GREAT.

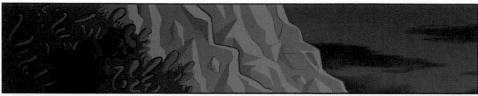

ARE YOU READY, NOLA?

YES...

I JUST NEED A SECOND TO GET USED TO THIS OUTFIT.

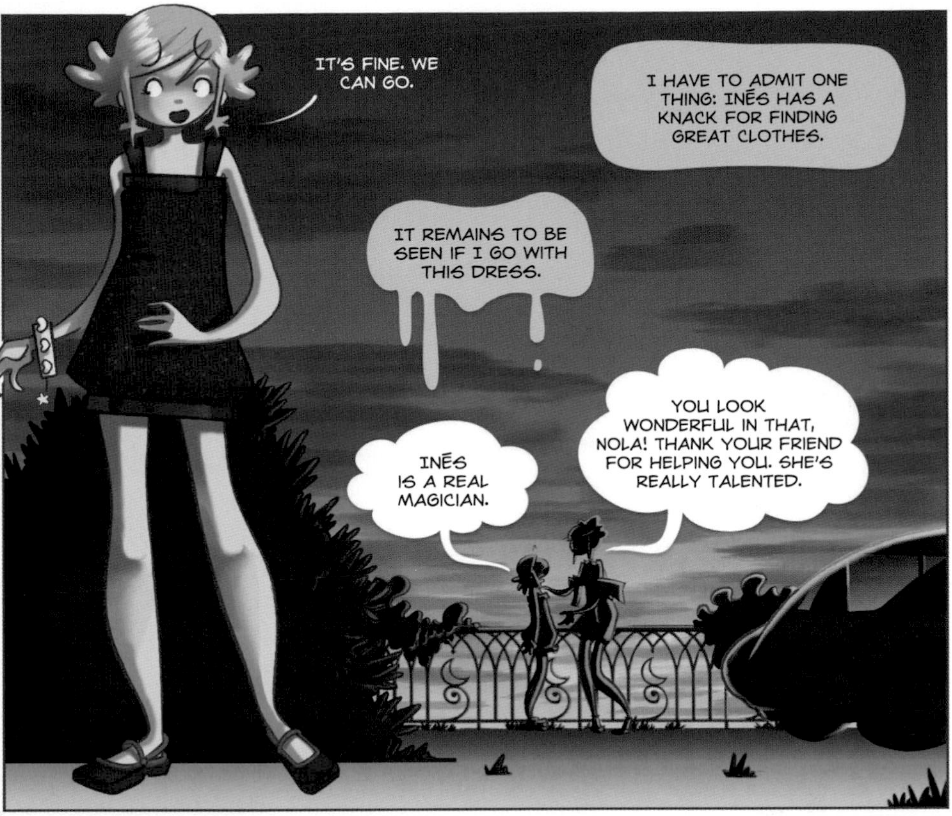
IT'S FINE. WE CAN GO.
I HAVE TO ADMIT ONE THING: INÉS HAS A KNACK FOR FINDING GREAT CLOTHES.
IT REMAINS TO BE SEEN IF I GO WITH THIS DRESS.
YOU LOOK WONDERFUL IN THAT, NOLA! THANK YOUR FRIEND FOR HELPING YOU. SHE'S REALLY TALENTED.
INÉS IS A REAL MAGICIAN.

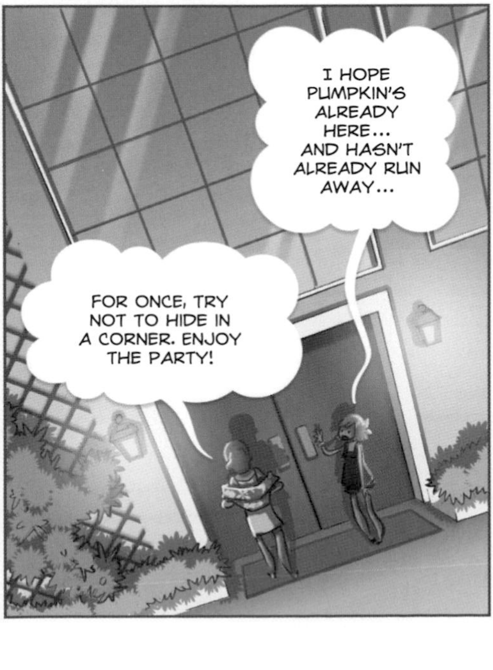
I HOPE PUMPKIN'S ALREADY HERE... AND HASN'T ALREADY RUN AWAY...
FOR ONCE, TRY NOT TO HIDE IN A CORNER. ENJOY THE PARTY!

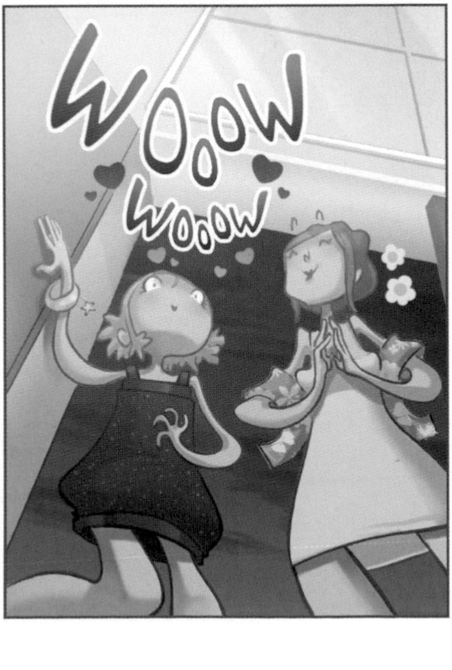
WOoOW
WOoOW

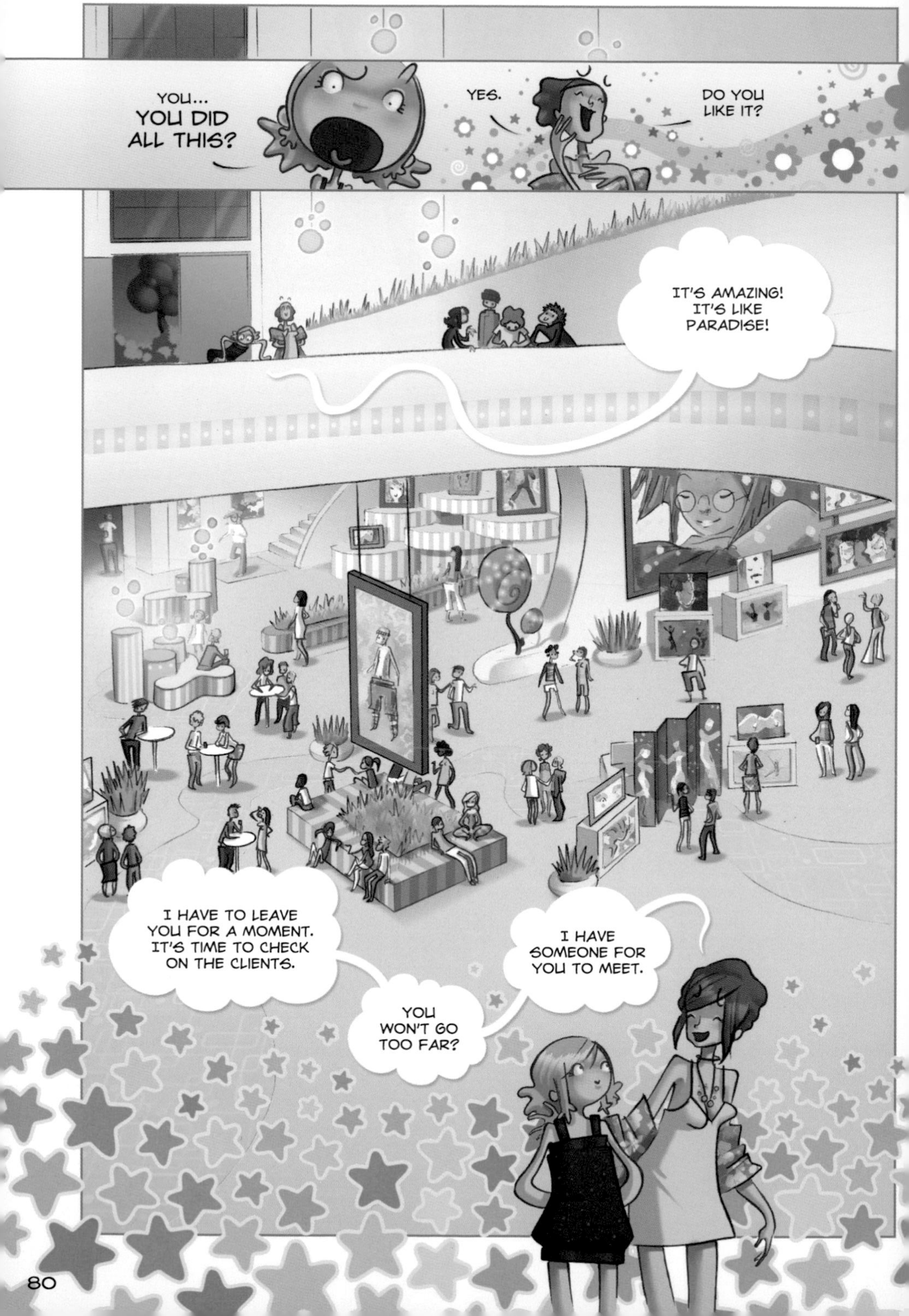
YOU...
YOU DID ALL THIS?
YES.
DO YOU LIKE IT?
IT'S AMAZING! IT'S LIKE PARADISE!
I HAVE TO LEAVE YOU FOR A MOMENT. IT'S TIME TO CHECK ON THE CLIENTS.
YOU WON'T GO TOO FAR?
I HAVE SOMEONE FOR YOU TO MEET.

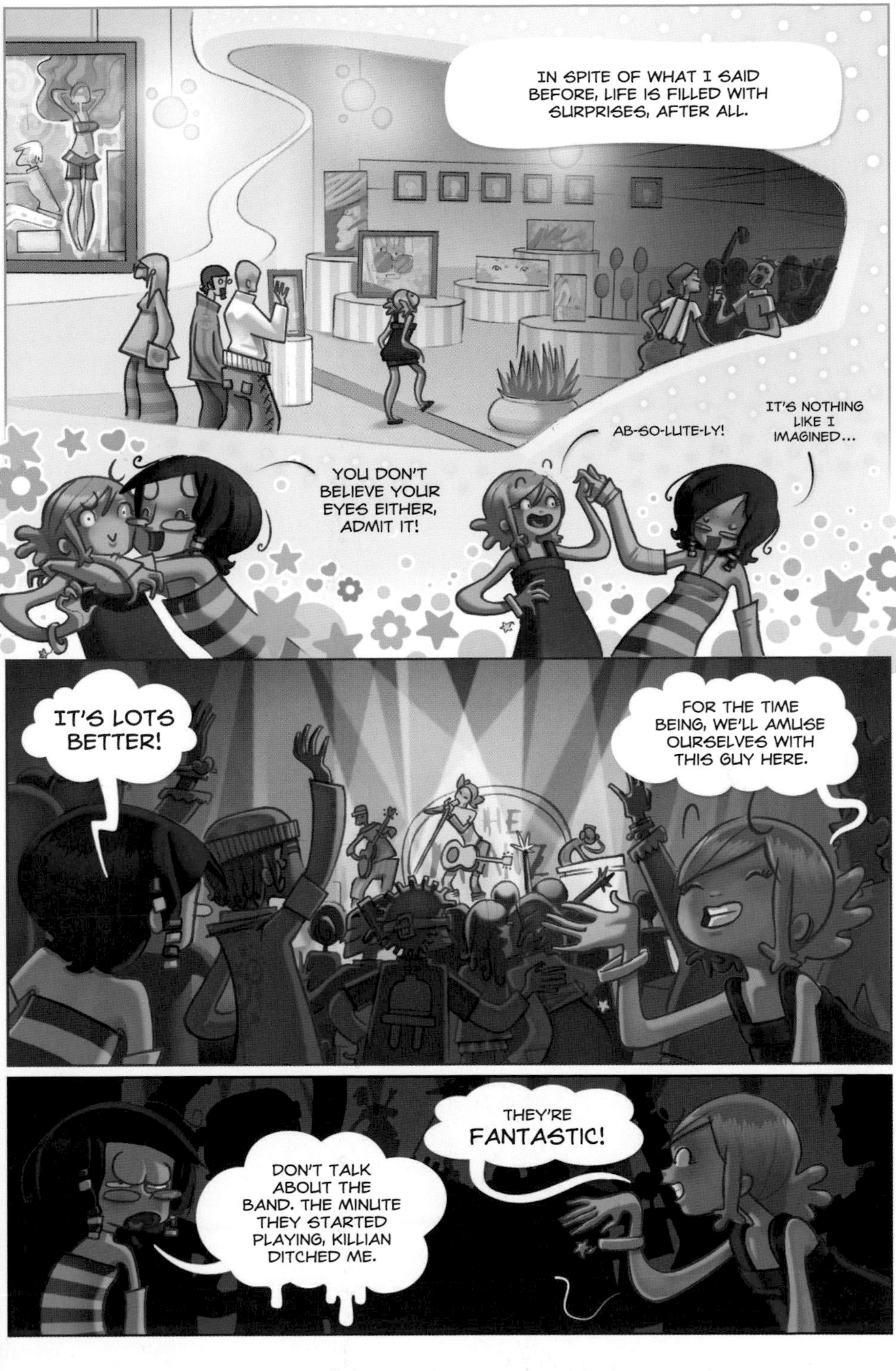
IN SPITE OF WHAT I SAID BEFORE, LIFE IS FILLED WITH SURPRISES, AFTER ALL.
YOU DON'T BELIEVE YOUR EYES EITHER, ADMIT IT!
AB-SO-LUTE-LY!
IT'S NOTHING LIKE I IMAGINED...
IT'S LOTS BETTER!
FOR THE TIME BEING, WE'LL AMUSE OURSELVES WITH THIS GUY HERE.
THEY'RE FANTASTIC!
DON'T TALK ABOUT THE BAND. THE MINUTE THEY STARTED PLAYING, KILLIAN DITCHED ME.

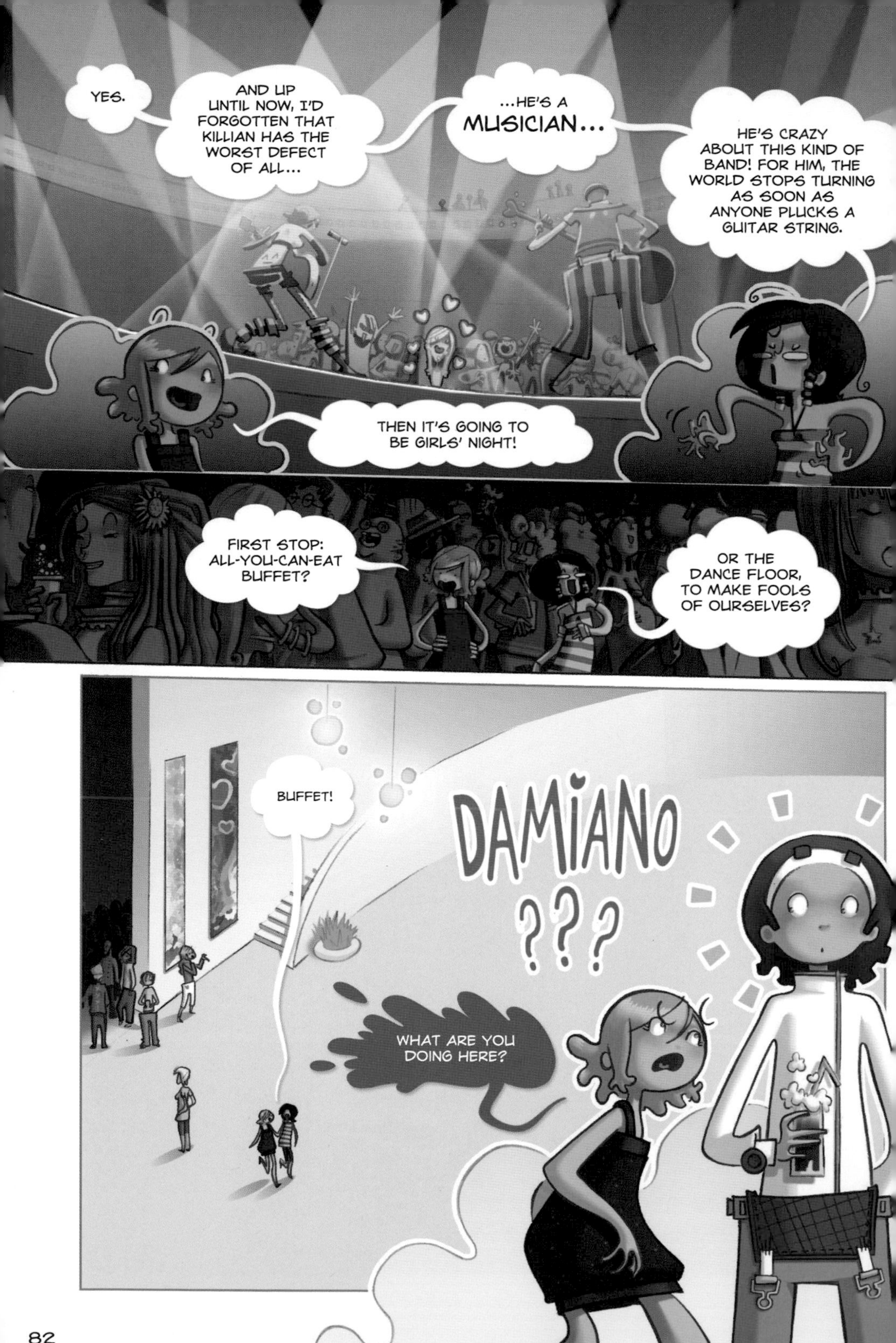

YES.
AND UP UNTIL NOW, I'D FORGOTTEN THAT KILLIAN HAS THE WORST DEFECT OF ALL...
...HE'S A MUSICIAN...
HE'S CRAZY ABOUT THIS KIND OF BAND! FOR HIM, THE WORLD STOPS TURNING AS SOON AS ANYONE PLUCKS A GUITAR STRING.
THEN IT'S GOING TO BE GIRLS' NIGHT!
FIRST STOP: ALL-YOU-CAN-EAT BUFFET?
OR THE DANCE FLOOR, TO MAKE FOOLS OF OURSELVES?
BUFFET!
DAMIANO ???
WHAT ARE YOU DOING HERE?

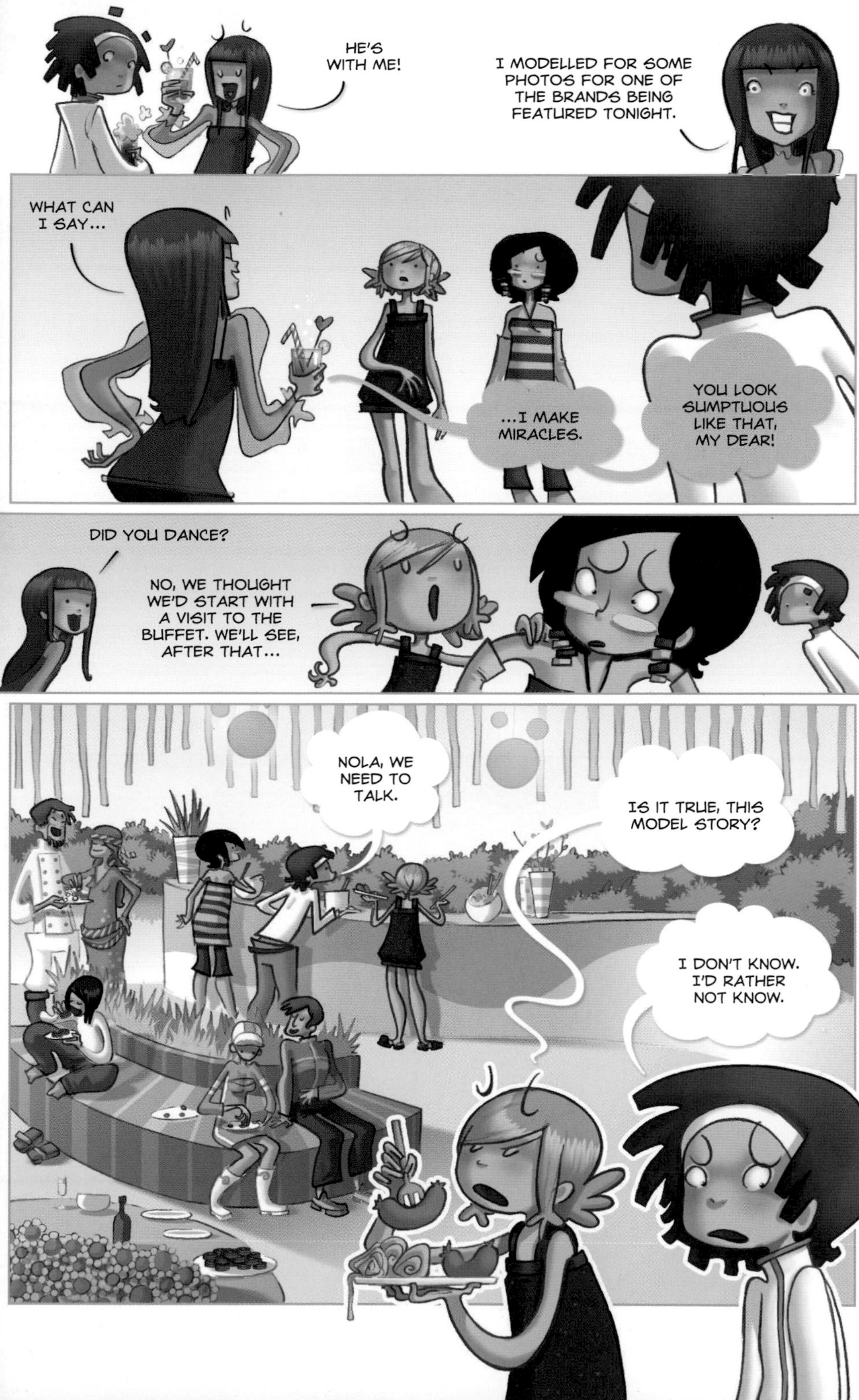
HE'S WITH ME!
I MODELLED FOR SOME PHOTOS FOR ONE OF THE BRANDS BEING FEATURED TONIGHT.
WHAT CAN I SAY...
...I MAKE MIRACLES.
YOU LOOK SUMPTUOUS LIKE THAT, MY DEAR!
DID YOU DANCE?
NO, WE THOUGHT WE'D START WITH A VISIT TO THE BUFFET. WE'LL SEE, AFTER THAT...
NOLA, WE NEED TO TALK.
IS IT TRUE, THIS MODEL STORY?
I DON'T KNOW. I'D RATHER NOT KNOW.

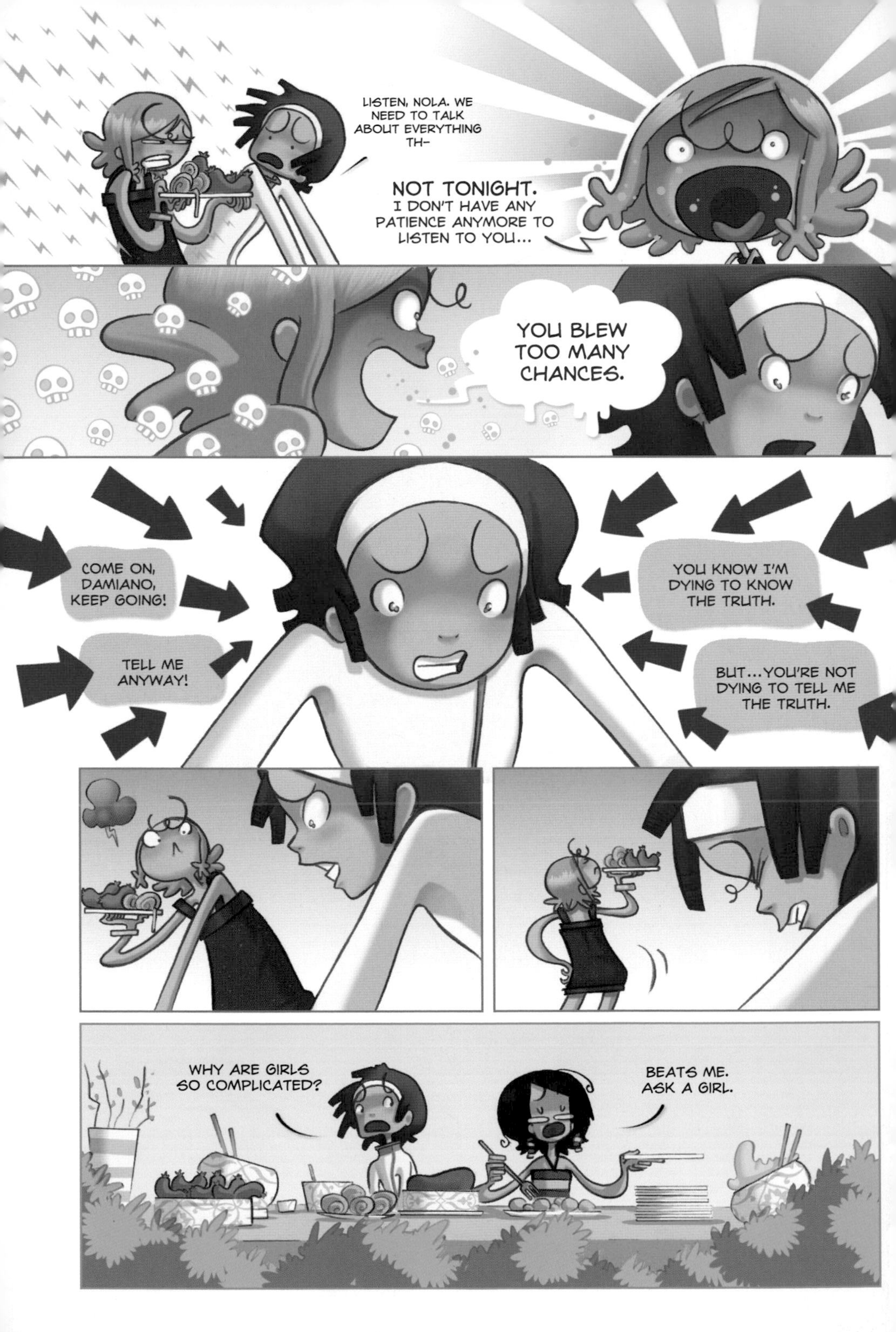
LISTEN, NOLA. WE NEED TO TALK ABOUT EVERYTHING TH-
NOT TONIGHT. I DON'T HAVE ANY PATIENCE ANYMORE TO LISTEN TO YOU...
YOU BLEW TOO MANY CHANCES.
COME ON, DAMIANO, KEEP GOING!
YOU KNOW I'M DYING TO KNOW THE TRUTH.
TELL ME ANYWAY!
BUT...YOU'RE NOT DYING TO TELL ME THE TRUTH.
WHY ARE GIRLS SO COMPLICATED?
BEATS ME. ASK A GIRL.

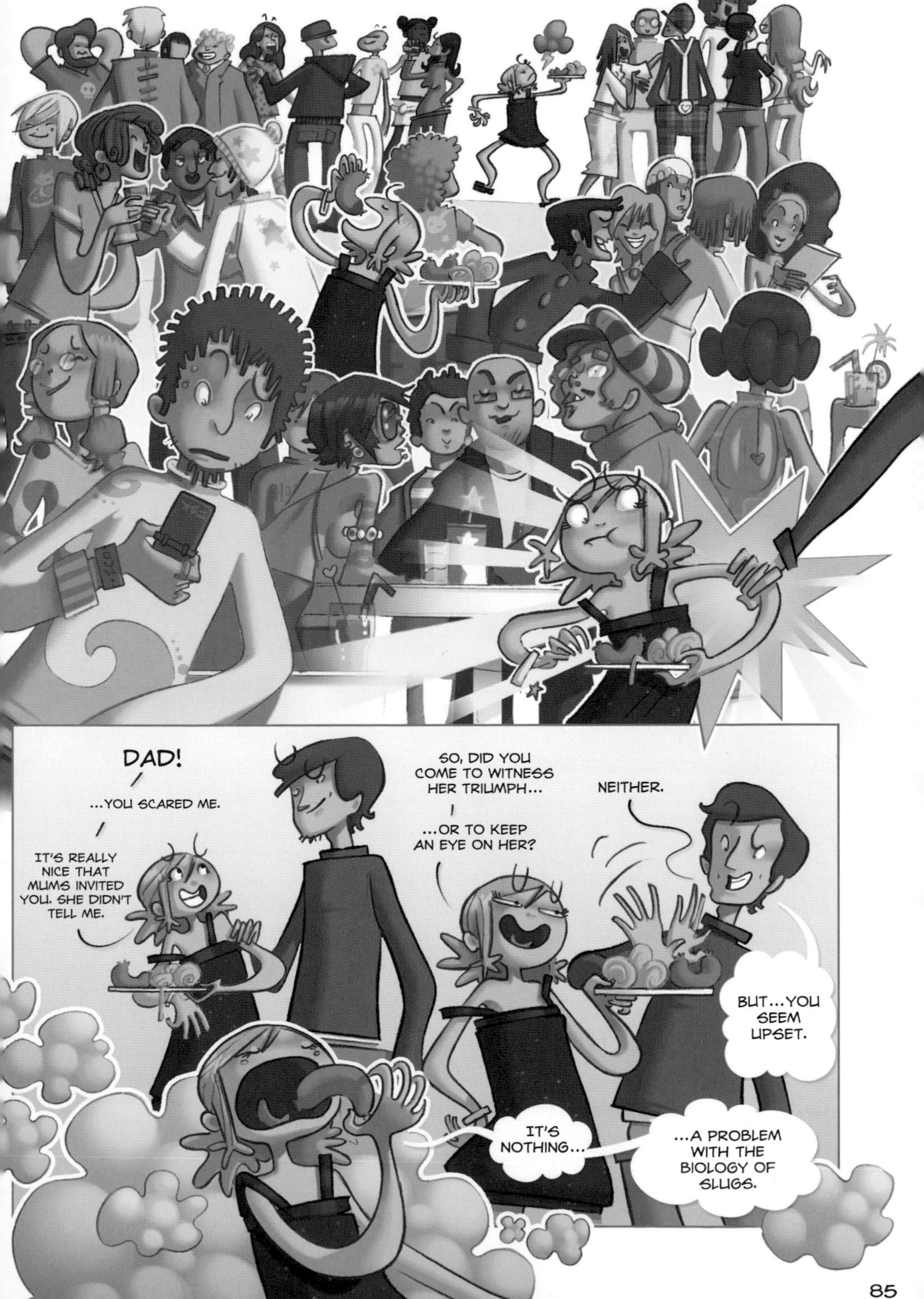
DAD!
...YOU SCARED ME.
IT'S REALLY NICE THAT MUMS INVITED YOU. SHE DIDN'T TELL ME.
SO, DID YOU COME TO WITNESS HER TRIUMPH...
...OR TO KEEP AN EYE ON HER?
NEITHER.
BUT...YOU SEEM UPSET.
IT'S NOTHING...
...A PROBLEM WITH THE BIOLOGY OF SLUGS.

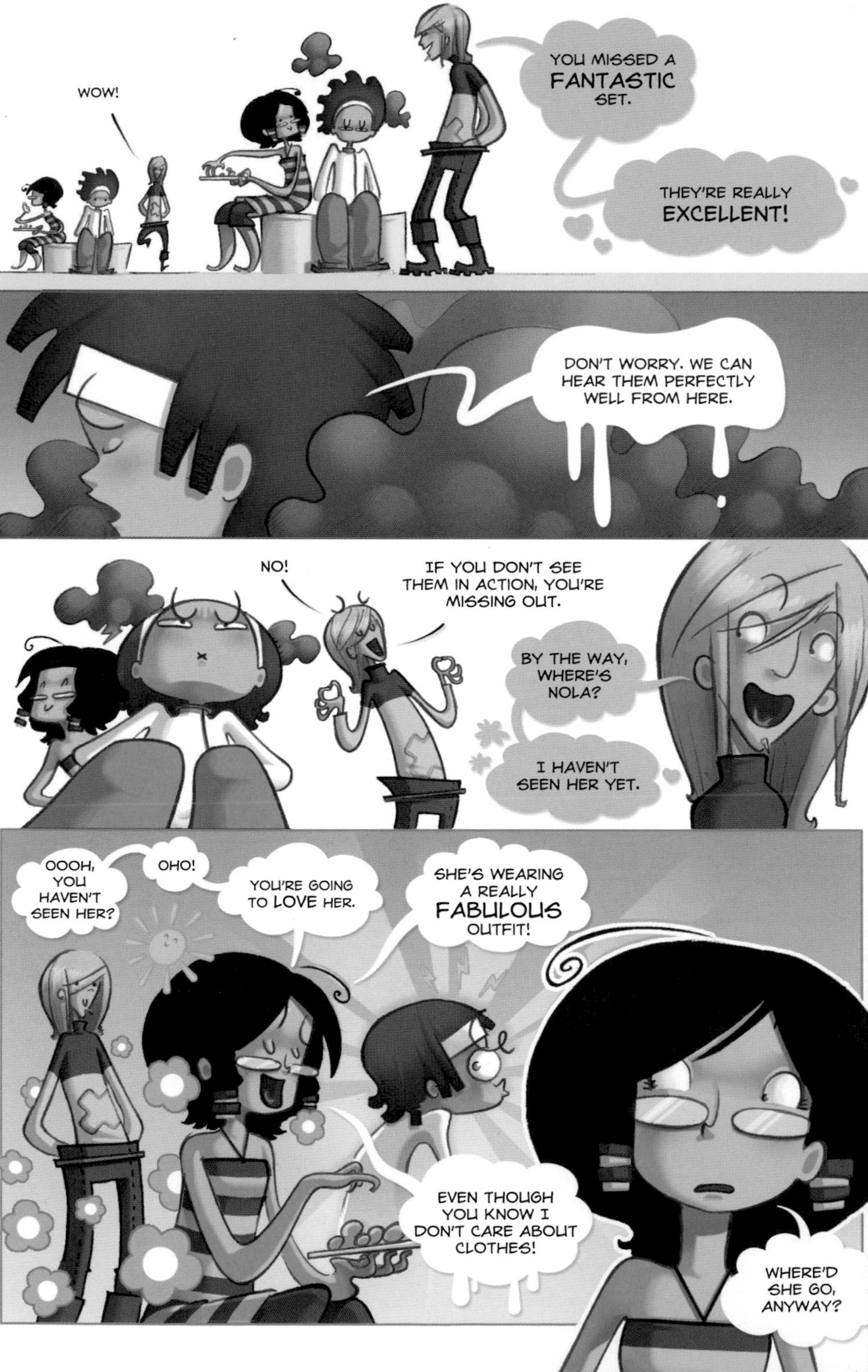
WOW!
YOU MISSED A FANTASTIC SET.
THEY'RE REALLY EXCELLENT!
DON'T WORRY. WE CAN HEAR THEM PERFECTLY WELL FROM HERE.
NO!
IF YOU DON'T SEE THEM IN ACTION, YOU'RE MISSING OUT.
BY THE WAY, WHERE'S NOLA?
I HAVEN'T SEEN HER YET.
OOOH, YOU HAVEN'T SEEN HER?
OHO!
YOU'RE GOING TO LOVE HER.
SHE'S WEARING A REALLY FABULOUS OUTFIT!
EVEN THOUGH YOU KNOW I DON'T CARE ABOUT CLOTHES!
WHERE'D SHE GO, ANYWAY?

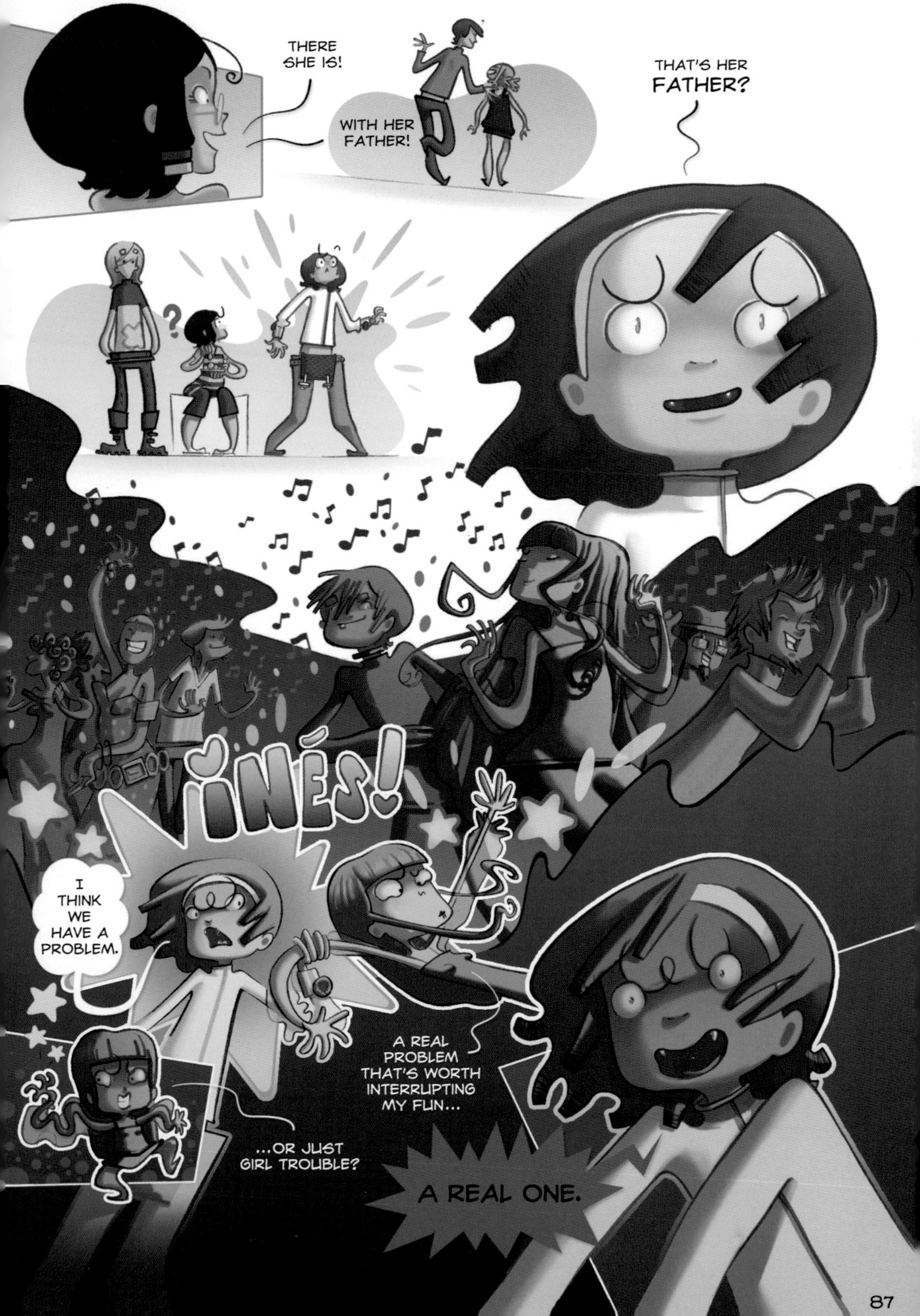
THERE SHE IS!
WITH HER FATHER!
THAT'S HER FATHER?
INÉS!
I THINK WE HAVE A PROBLEM.
A REAL PROBLEM THAT'S WORTH INTERRUPTING MY FUN...
...OR JUST GIRL TROUBLE?
A REAL ONE.

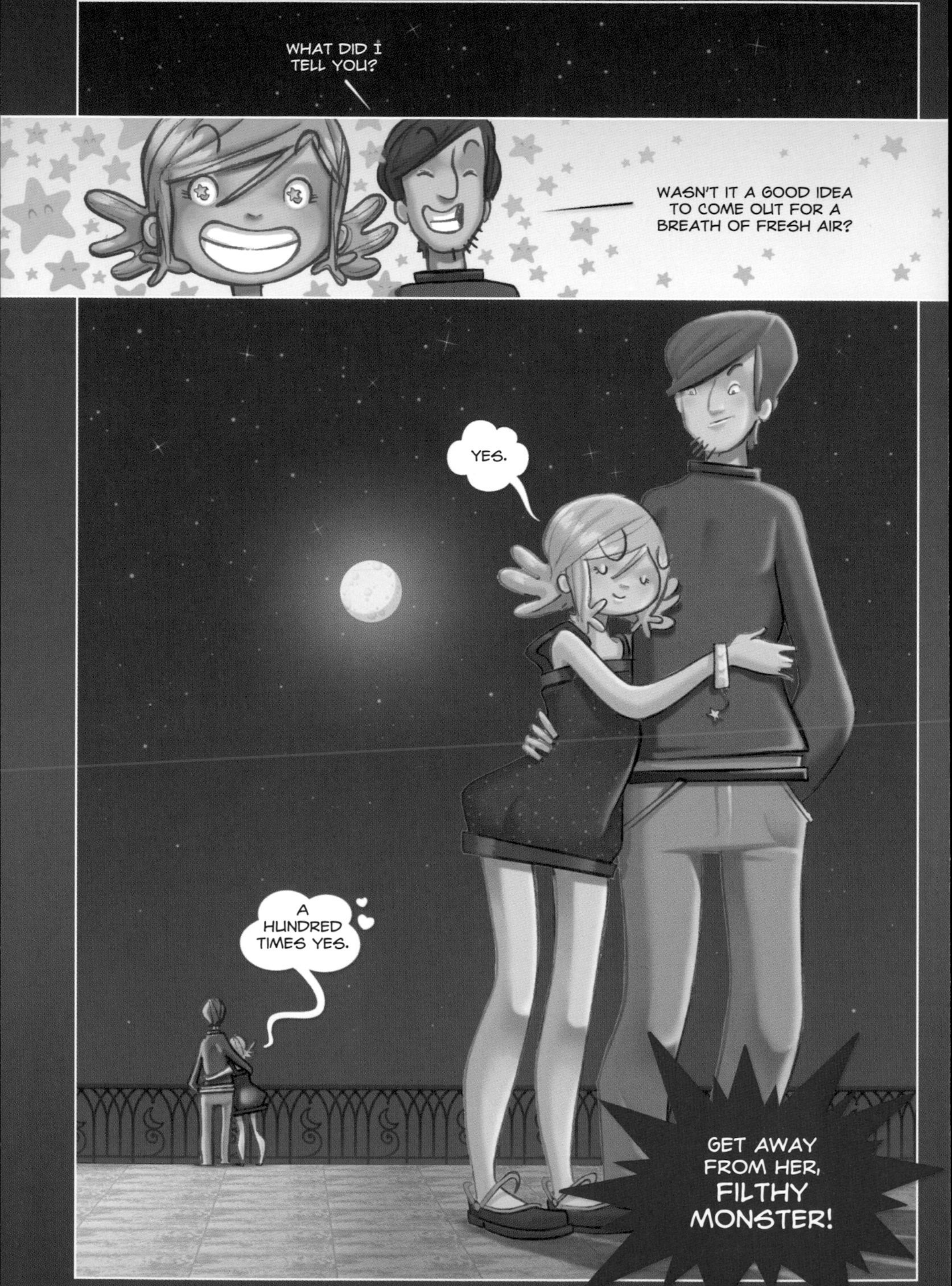
WHAT DID I TELL YOU?
WASN'T IT A GOOD IDEA TO COME OUT FOR A BREATH OF FRESH AIR?
YES.
A HUNDRED TIMES YES.
GET AWAY FROM HER, FILTHY MONSTER!

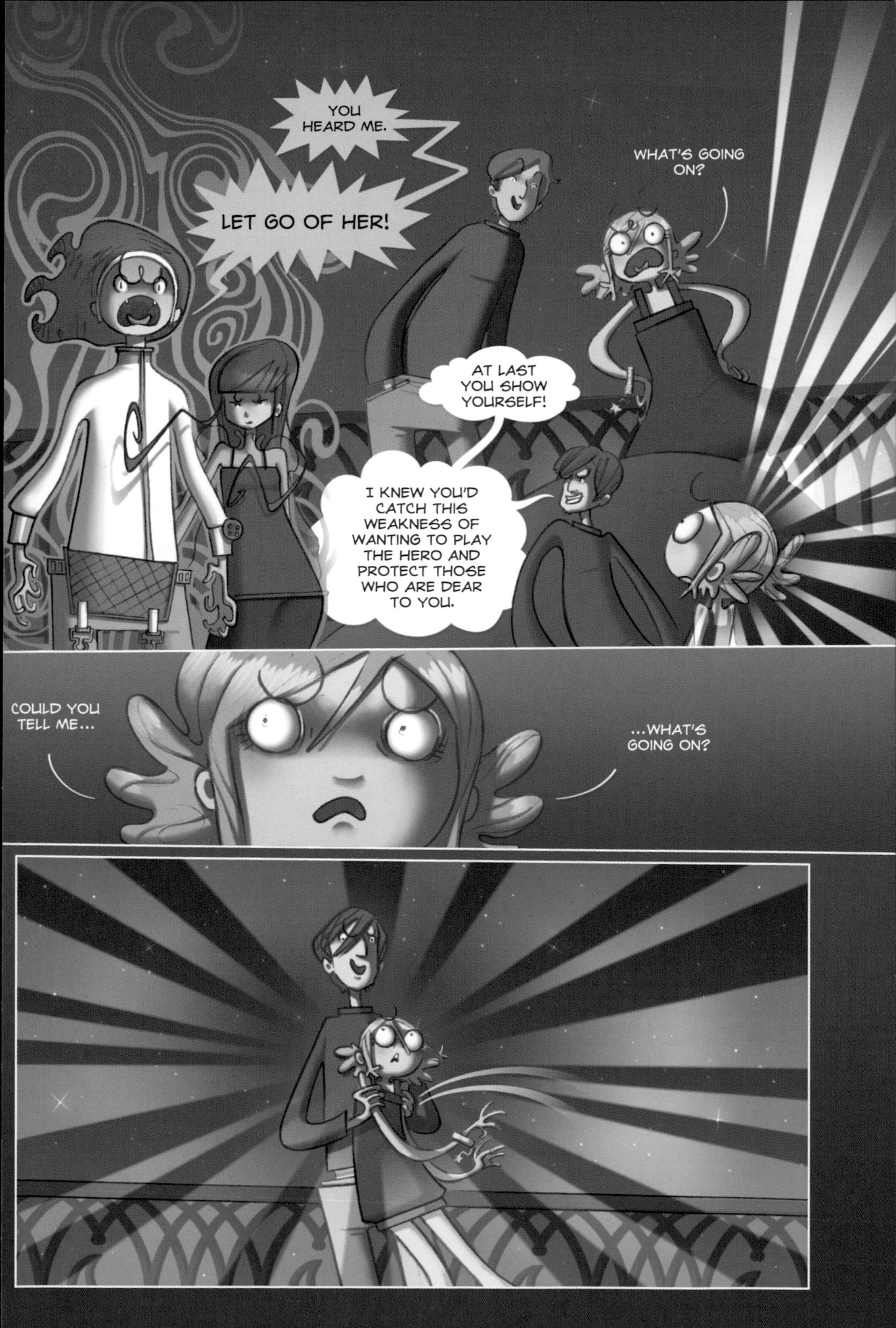
YOU HEARD ME.
LET GO OF HER!
WHAT'S GOING ON?
AT LAST YOU SHOW YOURSELF!
I KNEW YOU'D CATCH THIS WEAKNESS OF WANTING TO PLAY THE HERO AND PROTECT THOSE WHO ARE DEAR TO YOU.
COULD YOU TELL ME...
...WHAT'S GOING ON?

NOW, DAMIANO, IF YOU DON'T WANT HER TO HAVE A REGRETTABLE ACCIDENT...

WHAT ARE YOU DOING, DAD?

...YOU'LL AGREE TO FOLLOW ME PEACEFULLY.

THE SAME GOES FOR THE BEAUTY QUEEN.

DAD, THIS ISN'T FUNNY!

AGREE TO GO BACK WITH ME TO WHERE YOU CAME FROM, BOTH OF YOU, AND EVERYONE WILL BE SAFE AND SOUND.

DAD, I'M BEGGING YOU!!!!

I'M NOT LAUGHING AT ALL!

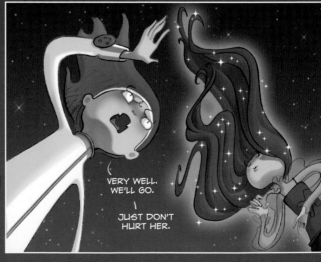

VERY WELL. WE'LL GO.

JUST DON'T HURT HER.

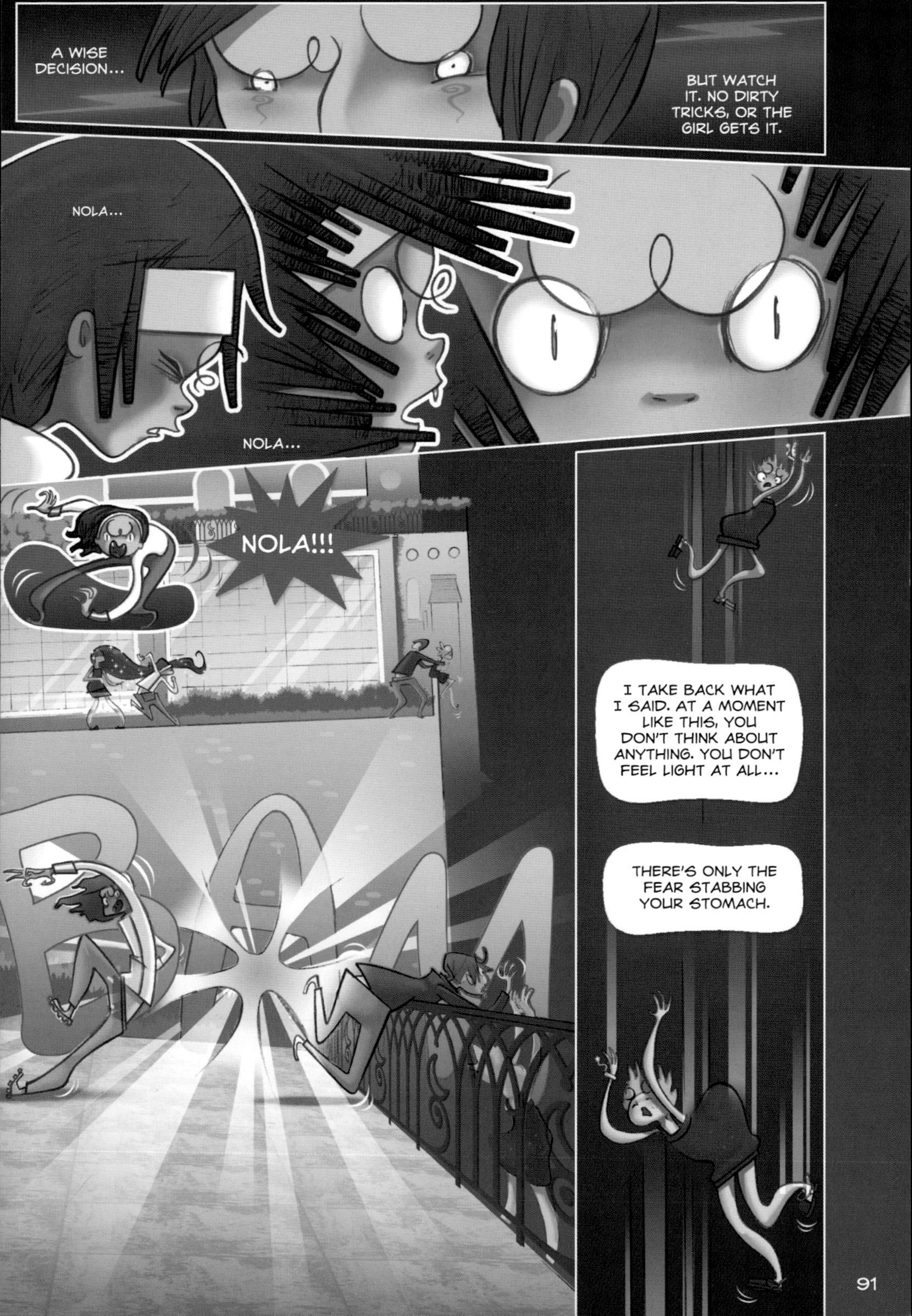
A WISE DECISION...
BUT WATCH IT. NO DIRTY TRICKS, OR THE GIRL GETS IT.
NOLA...
NOLA...
NOLA!!!
I TAKE BACK WHAT I SAID. AT A MOMENT LIKE THIS, YOU DON'T THINK ABOUT ANYTHING. YOU DON'T FEEL LIGHT AT ALL...
THERE'S ONLY THE FEAR STABBING YOUR STOMACH.

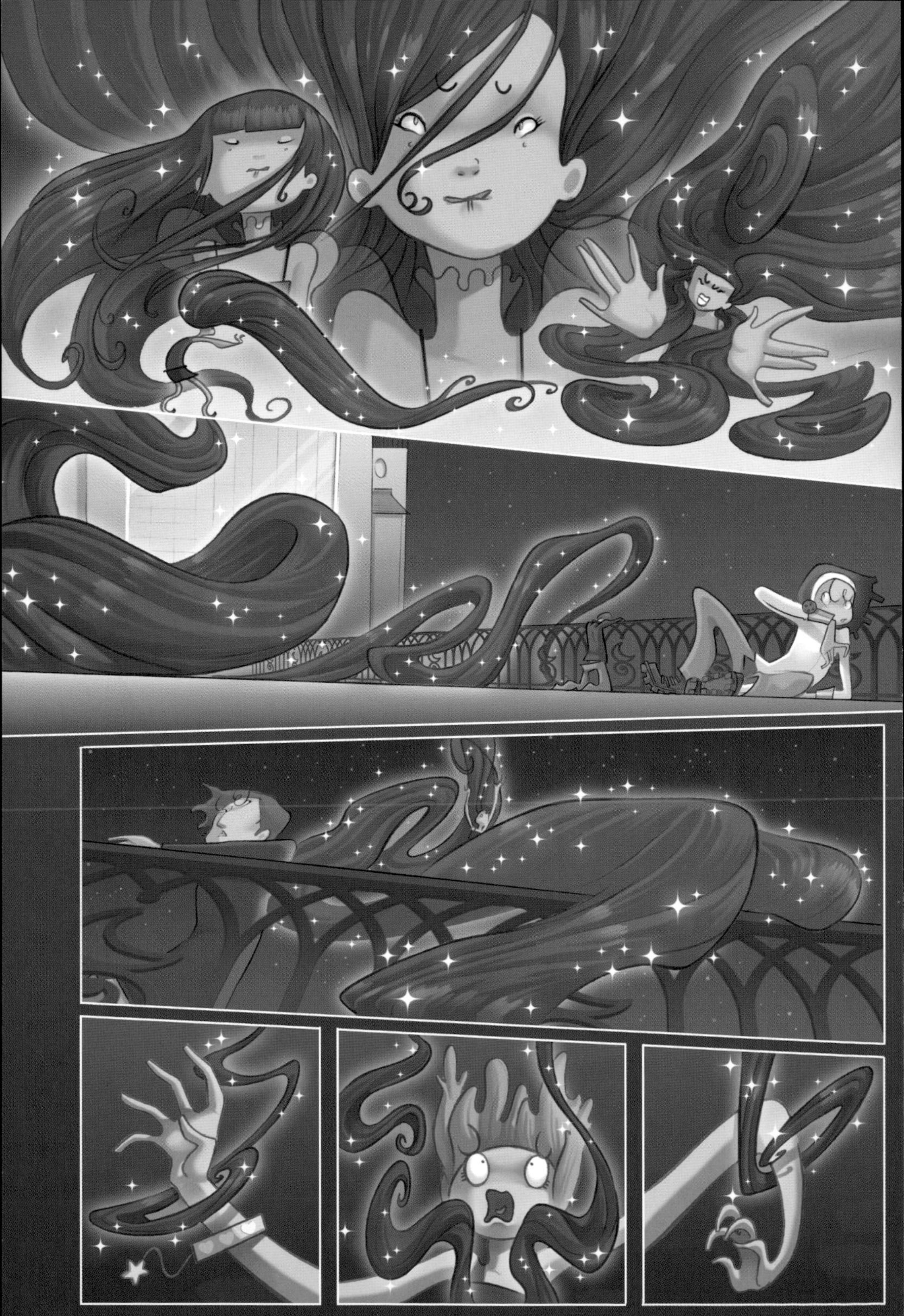

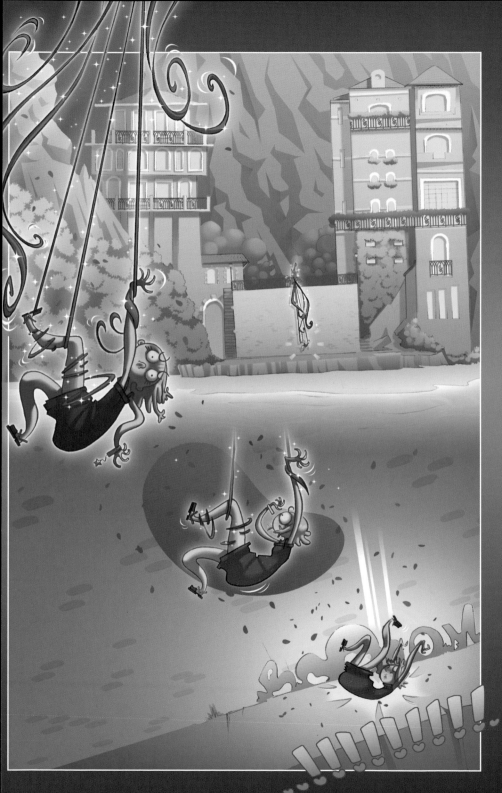

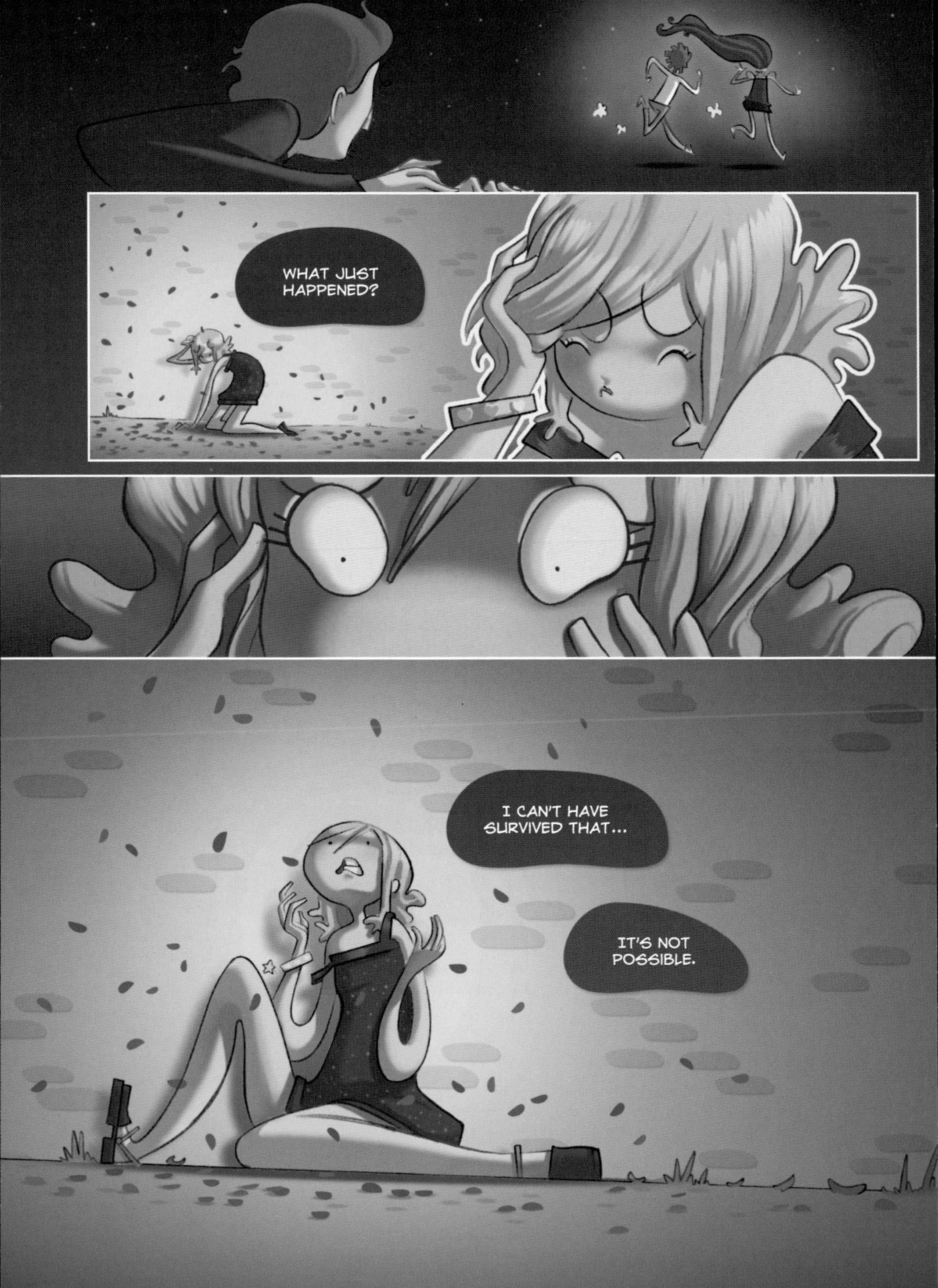
WHAT JUST HAPPENED?
I CAN'T HAVE SURVIVED THAT...
IT'S NOT POSSIBLE.

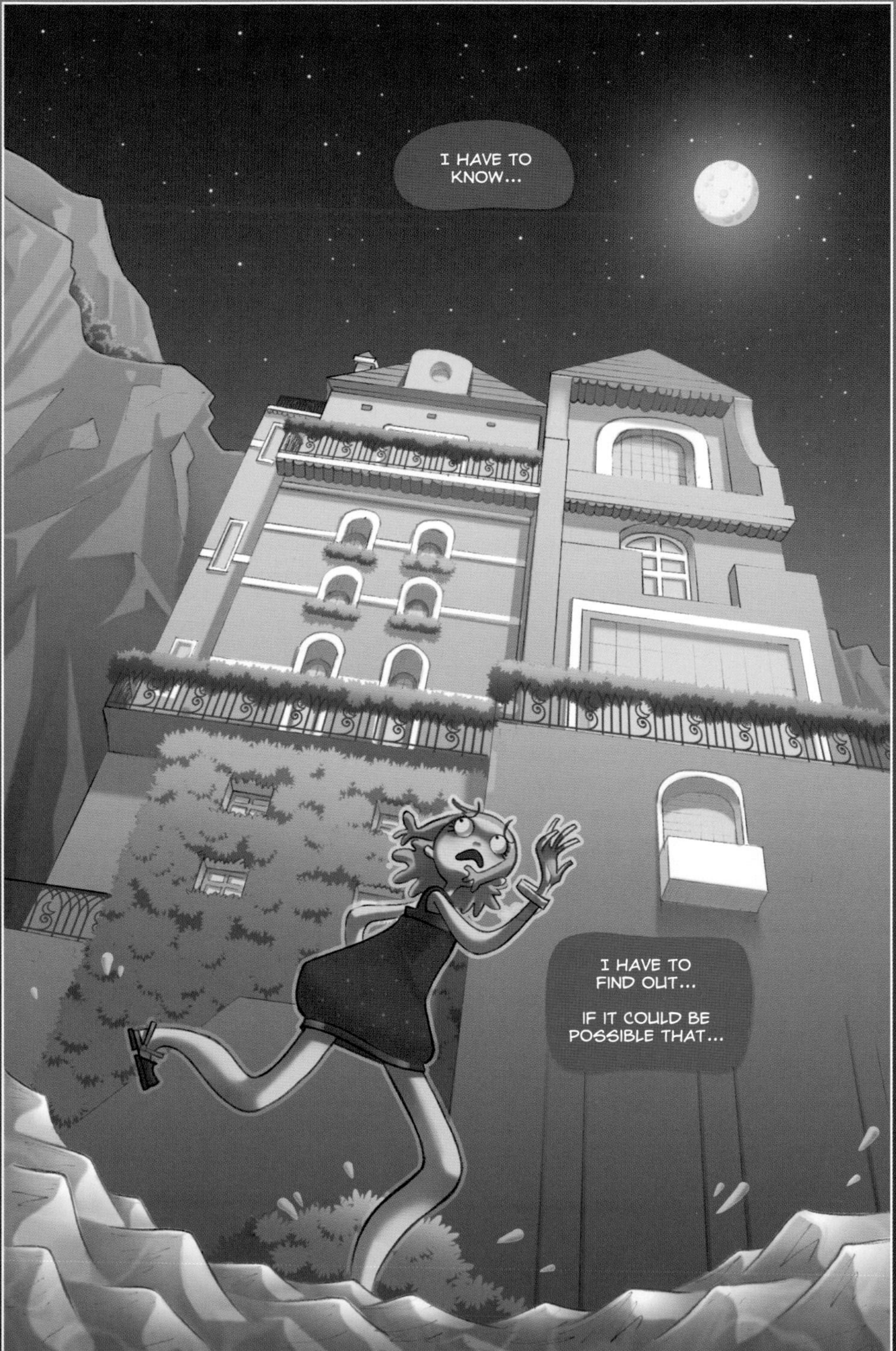
I HAVE TO KNOW...
I HAVE TO FIND OUT...
IF IT COULD BE POSSIBLE THAT...

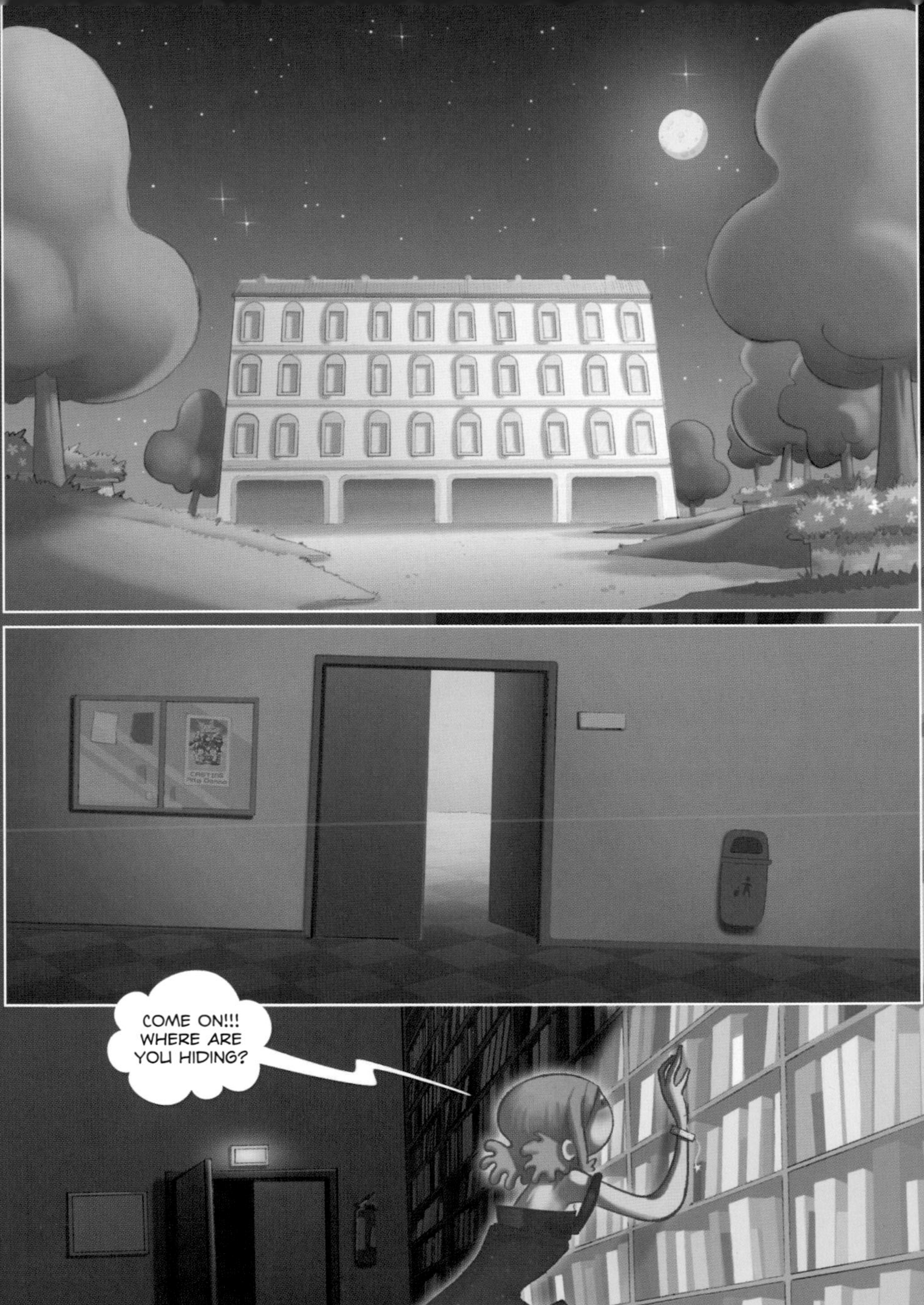
COME ON!!!
WHERE ARE
YOU HIDING?

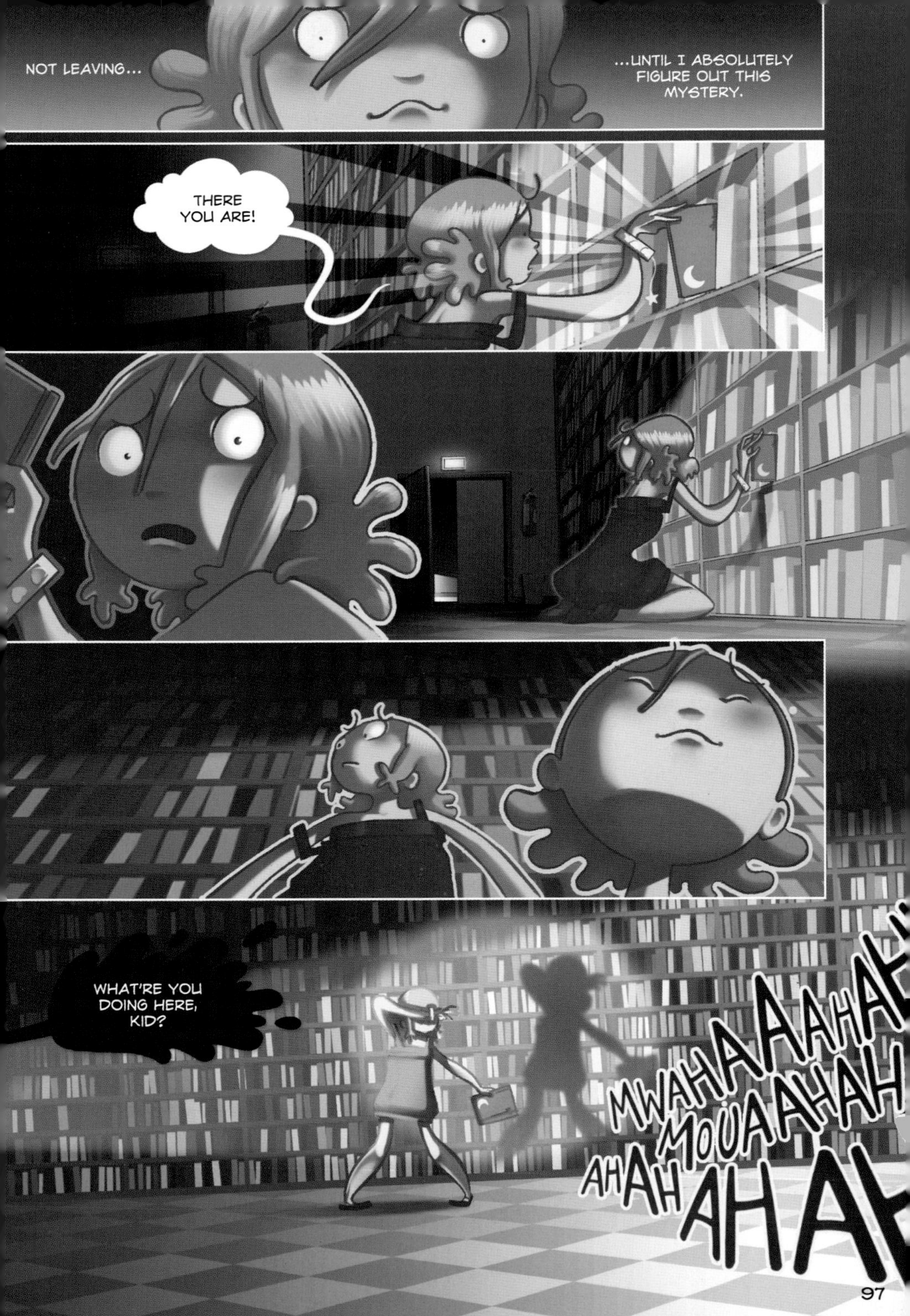
NOT LEAVING...
...UNTIL I ABSOLUTELY FIGURE OUT THIS MYSTERY.
THERE YOU ARE!
WHAT'RE YOU DOING HERE, KID?
MWAHAAAAHAH MOUAAHAH AHAH AHAH

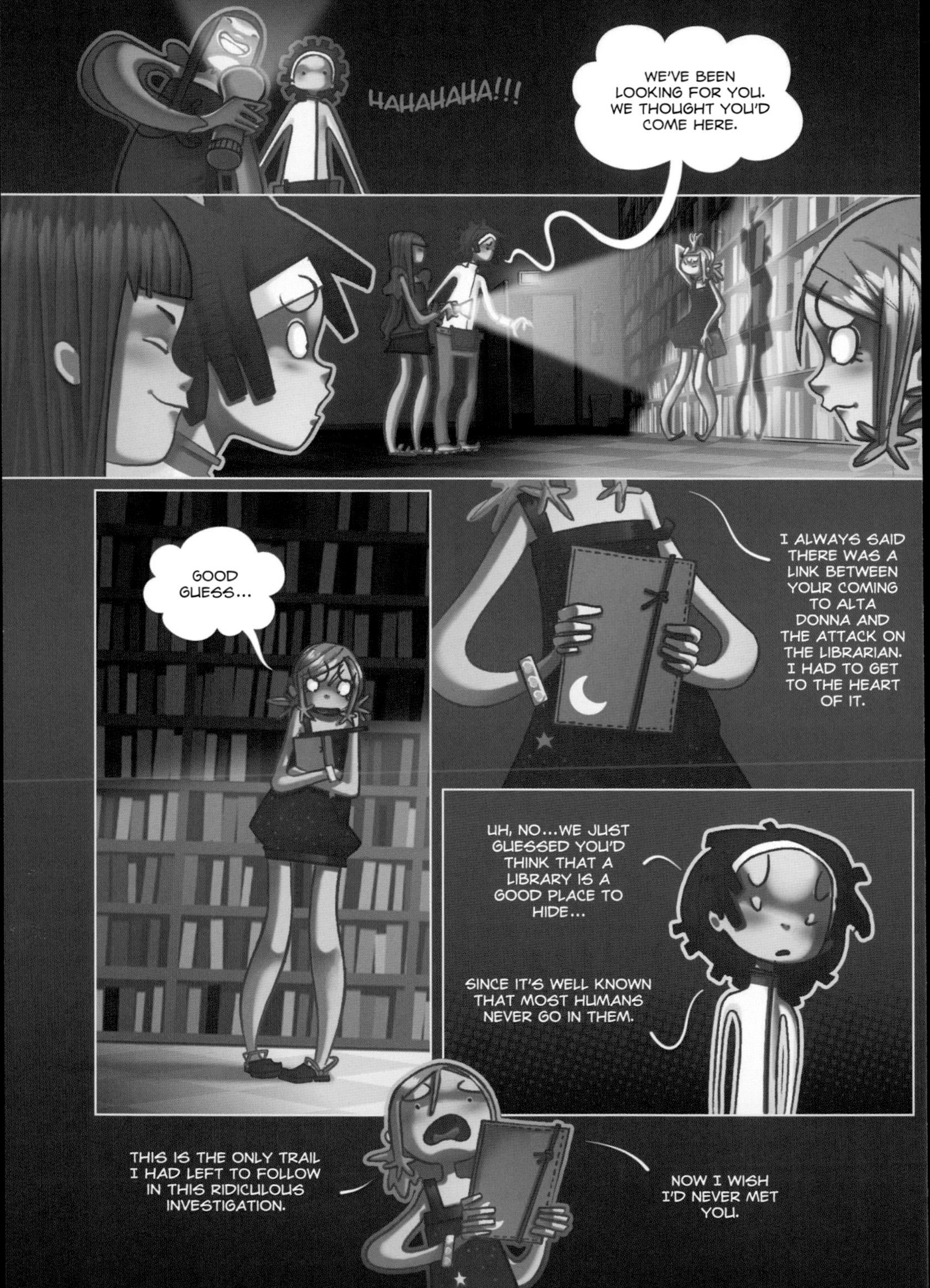
HAHAHAHA!!!
WE'VE BEEN LOOKING FOR YOU. WE THOUGHT YOU'D COME HERE.
GOOD GUESS...
I ALWAYS SAID THERE WAS A LINK BETWEEN YOUR COMING TO ALTA DONNA AND THE ATTACK ON THE LIBRARIAN. I HAD TO GET TO THE HEART OF IT.
UH, NO...WE JUST GUESSED YOU'D THINK THAT A LIBRARY IS A GOOD PLACE TO HIDE...
SINCE IT'S WELL KNOWN THAT MOST HUMANS NEVER GO IN THEM.
THIS IS THE ONLY TRAIL I HAD LEFT TO FOLLOW IN THIS RIDICULOUS INVESTIGATION.
NOW I WISH I'D NEVER MET YOU.

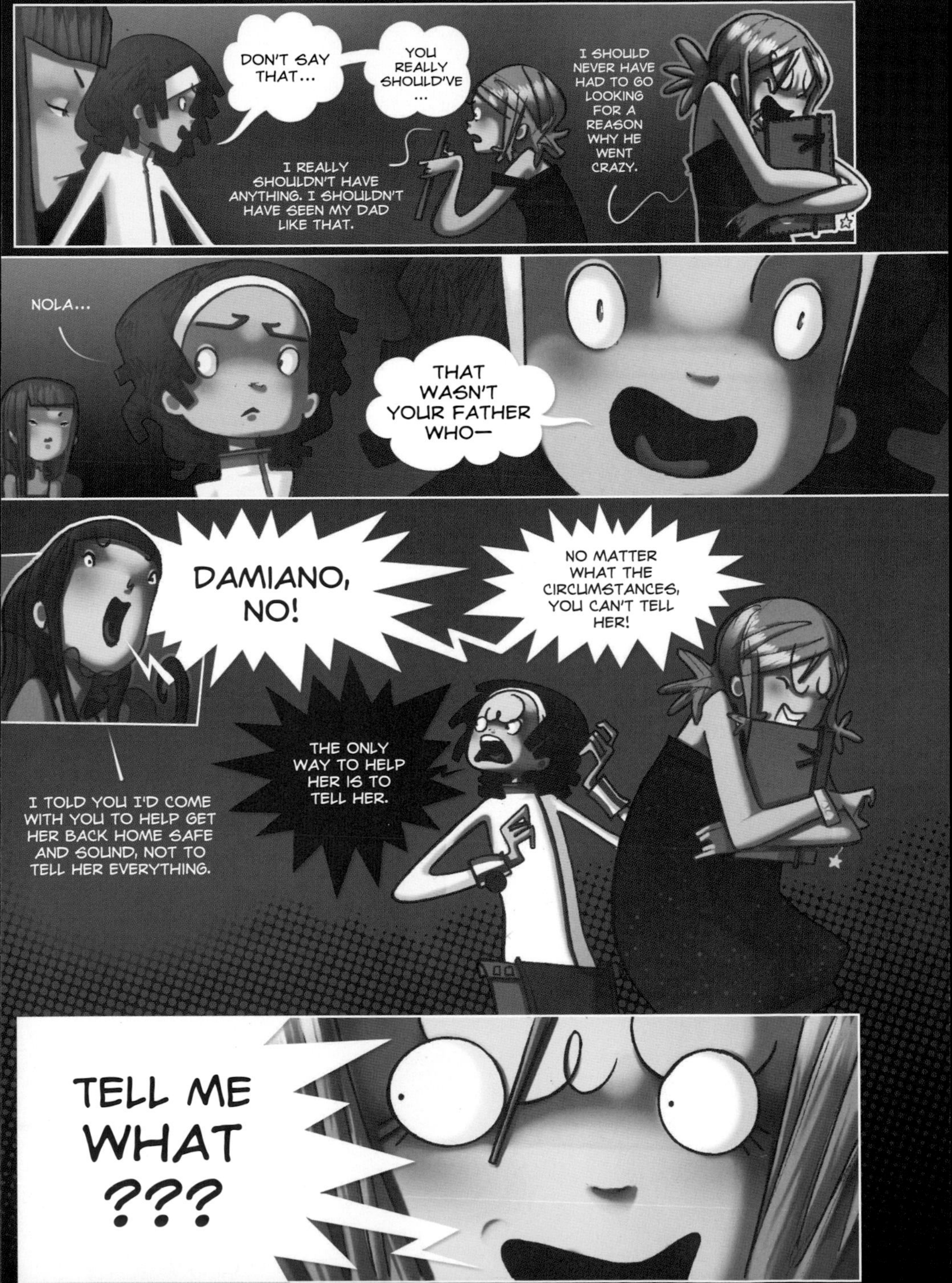
DON'T SAY THAT...
YOU REALLY SHOULD'VE ...
I REALLY SHOULDN'T HAVE ANYTHING. I SHOULDN'T HAVE SEEN MY DAD LIKE THAT.
I SHOULD NEVER HAVE HAD TO GO LOOKING FOR A REASON WHY HE WENT CRAZY.
NOLA...
THAT WASN'T YOUR FATHER WHO—
DAMIANO, NO!
NO MATTER WHAT THE CIRCUMSTANCES, YOU CAN'T TELL HER!
I TOLD YOU I'D COME WITH YOU TO HELP GET HER BACK HOME SAFE AND SOUND, NOT TO TELL HER EVERYTHING.
THE ONLY WAY TO HELP HER IS TO TELL HER.
TELL ME WHAT ???

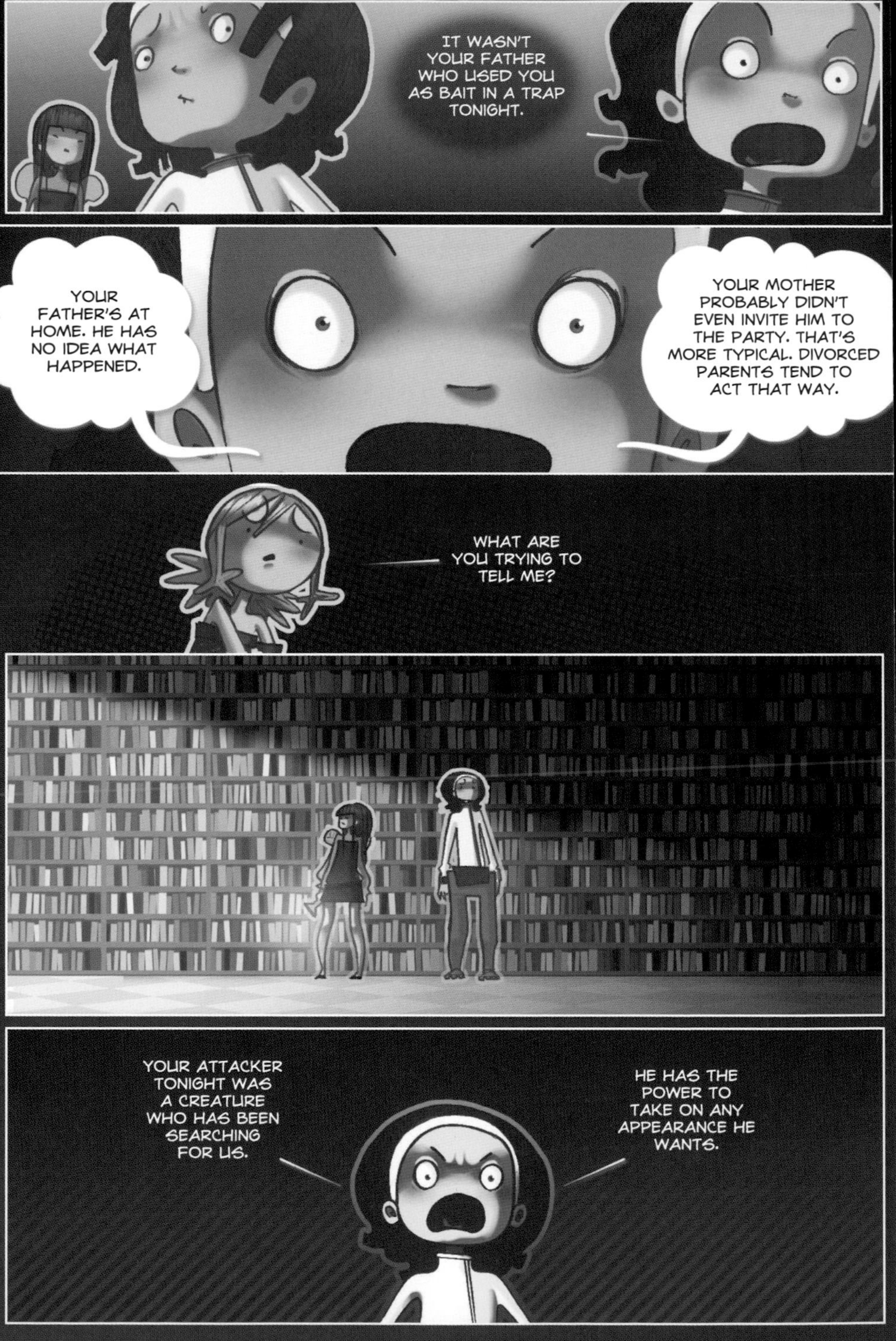
IT WASN'T YOUR FATHER WHO USED YOU AS BAIT IN A TRAP TONIGHT.
YOUR FATHER'S AT HOME. HE HAS NO IDEA WHAT HAPPENED.
YOUR MOTHER PROBABLY DIDN'T EVEN INVITE HIM TO THE PARTY. THAT'S MORE TYPICAL. DIVORCED PARENTS TEND TO ACT THAT WAY.
WHAT ARE YOU TRYING TO TELL ME?
YOUR ATTACKER TONIGHT WAS A CREATURE WHO HAS BEEN SEARCHING FOR US.
HE HAS THE POWER TO TAKE ON ANY APPEARANCE HE WANTS.

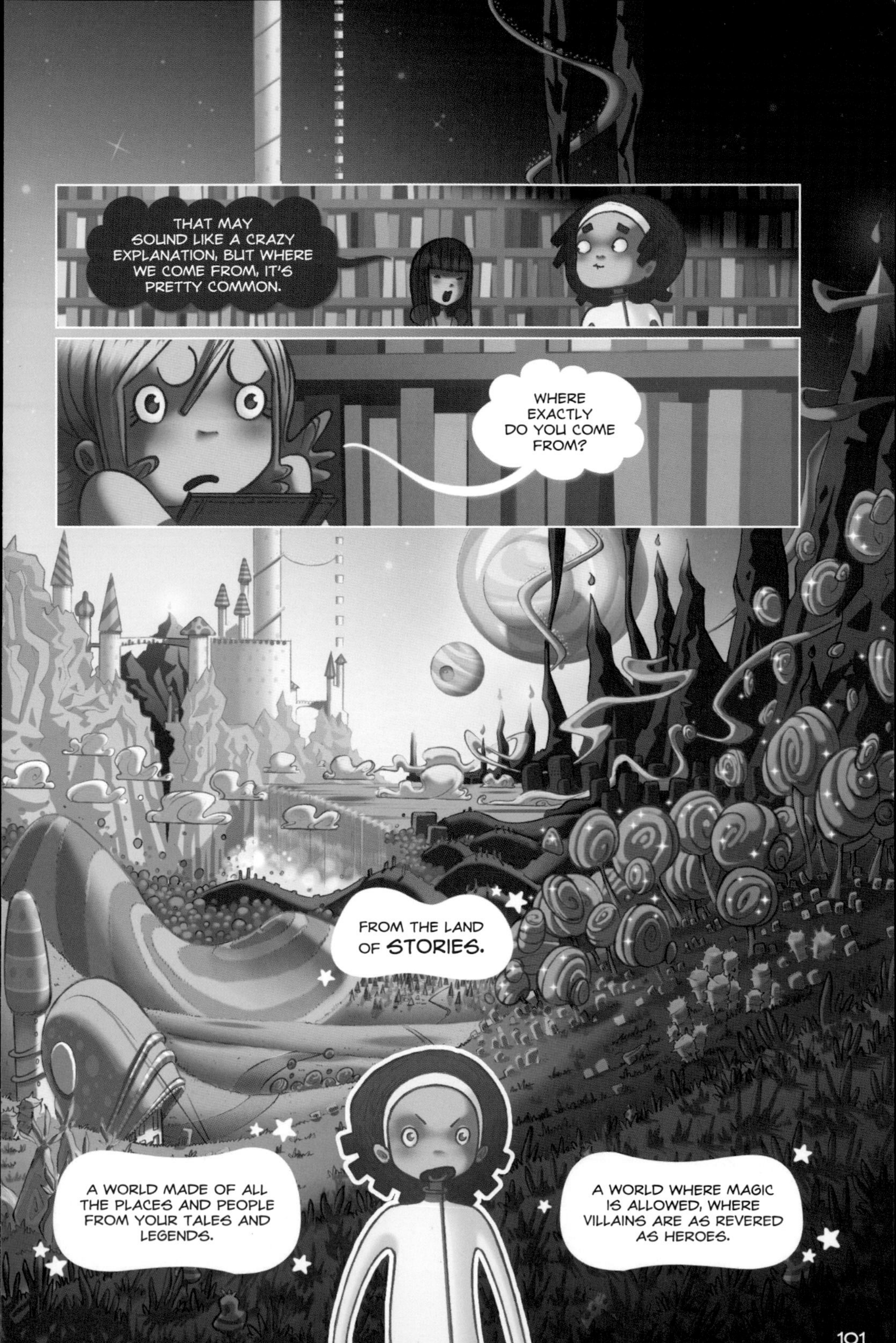
THAT MAY SOUND LIKE A CRAZY EXPLANATION, BUT WHERE WE COME FROM, IT'S PRETTY COMMON.
WHERE EXACTLY DO YOU COME FROM?
FROM THE LAND OF STORIES.
A WORLD MADE OF ALL THE PLACES AND PEOPLE FROM YOUR TALES AND LEGENDS.
A WORLD WHERE MAGIC IS ALLOWED, WHERE VILLAINS ARE AS REVERED AS HEROES.

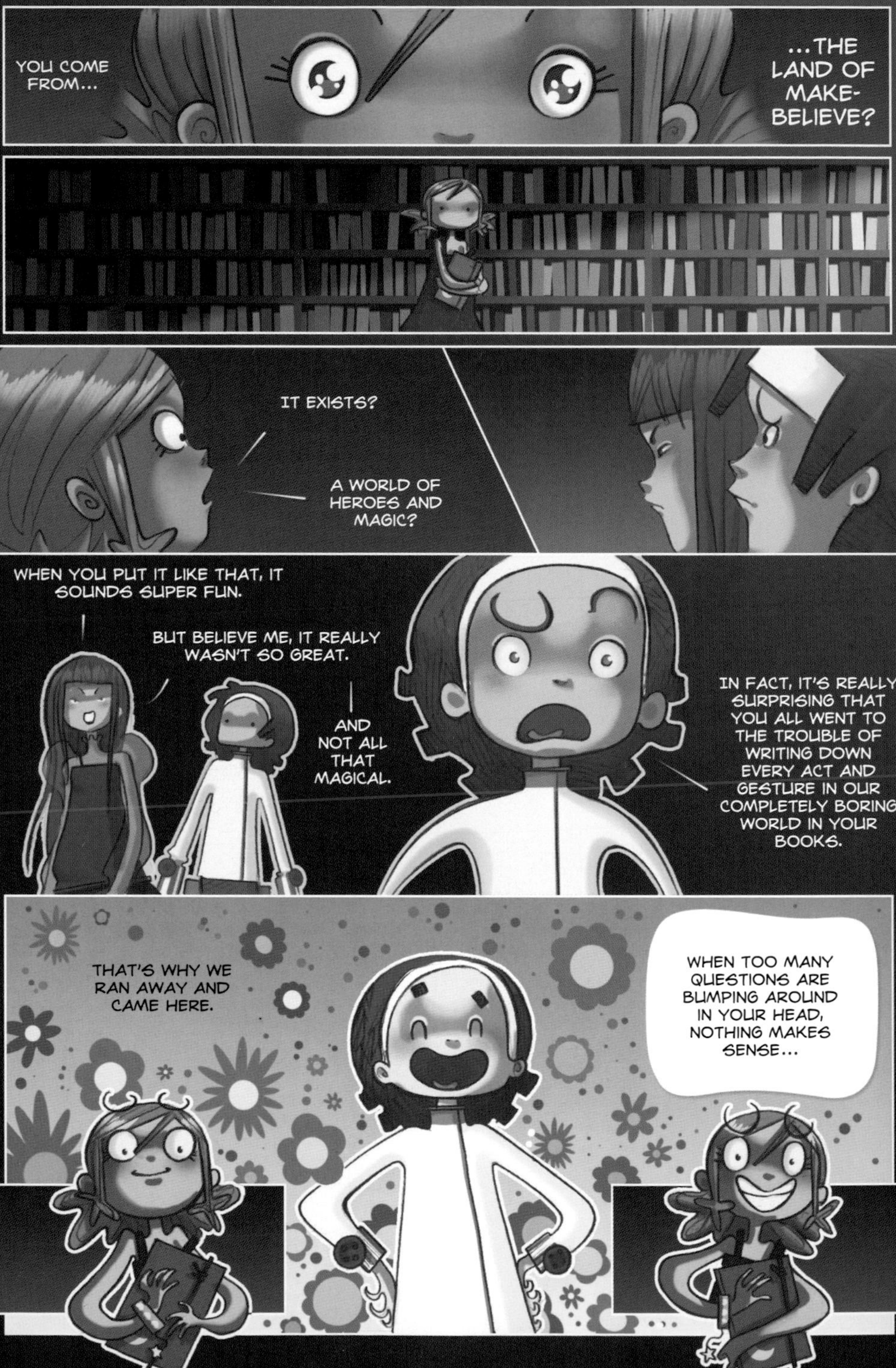
YOU COME FROM...
...THE LAND OF MAKE-BELIEVE?
IT EXISTS?
A WORLD OF HEROES AND MAGIC?
WHEN YOU PUT IT LIKE THAT, IT SOUNDS SUPER FUN.
BUT BELIEVE ME, IT REALLY WASN'T SO GREAT.
AND NOT ALL THAT MAGICAL.
IN FACT, IT'S REALLY SURPRISING THAT YOU ALL WENT TO THE TROUBLE OF WRITING DOWN EVERY ACT AND GESTURE IN OUR COMPLETELY BORING WORLD IN YOUR BOOKS.
THAT'S WHY WE RAN AWAY AND CAME HERE.
WHEN TOO MANY QUESTIONS ARE BUMPING AROUND IN YOUR HEAD, NOTHING MAKES SENSE...

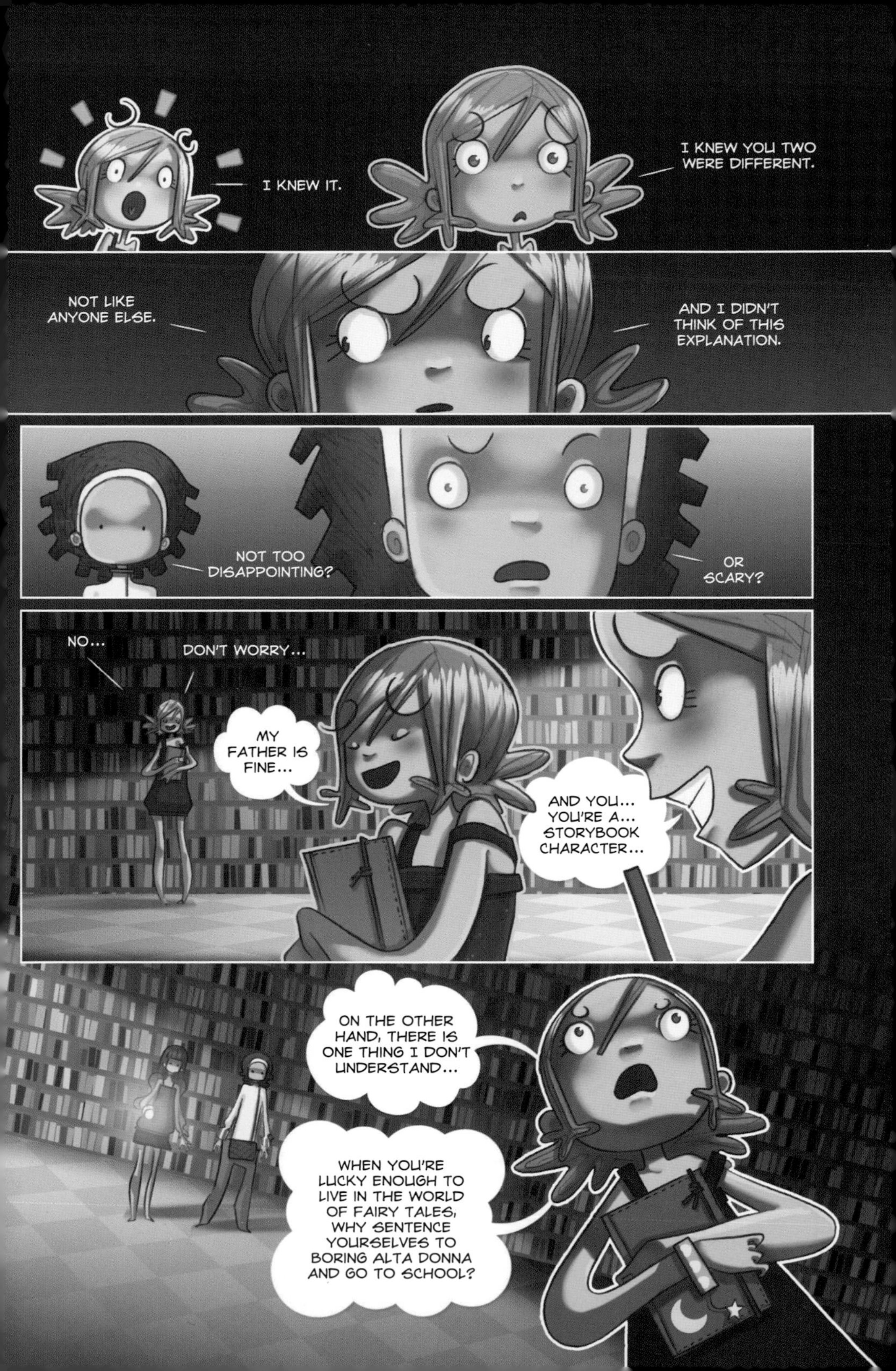

I KNEW IT.
I KNEW YOU TWO WERE DIFFERENT.
NOT LIKE ANYONE ELSE.
AND I DIDN'T THINK OF THIS EXPLANATION.
NOT TOO DISAPPOINTING?
OR SCARY?
NO...
DON'T WORRY...
MY FATHER IS FINE...
AND YOU... YOU'RE A... STORYBOOK CHARACTER...
ON THE OTHER HAND, THERE IS ONE THING I DON'T UNDERSTAND...
WHEN YOU'RE LUCKY ENOUGH TO LIVE IN THE WORLD OF FAIRY TALES, WHY SENTENCE YOURSELVES TO BORING ALTA DONNA AND GO TO SCHOOL?

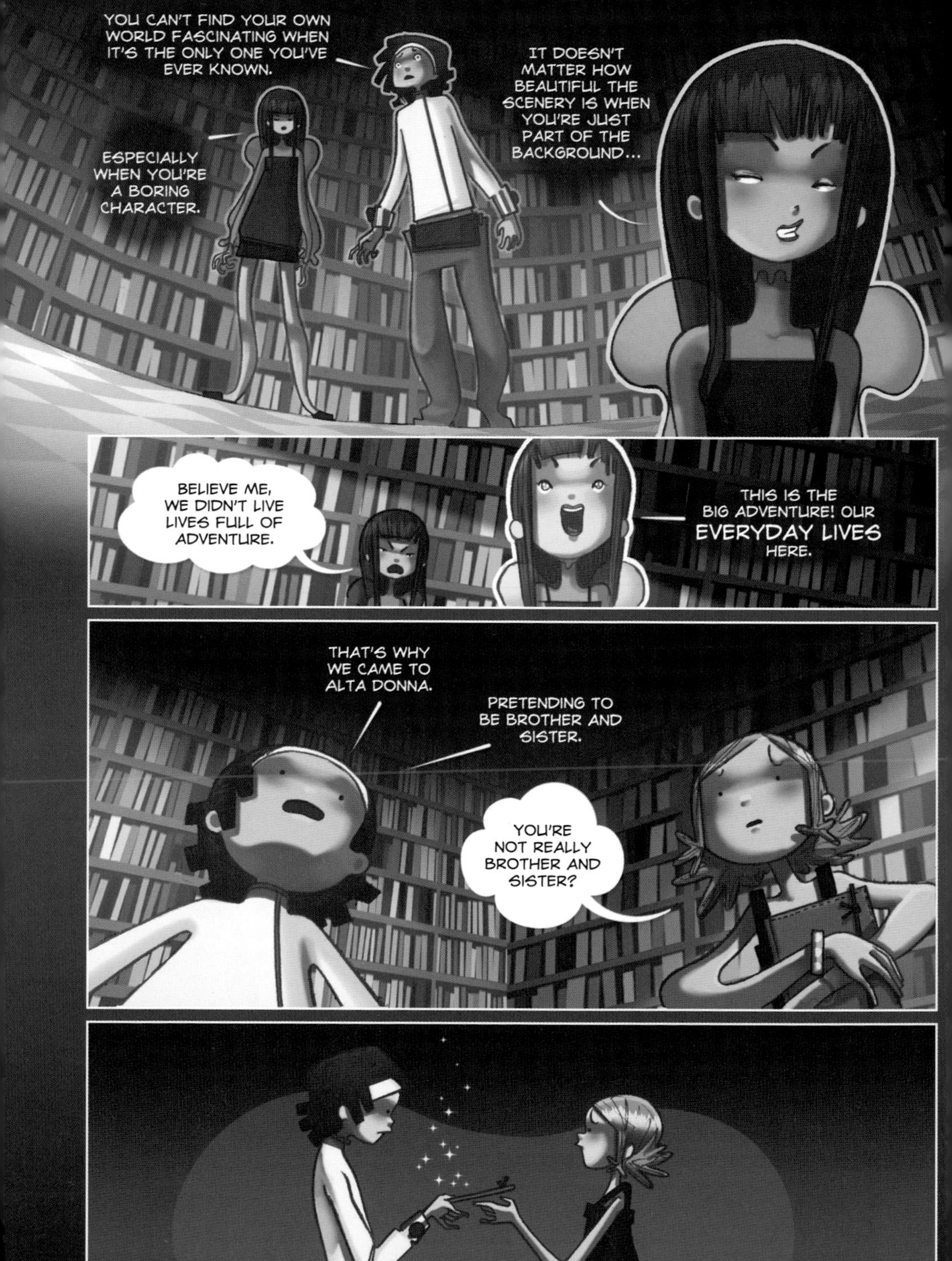

YOU CAN'T FIND YOUR OWN WORLD FASCINATING WHEN IT'S THE ONLY ONE YOU'VE EVER KNOWN.
ESPECIALLY WHEN YOU'RE A BORING CHARACTER.
IT DOESN'T MATTER HOW BEAUTIFUL THE SCENERY IS WHEN YOU'RE JUST PART OF THE BACKGROUND...
BELIEVE ME, WE DIDN'T LIVE LIVES FULL OF ADVENTURE.
THIS IS THE BIG ADVENTURE! OUR EVERYDAY LIVES HERE.
THAT'S WHY WE CAME TO ALTA DONNA.
PRETENDING TO BE BROTHER AND SISTER.
YOU'RE NOT REALLY BROTHER AND SISTER?

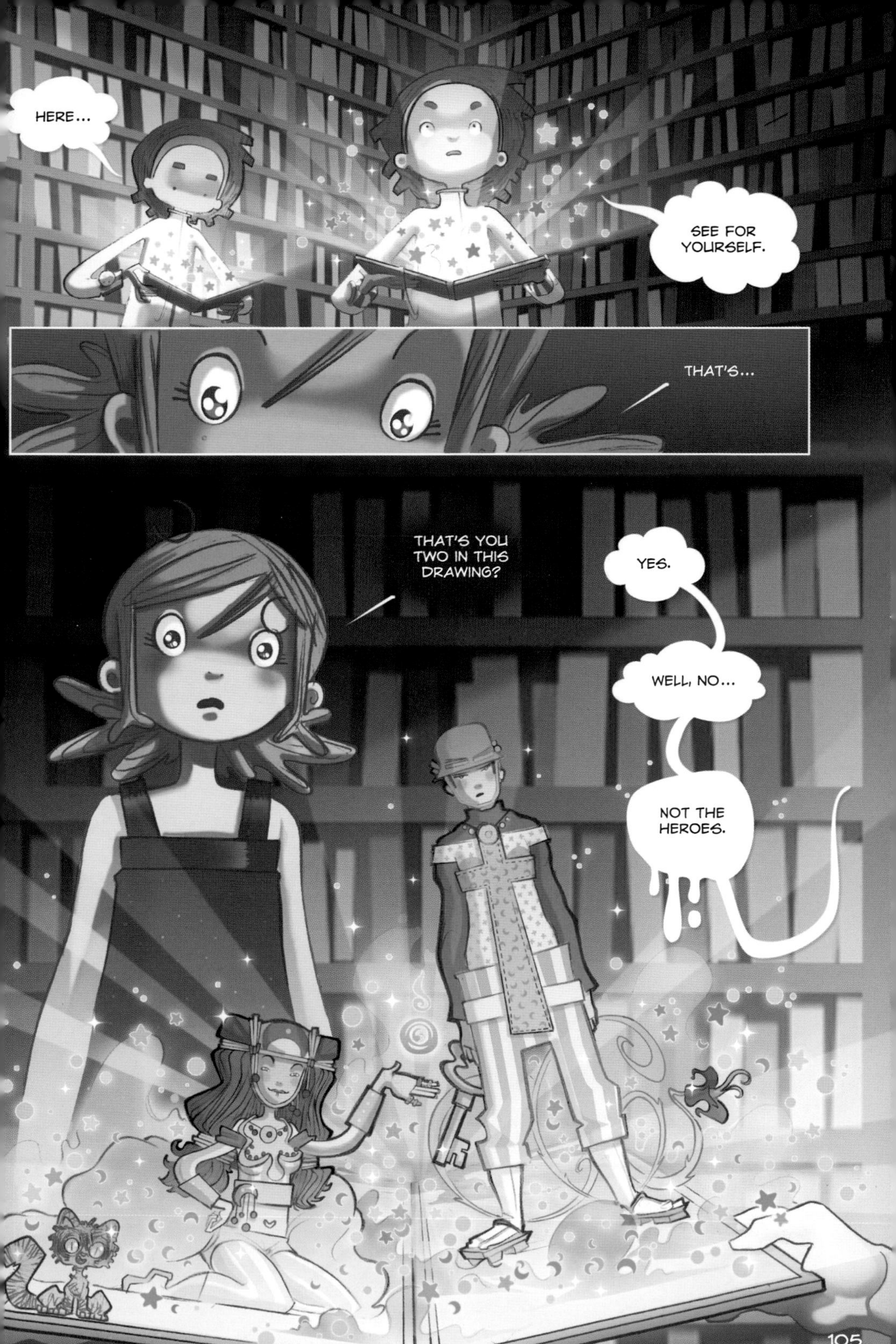
HERE...
SEE FOR YOURSELF.
THAT'S...
THAT'S YOU TWO IN THIS DRAWING?
YES.
WELL, NO...
NOT THE HEROES.

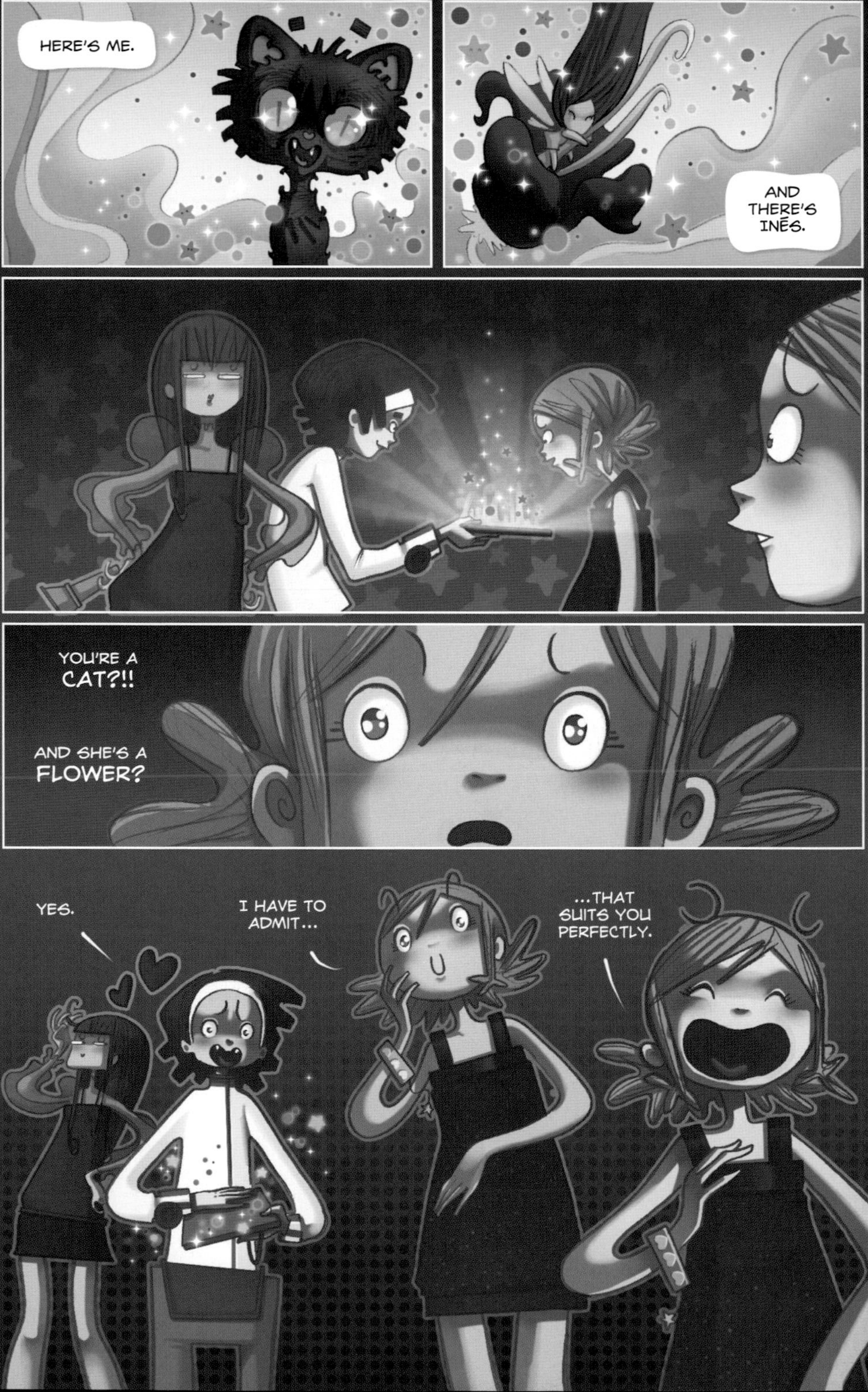
HERE'S ME.
AND THERE'S INÉS.
YOU'RE A CAT?!!
AND SHE'S A FLOWER?
YES.
I HAVE TO ADMIT...
...THAT SUITS YOU PERFECTLY.

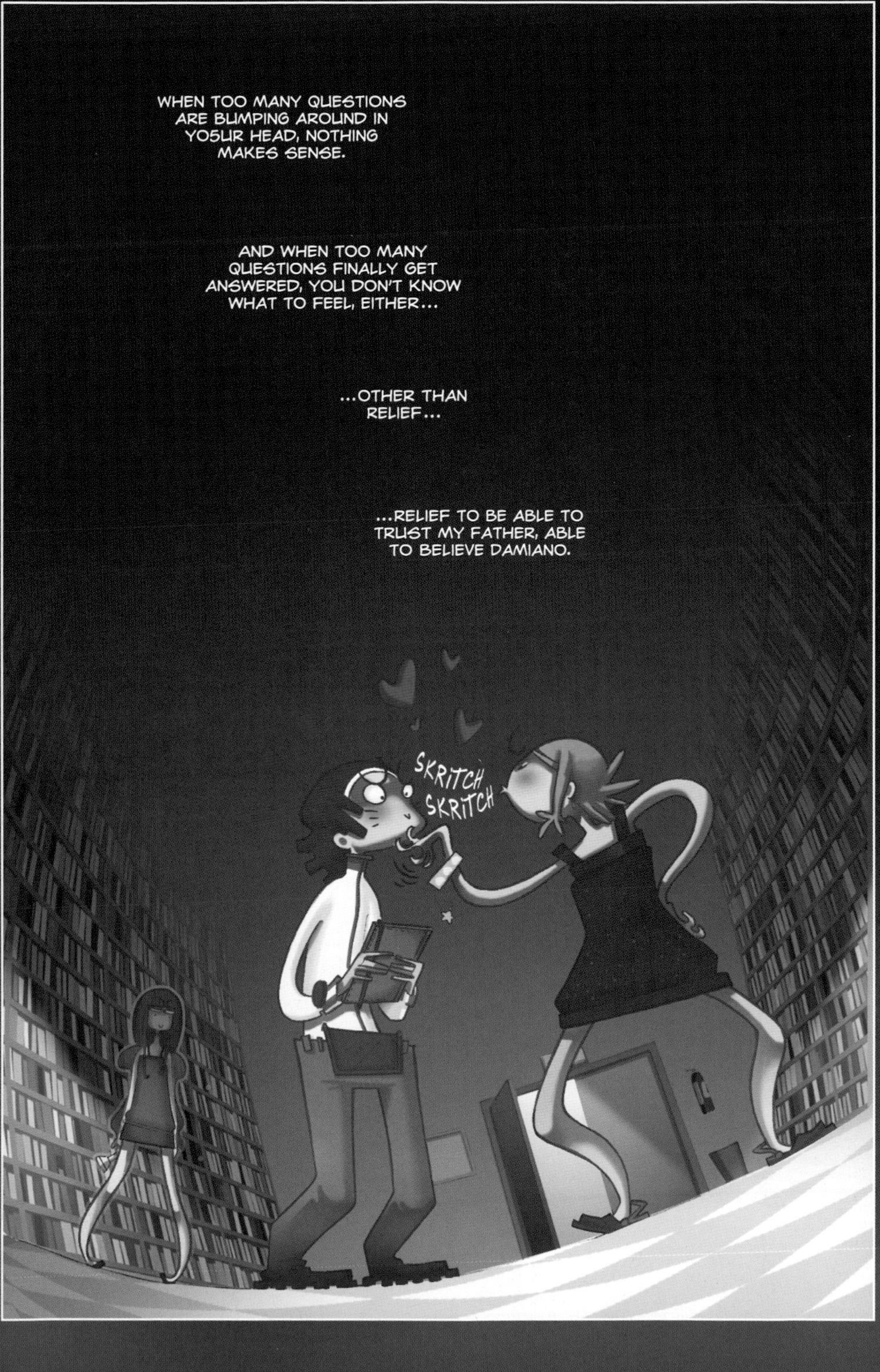
WHEN TOO MANY QUESTIONS ARE BUMPING AROUND IN YO5UR HEAD, NOTHING MAKES SENSE.
AND WHEN TOO MANY QUESTIONS FINALLY GET ANSWERED, YOU DON'T KNOW WHAT TO FEEL, EITHER...
...OTHER THAN RELIEF...
...RELIEF TO BE ABLE TO TRUST MY FATHER, ABLE TO BELIEVE DAMIANO.
SKRITCH SKRITCH

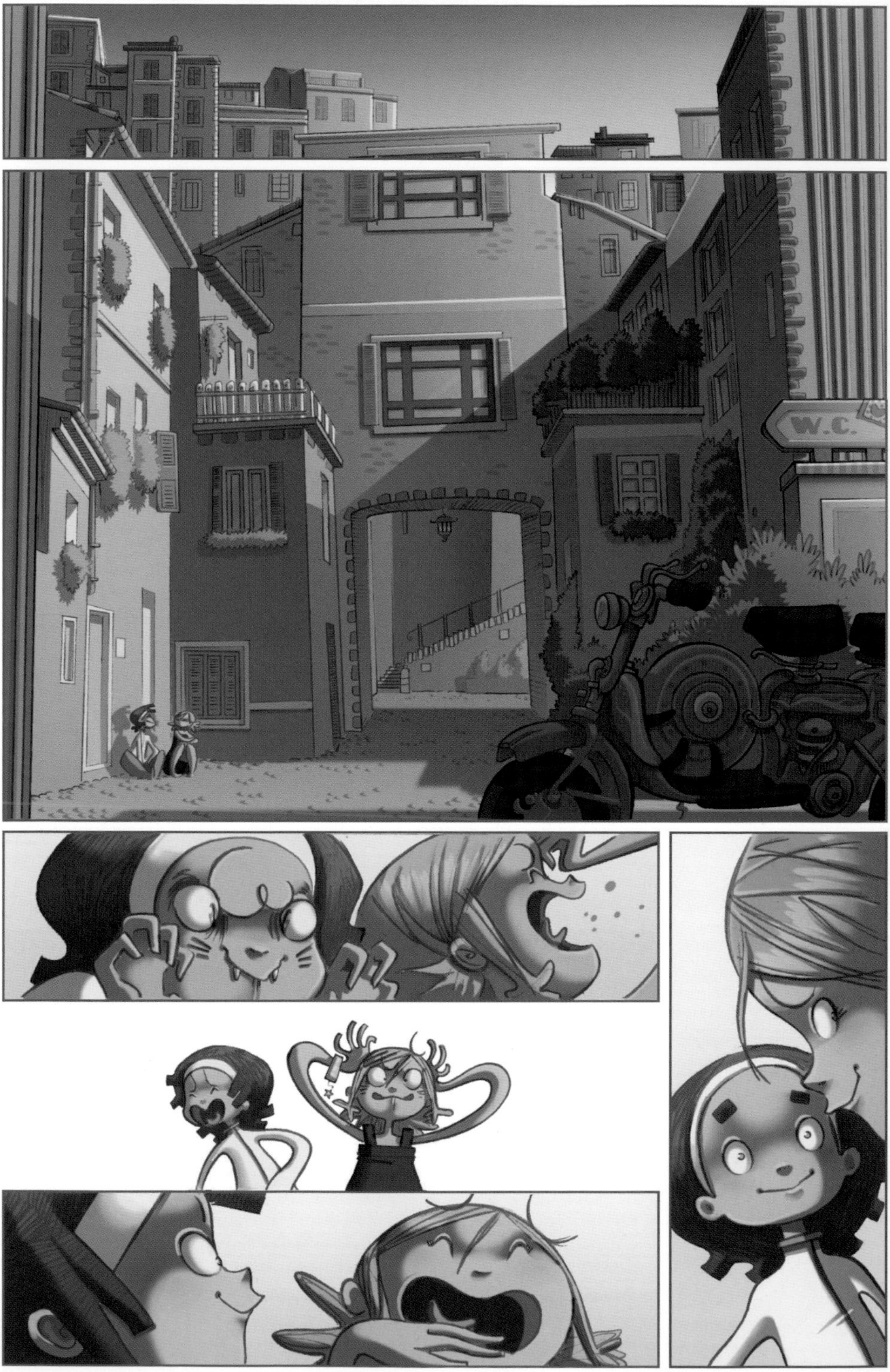
W.C.

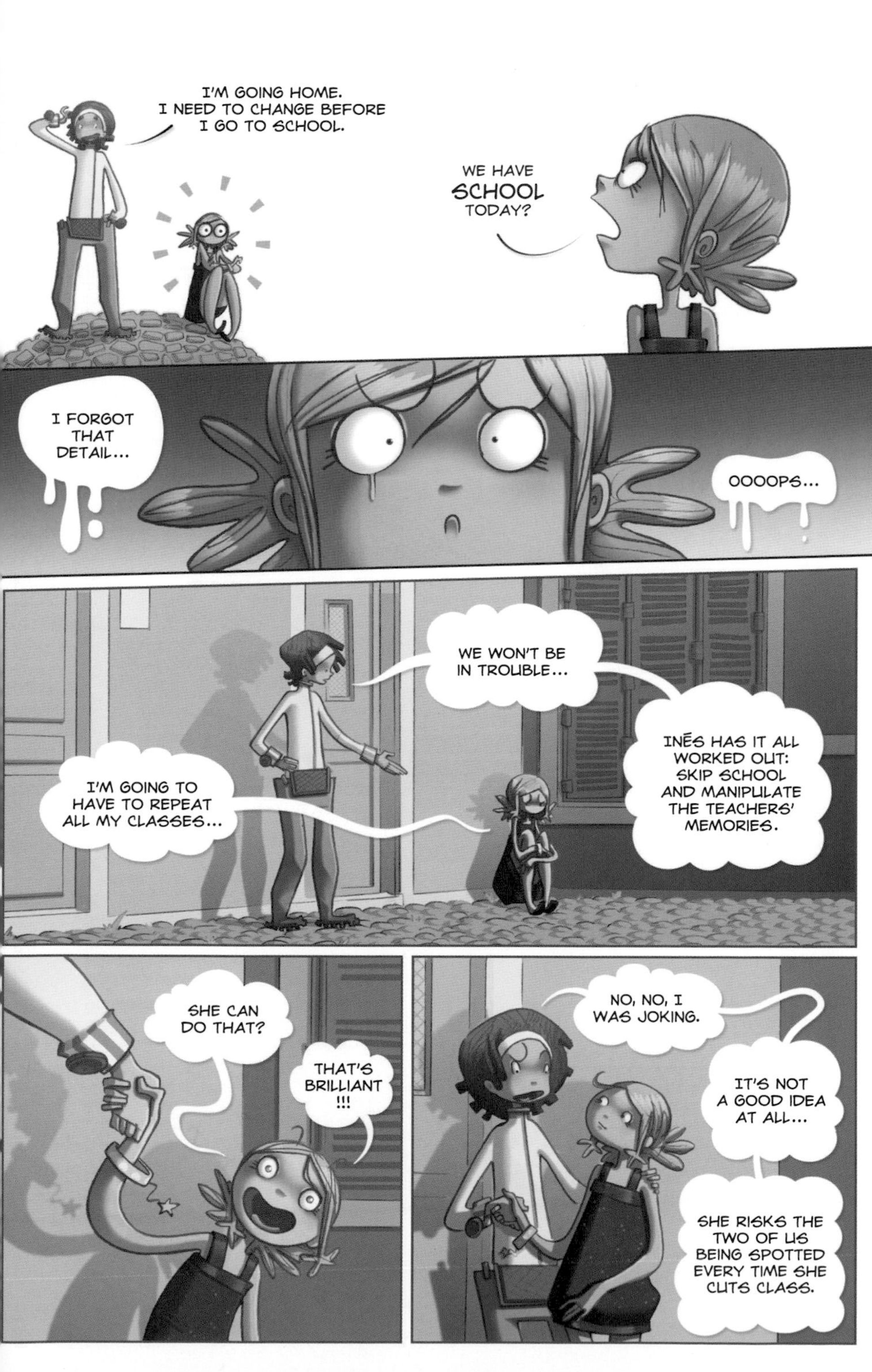
I'M GOING HOME. I NEED TO CHANGE BEFORE I GO TO SCHOOL.
WE HAVE SCHOOL TODAY?
I FORGOT THAT DETAIL...
OOOOPS...
WE WON'T BE IN TROUBLE...
INÈS HAS IT ALL WORKED OUT: SKIP SCHOOL AND MANIPULATE THE TEACHERS' MEMORIES.
I'M GOING TO HAVE TO REPEAT ALL MY CLASSES...
SHE CAN DO THAT?
THAT'S BRILLIANT !!!
NO, NO, I WAS JOKING.
IT'S NOT A GOOD IDEA AT ALL...
SHE RISKS THE TWO OF US BEING SPOTTED EVERY TIME SHE CUTS CLASS.

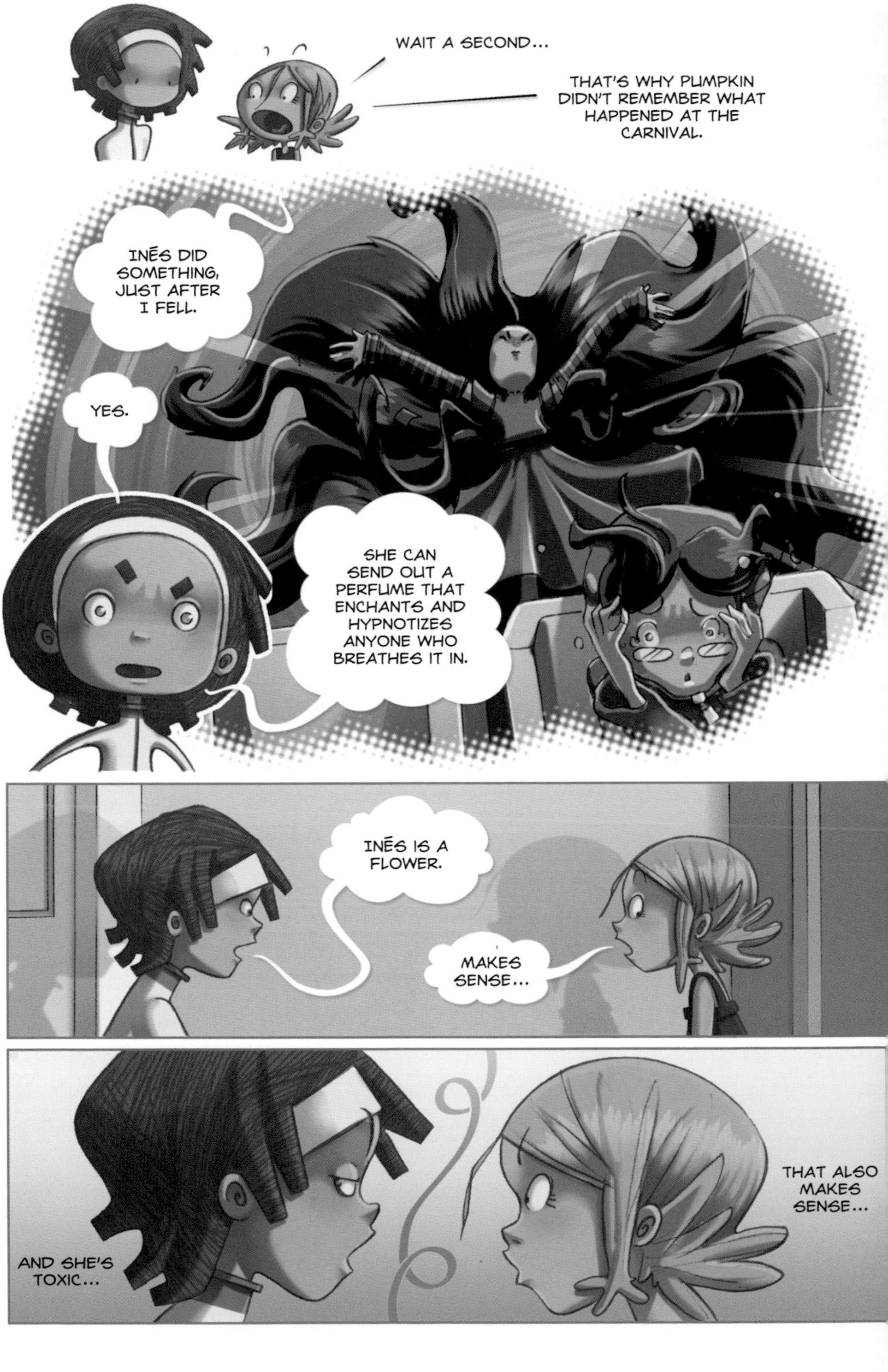
WAIT A SECOND...
THAT'S WHY PUMPKIN DIDN'T REMEMBER WHAT HAPPENED AT THE CARNIVAL.
INÉS DID SOMETHING, JUST AFTER I FELL.
YES.
SHE CAN SEND OUT A PERFUME THAT ENCHANTS AND HYPNOTIZES ANYONE WHO BREATHES IT IN.
INÉS IS A FLOWER.
MAKES SENSE...
AND SHE'S TOXIC...
THAT ALSO MAKES SENSE...

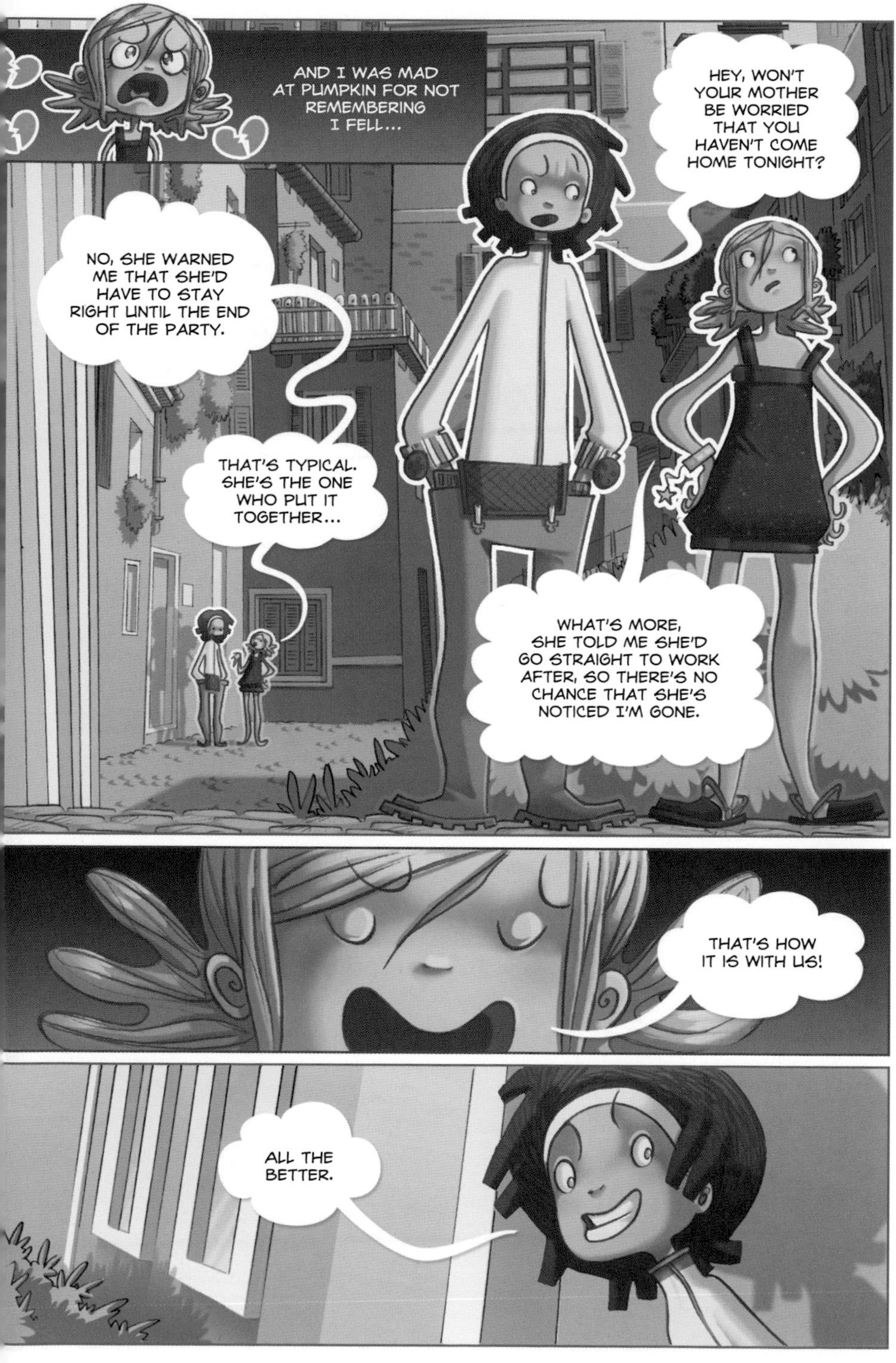
AND I WAS MAD AT PUMPKIN FOR NOT REMEMBERING I FELL...
HEY, WON'T YOUR MOTHER BE WORRIED THAT YOU HAVEN'T COME HOME TONIGHT?
NO, SHE WARNED ME THAT SHE'D HAVE TO STAY RIGHT UNTIL THE END OF THE PARTY.
THAT'S TYPICAL. SHE'S THE ONE WHO PUT IT TOGETHER...
WHAT'S MORE, SHE TOLD ME SHE'D GO STRAIGHT TO WORK AFTER, SO THERE'S NO CHANCE THAT SHE'S NOTICED I'M GONE.
THAT'S HOW IT IS WITH US!
ALL THE BETTER.

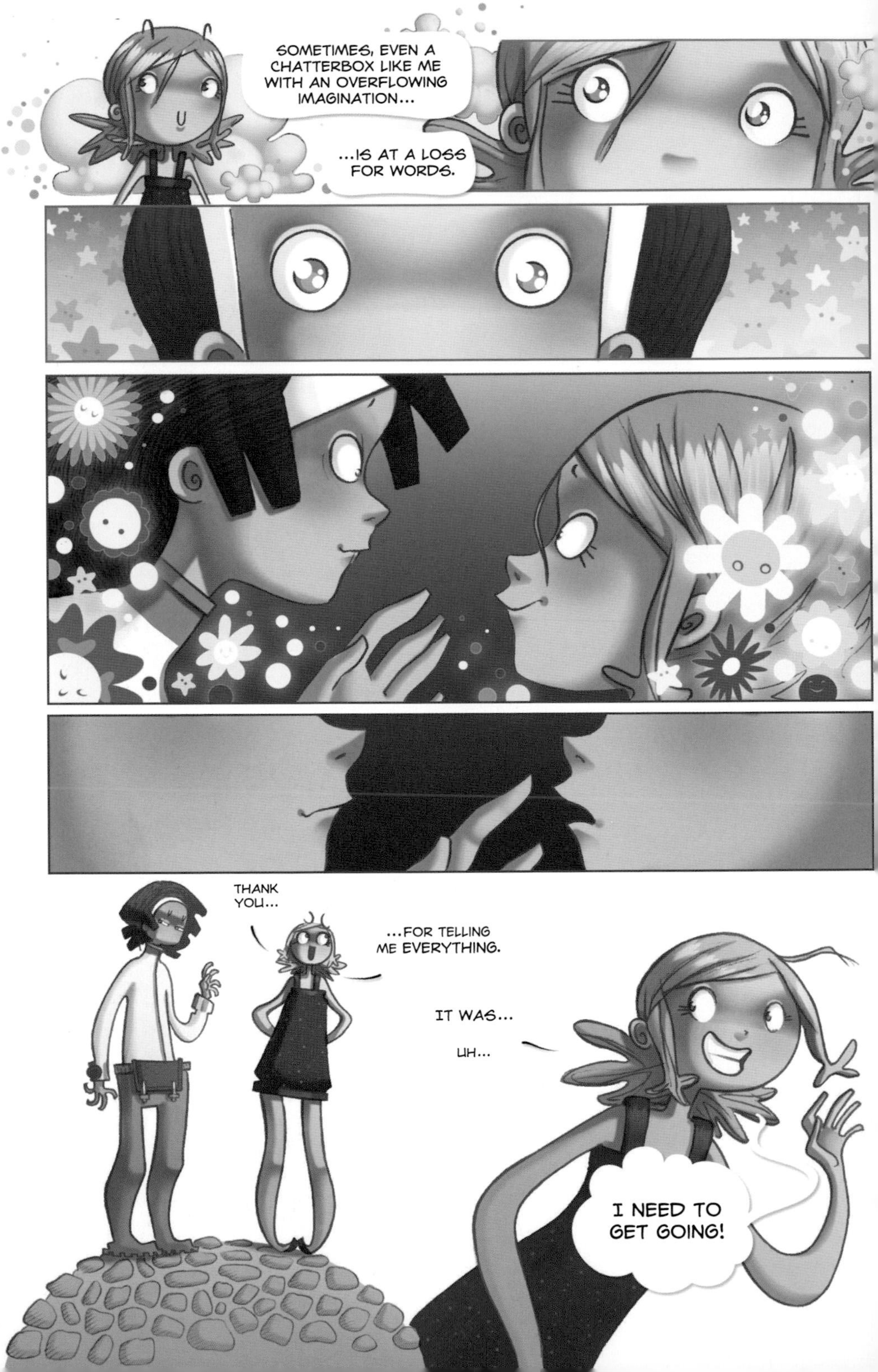
SOMETIMES, EVEN A CHATTERBOX LIKE ME WITH AN OVERFLOWING IMAGINATION...
...IS AT A LOSS FOR WORDS.
THANK YOU...
...FOR TELLING ME EVERYTHING.
IT WAS...
UH...
I NEED TO GET GOING!

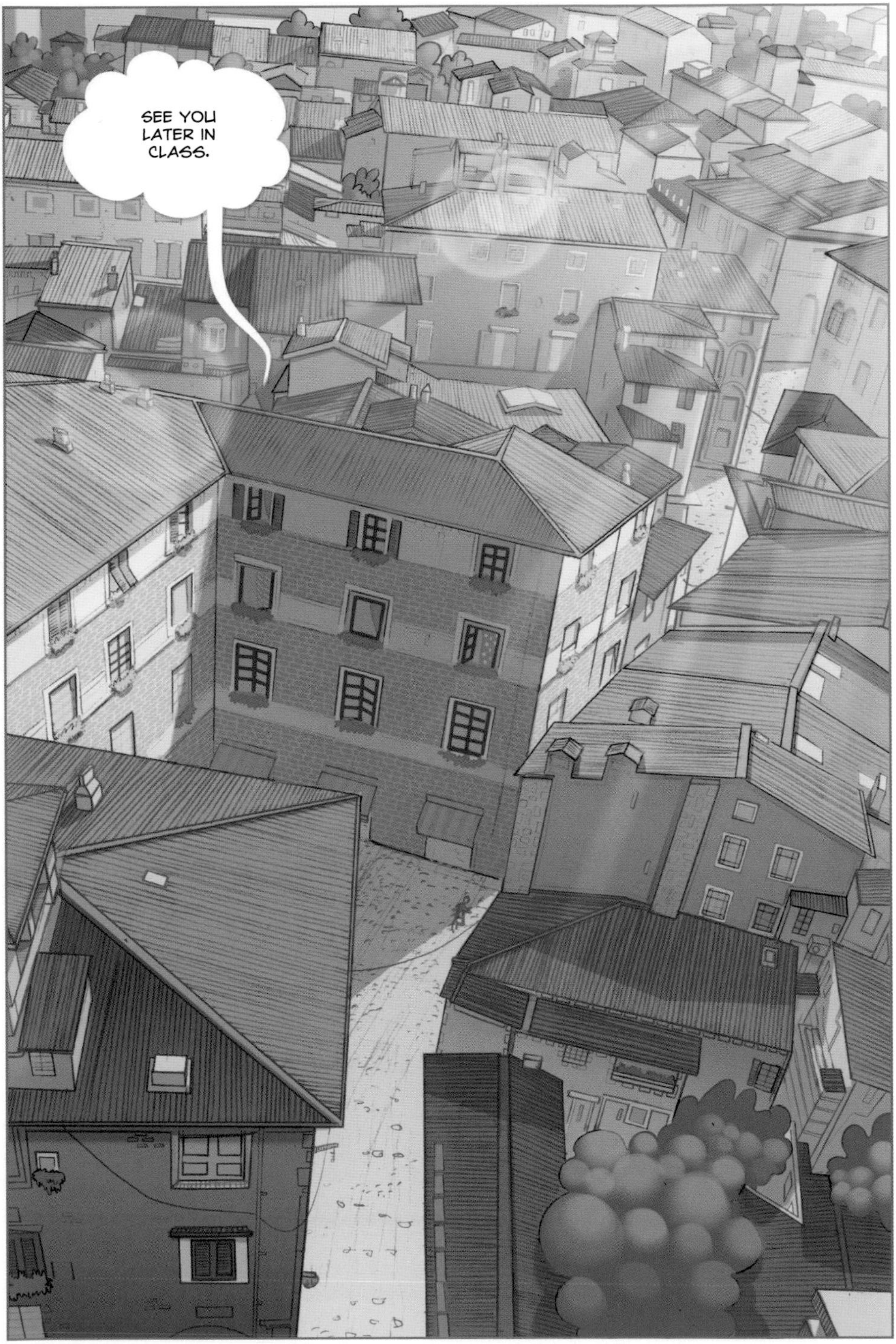
SEE YOU LATER IN CLASS.

EVERYTHING'S QUIET.

NO PROBLEMS IN SIGHT.

I CAN FINALLY GET BACK TO LOOKING HUMAN!

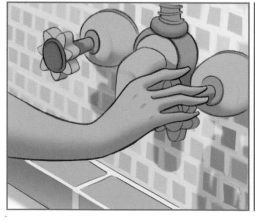

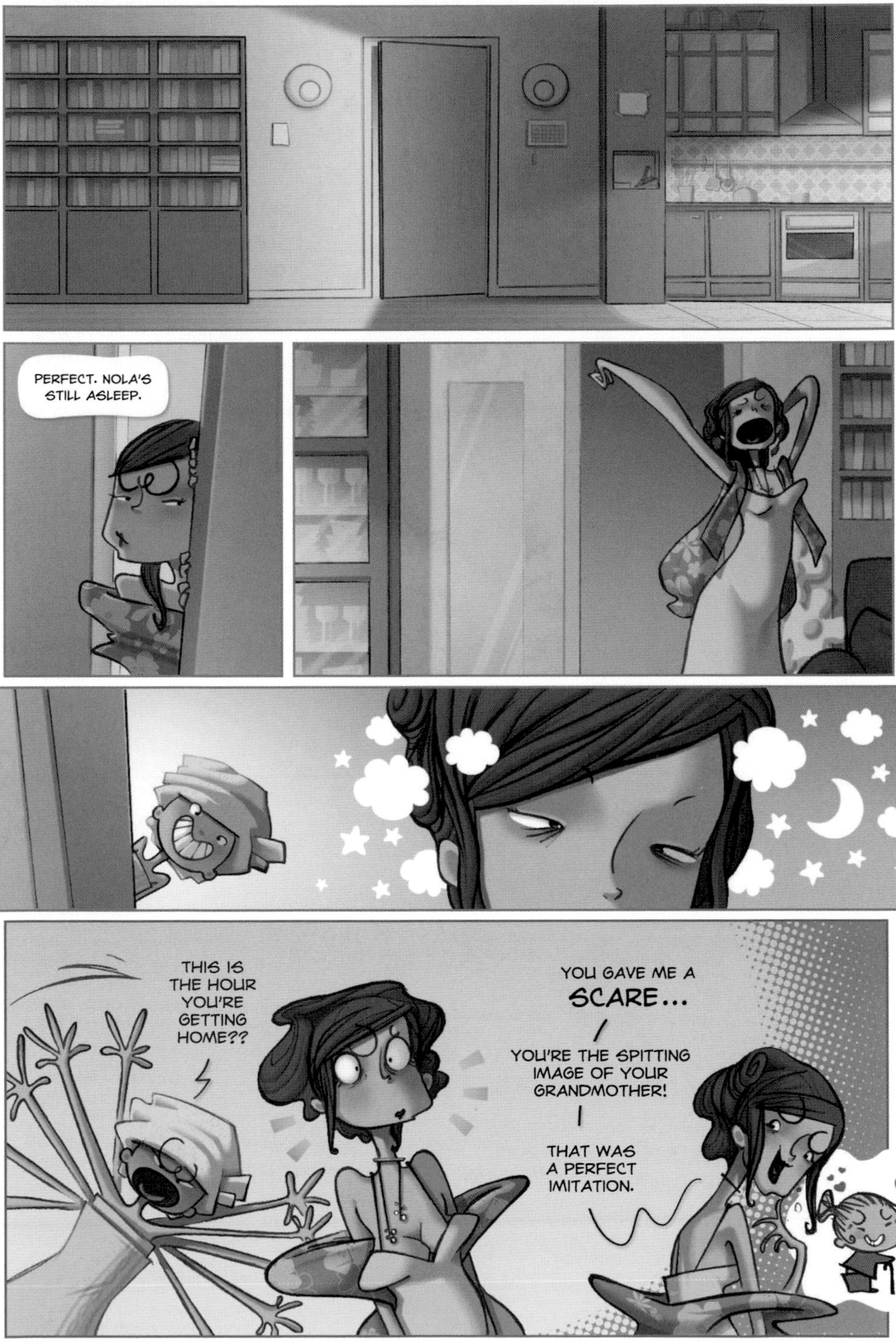
PERFECT. NOLA'S STILL ASLEEP.
THIS IS THE HOUR YOU'RE GETTING HOME??
YOU GAVE ME A SCARE...
YOU'RE THE SPITTING IMAGE OF YOUR GRANDMOTHER!
THAT WAS A PERFECT IMITATION.

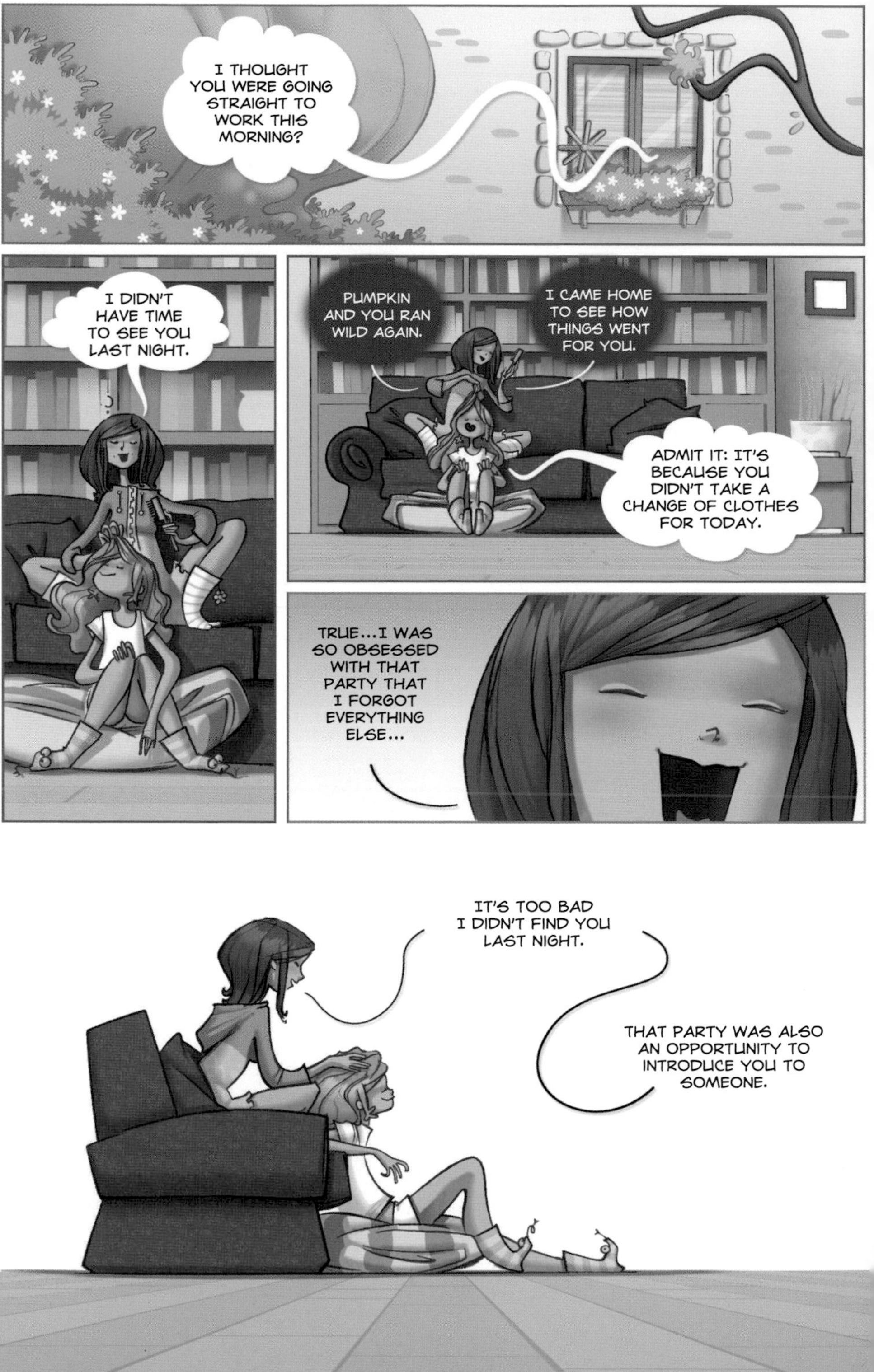
I THOUGHT YOU WERE GOING STRAIGHT TO WORK THIS MORNING?
I DIDN'T HAVE TIME TO SEE YOU LAST NIGHT.
PUMPKIN AND YOU RAN WILD AGAIN.
I CAME HOME TO SEE HOW THINGS WENT FOR YOU.
ADMIT IT: IT'S BECAUSE YOU DIDN'T TAKE A CHANGE OF CLOTHES FOR TODAY.
TRUE...I WAS SO OBSESSED WITH THAT PARTY THAT I FORGOT EVERYTHING ELSE...
IT'S TOO BAD I DIDN'T FIND YOU LAST NIGHT.
THAT PARTY WAS ALSO AN OPPORTUNITY TO INTRODUCE YOU TO SOMEONE.

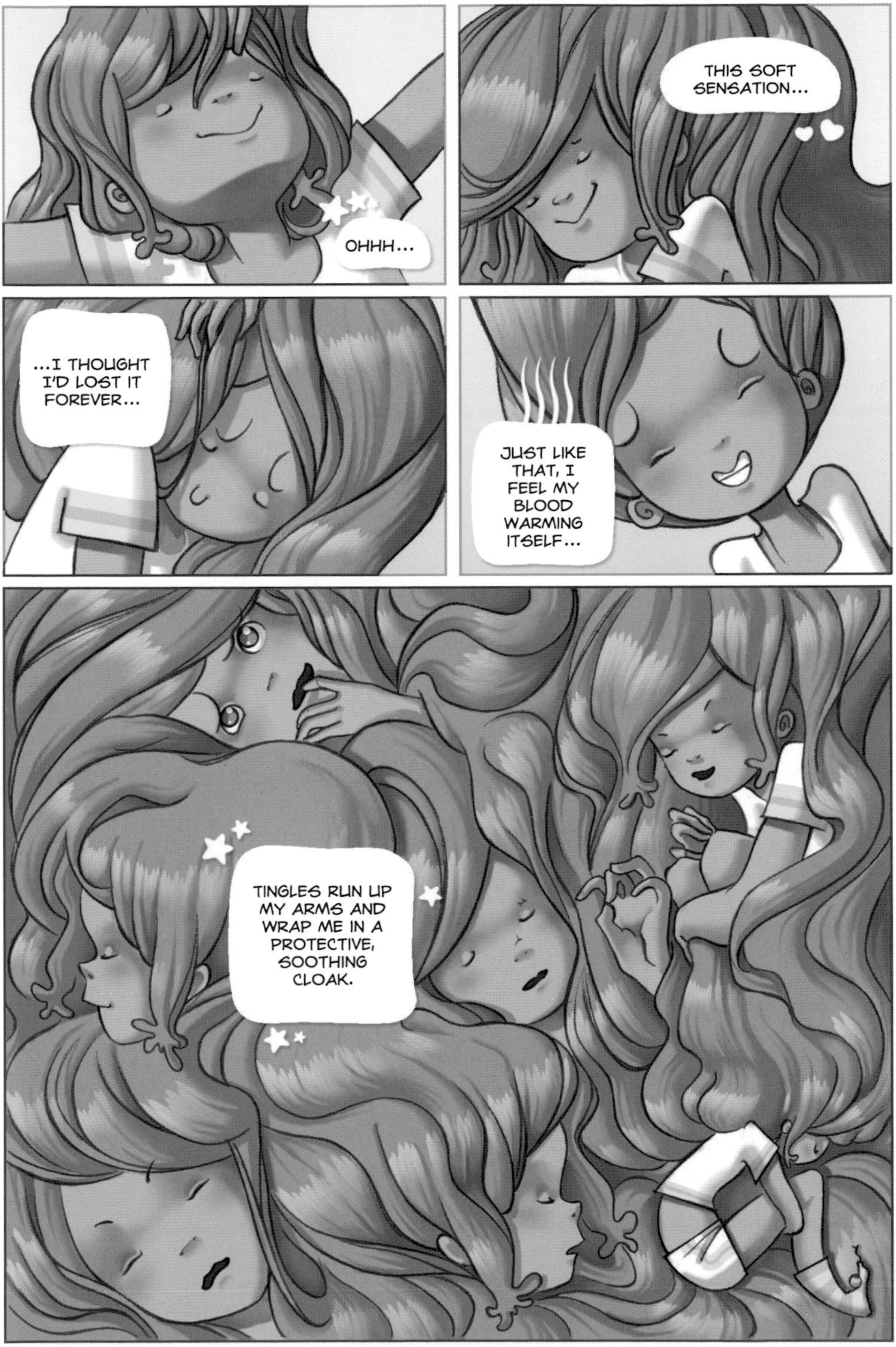
OHHH...
THIS SOFT SENSATION...
...I THOUGHT I'D LOST IT FOREVER...
JUST LIKE THAT, I FEEL MY BLOOD WARMING ITSELF...
TINGLES RUN UP MY ARMS AND WRAP ME IN A PROTECTIVE, SOOTHING CLOAK.

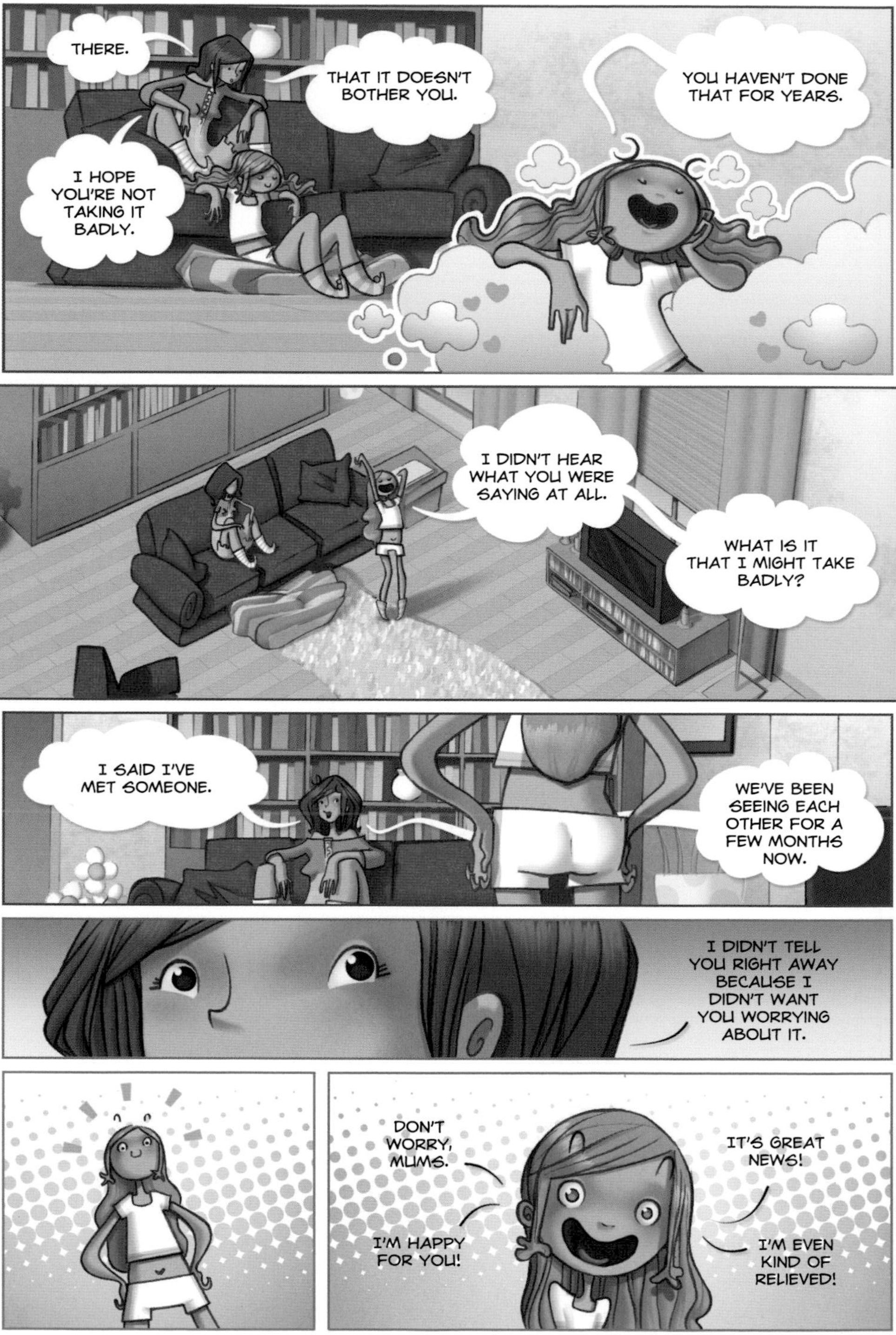
THERE.
I HOPE YOU'RE NOT TAKING IT BADLY.
THAT IT DOESN'T BOTHER YOU.
YOU HAVEN'T DONE THAT FOR YEARS.
I DIDN'T HEAR WHAT YOU WERE SAYING AT ALL.
WHAT IS IT THAT I MIGHT TAKE BADLY?
I SAID I'VE MET SOMEONE.
WE'VE BEEN SEEING EACH OTHER FOR A FEW MONTHS NOW.
I DIDN'T TELL YOU RIGHT AWAY BECAUSE I DIDN'T WANT YOU WORRYING ABOUT IT.
DON'T WORRY, MUMS.
I'M HAPPY FOR YOU!
IT'S GREAT NEWS!
I'M EVEN KIND OF RELIEVED!

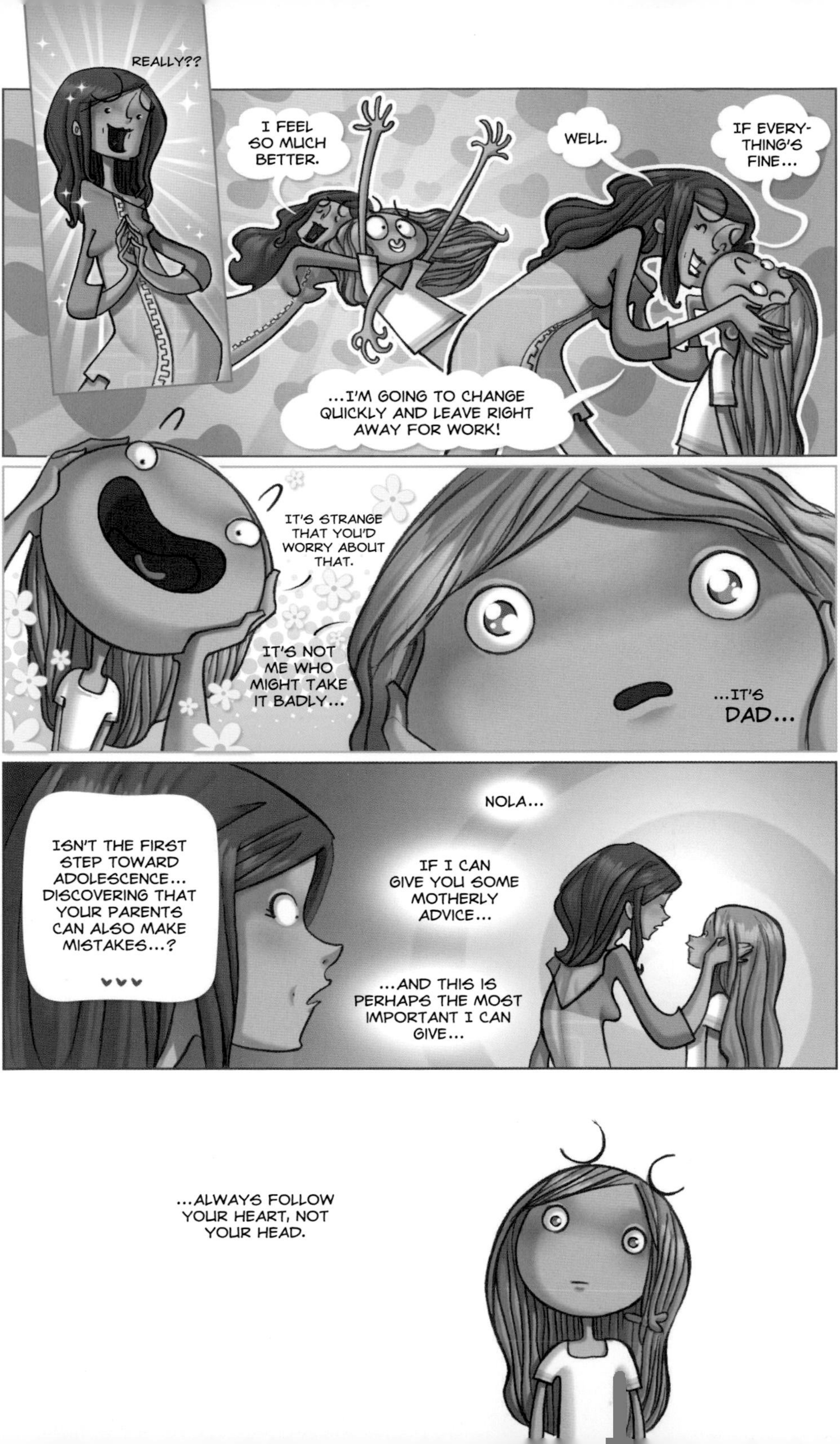
REALLY??
I FEEL SO MUCH BETTER.
WELL.
IF EVERY-THING'S FINE...
...I'M GOING TO CHANGE QUICKLY AND LEAVE RIGHT AWAY FOR WORK!
IT'S STRANGE THAT YOU'D WORRY ABOUT THAT.
IT'S NOT ME WHO MIGHT TAKE IT BADLY...
...IT'S DAD...
NOLA...
IF I CAN GIVE YOU SOME MOTHERLY ADVICE...
...AND THIS IS PERHAPS THE MOST IMPORTANT I CAN GIVE...
ISN'T THE FIRST STEP TOWARD ADOLESCENCE... DISCOVERING THAT YOUR PARENTS CAN ALSO MAKE MISTAKES...?
...ALWAYS FOLLOW YOUR HEART, NOT YOUR HEAD.

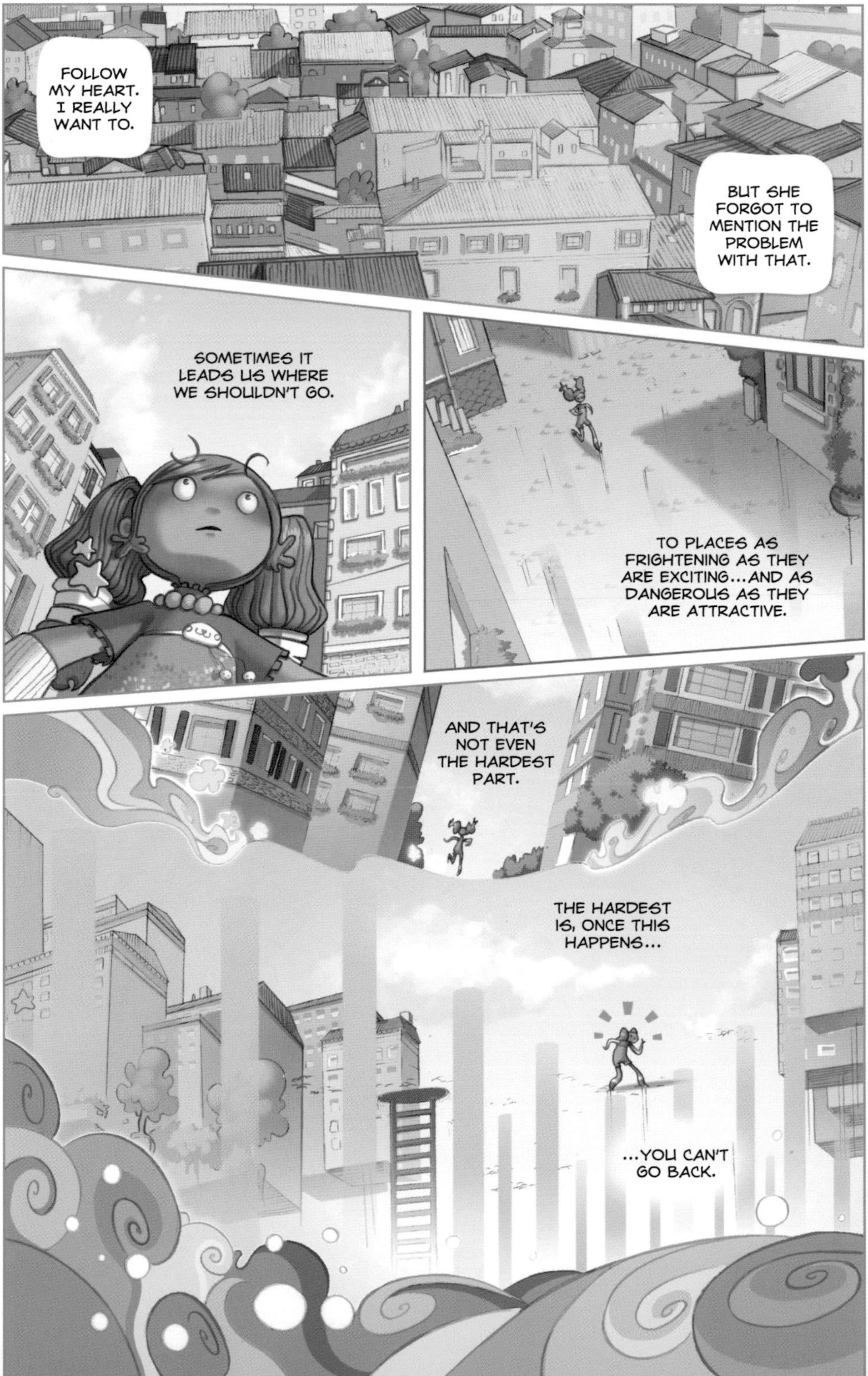
FOLLOW MY HEART. I REALLY WANT TO.
BUT SHE FORGOT TO MENTION THE PROBLEM WITH THAT.
SOMETIMES IT LEADS US WHERE WE SHOULDN'T GO.
TO PLACES AS FRIGHTENING AS THEY ARE EXCITING...AND AS DANGEROUS AS THEY ARE ATTRACTIVE.
AND THAT'S NOT EVEN THE HARDEST PART.
THE HARDEST IS, ONCE THIS HAPPENS...
...YOU CAN'T GO BACK.

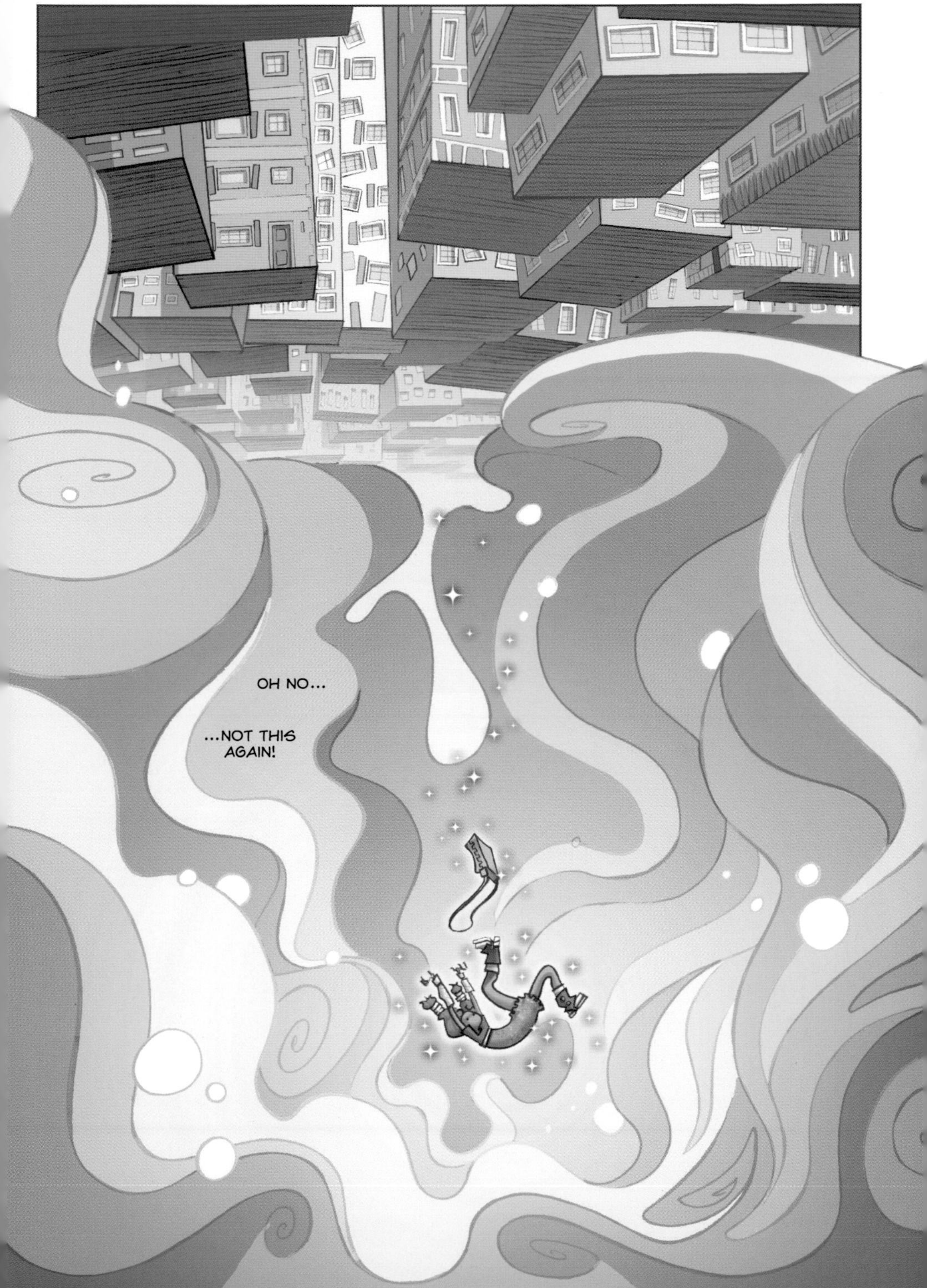
OH NO...
...NOT THIS AGAIN!

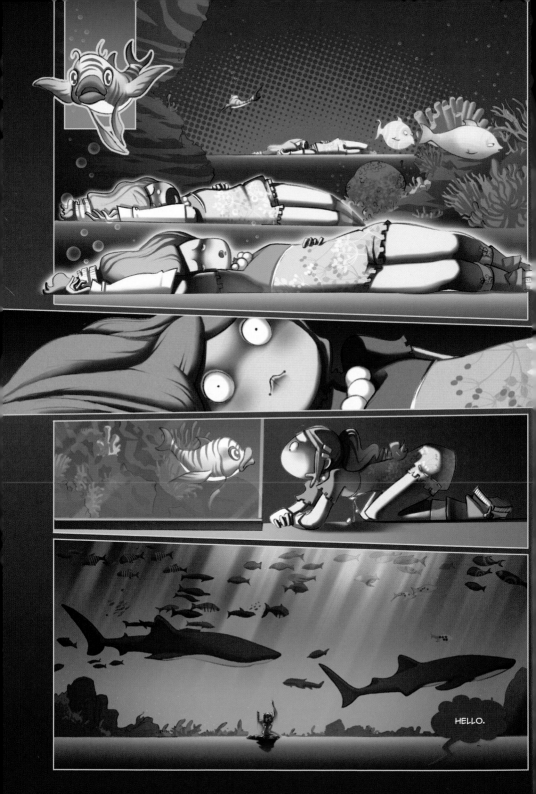

HELLO.

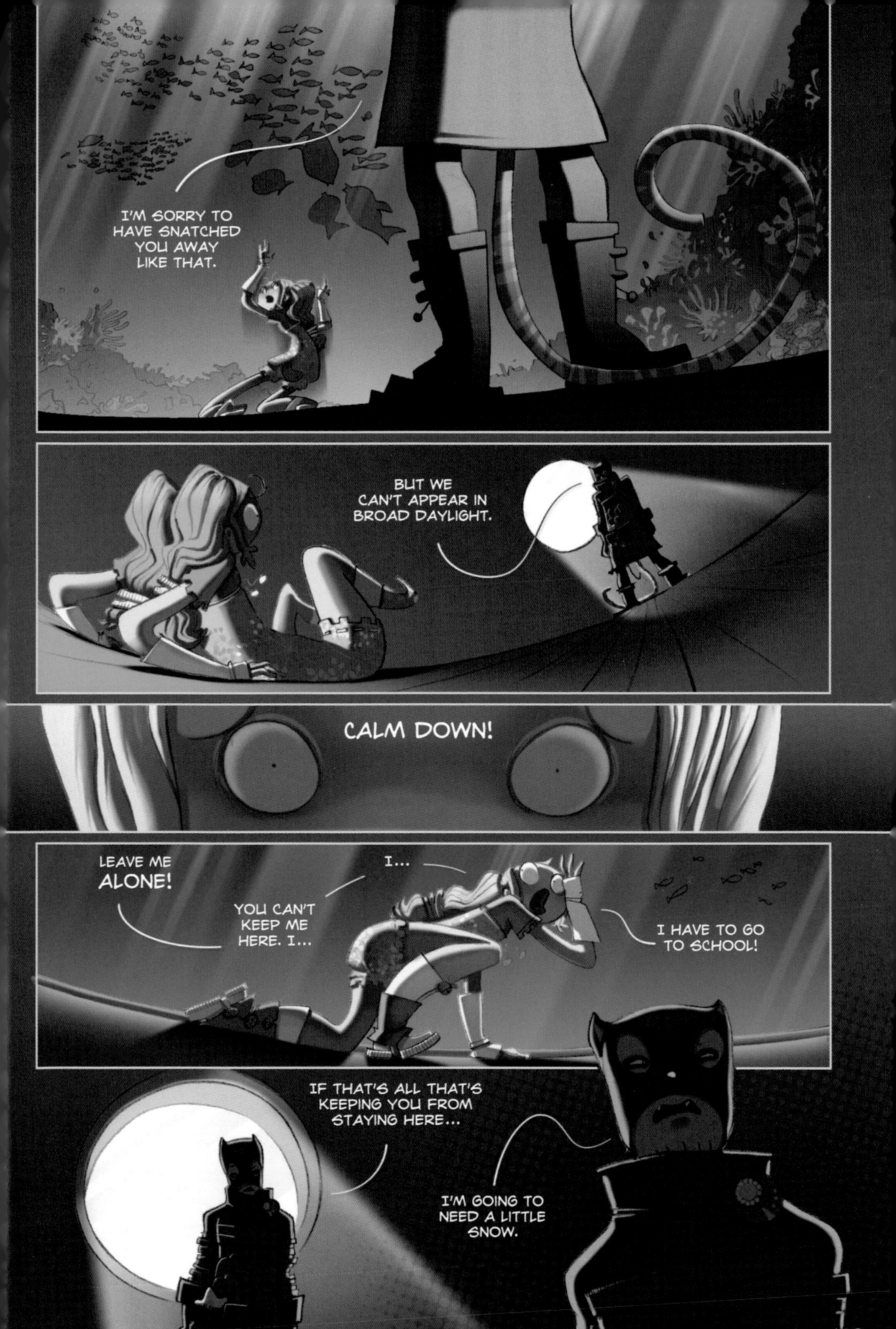
I'M SORRY TO HAVE SNATCHED YOU AWAY LIKE THAT.
BUT WE CAN'T APPEAR IN BROAD DAYLIGHT.
CALM DOWN!
LEAVE ME ALONE!
I...
YOU CAN'T KEEP ME HERE. I...
I HAVE TO GO TO SCHOOL!
IF THAT'S ALL THAT'S KEEPING YOU FROM STAYING HERE...
I'M GOING TO NEED A LITTLE SNOW.

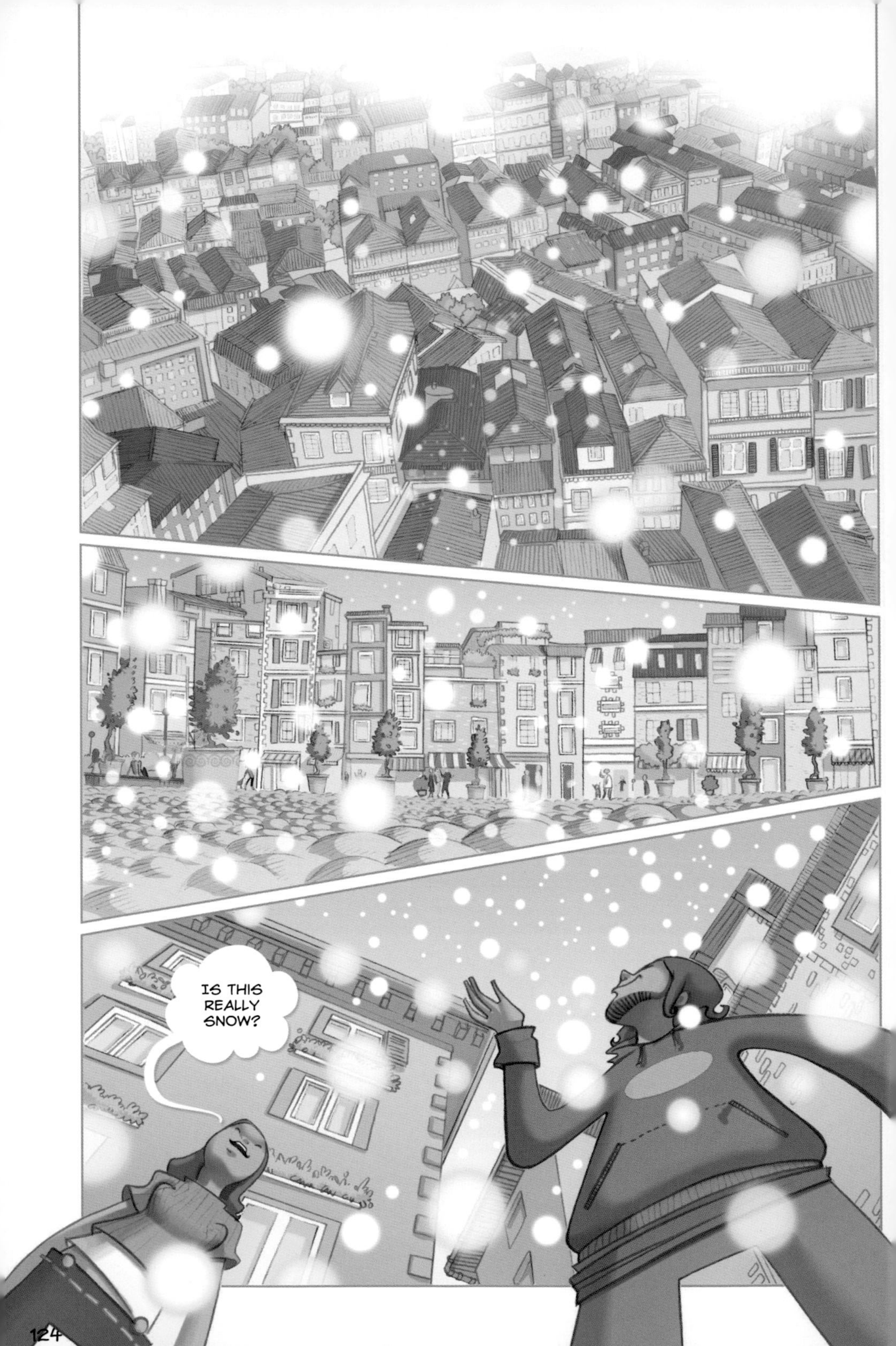
IS THIS REALLY SNOW?

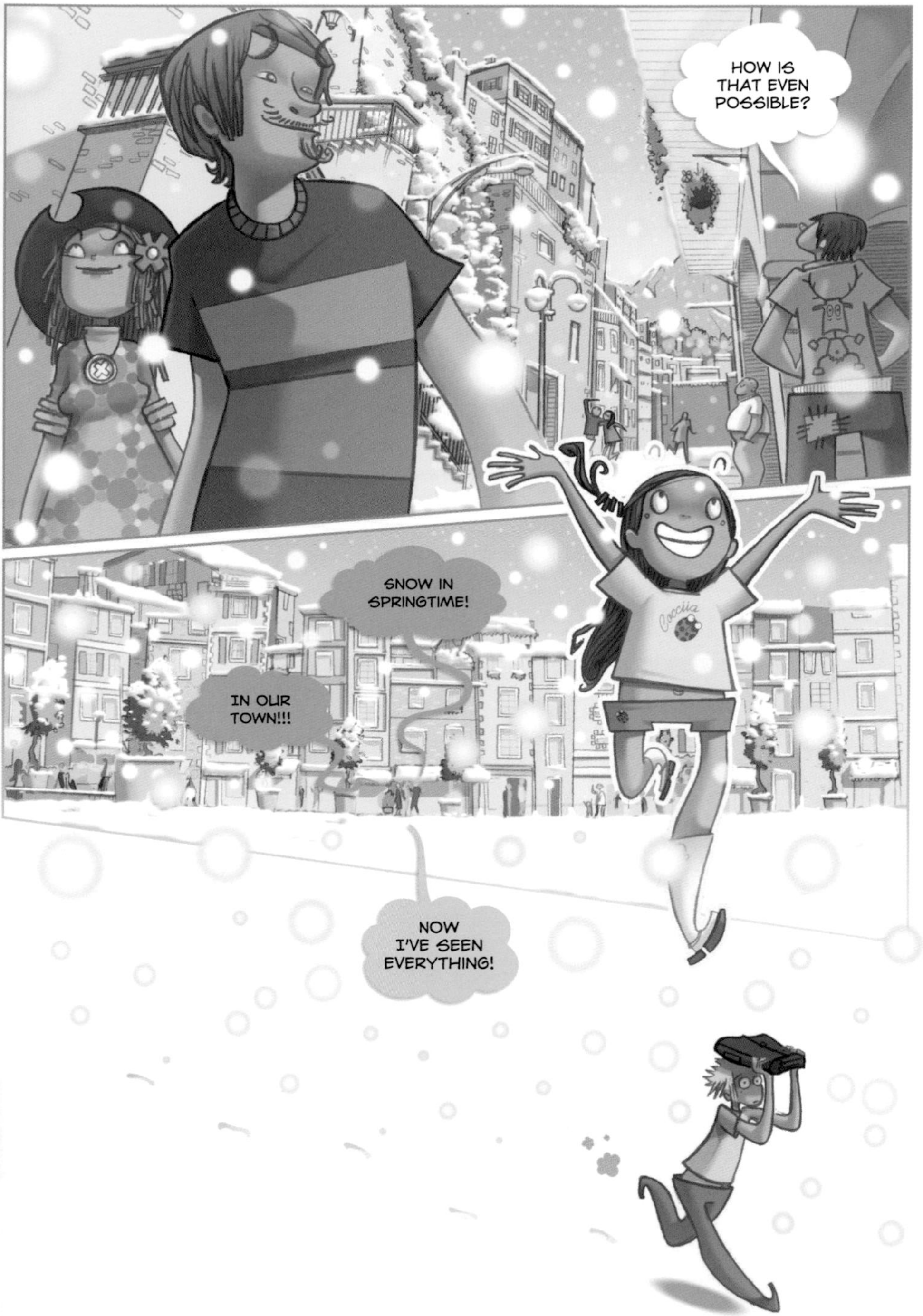
HOW IS THAT EVEN POSSIBLE?
SNOW IN SPRINGTIME!
IN OUR TOWN!!!
NOW I'VE SEEN EVERYTHING!

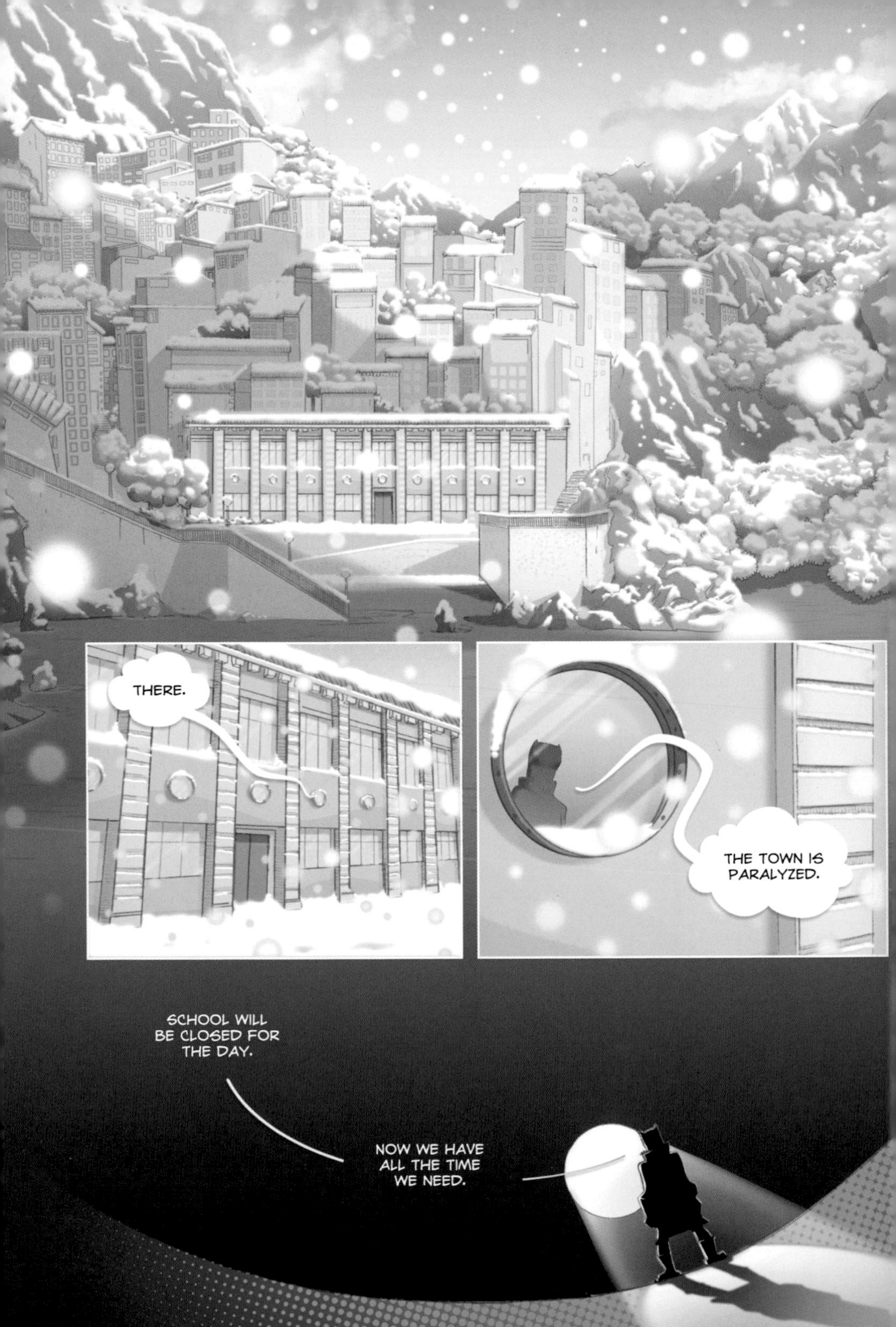
THERE.
THE TOWN IS PARALYZED.
SCHOOL WILL BE CLOSED FOR THE DAY.
NOW WE HAVE ALL THE TIME WE NEED.

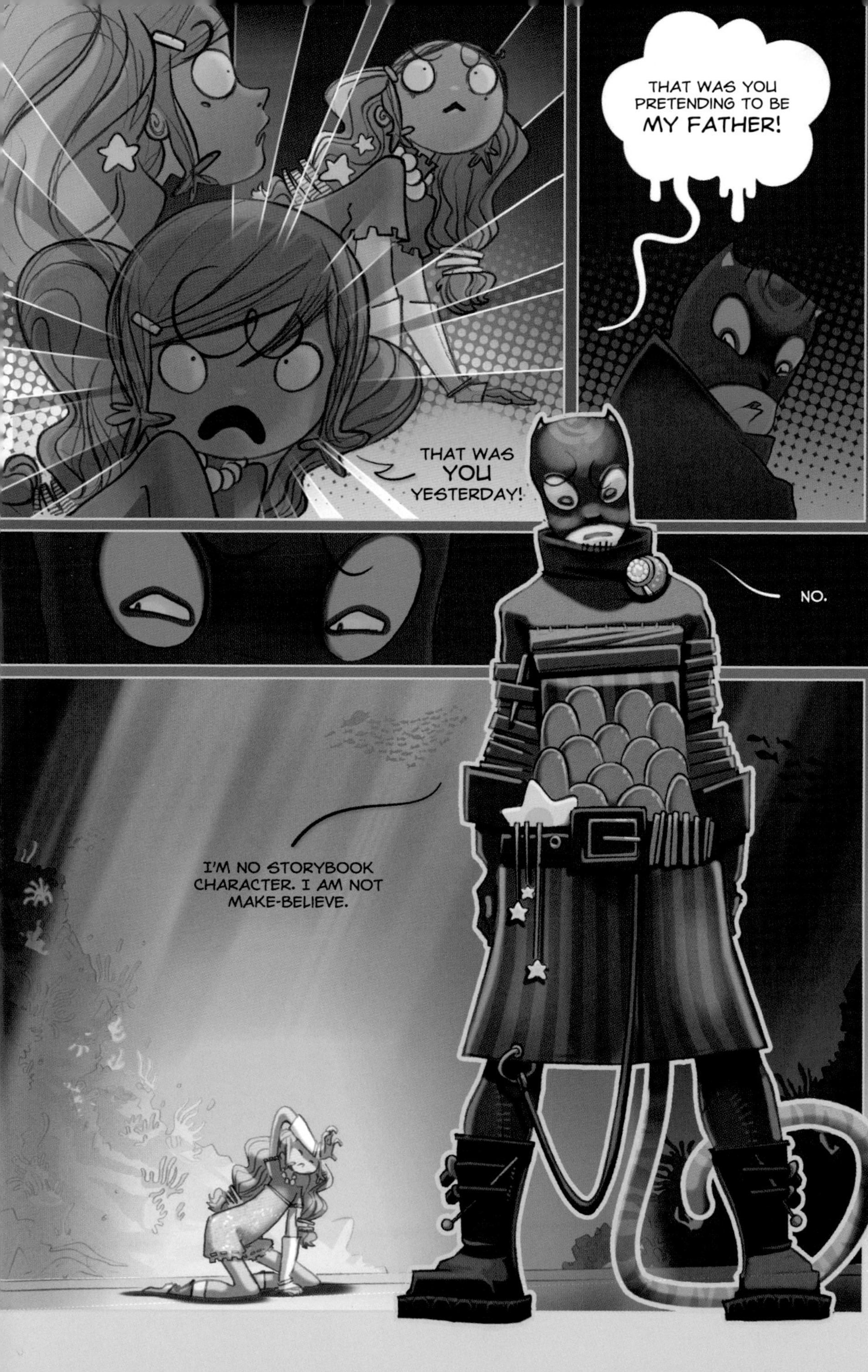
THAT WAS YOU YESTERDAY!
THAT WAS YOU PRETENDING TO BE MY FATHER!
NO.
I'M NO STORYBOOK CHARACTER. I AM NOT MAKE-BELIEVE.

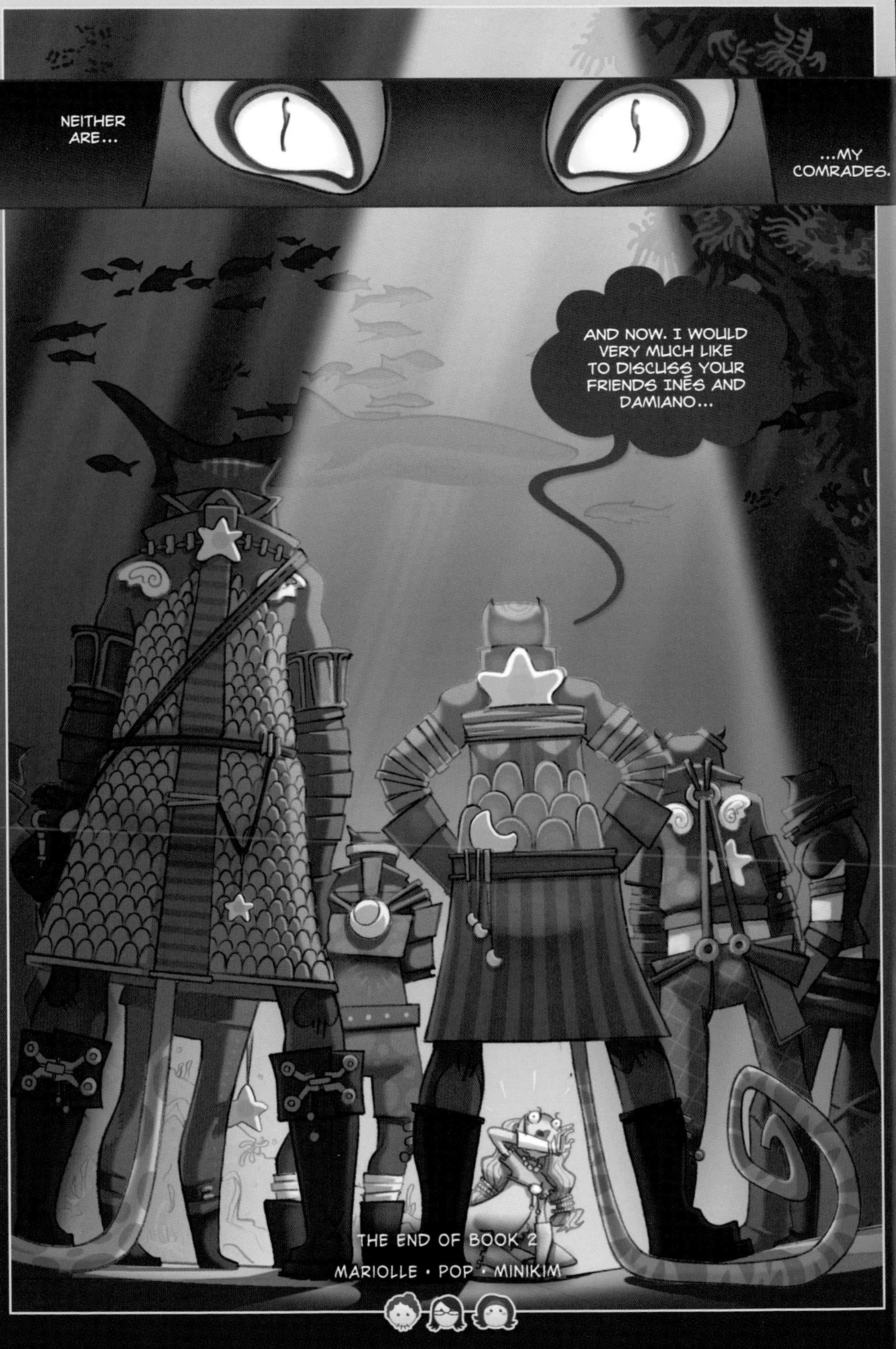

NEITHER ARE...
...MY COMRADES.
AND NOW. I WOULD VERY MUCH LIKE TO DISCUSS YOUR FRIENDS INÊS AND DAMIANO...
THE END OF BOOK 2
MARIOLLE • POP • MINIKIM

coming in Nola's Worlds #3...

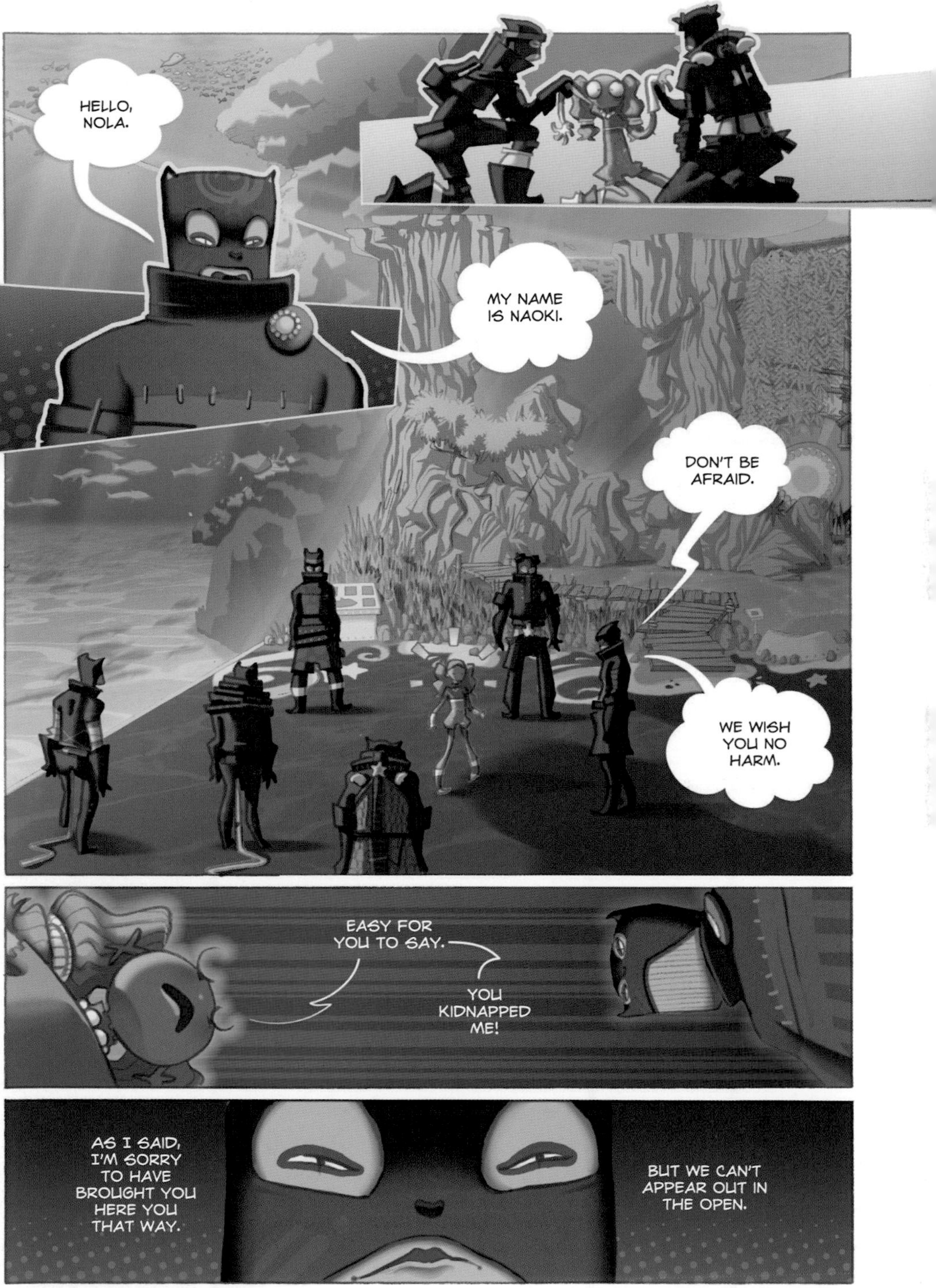
HELLO, NOLA.
MY NAME IS NAOKI.
DON'T BE AFRAID.
WE WISH YOU NO HARM.
EASY FOR YOU TO SAY.
YOU KIDNAPPED ME!
AS I SAID, I'M SORRY TO HAVE BROUGHT YOU HERE YOU THAT WAY.
BUT WE CAN'T APPEAR OUT IN THE OPEN.

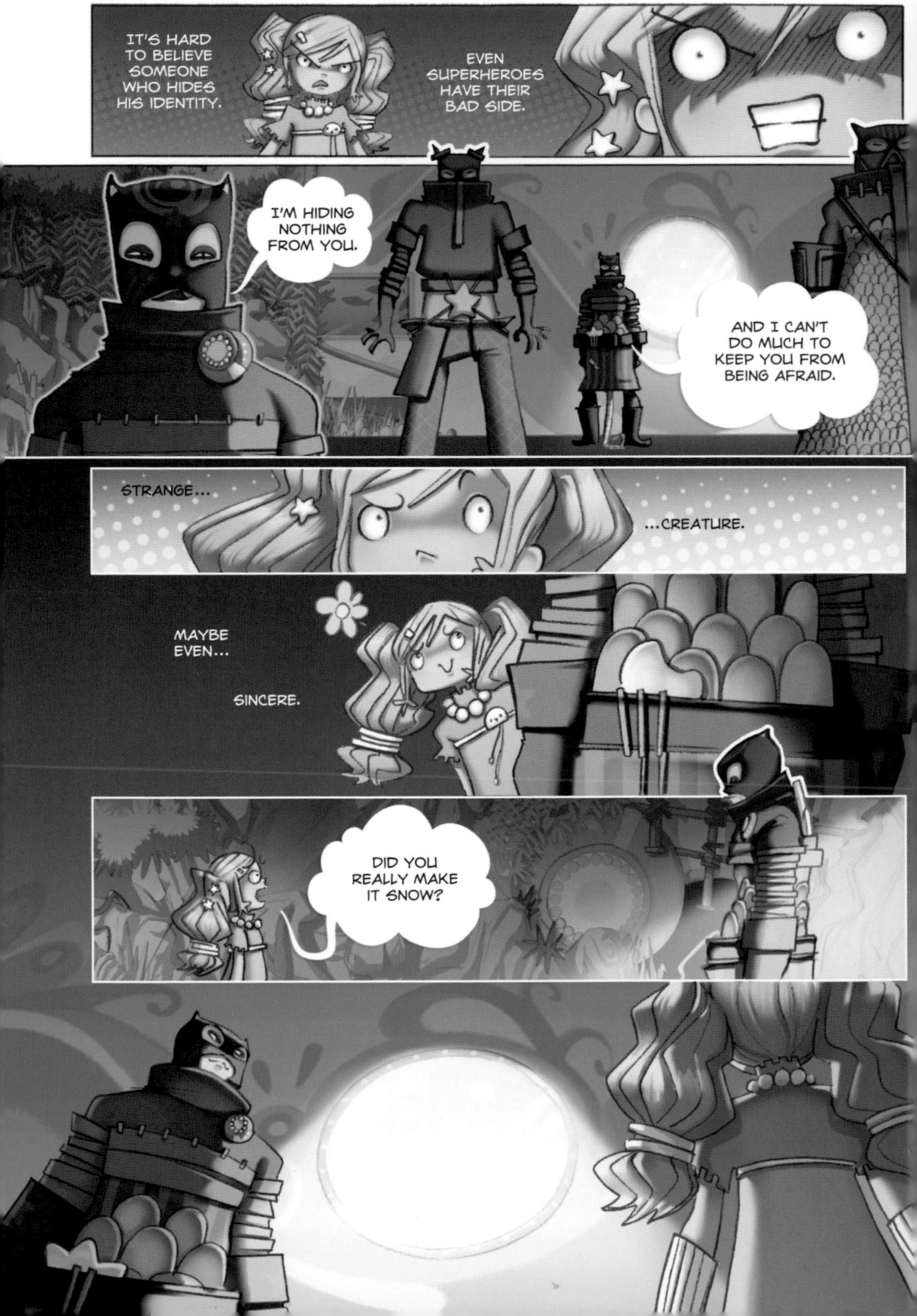
IT'S HARD TO BELIEVE SOMEONE WHO HIDES HIS IDENTITY.
EVEN SUPERHEROES HAVE THEIR BAD SIDE.
I'M HIDING NOTHING FROM YOU.
AND I CAN'T DO MUCH TO KEEP YOU FROM BEING AFRAID.
STRANGE...
...CREATURE.
MAYBE EVEN...
SINCERE.
DID YOU REALLY MAKE IT SNOW?

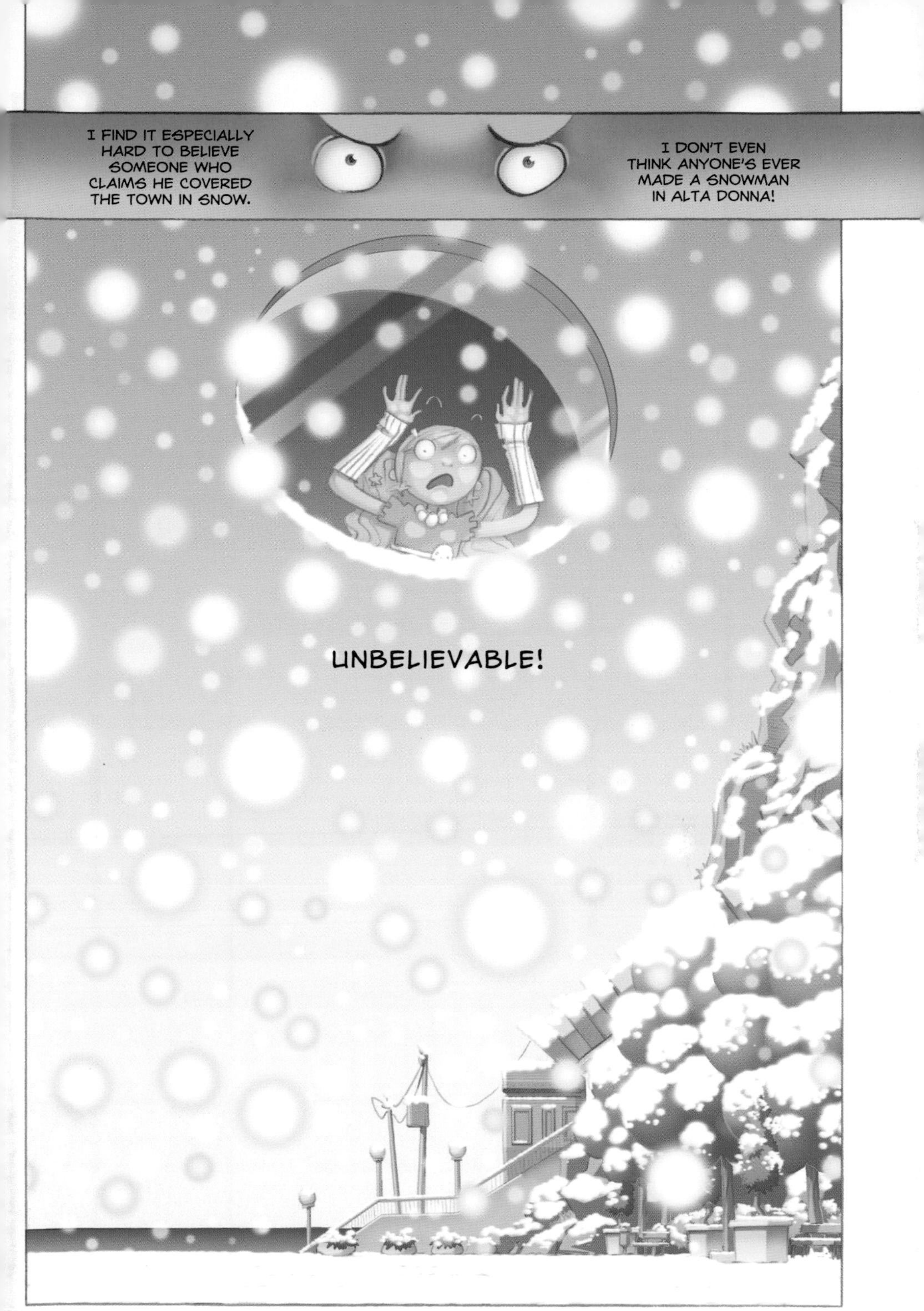
I FIND IT ESPECIALLY HARD TO BELIEVE SOMEONE WHO CLAIMS HE COVERED THE TOWN IN SNOW.
I DON'T EVEN THINK ANYONE'S EVER MADE A SNOWMAN IN ALTA DONNA!
UNBELIEVABLE!

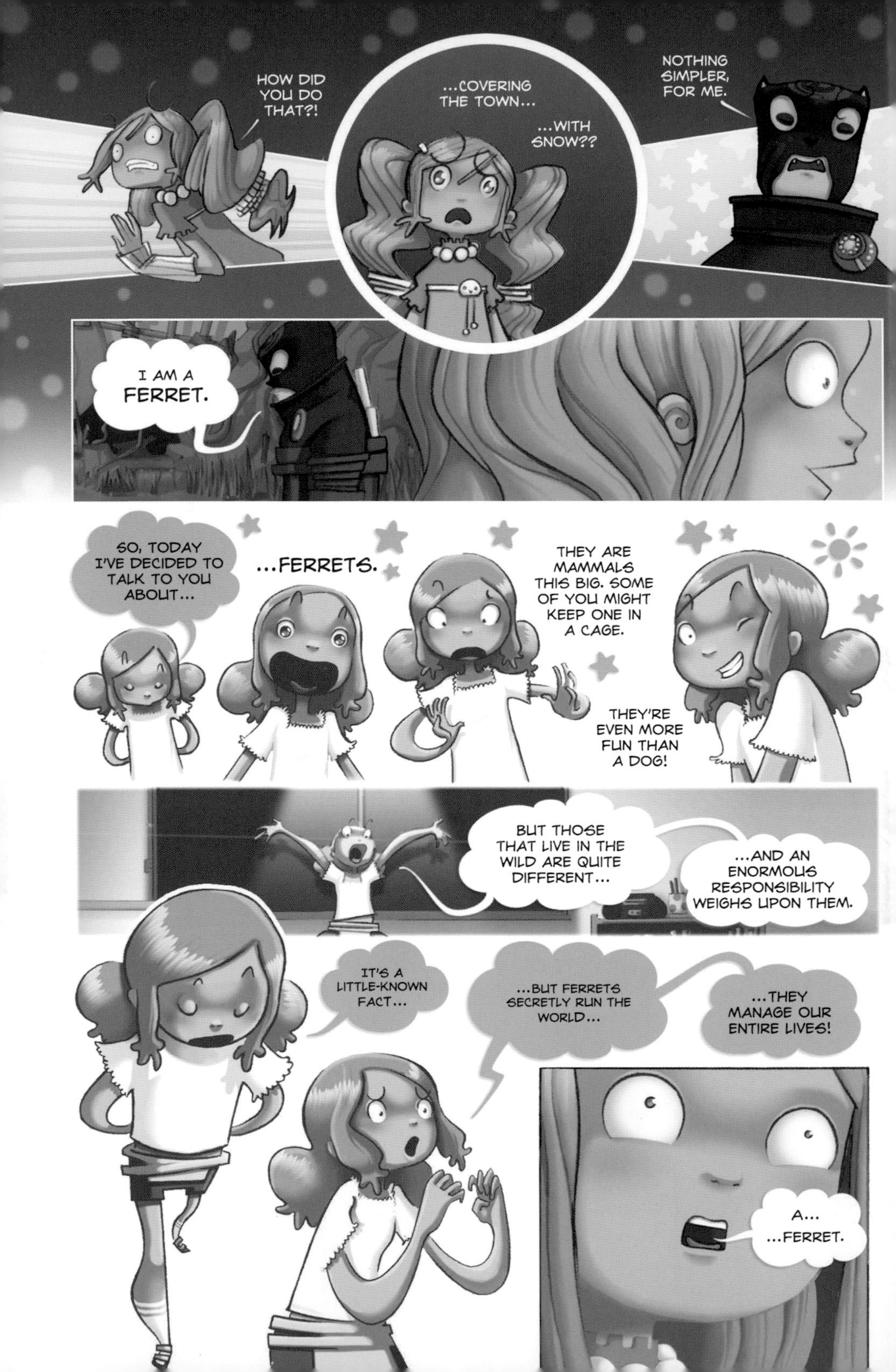
HOW DID YOU DO THAT?!
...COVERING THE TOWN...
...WITH SNOW??
NOTHING SIMPLER, FOR ME.
I AM A FERRET.
SO, TODAY I'VE DECIDED TO TALK TO YOU ABOUT...
...FERRETS.
THEY ARE MAMMALS THIS BIG. SOME OF YOU MIGHT KEEP ONE IN A CAGE.
THEY'RE EVEN MORE FUN THAN A DOG!
BUT THOSE THAT LIVE IN THE WILD ARE QUITE DIFFERENT...
...AND AN ENORMOUS RESPONSIBILITY WEIGHS UPON THEM.
IT'S A LITTLE-KNOWN FACT...
...BUT FERRETS SECRETLY RUN THE WORLD...
...THEY MANAGE OUR ENTIRE LIVES!
A...
...FERRET.

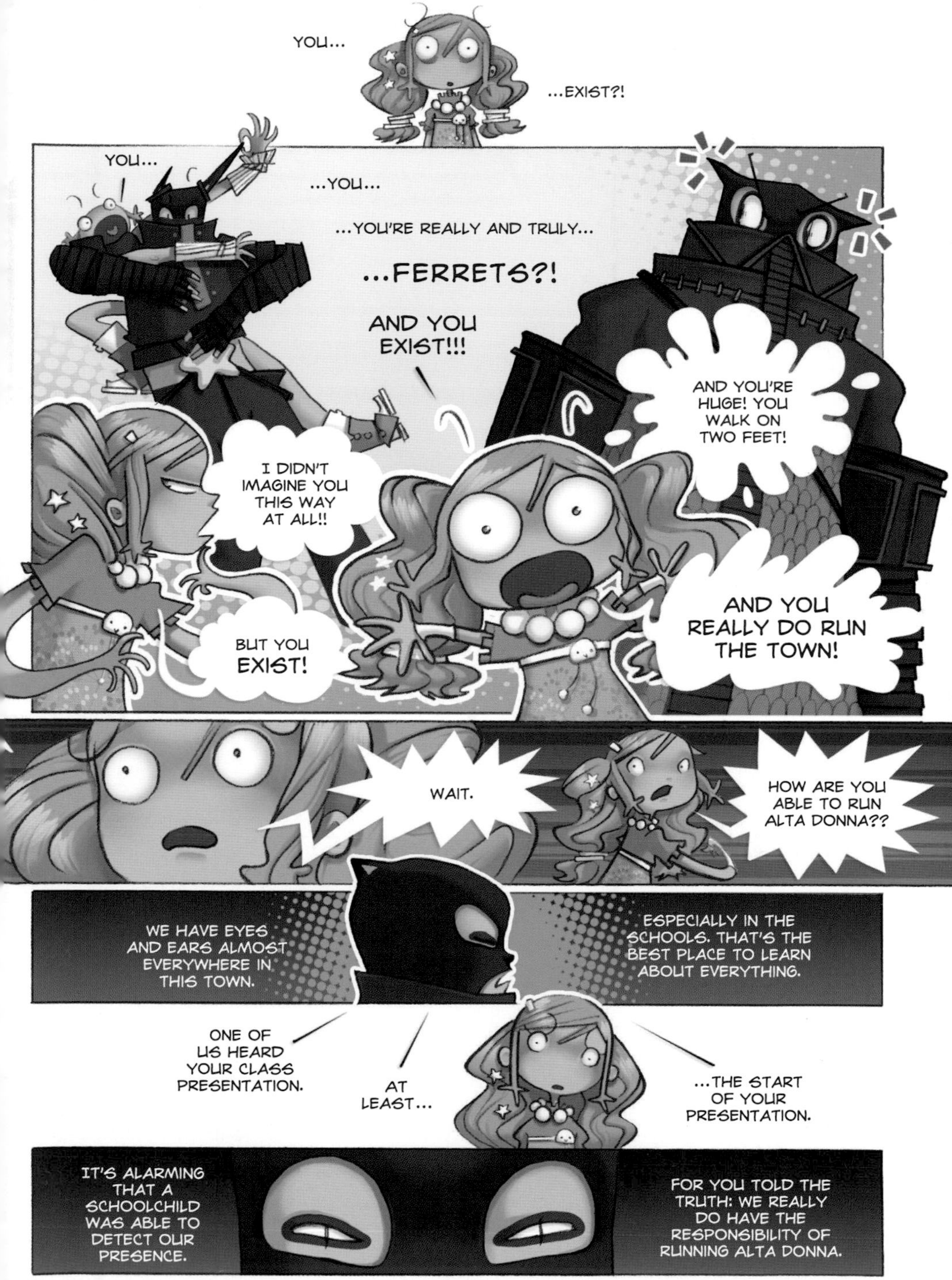
YOU...
...EXIST?!
YOU...
...YOU...
...YOU'RE REALLY AND TRULY...
...FERRETS?!
AND YOU EXIST!!!
AND YOU'RE HUGE! YOU WALK ON TWO FEET!
I DIDN'T IMAGINE YOU THIS WAY AT ALL!!
BUT YOU EXIST!
AND YOU REALLY DO RUN THE TOWN!
WAIT.
HOW ARE YOU ABLE TO RUN ALTA DONNA??
WE HAVE EYES AND EARS ALMOST EVERYWHERE IN THIS TOWN.
ESPECIALLY IN THE SCHOOLS. THAT'S THE BEST PLACE TO LEARN ABOUT EVERYTHING.
ONE OF US HEARD YOUR CLASS PRESENTATION.
AT LEAST...
...THE START OF YOUR PRESENTATION.
IT'S ALARMING THAT A SCHOOLCHILD WAS ABLE TO DETECT OUR PRESENCE.
FOR YOU TOLD THE TRUTH: WE REALLY DO HAVE THE RESPONSIBILITY OF RUNNING ALTA DONNA.

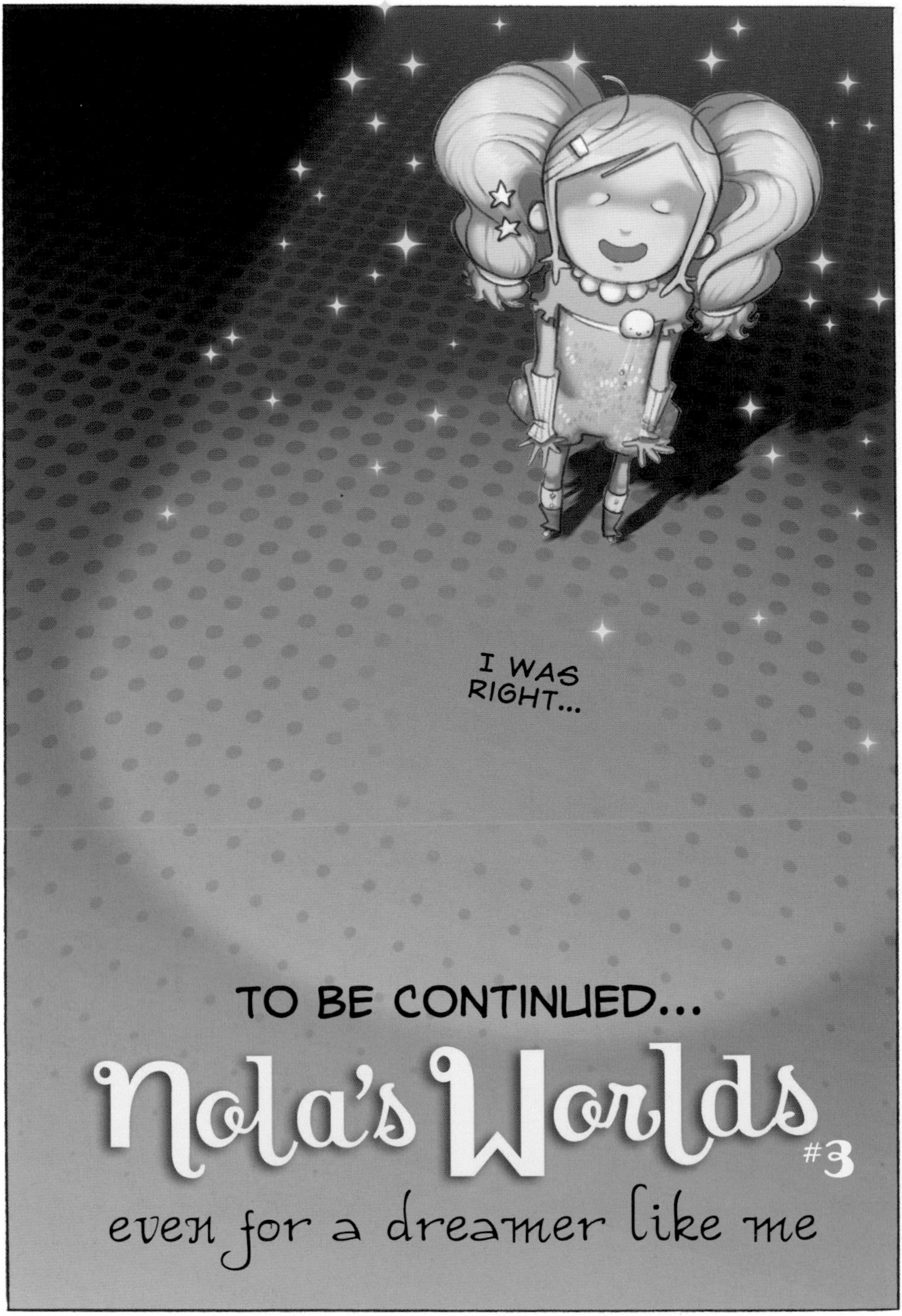
I WAS RIGHT...
TO BE CONTINUED...
Nola's Worlds
#3
even for a dreamer like me